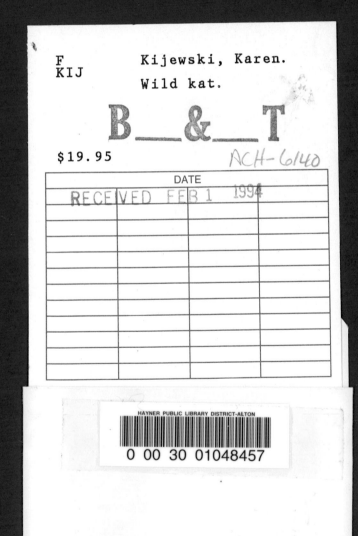

# WILD

# KAT

# WILD

# KAT

Karen Kijewski

DOUBLEDAY

NEW YORK  LONDON  TORONTO  SYDNEY  AUCKLAND

PUBLISHED BY DOUBLEDAY
a division of Bantam Doubleday Dell Publishing Group, Inc.
1540 Broadway, New York, New York 10036

DOUBLEDAY and the portrayal of an anchor with a dolphin
are trademarks of Doubleday, a division of
Bantam Doubleday Dell Publishing Group, Inc.

*Book design by Tasha Hall*

Library of Congress Cataloging-in-Publication Data

Kijewski, Karen.
Wild kat / Karen Kijewski. — 1st ed.
p.   cm.
1.   Colorado, Kat (Fictitious character)—Fiction.   2.   Women detectives—
California—Fiction.   I. Title.
PS3561.I364W5   1994
813′.54—dc20                                                          93-25740
CIP

ISBN 0-385-46851-2
Copyright © 1994 by Karen Kijewski
All Rights Reserved
Printed in the United States of America
February 1994
*First Edition*

1   3   5   7   9   10   8   6   4   2

# WILD

# KAT

# 1

## CAVEAT EMPTOR

~~~~~~~~~~~~~~~~~~~~~~~~~~~~~~~~~~~~~~~~~~~~~~~~~~~~~~~~

The burnished metal plate outside said 1453 ABC. The door was ajar. I pushed it all the way open and walked in.

B was the only bed with a body in it. A big, handsome body with bandages and bare tanned skin, blond hair, dark eyes and a blank stare. Outside in the corridor a loudspeaker droned for Dr. Sanchez, Dr. Romana Sanchez *please*. The room smelled of medicine and antiseptic, hatred and fear. It wasn't cold but I shivered as I waited at the end of the bed for the vacant eyes to focus and turn toward me.

Nothing. The porch light was out. No one was home.

It started looking like a long wait and patience isn't my strong suit. I cleared my throat. Someone walked in behind me and over to the head of the bed. Another big man, this one in street clothes and no bandages.

"Jude. Hey, you got company." The man's voice was soft—insistent, not gentle.

After a pause long enough to recite the alphabet backward and count to a thousand by twos, Jude looked at me from hospital bed 1453 B.

My cue. Good. "Kat Colorado. I came to see how you were doing."

"Fuck you."

I was glad I hadn't bothered with flowers.

*Yesterday.*

*Yesterday I was supposed to be in Fresno for a nine o'clock appointment. Five-thirty and I'm on 99 South just outside of Sacramento County limits, half-awake/half-asleep, the sun pushing up into the dark with pale promise, the sky sullen and sulky still, unwilling to give up night and coolness to a hot summer day in California's central valley, 112° today easy. I had shivered in the cool morning air.*

*The lights in the rearview mirror startled me first. Then they scared me. They were live crazy things, moving erratically and way too fast, passing me up at 80, 85 mph, then the vehicle skidded into the lane in front of me, back into the fast lane, brake lights on/off/on/off. A front tire blew, the car yawing, veering wildly, then sliding toward the shoulder, soft shoulder, over-correcting, out-of-control and headed for the center divider, caroming off the oleanders, rolling once over easy, spinning in the gravel, on the freeway, and sliding, resting finally in the oleanders. Pink and white and now smashed.*

*I stopped the Bronco ten yards or so down the highway and ran. I was wearing a short flared skirt, silk shirt and pumps. The pumps went first, then the panty hose. I ran on the pavement, the gravel hurt like hell. Ran hard. Ran fast.*

It was an old, now beat-up white Cadillac, its rounded fenders and cocky hood ornament stuck in pink oleanders. There was broken glass everywhere. The driver was crumpled up, pink and white and smashed.

The oleanders didn't smell, they never do. The car did. Burned rubber. Gas. Something else I couldn't identify. My stomach heaved. I choked on bile and raw terror. I hate fire, fear it almost more than anything. I am not brave around fires, won't even roast wienies, marshmallows either and I love them. Still running. Almost there. My feet hurt. In the cool of the morning I was sweating. The smell of gas was stronger. Dear God.

The driver's door was banged and dented, buckled and warped beyond imagination. I tore at it, hauled at it, kicked and swore at it. I gave it everything I had. Finally it moved, but barely. Maybe three inches. Maybe. Again. A little more. Five inches. Gas. Harder. A foot this time. I hauled on the driver, forgetting about his seat belt.

Damn!

Blood. Glass. Gas.

I cut myself yanking on the buckle, wrenching it off, hauling on the guy. He looked to be six-one, two-ten, easy. I'm five-seven, one-thirty-five, and I've never bench-pressed two-ten in my life. Or hauled it. Gas. Hey, no time like the present. There's a first time for everything. He groaned. Blood everywhere. His face was white. Pain. His and mine, but mine was conscious. Blood on my hands, my feet all torn up. Goddamn! Fresno is no great shakes but it's better than this.

No kidding.

My breath came in ragged sobs. His flesh, slippery with blood, was impossible to hold onto. I got a hand under his armpit, heaved, hauled. His sleeve snagged on the door handle. Held. Damn! I yanked. He moaned in response. The smell of blood and gas stuck in my throat, gagging me. The sleeve ripped free. Where was a cop when you needed one? Or a trucker? Even a tourist? I pulled him out of the car. Three feet. Not enough. Everything was slippery now, slick with blood, with sweat. I wiped my hands on my sixty-five-dollar silk shirt and hauled. Five yards. Still not enough. Gas. Too much blood, and he was too white.

*Ten yards.*

*I tripped and fell. Or maybe it was the explosion that knocked me —blasted me—over. Light and heat and fire. Some of it, the fire, on us, mostly him. I pounded out the flames with bloody hands. Sobbing. Swearing. The cloth of his shirt stuck to his body, gummed up in polo shirt cute little animal synthetic fiber napalm. It stuck to my hands. I tried to pull it off his body.*

*The skin started coming too.*

*I ran for the Bronco, the cooler, the ice. Dumped the ice and water on him. And then the drinks, all six cans of diet Dr Pepper, a hot day's stash. He was cool to the touch then, cool and pale and still bleeding.*

*"Breathe!" I screamed at him. "Breathe, dammit! I hauled you all this way. I saved your ass from a fire. Don't even* think *about dying!"*

*I was doing CPR and swearing when the eighteen-wheeler pulled up.*

*"Je-sus Chri-i-ist," the truck driver muttered under his breath as he stood and stared down at us. And, really, who could blame him?*

*"Get help," I gasped at him.*

*"I called, lady, honest-ta-god, I called 'fore I got outta the rig, they're on the way." He clenched and unclenched his big hands, shifted his weight from one foot to the other, cracked his knuckles, stuck his tongue in his cheek. Moral support, I guess.*

*Five days weeks years later the cops came. And the fire trucks and the ambulance. They had to haul me off him. "Breathe dammit!" I was still hollering. "Breathe!"*

*The emergency medical technician was swell. She wrapped me up in a blanket, bandaged my hands and feet and let me swear. She didn't want me to drive.*

*"I'm okay," I said finally, and without swearing, so maybe I was. She shook her head no. I ignored it. I drove, but not to Fresno. I was all torn up, bloody, and missing a shoe. A pickup had run over it, turned it into road kill.*

*I didn't know if the guy was alive or, if he was alive, if he'd live long. But I'd tried.*

"Fuck you."

So now I knew: He was alive. I flexed my fingers inside the bandages. They hurt. So did my feet, even in sneakers with extra thick socks. And the muscles in my arms, legs, back. I turned and reached for the door.

"Kat Colorado? Hey," the other big guy said as he walked over and engulfed me in a bear hug. "Jude, this is the gal who pulled you out, saved your life!" He let go of me and stepped back, beaming at me and at the man in the bed.

Jude looked up at me. Someone was home, the porch light a dim bulb. "Yeah? First you set me up, then you pull me out. And I'm supposed to goddamn thank you for saving my goddamn life? Bullshit."

What was there to say? Not much. Not much at all. I could ask: *What setup? What bullshit?* But why bother?

"No," I answered instead as I turned again and started out, away from the hospital smells, the fear and the hatred, away from the life he threw in my face and the thanks I wasn't going to get. Life's a crapshoot. No kidding.

Before I got out the door my orneriness got the better of me. I turned and faced him. Our eyes met, mine as cold and hard as his.

"You owe me, pal. For sure. You were on fire and I put it out. It cost me a six-pack of diet Dr Pepper. Two dollars and fifty-nine cents. Plus tax."

I didn't say *fuck you,* I just thought it. I did walk out. Walking down the hallway, my hands hurt—I tried to stop clenching them. How much did a six of diet Dr Pepper cost? Maybe $2.59 was too high? Or too low?

Ask me if I cared.

*I'm supposed to goddamn thank you for saving my goddamn life?*

Sure. Why not? Isn't that what we do?

"Here's your change, sir." *Thank you.*

"Go two blocks, turn left, and it's right there, you can't miss it." *Thank you.*

"Wonderful evening, great dinner." *Thank you.*

"Here's your life." *Thank you.*

Sure. Why not.

I pounded an icy frozen margarita after work. Why not?

I hate tequila.

# 2

Dear Charity,

My boss wants me to lie. I'm supposed to write up results to show that a product has passed safety tests when it hasn't. If I don't do this I'll lose my job, which I *need*. Help!

Don't Want To Lie

Dear DWTL,

I think the hideous orange jumpsuit they make you wear in jail is the most unflattering thing in the world. Personally, I'd rather look for another job.

Charity

~~~~~~~~~~~~~~~~~~~~~~~~~~~~~~~~~~~~~~~~~~~~~

"You're a private investigator?"

"Yes."

The light behind his back framed him in the doorway. I couldn't see his face.

"I want to hire you."

"No."

"And I owe you an apology." He said it in the way of a man used to having his apologies accepted, even welcomed.

"No." I'm used to a lot too, although not that.

He dropped a six-pack of diet Dr Pepper on a stack of papers on my desk, the cans icy-cold and beaded with moisture. "Someone's trying to get at my wife. It was her car I was driving, her car that was sabotaged." He ran his hand through sun-bleached blond hair. "In the hospital, with the drugs, I got confused. I thought you were one of them. I didn't get it, didn't get it that you were helping. Like I said, I'm sorry."

I reached out for a can of soda, popped the tab and slugged it down. I didn't offer him one. He didn't take one. Just as well.

He took out his wallet.

And then a photograph.

I haven't described Jude, not to do him justice. Picture a Nordic-god type with dimples, Nautilus muscles, a tight ass, a fuck-me smile and cowboy boots. Picture a Cosmo girl's hot and sticky dream.

But I'm no Cosmo girl.

The photo was of him, looking gorgeous, and a young woman. To say she was plain is to give her a break. Standing next to him didn't help of course. Jude's arm was around her and love was stated in his casually posed stance, his possessive eyes, his toothpaste-ad smile.

"That's Amanda. My wife."

Plain Jane Amanda, I thought.

"Someone is trying to kill her. The cops don't think so, but I do. And they tried to get me, would of, but for you. They set up the car accident last week. Look, I need help. Your help. I want to hire you."

I didn't ask the obvious or standard questions. *They who? Why? What for?* I didn't ask for details, I just shook my head. I wasn't even tempted. And I was scheduled to go to Fresno today. Again.

"I'm not asking for me." He shrugged, acknowledging that he'd been a jerk. "For Mandy. Do you know what it's like trying to protect a defenseless person who ignores threats and danger, who won't even see that there's a problem?"

I did. He saw the flicker in my eye. So much for Poker Face.

"Just listen to me, please." Jude started to sit down, read the expression on my face and remained standing. "Mandy's five-foot-three and ninety-eight pounds of determination. If she thinks she's right about something she's bullheaded as all git out. It's piss and vinegar then, not just determination."

I made an impatient gesture.

"Yeah," he said. "Okay, I'll get to it. She blew the whistle at work. Big time. What she did could curtail output, even shut down the company. That might leave her company, Louden, open to lawsuits, might put a lot of folks out of work. Good for her. No shit." He said this with admiration. "But it didn't exactly make Mandy the Queen of the Hop out there."

"It's a big jump from not being the Queen of the Hop to premeditated murder." I said it in spite of myself. Dammit anyway.

"Yeah," Jude said. "Yeah, it is. I agree with you." He shifted his weight from one foot to another, then planted his left foot on the chair, his elbow on his knee, hands gripped together, and leaned toward me. "At work she gets anonymous messages—threats in the interoffice mail and on her computer screen. Her desk gets messed up or trashed, the wastebasket turned over. A sweater she keeps there because of the air-conditioning goes missing, then turns up smeared with shit. And nobody sees anything, hears anything, knows anything."

"Mandy doesn't see there's a problem?" I asked in amazement.

"Yes and no." He shrugged helplessly, muscles rippling. "There's a problem, yeah, a big one, and it's getting to her. But she feels she's doing the right thing. She sees it as their problem, not hers."

"Is she doing the right thing?"

"Yes. No question." He said it without hesitation.

*No question? None? As if life were black and white and not shades of gray? As if one person or faction's interest wasn't opposed as often as not to another's. As if one truth wasn't another's lie.*

"At first I was all out for it, proud of her, proud she had the courage to walk a tough road. But, I'll be honest here, that wore off mighty damn quick. Now I just want to see her smiling again, not all jumpy and scared. I want to see her happy, happy and alive, more than I want to see her right. Damn straight." He said it grimly.

"And Mandy?"

9

"She won't back down. She's as hot as a dog on a rat about it. It's the principle, she says, and she won't walk away from it."

"What is it, this principle of hers?"

"Babies, old folks, people like you and me even."

I stared blankly at him. It wasn't enough of a clue.

"Anyone—"

*Anyone.* He paused and invested the word with weight and meaning, made it echo, *anyone . . . anyone . . . anyone . . .* made the listener realize that that anyone could be you, me, made all of that ugly.

"Anyone who received a heart valve made by Louden Medical Supply in the last two years or so is at risk. It fails, you're most likely done for. And it has failed, Mandy says. Not a couple of times, or tens of times, but hundreds."

"And failure is—" I asked, pretty clear on the answer.

"Death."

So there it was.

A kid on the street outside yelled and another answered. I heard the sounds of laughter and the rough-soft noise of in-line skates, felt the sun on my skin. It was still cool but I would have to turn on the air-conditioning soon.

"Sit down, Jude."

His cowboy boot disappeared from view as he lowered himself into the big wooden chair, dwarfing it.

I straightened a paper on my desk that didn't need straightening before I asked, "What do you want from me?"

"Two things. I want you to help me keep Mandy safe, and I want you to find out who's responsible for this." He clenched a fist, opened it. "Yesterday she found a plastic kid's whistle. A black whistle on a red string. It was on her desk at work. Smashed." He looked at me. "Just find out, okay, I'll take it from there. Fight fire with fire," he said grimly. "End this shit once and for all."

"You planning to round up a posse and ride the bad guys out of town?"

He grinned suddenly. Three-D gorgeous Technicolor cowboy. "Whatever."

"How about turning them over to the police?"

"That'd work," he agreed, keeping his options open. "Mandy's first, though, Mandy's number one. I'm leaving town on business in two days. I won't leave her alone and she won't come with me."

"It's almost impossible to watch over someone who fights you on it."

"She won't. Not now. She's worn down and out and scared and she damn well didn't figure being Queen of this Hop. The crown's sitting pretty heavy on her head," he said softly. "She wants to do what's right, she's determined—but she didn't figure it to get this bad. Shit on her sweater." He shook his head.

Yes. Exactly.

"And she doesn't figure to die for it, or watch me taken out either."

*To die for it.* It wasn't the kind of job I liked. It wasn't the kind of job I took. It also wasn't that simple.

I thought about Lindy, one of my favorite people, a kid I'd pulled off the streets and out of prostitution. She lived with Alma, my adopted grandmother, now. I thought, too, of Lindy's sixteen-year-old friend, Mary Beth. Smart, funny, a natural athlete, Mary Beth had a congenitally defective heart. Now, after surgery and an artificial heart valve, Mary Beth was "as good as new." What kind of a heart valve? Louden?

"Ms. Colorado?"

"Kat," I said automatically.

"Kat, will you do it?"

"I want Mandy in my office this afternoon."

"I can't do it, not without tipping them off at work and I—"

"Tomorrow, nine o'clock," I said, looking him straight in the eye. "And alone."

"Yeah. Okay."

I never did go to Fresno.

# 3

Dear Charity,

My dad says that everyone has to work real hard to make the world a better place. Well, I think that's stupid and that working hard and making a lot of money is enough. I mean, I spend a lot of money, too, and that helps the GNP. What do you think?

Give Me A Break

Dear Gimme,

I think you should listen to your dad.

Charity

~~~~~~~~~~~~~~~~~~~~~~~~~~~~~~~~~~~~~~~~~~~~~~~~~~~~

They were in my office at ten minutes of nine, Mandy a pale silhouette at Jude's side. Amanda Hudson was her husband's opposite in every way. He was large, blond, muscular and expansive. She was small, slim, dark, intense. Her clothing was shades of pale, cream-colored slacks, a crisp off-white cotton shirt and matching linen jacket. Her dark hair was pulled back in a ponytail and tied with a scarf that matched earrings and a necklace. Makeup was the only color in her face. Her smile was forced but the hand I shook cool and firm.

"You saved my husband's life. Thank you."

Her voice shook slightly. Her eyes, a clear deep brown, met mine and held. When she glanced at Jude he smiled, then leaned down to kiss her.

"I'll wait outside in the truck." His hand rested on her shoulder, then he nodded at me and left. We sat down.

"I think that scared me more than anything. That's why I'm here."

"The car accident?"

"Yes. They don't care who they hurt. It could have been me, it could have been Jude, it almost *was* Jude. If it was a warning it went too far, if it was an attempt . . ."

"It wasn't just mechanical failure?" I asked. "It was an older car."

"Oh no. Jude makes sure everything is running well, *especially* a car I use."

"How was it sabotaged?"

"I'm not sure, it's not something I understand very well, but apparently it was rigged so the effect was of the accelerator wide open. Then the brakes started to fail. A tire blew out too. It was out of control."

"Like at your job?"

"What?" she questioned, puzzled. "I don't get it."

Time to slow down. I had jumped a connection. Or two. Time to backtrack. "Why did you get involved?" I wanted to know more about her before I asked about work. "Most people would look the other way, transfer, quit, change jobs."

"I'm not sure. It's not that I'm brave or special, I'm not either of those things. Not at all." She tossed her head and the scarf flipped around her ears, flashed briefly, brightly, then settled down docilely. "You know when you're a kid and you say: When I grow up, I'm *never* doing that?"

I nodded. I remembered my mother, her face contorted in a drunken rage. I knew.

"My dad's boss used to come over to the house and push him

around in front of us kids. And my dad always took it. Later he tried to make a joke of it, but it wasn't a joke and we knew it. The butcher could give another customer a special roast Mom had ordered days before, right in front of her practically, and give us something ordinary and she'd never say anything. 'Don't make trouble.' 'Be nice.' 'Be polite.' 'Smile no matter what.' That's how I was brought up."

She was very angry. Give her nails, she'd chew them up and spit tacks.

"I have a hard time respecting my parents. I have nothing but contempt for the way they were. I won't do that."

Her voice rang out. Echoes, shades of Patrick Henry. Admirable, no question.

"Doing what's right is *not* making trouble, it's doing what's *right,*" she said fiercely.

"Doing what's right often causes trouble for someone," I pointed out reasonably.

"Of course." Her hand waved, dismissing my point. "But so what? It *has* to be done."

"And it can be a dangerous thing to do." Thoughts of Karen Silkwood had crossed my mind. Did they ever cross hers?

She ignored my comment. "Do you remember the drug thalidomide?"

I nodded.

"One doctor had the courage to blow the whistle on thalidomide in the United States. Without her the drug could have, would have gone out to pregnant women all over the country. And their babies . . ."

Yes, the babies. Little ones born without arms or legs, with hands and feet attached to the trunk, with minds clear and untouched in bodies beyond anything even Bosch on a bad day had contemplated.

"Watergate, Three Mile Island, thalidomide, the *Challenger,* defective medical supplies . . ." Her voice was low but intense, clear, passionate, the words charged with energy. "How can *anyone* forget the past or ignore such things in the present? How?"

Her cheeks were flushed, her eyes sparkling, her question a battle cry. She had the simple, single-minded, passionate fervor of a Joan of Arc: *This is right. It must be done. I must do it, whatever the cost.* St. Joan. One does not become a saint by merely doing good works and living a blameless life. Very few saints—any? I didn't know—died in their beds of old age. They were crucified, or stoned, or drowned, fried like griddle cakes, fed to the lions, crushed beneath . . .

"I can't just forget it. I can't ignore it. The thing is, Ms. Colorado, mistakes can happen, I know that. People aren't perfect, companies aren't either. But when you make a mistake and then find out, you correct it, right? They should be *thankful* for my help!"

"Only in the best of all possible worlds. In reality—"

Her words rushed over mine, tumbled them about like cars on an L.A. freeway in a wild crash. Simplistic fervor doing a 100 mph. I quit talking.

"Not only does Louden not admit the mistake, they're *covering* it up. People will continue to suffer and die. I won't be part of the cover-up, I *won't*. I feel so tricked, so duped. I worked hard for this company. I helped make it a better and more efficient business, and for what? So they could continue to put a faulty product on the market. That's what! *Money* is more important to them than *safety!*"

"It often is, Amanda," I said, though she wasn't listening. As she raged on, I remembered the exploding gas tank of General Motors vehicles. *Fiery crashes. That's what.* Bic lighters that failed to extinguish or exploded. *Burn victims. That's what.* Drugs with known and lethal side effects. *Grave physical damage and death. That's what.* Asbestos exposure, lead exposure. *Cancer, death. Untold human pain. That's what.*

"So, I can't be part of a cover-up. It's just as bad to *know* that something's wrong and not do anything as it is to do it. I have to do something, but Kat— May I call you that?" She rushed on without waiting for an answer. "I just didn't know that all these awful things were going to happen."

The fire-breathing, sword-slashing Angel of Righteousness melted away. I was looking at a very frightened young woman.

"Tell me."

"At the beginning, when things started happening, I said I wasn't going to let it bother me and . . . and I'm good at that but . . . but I just had no idea." Her voice ran down like a tired old sewing machine on a hem put up too many times. "No part of my life was too everyday, too humdrum and no account but they'd get into it, make me feel watched and *violated*. Do you understand?"

Yes. It had happened to me. It had terrified me but it had also made me angry, made me want to fight. I glanced over at Amanda. The fight in her was gone.

"I was prepared for it at the office, but not at home. In the middle of the night there'd be noises, especially if Jude was away. And he's away a lot." I raised an eyebrow in silent question. "He sells farm equipment. For John Deere. His territory is pretty big so he travels a lot."

She quieted and shivered. "Anyway, at first I was brave. I had a gun; I had the dogs inside the house with me." She took a deep breath and filled her fragile-looking chest with air. "Or was it stupid? I'd call the dogs, take a flashlight and the shotgun, and go out. Nobody. He. She. They. All gone. But the message was there." She pulled her hand aimlessly across her face, then pushed a stray strand of hair behind her ear. It fell forward again almost immediately.

"The lights in the barn would be on or the windshield wipers on my car would be going. The gate would be open and a rake tossed out in the drive, prongs up. I kept telling myself it wasn't going to get to me." She stopped, then said, "Two months ago if Jude had asked me to come talk to you I would have laughed at the idea."

I looked at Amanda, her slender body rigid, her face immobile, cold with righteousness or fear.

"But now I'm scared. We—I—do need help. This *can't* go on. I realize that in doing this I didn't and don't know what I'm doing exactly. I thought if I found out about the facts, talked about the situation, wrote to everyone I could think of, something might work, somebody might notice."

It had worked. Somebody had noticed.

"You got it started. Now let someone else finish. Let someone else carry the ball."

"I almost wish I could, but I can't." She sounded wistful. "No one wants it."

Not surprising. Hot potatoes are not particularly popular.

"So, I'm stuck. I can't quit until I can prove it, nail them, stop it. I *can't*." There was fear in her voice but what drove her was something stronger than that fear. "All those people who don't know, who think they're safe . . ."

I thought again of Mary Beth.

"And there will be more, Kat. It will happen. These are not just statistics, these are people. So it has to stop. I have to stop it. And I need your help."

My mind slipped into the past.

*Mary Beth smiled at me. "Yo!" Lindy yelled. "C'mon, Kat. Catch us!" The two girls raced off, the dogs wild and running, all of us yelling, hollering, having a good time. I caught them. Barely. And only because we piled up in a dead end behind Charity's barn, the horses whinnying and snorting and wound up in our fever. "I would have beaten you." Mary Beth threw back her head and laughed. "I would have; I thought there was a gate here." We all laughed with her because it was true and because we were glad, because the heart operation had made her as fast, faster than we were. "Now you're IT, Kat!" Mary Beth called, and they took off like bugs on a hot fry pan. "You're IT."*

It.

"Kat?"

An impatient voice tugged at me.

"Kat?"

I was IT. "Yes," I told Amanda Hudson. "What kind of help do you need?"

"Thank you. I want somebody on my side, somebody who is not afraid, who will fight back." There was a question there.

I answered it. "Like me."

"Like you," she said in relief.

"At work?" I asked, wondering how we would pull that one off.

"No. It's horrible, nasty, and mean." She thought about it. "It's even threatening, but it's not life-threatening, no matter what Jude thinks. I try to look at things through their eyes and I know that they're afraid too, for their jobs, their lives as they have them now, their security. They just don't see yet. How can you build your security on someone else's loss? You can't. They don't see yet that it really affects us all, that we're all in this together."

I thought she might be grossly overestimating the altruism of the average worker, that she was being wildly optimistic. I thought, too, that she might be the shortsighted one.

"They may never see that, Mandy."

"Amanda," she corrected firmly.

"Amanda," I amended. "Many people never see past a paycheck, never see past tomorrow or at most the day after."

"Oh, I think they will," she said, idealism and youth piling into the elevator marked HOPE, pushing the penthouse button, heading for HEAVEN. "Of course they will, but it takes time. I understand that, you know. Definitely," she said to the green eyes I had deliberately made go blank.

"Definitely!" she repeated.

All right. That made one of us who was convinced.

"Anyway . . ." she continued, with a slight note of exasperation at my cynicism.

"Do you still wear the sweater?"

She frowned. "What sweater?"

"The one you had at work. The one you found soiled with excrement."

"*Really,* Kat! I . . ."

"Do you?"

"I don't know what you're . . ." Color flared in her cheeks.

"See you, Amanda," I said as I stood up, pushing the chair behind me, preparing to escort her to the door.

"No!"

Her eyes met mine, then dropped to hands folded tightly in her lap. She was holding something back.

"No, I don't. I threw it away. I wanted to flush it down the toilet but of course I couldn't do that. I wanted to do something horrible back but I didn't do that either. It just made me more determined to get to the bottom of this, to use my mind, my intelligence and determination."

"What, specifically, do you want from me, Amanda?"

"Jude's going away on business. He thinks . . . I . . . we . . ." She stuttered along like a badly tuned motorbike, then took a deep breath and said what she should have said when she first entered my office. "Could you stay with me then? Please. I don't want to be alone. Just the thought of having someone there makes me feel so much better."

Intelligence, determination, and muscle.

I was the muscle.

*St. Joan. Thalidomide babies. Mary Beth.*

"Yes. Go get Jude. We'll work it out."

I hadn't chosen this job. It had chosen me. *Be gracious with the inevitable, Kat,* Alma, my grandmother, had taught me. There you go. In the silence of my office and my mind the Maid of Orleans gazed at me. Idealistic, passionate young Joan, with God in her soul and the angel's voice in her mind, heart and dreams. There were no angels' voices ringing in my mind, just Mary Beth's and the cries of deformed children. And Joan's, tied to a stake at nineteen with dry branches, desperadoes and fanatics all around her.

A spark was all it took.

# 4

Dear Charity,

I got in BIG trouble with my coach 'cause I stood up for my friend who is visually handicapped and wants to play on our softball team. I say give her a chance and so what if she misses the ball sometimes. The coach said I had to *Put up, shut up and follow orders, period.*

Left Field

Dear Left Field,

You may be out in left field but you're hitting home runs! Good luck to you and your friend.

Charity

～～～～～～～～～～～～～～～～～～～～

"You hate it, don't you?"

I was inferring from body language and it wasn't a tough call. Amanda sat in the passenger seat of my Bronco, her slight body rigid with tension, her face ashen, a pulse thudding in her temple. Jude had left early this morning for the airport and an out-of-state sales conference; I had arrived as he was leaving; now I was driving Amanda to the Louden Industries plant. That was the plan.

"I used to love going to work, Kat. Now—"

I braked suddenly as a red Hyundai driven (sic) by a teenage hotshot with racing stripes shaved into the side of his head darted in front of me, missing us by inches, and squealed into the left-turn lane. Amanda gasped.

"You need to explain, Amanda. I need to know more about Louden, your job, the people you work with, the situation in general. I need to know who 'they' are."

"They?"

"Who's threatening you?"

"I don't know."

"Who could be doing this?"

"I . . . I don't know."

"Let's back up," I said gently. "Let's start with the basics."

So she did. It was a smooth, easy recitation, the kind I'd expect from an MBA making a corporate presentation at a board meeting.

"Louden Industries manufactures medical devices—heart valves, pacemakers, that kind of thing. Our manufacturing plant is located in Texas. These devices have to be made, handled and packaged in a 'clean room,' a sterile environment. Production is therefore concentrated in the Texas plant. There are two other shipping and receiving areas in addition to the one at the main plant, one here in Rancho Cordova and one in Illinois. We handle shipping to the western U.S.; Illinois handles the midwest to the eastern seaboard, and Texas the rest. Our plant is not sterile, so we just do the shipping and receiving, handling and processing incoming orders, sending them out to medical facilities and hospitals." She paused for a quick glance at me.

"Got it."

I stopped for a yellow light where a McDonald's, a gas station, a wallpaper store and a dumpster competed for our attention. Tough call. No trees, no flowers, no shrubs, nothing green or alive, just an asphalt, concrete and plastic bummer. California, the Golden State, the Flower of the West, is disappearing.

Two cars in the lane next to ours hit the gas and sailed through in a big hurry to stop at the red light in the next block. Maybe it was the lure of the Taco Bell there. *Yo! Nachos! Tacos! Enchiladas! Tostadas!*

"I'm an accountant by training."

An accountant, not an MBA. And a whistle-blower?

"Some accountants are really just number people: add, subtract, multiply, divide. They don't see behind or beyond the numbers. They don't have any creative or critical facility at all. More and more, computers do the routine work, but you still need a person there to take in, sort and process the information. A lot of accountants are afraid of life and people, I think. They feel more comfortable with numbers; they take refuge there."

I thought about the accountants I knew and decided they all fell in that category.

"But accounting isn't just numbers any more than a painting is just used art supplies. They're both pictures."

Her soft voice was passionate and I was intrigued. I'd never known an accountant like this before.

"And these pictures reveal information about people, about situations, about . . ." She stared in the direction of a lone cottonwood tree that someone had forgotten to cut down to make way for urban ugliness.

"Companies," I finished.

"Yes. And here's the talent I have: I can spot inefficiency, cost overruns, and production mismanagement by looking at figures, spread sheets . . ." Amanda caught my eye and laughed. "Am I out of your league?"

"Not yet, but you will be soon."

"Okay. Anyway, by looking at the available production and distribution, at projections and financial data, I can extrapolate and make recommendations. My recommendations saved the company time and money. I wasn't just an accountant long."

"I bet."

"Oh, Kat, it was wonderful! I loved being a problem spotter and solver for the company. I loved making things better and cheaper and right. It was like being a kid again, adding up a long column of six-figure numbers and having them come out right the first time. It was a rush!"

"You can do that?"

"What?"

"Add up a long column of big numbers and have them come out right the first time?"

"Of course. You can't?"

"Not necessarily." That was a decided understatement. Not the first time, not the second. Maybe the third. Maybe.

"Oh," she said. "Well, anyway, it went pretty fast from there on out. They loved what I did at the plant. I was promoted and given bonuses, made the employee of the month, the whole bit. The president of Louden even phoned to congratulate me. I could do no wrong." She said it without arrogance.

We'd been on surface roads and then the freeway for about twenty minutes. Highway 50 is a major commuter corridor in and out of Sacramento, always busy these days and often packed or slow-and-go at rush hour. It's not scenic anymore. The open fields and prime agricultural land of California's Central Valley are disappearing. Industrial complexes, midlevel chain eateries, and business high-rises thumb their noses and smirk insolently as you zip past in polluted air. I'm a native Californian. It makes me sad, or mad. Depends.

"Bradshaw?" I asked, referring to an exit that was coming up.

"Yes."

We were, I figured, about five minutes from the Louden plant.

"Stop," Amanda said, as we exited. "Please. We're twenty minutes early. I haven't finished telling you and I don't want to get there early."

"Do you want coffee?" We were passing a coffee shop.

"No. Not really. I just want to talk, to finish telling you this. Can you park somewhere?"

I pulled into the parking lot of a carpet store and looked at rolls of carpet stacked outside the store that I wouldn't consider using for anything off a black-and-white movie set. Maybe not even that. When I killed the ignition the silence was thick. I rolled down the window and heard cars and an occasional brash, bold and gutsy bird singing its heart out, doing soprano to the bass of traffic in brave defiance of the auditory odds.

Amanda folded her hands in her lap. "After I got promoted they

23

asked me if I would act as a management consultant and do the same work at the other plants. I was pretty excited by the prospect. Excited? Shoot, I jumped on it. They sent me to Texas first. I was to work with a couple of people there, help train them and set up the kind of programs and systems I'd put into effect here."

I gazed at a roll of carpet. *Sculptured Pile!* the sign proclaimed. The carpet was done in about four different shades of green and brown and I swiftly averted my eyes. *Oatmeal Elegance* was better, but not by much, for sure nothing to write home about. Amanda was briefly silent, apparently in rapt contemplation of *Persimmon Passion—Perfect for YOUR Bedroom!*

"And you uncovered more than they expected or wanted?"

"Yes. How did you know?"

"Well, there you go. You hired an investigator—that's how it works. A lot more?" I prompted.

"A lot more," she agreed. "A whole lot more. I had the run of the place, of course, and I spent a lot of time going through files and examining data."

I zoned out. I didn't mean to or want to but I did. One moment I was watching and listening to Amanda Hudson with complete attention and the next I was wondering at the incongruity of a high-powered corporate hotshot professional mind and perception packaged in such an unpreposing, unassuming, almost meek and mild manner and person—like Superman and Clark Kent. I could hear Alma's voice in my mind. *Don't judge a book by its cover, dear. So tempting, so misleading.* Yes. I wrenched my mind out of dual personalities and book covers and back to Amanda.

"I was working ten, twelve, fifteen hours a day. Why not? It was interesting, enormously challenging, and Jude wasn't there to go home to."

*Indoors! Outdoors!* the sign screamed at me. *Perfect Anywhere!* It was mustard. Mustard carpeting by definition goes nowhere and is not perfect.

"And late one night you found something."

"Yes." She wrinkled her nose.

*Ideal for YOUR Bathroom! Hides Everything!* It was dark brown pile. I shuddered.

"I accessed a file—actually it took me a while to find it because, although it was referenced in several places, I had a time tracking it down. And the references to it kept changing. Once it was listed under payouts, then as miscellaneous expenses, then overhead."

"How much?"

She nodded. "Yes. That's it, you're right, and that's what caught me too. It was a million and a half. *For this year alone!* Over a two-year period it came to almost four and a half million dollars. I couldn't access records older than three years. And I couldn't figure out what it was for."

"Was this all on the computer or were other records available to you?"

"Both. Up to that point I'd primarily used the computer. It's faster, easier, more efficient. After that I started digging through the files for hard copy. I found it." She looked at me expectantly.

"Out-of-court settlements for product failure."

"Yes."

I think she expected me to be surprised.

"How did you know?"

"Amanda, I'm an investigator. I have an IQ in triple digits and I can add two and two without a calculator, but basically you led me to it, okay?"

"Okay." She sounded subdued.

"And?"

"And I couldn't believe what I read. I wasn't prepared for it."

*Understated Elegance! Fashion! Price! Looks! Rugs Rugs Rugs!*

"Here I was on assignment to streamline operations, pare down cost overruns and reorganize in order to save Louden money in the hundreds and the thousands of dollars and I'd stumbled onto cost overruns in the *millions*. But it wasn't just that, Kat."

No. It wasn't.

She glanced at me, pretty brown eyes that were young, old, and confused. "It wasn't just the money, the millions. It was what it meant."

Yes.

"Do you know what you have when you pay out that kind of money?"

"Serious liability, I imagine. Permanent disability. Death."

"You got it."

"What is the problem?"

"Heart valves. Either strut fracture, or the wire that makes a disc inside the valve open and close breaks. The most recent settlement was three months ago." She took a shuddery breath. "I made copies of all those records. Then I drafted a memo querying the advisability of marketing a product that left us wide-open to liability. Of course I also made suggestions for dealing with the problem. They were costly and long-term but still— People were losing their lives. It had to be done."

Her naïveté was simple and heartfelt. But it was not an *of course* situation. Not by a long shot.

"And then the shit hit the fan?"

"Yes. How did . . . Oh, never mind. Well, it did for sure. Management told me to lay off that entirely and concentrate on my job. I said that was my job. They said not anymore it isn't. And then they asked for all my notes and files on that 'angle,' as they called it."

"Did you turn everything in?"

"Oh yes. But before I did I made copies they didn't know about, though they may have guessed by now. I finished up my job in Texas, went to Illinois, did the same thing there minus that file. I never saw, could never find, actually, any further references in company files to that account. And I looked, you bet I did.

"They told me to forget about it, but I couldn't. They told me it was being handled, but I didn't believe them. When they spoke about it to me they kept using terms like: 'acceptable risk factor,' 'calculated losses,' terms that ignore the fact that we are talking about people's *lives* here, not wristwatches or toasters or underwear."

*Sale! Last Three Days! Prices Slashed!*

I started the car and pulled out of the parking lot. "Was that when it started getting ugly?"

"No. Not until I wouldn't drop it, until I wrote to the FDA and sent my boss copies of the letters. I wasn't trying to do anything underhanded, you see."

I groaned inwardly. Had I ever been that young, that naïve, that idealistic?

"That's when it started. They told me to lay off, to stop being a troublemaker. And I don't think I'm very good at being diplomatic, Kat."

I nodded. That thought had crossed my mind a time or two.

I drove past the big blue and white Louden Industries sign and pulled into the company lot and up to the plant. I looked over at Amanda, looked for a Superwoman cape. No. No hero statement—just ironed blah beige and pearls. Maybe she'd left her cape at home.

"Why did—do you keep on?"

"I told you."

"There's more."

There had to be. There always is.

The Bronco idled beneath us, the sound of the engine deadened by the drone of the air conditioner. I listened to the rush of air, not the rush of words, for some time.

"I was an ugly kid. Some people are ugly kids and grow out of it. I didn't."

I shook my head meaning, no, you're not ugly, not at all, but she wasn't looking at me.

"My sisters and cousins were pretty and cute. They were adorable, actually. I was plain. *Plain Amanda,* they said; and *Your name should have been Jane. Plain Jane, plain plain Amanda Jane.* She said the last in a sing-song taunting child voice.

Amanda's face and voice were otherwise without expression. If there was pain—and there had to be—she'd learned to hide it long ago.

"I worked hard, studied hard, did very well in school. Being the smart one was a lot better than being the plain one. People came to respect me. Awards and scholarships were all I've ever had to give; they were the only way I had of getting recognition and appreciation. Respect is a lot better than pity."

"You're an attractive woman and a good person. That's enough."

"No," she said firmly. "It's not and you wouldn't know anything about it. Nothing. You can't. You're pretty. " Her voice was acid-edged, harsh. She put her hand on the door handle and opened it.

"Four-thirty?" I queried, at a loss for other words.

She nodded.

"I'll be here."

She climbed out of the car, then leaned back in. "Nothing. You know nothing about it."

"Morning, Amanda." A stocky, beef-faced man in a one-piece gray coverall stood at the entrance. "Have a nice day." He grinned, then leaned forward and spit on the sidewalk in front of her, just missing her shoe, a beige open-toed sandal.

She ducked her head down and scooted inside. I caught a glimpse of stricken eyes in a frozen face and then the double glass doors closed. The man in the coverall folded his arms across his chest and stared at me. His name was stitched on his pocket: Buck. I stared back, held his glance until he looked away, walked away. Then I drove off.

Amanda was tough, idealistic, brave.

She was also way out of her league.

# 5

Dear Charity,

Do you believe that life is fair and that everyone, especially the bad guys, get their just desserts?

Hoping So

Dear Hoping,

It doesn't always work out that way in the short run. In the long run, what goes around comes around. By the way, there is no such thing as just when it comes to dessert. Dessert is one of the high points of life.

Charity

~~~~~~~~~~~~~~~~~~~~~~~~~~~~~~~~~~~~~~~~~~~~~~~~~~

"What do you want for dinner?" Amanda asked. Gone was the professional woman who'd spoken so passionately of her accomplishments earlier this morning.

"What happened at work, Amanda?"

"We could have Chinese or . . . I'm not hungry, Kat."

"Get in the car, lock your door, fasten your seat belt." I said it slowly and gently, as one would to a hurt child. "What happened?"

"If they're trying to scare me, make me quit, they're doing a pretty good job."

Her voice was supposed to sound stoic, I thought, but there was a quaver in it.

"Tell me," I requested again, looking at her briefly as I changed lanes and approached the freeway on-ramp. She was pale, too pale, and it was hot even with the a/c set on Alaska.

"There are always nasty jobs everywhere you work and no matter what you do. Always. And somebody has to do them—no problem. It's just that lately I'm invariably the somebody."

"Today?" I kept pushing. I needed specifics, not generalities or philosophical digressions.

"Today . . ." Her voice, uncertain and shaky, drifted off.

I glanced at her, decided to wait it out. We stopped for a yellow light. It went red, then green before she spoke.

"Today Al, my immediate supervisor, asked me to check accounts and figures by hand. There are no math mistakes in them, these are computer-generated figures. Data entry mistakes perhaps, but not math. After that I sharpened pencils and filed. That's not nasty of course, just demeaning and degrading since it's so far beneath my work and ability level, never mind my job description.

"After lunch I was asked to move stock around in the warehouse, clean out the men's room and—"

"The *men's* room?"

"Yes. Somebody locked the door from the outside so I was stuck there for close to an hour." Her face was expressionless, her voice as flat as yesterday's news. "I kept wishing I had cherry bombs to throw in the toilets."

She grinned just a little. Good. Much better than her beaten-up-poor-little-downtrodden-and-suffering-but-still-savior-of-the-human-race look.

"How did you get out?"

"Barry, the maintenance man. He's a nice guy, really, decent. He shows me pictures of his grandkids all the time. He was very embarrassed about the whole situation, my being assigned to do his job."

I changed lanes on Highway 50 without signaling. Why should I be any different from all the people (not Californians!) who'd moved here from New York, New Jersey, and Massachusetts? "Amanda, I want you to scoot around in your seat and take a quick look at the white Honda two-door behind us. Tell me if you recognize the car or driver. Be low-key."

Amanda swerved around and practically climbed into the backseat for a better view. So much for low-key.

"Where is it? I don't see it."

"Two car lengths behind, one over, fast lane. Try for cool, okay?"

She glanced at me contritely. "Sorry." Then she reached into the backseat for the newspaper I'd been reading while I was waiting for her. She held the paper partly up, as if reading, and swiveled around slowly behind it to observe the roadway. Better, but not by much.

"While I was working in the warehouse shifting stock and stuff?"

"Yes."

"I was working in the same area as a guy on a forklift. In fact I was doing by hand what he was doing by machine, so go figure. Anyway, a stack of boxes tumbled over, just missing me."

"Just?"

"Six inches. As I left, Jim, one of the warehouse foremen, stopped me. 'About that accident,' he said, and then he winked. 'Maybe you better watch your step a little more closely. Maybe then there'll be no more accidents.' "

I changed lanes.

"The Honda still with us?"

"Yup, changed lanes too. I can't tell about the car, Kat. There're a million of them around, especially old beat-up ones."

Yes, it was a perfect choice for a tail, if it was a tail.

"What was in those boxes? How heavy were they?"

"Would I have been badly hurt, you mean?"

"Yes."

"Not too heavy. For sure I would have been bruised and banged up."

"Could it have been an accident? Maybe the foreman just said that afterwards to scare you?"

"Maybe. And it could have been an accident that I was locked

31

into the men's room, too. It could have been an accident that I was given ridiculously stupid work assignments outside my area of expertise and experience. It could have . . ." Her voice was raw and shrill and starting to spiral out of control.

"Amanda, stop it. I'm on your side. I believe you." Briefly I touched her cool hand. "If we're going to figure out the pattern here, see who could be responsible, we need to separate the deliberate from the accidental or coincidental."

Or paranoid, I thought. I watched the Honda in the rearview mirror. I was in the center lane and it was in the fast. We were in rush-hour traffic, heavy but steady and moving right along at 65 mph. At the last moment, no blinker, I slid over into the right lane and exited the freeway.

"Where are we going? What are you doing?"

"Losing the Honda." We stopped at a light, then I crossed over the freeway going south to pick up a back road. We would drive surface streets to Amanda's home in Elk Grove.

"White male, probably mid-thirties, dark hair brushed back off his face, dark complexion, wide shoulders, reflector sunglasses?"

"Huh?"

"The driver of the Honda. Does he sound familiar?"

"I don't know." She shrugged, looking straight ahead out the windshield. "There could be a dozen guys in the warehouse like that. Did you lose the car?"

"Yes."

"Nice work!"

She sounded jubilant. I didn't tell her that it didn't matter, that ten to one they knew where she lived and could pick us up anytime. It was good to see her smile, however briefly.

"Let's stop for a pizza, okay? We can take it home, eat there."

So we did and Mama's Italian (was there any other kind?) Pizzeria said they were glad to see us. Amanda's appetite and faint color were back. Good news. We drank iced tea while we waited for our order.

"What happened when you wrote the FDA?"

"Nothing."

"What did your letter say?"

"I told them what I found out, including names, dates and dollar amounts. I noted that all the examples cited seemed to be associated with one specific Louden product, a heart valve. I stated that there was absolutely no reason for large sums of money to be paid out like this unless there was a defective product involved."

There she was again, the competent professional, the woman who was an accountant and sounded like an MBA. The scared little thing was gone.

"I wrote that the cash payouts all seemed to be made to relatives of the heart valve recipient, not to the actual patient, which indicated to me that this product was not only defective but life-threatening. I quoted figures to show that the Louden valve was in wide and current circulation. I said I could find no records indicating testing, modification, or other appropriate action on the part of Louden."

"Was your letter acknowledged?"

"No. Nothing. So I wrote again, sending a copy of the first letter and enclosed data, just to be sure. I asked for the courtesy of an acknowledgment."

"And?"

"Nothing, at least not yet."

"Did you write these letters at work?"

"No."

"Mail them from there?"

"No."

"When did you mail them?"

"About a month ago, I think. I can check my file."

A fleshy, pimply kid who looked like he'd had too many pizzas washed down with too many chocolate sodas sullenly dropped our pizza on the table. "Here, have a nice day," he snarled, words and body language at opposite poles. Amanda and I looked at each other and started to laugh. He snarled sullenly again, a pimple bobbing on his chin. His was a limited repertoire but he did it pretty well. We grabbed the pizza and scrammed.

I hate driving with pizza. The choices are never good. Either you burn your mouth and spill stuff all over yourself, wishing you had thought of napkins, not that it would make any difference at all in the mess level, or you suffer as the smell of hot tomato sauce and cheese amps up every cell in your body, turning them into little rude cheerleaders screaming for immediate culinary gratification. Gimme a P, gimme an I, gimme a Z, gimme . . .

"Kat?"

"Hmmmm." Gimme a Z, gimme a . . .

"It's the next left, did you remember?"

I did. I had. Well, I would have except for the pizza. We were on a tree-lined two-lane road in the old part of Elk Grove. Here most of the houses were set on five-acre, ten-acre, or larger spreads. Many of them, like Jude and Amanda Hudson's place, were working farms and ranches. Amanda and Jude boarded horses, had a few of their own and ran some stock.

I turned off the air conditioner and rolled down my window. In the early evening I could hear the *snick snick* of sprinkler systems over the hum of the Bronco's engine. As the sun sank, the still hot air held out faint hot promise for a cool evening.

I studied the Hudson place as we approached. A wooden ranch house, it had been added on to over the years as generations of families with new kids, old grannies, and notions of coming up in the world had dictated. It was an old house but slick as a new penny, recently painted in white and trimmed out in dark green. The garage was detached and neatly painted like the house. The barn and pumphouse were a couple hundred yards from the house. Both had been painted long ago in now weather-beaten farm red.

The sun dipped behind the barn and everything exploded in the fireball red glow of hot valley sun. Cottonwoods and majestic valley oaks, neatly maintained houses and barns lit up against the red/pink, then the gray/azure blue electric flash of the breath-stopping, heart-stopping, memory-blocking evening horizon line. God, I love the valley, I love California. My heart sings at this kind of beauty, at the farms and the crops, at the old places and the memories of early pioneer dreams, at the struggling possibilities and hoped-for promises of the present in this hot, flat, glorious beautiful valley.

So I missed it.

"Kat! Oh my God! Oh no, no!"

Amanda hadn't missed it. The gate to their property was a standard farm gate, two metal gates hung at each side of the road and swinging open in the middle. This morning there had been a new chain and a padlock. I knew; I'd fastened it. There still was, but the chain had been cut and dangled limply, the padlock dragged in the dirt. The right-hand gate had been pushed open far enough for a car to get through.

Not good.

"Where's Georgie? Kat, where is he?"

Amanda grabbed for the door handle and started to slide out. I grabbed for her. She tried to yank away but I was into my Super Girl/ Super Glue routine, so no dice. Two can play this game.

"Georgie?"

"One of our dogs. He's always here to greet me. Always. And he would be barking because he wouldn't recognize the sound of your car yet."

Yes. I remembered now.

"Where are your nearest neighbors, Amanda?"

She pointed off to the right, pulling away from me. A row of trees screened anything beyond, but earlier I had seen a house and barn from the road.

"How far?"

"Not very. Five minutes."

"Get them." She started to protest. I stared her down.

She swallowed hard. "Okay."

"Good. I'll meet you up at the house."

She nodded, slid out of the Bronco and took off at a run. I

snapped open the glove compartment, pulled out my .380 and laid it on the seat beside me. Then I drove. Slowly. With the windows down. Paying attention. The still of a valley summer evening no longer seemed peaceful, tranquil and full of promise. Menace, like beauty, can be in the eye of the beholder.

The Bronco jolted along the packed dirt road, in and out of potholes raising dust and making a lot of noise. My arrival would not be a surprise. I didn't see any vehicles that didn't belong but the barn made a large screen. I didn't see Georgie. I could hear a number of dogs barking. I pulled the Bronco up so it blocked the driveway and the way out, turned off the ignition, pocketed the keys and stuck the .380 in the waistband of my jeans. Then I got out.

I could still hear the *snick snick* of the sprinklers, birds calling out in cloudless sky and hot evening air. A bee buzzed in the heat that buzzed in my ears. Dogs barked furiously from behind the barn or house. Chickens squawked and scattered at my approach. Over it all was the muted happy-go-lucky sound of ragtime piano music. For two minutes, I forced myself to stand absolutely still next to the car. I saw nothing else out of place, heard nothing more. There was nothing behind the barn or house. I checked. The piano played merrily on.

A vehicle approached behind me. I turned to see a beige pickup stop just short of the Bronco, next to a burned-out hulk that I assumed was Amanda's Cadillac. Amanda fell out of the truck and raced over toward me. A tall man of about seventy with shoulders stooped by age and work, white hair, a farmer's tan and a shotgun, laboriously got out of the driver's side of the truck. I walked around the house, checking doors and windows. Tighter than a drum. Then I walked out to meet him. I couldn't see Amanda. I assumed she was looking for Georgie.

He took in the .380, then me, at a glance, nodded in an abbreviated greeting. "Walk the place, I reckon."

"Yes," I agreed.

"Name's Todd."

"Kat."

He shifted the shotgun to his left arm and we shook hands, then started walking.

"Me and Daisy, the wife, got the place just south of here. These here are nice kids. I don't like what's happening, not a bit. Glad to help out. This ain't like Elk Grove."

"I don't think it is Elk Grove."

His eyes didn't change. Old eyes. Beyond-surprise eyes. "Yeah. I didn't reckon it was. I don't have to know. Still glad to help."

"I wish you were *my* neighbor."

He grinned at me. "We'll hafta git you out here then."

The horses heard us and came dancing out of the barn and into the corral, ears flicking, eyes curious, tails switching flies in the beginning of an evening breeze. The dogs barked wildly and raced around. Chickens squawked and scrabbled about in the dirt. Everything looked okay.

Almost everything.

I looked at an Appaloosa mare and gasped. Todd made a deep sound low in his throat. The Appy's mane and tail had been hacked off in ragged sawtooth fashion. She hung her head and looked at us sideways, her haunches twitching and skittering. Embarrassed, I thought.

"Todd—?" I looked the question at him. The mare didn't always look like this, surely.

"Someone's been at her." He unlatched the gate and strode into the corral, ran his hands soothingly over the mare, calming her, talking sweet to her. She knickered and nuzzled him. He gave her a last pat and we continued our look-see. Nothing else was unusual or out of place. Ditto in the backyard and spa area, although I noticed a string of lights coming loose over the hot tub. And I admired the roses and summer flowers.

Back in the front of the house we found Amanda cradling Georgie in her arms. The dog was madly licking her cheek. "Oh, thank God he's okay—that they're all okay." There was a crescendo of piano notes, a final riff. Silence. Then it began again. Amanda seemed oblivious.

"May I have the house keys, Amanda?"

"Hmmm? Oh yes, of course. Over there."

She waved vaguely in the direction of a purse tossed in the late-afternoon sunshine of the new-mown lawn. I retrieved the keys, leaving the purse, and walked up the steps to the porch. Todd was leaning on the porch rail chewing a piece of grass and measuring life with eyes that had seen two generations of it. He was still cradling the shotgun.

Inside the house was cooler than outside and would be for another hour yet. Then, with luck, the cool Delta breezes would kick up, push through hot air and across our faces. It would be time to open the windows and doors, let the cool in. I know the way it is and broke the unwritten rule as I left the front door wide open, letting the hot air waltz in, settle down and make itself at home. Todd didn't close the door either.

With the heat pulsing at our backs and ragtime piano pounding in our ears we surveyed the front room. I walked over to the stereo setup and punched the power button on the compact disc player. In the silence I could hear the *snick snick* of the sprinklers again.

"You checked the outside, the doors, you said," he commented.

"Yes."

"Locked up tight?"

"Yes."

He didn't ask me if I was sure. I liked that. I liked him.

"We got us something kinda nasty here then."

"Yes."

Nasty. Amanda had used the same word earlier. My flesh crawled in the heat. I thought I smelled blood, or was it just dread? Amanda's footsteps closed in on us.

"Georgie, *c'mon.* Here. *Good* boy, *good* dog. Kat? Todd?" Amanda's voice bumped at our backs. "Georgie's fine. Thank goodness."

She was close enough now to see the room in which Todd and I stood. The silence that lasted for a long time was broken finally by her gasp, then by a low keening, and then by the barking of the dog.

# 6

Dear Charity,

I put a snake in my girlfriend's bed as a practical joke. She says it really scared her and now she won't speak to me. Hey, it was only a joke!

**Good Humor Guy**

Dear Guy,

Maybe your girlfriend doesn't like snakes, reptile or human.

**Charity**

~~~~~~~~~~~~~~~~~~~~~~~~~~~~~~~~~~~~~~~~~~~~~~~~

Amanda stopped crying, but not right away. I soothed the dog. In the silence Amanda's breathing was harsh and ugly; the dog panted and kept to her side.

The furniture was old and heavy. It had been the honeymoon dream of someone's grandmother, perhaps even great-grandmother. Solid and stable, it looked centered and right in the big room.

Remember the kid puzzle page in the comics? *What's missing in this picture? What's wrong with this picture?* At first glance everything looks okay, looks fine. But it isn't. *Find ten things that are wrong.* That's what we had here.

The furniture was old-fashioned but attractive. The arms of the sofa and wing-back chairs were worn, in some cases ripped. The doilies that had covered them this morning were stacked neatly on the grate in the fireplace. They hadn't been thrown in but carefully placed, like frail lacy logs. *One.*

Books in the bookshelf had been removed and replaced with their spines to the wall. *Two.* The fresh-cut flowers, roses in pinks, yellows and oranges, were limp and wilted. The water in the vase had been poured out. *Three.* A group of framed family photos had been pushed sideways on their wires and the subjects lurched and smiled drunkenly in their odd disorder. *Four.* An oil painting of a hard hot high-noon summer day in the California desert had been hung upside down over the fireplace. *Five.*

A mirror had been taken down and placed carefully and exactly on the floor beneath the nail on which it had been hung. All the lightbulbs in the overhead chandelier had been removed and placed in a neat row on the coffee table. The morning paper lay next to them carefully folded inside out. The cushion of the rocking chair was upside down, its zipper showing. The birdcage was empty. *Six. Seven. Eight. Nine. Ten.*

I didn't want to go any higher.

And the smell of blood was still with me.

"They've never come inside before." Amanda's voice had a childlike singsong quality to it, and an edge of fear. It bothered me. But not as much as the house. Deliberate and delicate viciousness is much more horrific than unplanned, unchoreographed violence.

Todd stood at Amanda's side, quiet and sad. He didn't care for this at all.

I walked into the kitchen. Nothing was broken, nothing seemed out of place. Except for the kitchen chairs with their backs to the table. And the cupboard doors. All open. I looked at the heavy glass jars on the counter: flour in the sugar; sugar in the rice; rice in the pasta.

The tags had all been pulled off the tea bags and there were M&Ms in the coffee beans. It was adding up. We were way over ten now. Absently I picked up a few M&Ms and munched them as I started toward the bedroom.

Amanda was crying again. I didn't blame her.

The smell. The bedroom looked okay, although the bed was un-made, a small—so what?—housekeeping detail in a house turned around as oddly as this one was. The smell. What? Not blood. I pulled back the rumpled bedcovers that nearly reached the pillows. Not blood, no, a cat box that hadn't been changed in days had been dumped into the open bed. I wondered where the cat was.

Behind me Todd made a growling sound. "City stuff."

"Yes."

In the bathroom the toilet paper had been unwound and tossed around the room in the style of an exuberant two-year-old. Shampoo and conditioner bottles had been opened and squirted into the sink and tub. On the vanity mirror a round happy face had been drawn in shaving cream.

Todd picked up a towel and started toward the mirror.

I held out a hand. "Better to let her see it, don't you think? She needs to know."

He made a noise signifying disgust, and dropped the towel. That about summed it up, all right.

"Needs to know what?" she asked behind us and then let her eyes meander along the same paths ours had taken. "Oh."

I don't think Amanda was capable of taking any more in. She sounded emotionally played out, into shock and out and beyond, past and lost. I put my arm around her and we walked the rest of her house, the spare bedroom, the laundry, the screened porch. I didn't see any-thing. I couldn't smell anything. Of course that didn't mean much. There were as yet unnoticed, uncounted surprises, I was sure of it.

We went back to the living room.

Todd propped the shotgun in the corner and he and I got to straightening out. Amanda stood dazed, propped up against the wall and as useless as Todd's gun. Smells. That reminded me. I left Todd

41

working in grim silence around the dazed Amanda and went back into the bedroom. I stripped the linens off the bed, dumped the cat litter outside and away from the house and piled the bedding into the washing machine. Mattress pad too. Scalding hot water and extra bleach.

It took us an hour and more. Us: Todd and me. After a while we got Amanda to sit down and clutch a glass of water, which she wouldn't drink. She didn't speak either. Georgie sat at her feet, head on her knee. I saw the cat under the sofa but it wouldn't come out, even when Amanda called. I had tossed the bedding into the dryer in the middle of the hour and then made up the bed again: fresh and sweet-smelling, bleach-smelling, safe-smelling.

Todd's wife called, then came over with a pitcher of iced tea and a plate of cookies. Daisy was a lovely dumpling of a woman with white hair braided and wrapped around her head, pink cheeks and farmer's overalls over a Todd-sized T-shirt. When she arrived we took a break, ate cold pizza and cookies, drank the strong sweet/tart iced tea with fresh mint leaves floating in it. Amanda had a plate of food, though I hadn't seen her eat yet.

"You oughten to stay here, Amanda Rose. You'll stay with us and that's settled." Daisy's voice was firm. Todd nodded his agreement and reached for another piece of pizza. Good thing we'd gotten a large. Georgie was on his second piece, thanks to Amanda, and in dog heaven over it.

"I won't be alone. Kat's staying with me."

Daisy was unconvinced. "You oughten, even the both of you, to be here. Not alone. Not till Jude gets back. Not just you girls."

Just us girls and my .380. I caught Todd's eye. He winked, I swear.

"How did they get in?" Daisy still. Still fussing. Still worried. Still right. "Didn't you lock your door?"

"I think so, I'm not sure. We used not to bother but I always try to remember now." Amanda's voice broke.

Which reminded me.

I got up and headed for the phone, looked for the phone book, then gave up and called information. Harry caught it on the second bounce. "Harry the Houdini of Locks" is what his advertising says.

"Harry, it's Kat. I've got a job for you: dead bolts, window locks and stops." I rattled off the specifics. "And bring me—" I turned my back to the room and lowered my voice. He laughed and said he would. I gave him directions; he said he'd be here pretty damn quick. Harry's a good one and his locks couldn't be slipped like the Hudsons'.

I hung up and started over to the last piece of pizza. *The smell. What? Not pizza.* Amanda beat me to it. Okay. She needed it for sure, and more than I did. Also for sure. Georgie whimpered in surprise and delight as Amanda reached down to pet him and offer him the slice. I whimpered too, but not in delight.

Todd chuckled at me, then spoke to Amanda. "Amanda, girl, you're gonna need a new chain on that gate. You got one?"

"I don't know . . . I think . . . Jude usually . . ."

"I reckon I'll jist check it out." Todd got to his feet and ambled off, Amanda behind him.

I'd quit watching the dog eat pizza—I was still hungry and the sight was too painful—and was lining up books and knickknacks and arranging them neatly, if not particularly domestically, on their shelves. The smell was stronger. I fought back an impulse to walk outside.

I moved to the couch to straighten the cushions.

"Daisy," I said as I moved the last cushion and saw it. She came and stood beside me in silence. Then her strong and calloused hand took mine.

It wasn't just that the bird was dead. I thought, and started to gag at the notion, that someone had torn its head off. I wasn't sure, but then I didn't want to be. And I was glad, after all, that Georgie had had that last piece of pizza, not me.

"Amanda shouldn't see this," Daisy said firmly, her hand warm and comforting around mine. She headed for the kitchen and returned with a roll of paper towels, moved quickly, took it away. The smell stayed, I thought, but maybe it was in my mind now, not in my nose.

Amanda did not take the news well.

Who could blame her?

That was before I found the card in the bottom of the birdcage. Amanda left the room as I read it.

Who could blame her?

It was bad. Bad find, bad timing, bad news. Bad all around.

The card was white, an expensive one done entirely in silver and gold. And embossed. On the front a magnificent wreath of delicate flowers, leaves and tendrils hung on a tombstone. The crisp, freshly carved lettering said: *In Memory.* Georgie pushed his pizza breath in my face as I plopped down on the floor and opened the card.

> *Yea, though I walk through the*
> *Valley of the Shadow of Death, I*
> *shall fear ~~no~~ Evil for the Lord is* **NOT**
> *my Shepherd and I shall ~~not~~ want.*

> *In this time of sorrow we send you*
> *the bountiful blessings of, ~~hope,~~*
> ~~*comfort and love.*~~   HA HA HA
>    A WARNING        A FRIEND

Daisy spoke to me twice before I heard her and looked up. I stood and handed her the card. My eyes roamed around the room. In search of what? Clues? Meaning? An explanation? I found nothing.

Daisy sucked her breath in with a sharp hiss. "Dear God in Heaven . . ."

Georgie, finished with the pizza and now thoroughly spoiled, had his eye on the plate of chocolate chip cookies. In that moment—who was choreographing this, anyway?—Todd and Amanda walked in.

I think I liked the last part the least. *A Friend.* It was such a mockery. It was such a lie.

The crying started again. To escape it, I went out on the porch.

.  .  .

"After a while, you see, it doesn't take much to get you, you're already worn down. It comes at you all the time but you never know exactly when, exactly where, so you're always trying to be prepared, be ready. Every odd little noise or thing out of place, every unusual occurrence sends the adrenaline rushing through your body, makes your heart thud wildly and the blood beat in your ears. You hold your breath or you breathe too fast."

Todd and Daisy had gone home without us and were not happy about it. Harry, too, had come and gone and now we had dead bolt locks, window locks and stops so that the windows would open far enough for ventilation but not far enough for entry. Four dogs were running loose in the yard, not penned up behind the barn. Georgie stayed in the house, eating the last chocolate chip cookie as we spoke.

Amanda is telling me what it's like and I am listening, but only because I have to, not because I want to. It's not the kind of thing I like to listen to because I've been there and I know it's not a nice place.

"Your mind gets screwed up. You get jumpy and paranoid and cry for no reason. It seems like it will never end and you know you can't bear that. Then, finally, you wish desperately that it would end. You wish that it would be absolutely over so you would *never* have to worry about it again, or face it, or feel it. And the only way that happens is if they stop, and you can't believe they will. Or if they get you," she whispered. "And you almost wish for that." The whisper drifted into a sigh.

"Because *then* it would be over." Her eyes stared out the window; they had refused to meet mine for some time now. She was drinking cold, dry white wine in gulps.

"So," she said flatly, "then you know: They did it. They won." Her voice stopped, as though it had run into a wall and given up.

"Then you hate yourself because you know you shouldn't let them do this to you. Because once they couldn't and now they can. Oh,

45

not right away. It took them three months to get to me. Three months. Only now it's not just me anymore so it's even scarier. They tried to hurt my husband and my dog. They killed my bird. They came into my home and . . . and I didn't stop it."

"Don't blame yourself for any of it," I said. "Don't help them victimize you."

"I—" She put her hand over her mouth and was still.

The phone rang. I got up to get it.

Silence. No words. No breathing. No nothing. Silence. Loud silence. Then a voice: *"Curiosity kills the cat!"* I broke the connection, took the phone off the hook.

Amanda poured more wine. "We have to leave the phone open so Jude can call."

"Call him."

"I don't know where he's staying."

It was three more calls, unpleasant silent messages, before the phone rang again and Jude was on the other end. I took them all and it started to make me jumpy and hateful too. When Jude finally did call Amanda wouldn't take it.

"I can't," she whimpered. "I'll talk to him tomorrow. I'm too upset tonight and he'll get mad over all this and . . . Don't tell him. Not yet. *Please.*"

I didn't lie, but I was brief and I omitted a lot. I thought he should know everything; I thought he should come home. But, for now anyway, I wasn't calling the shots. I told him we'd talk tomorrow and then I hung up, Jude clearly unhappy with the situation. Fine. That made two of us.

Amanda read it on my face before I could say it. "I know, Kat, it's just that I'm feeling so tired and beat up." She set the empty wineglass down and struggled to her feet. "Tomorrow, okay? I'll cope tomorrow. I'm going to bed now." Georgie padded after her.

"Amanda, victims aren't responsible for the crimes against them."

"I know."

"No, you don't, or you've forgotten, but they're not. You're not. Not now. Not *ever.*"

She shook her head and stumbled out of the room. Bad. The urge to hatred and revenge filled my mind, flooded my body. Worse.

And ugly. Very.

I hadn't found all the things wrong with this picture, I was certain of it.

I didn't have sweet dreams that night.

# 7

Dear Charity,

I think the most important thing in the whole world is to be beautiful. I buy all the fashion magazines and spend all my money on clothes and makeup. Last year I was Miss Corn Husk of Wannabe County! If only I could be Miss Universe!! I say I shouldn't have to study or go to school but my mom makes me.

Miss Corn Husk!!

Dear Miss Husk,

Your mom thinks you should have something inside your beautiful outside. I think she has a very good point. I mean, suppose you don't make Miss Universe?

Charity

~~~~~~~~~~~~~~~~~~~~~~~~~~~~~~~~~~~~~~~~~~

We were up with the first light. Amanda was a farm girl before she was an accountant. I was neither. And, for sure, not a morning person. Bartenders, ex in my case, hardly ever are. We had spent a quiet, if not a peaceful night. Thank God it was Friday. One more day, then the weekend.

"Call in sick," I ordered, pitching hay, opening stalls, filling troughs, running the dogs out and feeding the chickens. Todd had taken care of the chores the previous evening but there is always plenty to do on a working ranch.

"No *way.*" Her chin snapped up. Today she was a five-foot-three-inch hell-raiser mucking out stalls. "I had a bad day, Kat, and then a horrible night. I lost it last night. But that was last night and this is today. I'm up and running again."

She flashed a grin at me and shoveled horse manure. Life is one big metaphor sometimes. I shook my head. I'm thirty-three, eight years older than Amanda, but I feel a lot older than that. I've got guts and determination but not the mindless optimistic bounce-right-back of youth. It's admirable. It's also shortsighted. And sometimes it's dangerous.

"Take a day off, Amanda. Let's work on this a bit, figure it out some, lay out more of a plan. They're on a roll, whoever they are, with no indication of slowing down, never mind stopping. I don't like it. I don't want you rolled."

"I won't be, Kat. And I won't give them the satisfaction of knowing they scared me so badly."

I admired her even as I disagreed with her plan to go it as usual.

"Yesterday they beat me down something fierce."

Yes. No kidding.

"I'm not doing this just to get in their faces. That's part of it, yes, but mostly it's for me. *Don't let the bums get you down.* That's going to be my motto from now on. Kat, you won't argue with that, I know you won't."

I wouldn't, I couldn't, though I wanted to. Badly. She was brave, also terribly vulnerable, and she knew it as well as I. All right, not quite as well. Some of it lay beyond the boundaries of her experience, imagination, and optimism. I fell back to pick up on the remaining lines of defense.

"Call the phone company. Change your number to an unlisted one."

She frowned. "I can't. Our business, friends, everything. I can't."

"You can. The annoyance of informing friends and business associates of your new number is considerably less than the aggravation of threatening and frightening phone calls at all hours. And it makes you a doer, not a victim."

She leaned on her shovel for a while, then smiled. "Okay, I think you're right."

"And call Jude. He should know," I said. *He should be here* is what I thought.

"No. I don't want this to take over our lives or to interfere with his work, his job. And we need the money. If I lose my job and he can't travel because of me—" She let the words fall into a black hole somewhere. "You see, don't you?" It was a plea.

So I let it be.

We had a full morning. I got her to the Louden plant on time, but just barely. She bounced out of the car, all enthusiasm. The fear was there in the back of her eyes, underneath the bravado, but only if you looked closely.

I saw it when she turned to wave.


It was twelve-thirty when the cops called. I was at my office. Amanda Hudson was in the hospital. Could I come right over? My stomach knotted as I asked what had happened, was she okay, what was going on. The calm, uninflected, professionally impersonal voice asked again if I could come over. I practically begged the voice that sounded more like a machine than a person to tell me something. Could I come over, it repeated. I swore, banged the receiver down and drove to the hospital.

Nobody likes hospitals or emergency rooms. We're grateful for them but we don't like them. As I walked in, I choked on the sour smell of fear, blood and death. I tried to hold my breath and looked around for cops. Nothing. I asked a harried nurse.

"Officer Connors called me twenty minutes ago. Where would I . . ."

"The rape? Last door on the right."

*Rape.*

*It's threatening,* Amanda had said about work, *but not life-threat-*

*ening, not dangerous.* Rape was both of those. More. I knocked on the door. A uniform opened it.

"Kat Colorado," I said. "Officer Connors?"

She nodded and stepped aside. A slight, still form lay on a hospital bed covered by a sheet. I walked toward it. Flashes of Jude in a hospital bed, after the car crash, in my mind; flashes of Amanda mucking out the stalls this morning and smiling, laughing. *Don't let the bums get you down. That's going to be my motto from now on, Kat.* But they'd gotten her. She was down.

"Amanda." Nothing. I tried again. "Amanda, it's Kat."

She turned her head slightly to look at me. Her cheek was obscenely swollen, stamped with a large purple and blue bruise. "Take me home," she whispered.

A nurse moved out of the background and answered my unspoken question. "She should stay here overnight."

"Take me *home,* Kat. Don't leave me. Please don't leave me here."

"What happened?" I asked anyone and everyone.

Connors answered. "Ms. Hudson's statement indicates that she was sent on a job to the warehouse. There she was attacked from behind by a male, medium height, stocky build. He wore a ski mask. The assailant used obscene language and said he was going to get her for being a troublemaker. He punched her, threw her up against an inside loading dock and threatened her with a screwdriver. The assailant stabbed Ms. Hudson with the screwdriver in the arm and left breast. Ms. Hudson fought back. That and her screams attracted the attention of two other warehouse workers. They ran over, the assailant took off, they called us and an ambulance."

*Assault and attempted rape but not rape. Thank God.*

"Did you find him?" I asked it without much hope.

"No."

"I.D. him?"

"No." Connors spoke as an officer but the awareness of rape, a woman's knowledge, was in her eyes.

"Anybody know anything?"

"I haven't spoken to everyone yet."

"And they're lying?"

The cop's eyes flickered. "Too soon to tell," she said.

"Amanda?" I asked the still form on the bed.

"Yes." She spoke as if the word were a fragile thing that could shatter. But it wasn't the word that was fragile, it was Amanda. "That's what happened. He said he was going to fuck me, hurt me. He said he was going to teach me a lesson." Her eyes filled with tears. "Take me home, Kat."

"What is the extent of her injuries?" I asked the nurse.

"Several scrape and puncture wounds from the screwdriver, considerable bruising."

"And treatment?"

"The cuts and punctures have been sutured where necessary, tetanus shot, mild pain reliever. Patient is currently under observation." She shrugged. Amanda was a bed number, a case.

"Take me *home*, Kat. I *won't* stay here."

The nurse frowned.

"I *can't*," Amanda whimpered.

I looked at her bruised face, then at the nurse. "I'll keep an eye on her. Would you get her clothes, please?"

The nurse smiled in triumph—small-minded of her, I thought—and pointed to a pile on a nearby chair. They had cut the clothes off her to tend her wounds. Beige shreds.

"Amanda, I'm going to the car to get you some clothes. I'll be right back."

She stared blankly at me. I took it for assent. The officer and I walked out together.

"Did she fill you in on the larger picture?"

"That she blew the whistle at work? Somewhat. She's not in the best of shape to give me the whole story. Mostly I wanted to know if she could identify her attacker."

"And?"

"No."

"Nothing?"

"He had bad teeth and bad breath."

"That's something."

"You bet." Connors grinned. "I'll check it out, too."

I liked this slim, blond, pretty cop with bright red nail polish and professional attitude. "What are the chances of finding him?"

"Not great. We'll give it our best shot."

"May I call you?"

She handed me her card. "I'll know more in a day or so. They'll put a detective on the case, too."

I thanked her as we shook hands.

Amanda looked sort of silly, like an undersized waif in oversized running shorts and paint-spattered sweatshirt, but so what? We were way past silly. We started arguing the minute I got her in the Bronco. I hate to argue with someone who's just been beat up but I didn't have a lot of choice.

"Where would you be most comfortable, my house or a hotel?"

She looked at me blankly. "Huh?"

"We're not going back to your place, Amanda," I said gently, patiently. "How much evidence do you need that these guys mean business? They're not playing a game. They're dangerous. *Really* dangerous."

"I have to. The animals . . ."

"Todd offered to help out."

Her face was set in straight stubborn lines with bruises here and there like random checkers on a board. "I want to go home. They've practically taken my job away from me. I can't let them do that with my life, my home, my animals. I can't."

"Not forever, Amanda. For now. A temporary strategic retreat is often the most sensible move."

"I want to go home." She closed her eyes and leaned back.

We argued some more but I'd already lost and I knew it.

"The guy who attacked me?" She opened her eyes, still leaning back on the headrest. "He said I was as ugly as a gap-toothed toad, too ugly to even bother fucking."

Where to start putting on Band-Aids? *Ugliness has nothing to do with rape. Toads don't have teeth.* I didn't know. "He was trying to hurt you and scare you, to degrade you in any way. In every way. Ignore it. Consider the source."

"You can say that. You're not ugly."

"Neither are you."

Silence. I had picked the wrong Band-Aid.

"You don't know how that makes someone like me feel. You can't, you're beautiful."

I opened my mouth to say something that probably wouldn't work any better than the rest of it had but she ignored me, so I shut it again. And why were we talking about looks when someone had hurt her, had tried to terrorize and rape her?

"You're tall."

Five-seven isn't that tall.

"And slim."

Well, sort of, and sort of round, and I had muscles.

"And you have great breasts and pretty brown hair that always curls and bounces around your face."

Thanks to genes, luck, and my hairdresser I have a wash-and-wear haircut that always looks good. And blond streaks in it.

"And green eyes like, well, like emeralds."

Emeralds. How trite. She started crying so I didn't bother pointing that out.

"I'm short and flat-chested, with straight brown hair, blah eyes and the looks of a boring little mouse."

Okay, I had it finally. We weren't talking just looks here, we were talking self-esteem, self-worth. Amanda's sense of power and worth was tied up with her professional capability and they had taken away the importance of her job. Now she believed she had nothing. So? So I would try to do something about it but, dammit anyway, I'm an investigator, not a therapist.

"So?" Forget sensible, I was going for tough.

She cried harder.

"Neither of us had a choice in that. Those are the hands, the looks we were dealt. Why don't you do something about what you can change?"

"Wha-a-a-at?" she bleated at me.

Okay, now I was on shaky ground here, real shaky, but, undaunted, I was about to jump into where-angels-fear-to-tread territory. I am an expert on fashion the way Mike Tyson is an expert on dating etiquette. Mostly I wear jeans and sweaters and western boots or sneakers and I think I'm all dressed up when I wear a silk shirt and flats with my jeans. Once I wore a black pump on one foot and a navy one on the other, same shoe except for the color, and didn't notice it until someone pointed it out. You get the picture. There are six-year-old children who have more fashion sense.

She was sobbing now. Someone like me is a real find for a "helping profession." No kidding. I felt like a shit. No kidding. Had I called it wrong? I was trying to reach the Amanda who was a fighter, not the Amanda who had become a victim. We drove in silence. It took her another ten minutes of snuffling to notice we'd passed the turn off to the ranch and were going miles out of our way in the wrong direction.

"Where are we going?" she stammered out through sniffles and tear-soaked snotty tissues that were ending up on the floor of my vehicle, I noticed glumly. I'd asked for it, of course, but that didn't make me feel any better about it.

"Do you read the paper?"

"Where are—"

"Do you?"

"Yes." Her voice was sullen and angry, a big improvement over sad and beat-up. She blew her nose loudly and tossed the tissue on the floor. *So there, Kat.*

"Do you read *Dear Charity?*"

"The advice column? Of course. I love it."

"We're going to Charity's. She's my best friend."

Amanda gasped and was silent. The sniffles tapered off. Just before we got to Charity's ranch in Wilton—she breeds quarter horses as well as dishing out advice in her column—I spoke again. "Rape is a sexual crime but it has nothing to do with sexual attraction or the physical attractiveness of the victims. Eighty-year-old women are victims, three-year-old children are victims. So are beautiful women and boot leather barnside ugly women. Rape is a crime of violence, Amanda."

"I know." She spoke the words softly.

"Okay," I said, though it was a lie.

# 8

Dear Charity,

My mom says that *Beauty is only skin deep* and *Pretty is as pretty does* and *It's inner beauty that really counts.* Do you think so? I don't.

Kinda Plain

Dear Kinda,

No. If that were true, why would models make so much money? Beauty is important but so are a lot of other things. Learn to be beautiful in your own way. After all, butterflies were once caterpillars!

Charity

~~~~~~~~~~~~~~~~~~~~~~~~~~~~~~~~~~~~~~~~~~~~~~~~~

As we got closer to the house I saw Charity's BMW. Good. She was home. The dogs were out and making a racket. We waited in the car until either Charity came out or I was sure Jack the Ripper was chained. Jack is a horrible dog that has bonded to Charity but would cheerfully rip the throat out of anyone else, hence his name.

Charity bounced out the door in sweats—designer, I'd put money on it. Shoulder-length blond hair framed her exquisite Madonna face.

"She's shorter than I am," Amanda said.

"And chubby," I added. "And beautiful. Beauty comes in lots of shapes and sizes, Amanda."

Amanda was silent. I got out of the car and went around to help her.

"Amanda's had a hard day," I said to Charity, skipping the explanation that should have followed the intro. "A bad day."

"Oh."

Except in her love life, Charity is largely unflappable. Anyway, she would assume that Amanda was having a bad day. There was no reason to dress as Amanda had otherwise. Not to mention the bruise on her face. Not that Charity would mention any of it—she was far too well-bred.

"Come on in. Will you stay for dinner? I'll order Chinese. Yum. Do you like moo shu pork?"

Amanda nodded dumbly, dazed, in shock still perhaps—it was difficult to tell. My heart went out to her. She stumbled as we walked into the house. I caught her, held her around the waist. Charity looked at me.

I answered her silent question. "We need help, Charity."

Amanda shook her head. "No. I'm fine. Really. I—" Her eyes filled with tears and she sagged against me.

"We need a safe place for Amanda." I put my other arm around her and held on tightly as we walked in the front door.

Charity closed the door behind us, then supported Amanda so that she was securely tucked between us. "The guest room is this way." She spoke in a firm, pleasant voice. "Are you strong enough to walk with our help, Amanda?"

Amanda nodded, her head against Charity's shoulder. We steered our way to the guest room, a lovely room in yellow and blue chintz with lace curtains and fresh flowers. Charity had taken charge: She's wonderful with sick creatures, animal or human.

"You're too tired for a shower, aren't you? Yes, of course you are," she asked and answered in a matter-of-fact tone. Charity turned down the covers on the bed and we sat Amanda on the sheets.

"Kat, please help Amanda off with her things while I get a clean nightgown."

Amanda held her arms up like a cooperative two-year-old and I gently pulled the sweatshirt over her head. Her skin was cool to the touch and her eyes were empty. Charity walked in with a nightie in white cotton eyelet as I got the last of Amanda's things off. I put the gown over her head, easing it over her bandages. She struggled to get her arms into the sleeves and then fell back on the bed like an exhausted child. I tucked her legs in and pulled the covers up. Charity gently wiped Amanda's face with a cool cloth that smelled like lilacs and lavender.

"That smells so pretty. Thank you," Amanda murmured and almost smiled.

"Would you like something to drink?" Charity asked. "Water? Lemonade?"

"Lemonade," Amanda said, and closed her eyes.

Charity left to get it and I sat down in an antique rocker in the corner, watched Amanda, who lay without moving, and rocked. Charity reappeared with the lemonade and crossed to the bed, spoke softly to Amanda. No answer. She touched Amanda's shoulder. Nothing. Charity handed me the lemonade, pulled the chintz curtains closed over the lace ones, looked one last time at the slight, unmoving body under the flowered sheets. We left the room, pulling the door shut behind us.

In the kitchen I drank Amanda's lemonade thirstily.

"What happened?" Charity asked.

I drew her a rough sketch: the discovery of the scam at Louden; the husband out of town; the situation at work; the assault. A black and white and now black and blue and blood-red sketch.

Charity ran through an emotional gamut—pride in Amanda's courage, anger, distress, outrage—and all in record time. It left me exhausted and her revved up.

"She'll stay here, of course. You're no good at all with someone who's hurt, Kat."

I bristled a little at that. I'm okay, although not as good as Charity is, true. I was also enormously relieved. This was a safe place for Amanda, and Charity would take good care of her.

"When does her husband come home? She can't go back to work. Not until something's been done about this."

Yes. My thoughts exactly. "Jude will be back from Dallas Tuesday. I'll call Louden and tell them not to expect Amanda until Wednesday at the earliest. Can she stay here until then?"

Charity waved her hand, dismissing the question.

"Don't let her go *anywhere* alone."

"No. We'll be fine. What are you going to do? Be careful, Kat."

I nodded. No shit. "I'll follow up on this, talk to the cops, see what I can find out. I'll be staying at the Hudson ranch, so call me at the office or there if you need me."

I gave Charity a big hug and peeked in on Amanda before I left. She hadn't moved.

The next morning, Saturday, I called Charity. Amanda was still sleeping. By late afternoon she was up. She'd had a bath and a meal and smiled twice, Charity reported cheerfully. I spoke to Amanda briefly; she sounded subdued but okay. Charity told me not to bother coming out, Amanda was going back to bed.

Sunday Amanda did all of the same things plus she got dressed, they went for a walk, rented videos, and swam in the pool. Charity said she was teaching Amanda how to use makeup to cover her bruises. Ha. Good luck. I've tried that myself a time or six.

Nothing happened at the Hudson ranch all weekend. Todd and I did chores and I spun my wheels. I nosed around and I found out ZIP. Officer Connors had nothing new to report.

Monday I called Amanda in sick. Somebody who was paid to be polite faked a moderate level of concern. Pretty feeble. No flowers from her stunned friends at Louden. Big surprise. I checked in with Connors again and didn't find out anything I didn't know already. There are lots of days like this in my business.

Finally I gave up and worked at the office, cleaned off my desk.

Charity called at noon and asked me out to dinner at the ranch and would I please pick up Chinese—she had called in the order and it would be ready at five-thirty—and meet them out there at six and they were going out on an excursion now but they would see me later. She ran out of breath finally—ending her sentence on a slight gasp—which allowed me to graciously accept. Then I spun my wheels some more. Fun. I hate it when this happens. I hate days like this. At five I left the office and started out to Elk Grove.

Even though I was starving, I held myself back and didn't start eating until seven-thirty. I was partway through the egg rolls, dishing out a bowl of cold hot and sour soup and watching *Pretty Woman* on a video when I heard the dogs barking and then the car and the sound of slamming doors.

Charity was first, with bags and parcels and smiles.

I bounced up. "Hey, guys, did you have fun? Amanda, how are you?" I put my egg roll down and went to greet them. "How come you're so late?"

"I called this darling little boutique to tell them we were coming. They organized a special showing just for us."

There you go. That's the difference between expensive boutiques and blue-light specials. "Did you—" My brain stopped working first, then my mouth. I stood there and gaped.

The little brown mouse was history. Dead and buried.

Amanda Hudson still wasn't beautiful. But she was striking, arresting and eye-catching. I had never seen a smile like that on her face either.

"What do you think?" Charity demanded.

"Wow," I replied, with my usual semi-dazzling command of the English language.

Amanda's hair was a warm shade of honey-blond cut short everywhere except in the back, where it was long and curling about her neck. The expert cut revealed the beauty in the shape of her head, her

61

high cheekbones and fine features. Makeup made her eyes beautiful, her cheekbones bold and her mouth sensuous. She wore a dusty-rose suit (ridiculously expensive, it goes without saying) with a long slim jacket and a miniskirt. She looked exquisite.

"Wow," I said again, profoundly. They wanted to show me everything right away but I made them sit down and eat. I stared rudely at Amanda the whole time saying "wow," or sometimes "gee," or maybe "holy cow," for a change of pace. She loved it. Except for the bruises makeup couldn't cover, it was hard to see the woman I had picked up at the hospital three days ago. Wow didn't cover it.

It was late before we went to bed. Amanda modeled every one of her outfits. We opened another bottle of wine and I decided to spend the night on Charity's couch. Somewhere in there we called Jude in Texas to see what time he would be home tomorrow.

"He won't recognize you," Charity promised after Amanda had hung up. Amanda's eyes sparkled.

"It's *so* wonderful, Kat." She laughed giddily. "I feel like a different person." I smiled. I didn't have the heart to say what I was thinking.

At one-thirty they were still trying on, accessorizing and doing other things I didn't get. I went to bed to the sound of their excited voices.

# 9

Dear Charity,
I am 16 and my favorite people in the whole world are Dirty Harry and Rambo. I want to be just like them when I grow up. My mom says I'm nuts. What do you say?

Wannabe

Dear Wanna,
Dirty Harry and Rambo are *not* people. They are made-up characters with made-up lives and made-up happy endings. There's a *big* difference between movies and real life. If you act like them you will probably be dead before you grow up.

Charity

~~~~~~~~~~~~~~~~~~~~~~~~~~~~~~~~~~~~~~~~~~

I was up before eight. It was just the animals and me, the farm girls were still out cold. The three empty wine bottles littered around the kitchen explained why; there'd only been two when I went to bed. At eight-thirty I rousted them out. We're not talking a lot of sympathy here. Charity and Amanda were heavy-lidded and bleary-eyed and then, soon enough, smiling and giggling. After washing up Amanda appeared in tight (I mean *tight*) blue jeans with several layers of tops, all bright, and high-top sneakers. I gaped again. It was something.

Charity was right. At a first or quick glance Jude might not recognize
Amanda.

Then they disappeared into the bathroom with mugs of coffee—
makeup, mousse, and imaginations running wild. One of Charity's
dogs and I read the paper and waited hopefully for breakfast. We
weren't, any of us, in any hurry. Jude wasn't due back from the airport
before one and I had flatly refused to show up at the house before he
did.

They talked me out of that.

I didn't get breakfast either.

We compromised on a half hour before. I guess I got fed too, if
you can call a diet vanilla milk shake made with nonfat milk food.

"I can't have much food in the house, Kat. I'm on a diet," Charity
explained, smiling angelically.

"Bread?" I suggested. "Toast would be nice."

"Nope."

"Fruit? Peaches, strawberries, bananas, apples?" I asked in de-
scending order of interest.

"No."

I opened the cupboards. Cold cereal maybe? Nothing. I opened
the refrigerator. Nothing. This is not exaggeration or hyperbole; this is
fact. (I'm not counting pickles and mayonnaise.) What had they been
eating the last four days? Then, on a hunch, I opened the freezer.
Bingo. It was chock-full of Sara Lee goodies. Charity blushed prettily.
So we defrosted some kind of double fudge, double chocolate bliss and
a pound cake. Nothing like empty carbos and a sugar rush to start the
day.

At twelve-thirty we idled at the Hudsons' gate, the Bronco first,
Charity's BMW right behind us. Charity had come along for the ride
and she and Amanda were apparently fast intent on turning the whole
episode into a sideshow. All right, that's not fair, they were justifiably
excited by Amanda's new look. Me, too, but I was more excited by the
prospect of keeping Amanda well and safe.

Everything looked good so far. The gate was closed and chained, the dogs running free and barking, all paws accounted for. The house was shut, quiet and serene. The stock was fine, ditto the outbuildings. I let my breath out slowly, surprised that I'd been holding it.

When Jude pulled in shortly after one we were ready for him. The stage was set, the characters positioned and costumed, the scene rehearsed. Even I knew my lines. The dogs started barking excitedly as he pulled his pickup into the yard. Charity and Amanda were just as excited. We walked out to greet him as he climbed out of the truck.

"Hey, Jude!" I called across the yard and the barking dogs.

"Hi, Kat." He smiled. "Hullo, ladies." His eyes swept across them, looking for Amanda, then suddenly recognizing her.

"*Jesus* Christ!"

Jesus was apparently unavailable but Amanda was right there.

"Mandy, you look . . . you look . . . damn! Hot damn!"

They walked, well, charged really, into each other's arms. I hoped Amanda's new makeup was kiss-proof. Water-proof too—I saw a few tears. Charity simpered graciously on the sidelines.

Amanda turned her pretty face up to her husband's smiling one. "Now you'll *always* love me and *never* leave me because I'm pretty."

My heart constricted. I turned away.

He held her tightly and she smiled into his eyes. "No." He said it gently. "I'll always love you because you're *you*, Mandy." Then the makeup got another round of kisses.

I turned away again, my heart knotted up like old string. *Now you'll always love me because I'm pretty.*

Okay, that was the highpoint, it was downhill from there. We were sitting at the Hudsons' kitchen table amidst the debris of lunch. Amanda and Charity were still twittering away on clothes and girl-talk and Jude was enjoying it all and especially his happy pretty wife when I delivered the opening line to the next act. As far as Theater goes it was a hit: My audience sat in stunned silence.

"As long as we're doing show-and-tell here, Amanda Rose, why don't you show Jude your stab wounds and bruises?"

Jude recovered first. "What are you talking about?" He looked at

65

me. Just as well. Charity and Amanda weren't twittering anymore; they had clammed up.

"The cops called me from the hospital on Friday to tell me Amanda had been assaulted."

"Mandy?" The word almost exploded from his mouth. He grabbed her arm. She winced and he let go immediately.

"Show me," he said quietly.

She hesitated, then pulled up her sleeve. Jude looked at the bandage, then gently peeled it back. A small jagged wound was neatly stitched and healing nicely. He replaced the bandage and tugged the sleeve down.

"Tell me."

Jude looked at Amanda. Amanda looked at me. I looked at the ceiling. Finally she told him. Jude sat silent, his hands clenching and unclenching in an unconscious reaction. When she finished he got up and slammed out of the house. The screen door banged behind him.

It was fifteen minutes before Jude came back, still silent, face white with anger. We sat at the now cleared kitchen table, a tableau with untouched glasses of iced tea. I poured one for Jude, which made a matched set. He didn't touch his either.

"Why, didn't you tell me?" he asked his wife harshly.

"I was with friends. I was safe. I didn't want to worry you."

"Mandy, for godssake!"

"There was nothing you could do, Jude. It happened. It was over."

"There are things to be done *now*."

Good. My cue. I jumped right in. "We need some new ground rules. Amanda should take medical leave for a while. If and when she goes back to Louden it will be on the absolute understanding that she does the job she was hired for. No more bogus assignments in the warehouse or the men's room.

"For now, I don't want Amanda living here. Ideally she should leave the area, the state, visit family or friends elsewhere for a while. If you don't want to do that, Charity's invited you both to stay with her.

"This house should have an alarm system and we should con-

sider hiring someone to patrol when neither you nor I are here." I
caught the look in Jude's eyes. "This is temporary, stopgap only. We're
buying time until we figure it out. The cops are working on this now,
and I'll be able to get into the plant as well. After what just happened,
it will be real hard for anyone at Louden to refuse."

"No," Jude said.

No what? *No, I don't care for iced tea. No, I don't like one small
part of that plan. No, we can't afford to hire a guard, what else can we
do? No what?*

"No what?"

"No. We're not going to do it that way."

First he outlined his plan.

Then I quit.

Simple as that.

I didn't walk out. I couldn't. I had Charity and Amanda hanging
onto my elbows like trendy, well-dressed leeches so we talked about it
even though I wasn't going to change my mind and I didn't think for a
minute that Jude was going to change his.

Jude was acting and talking like a good old boy. Charity was
cheering him on; there's a lot of good old girl in her. Amanda was
showing some sense and demurring. In the middle of this Todd showed
up. He pulled up a chair, declined iced tea—why should he be different?—and agreed with Jude.

Son of a bitch.

"Thing is, Kat," Todd explained, "we take care of our own and we
take care of each other. The time has come to take care of this."

"That's what I like about you country boys, the cowboy and vigilante side: *Let's round up a posse and take care of the problem.*"

"You got it," Jude said.

"But the police—" Amanda began.

Jude interrupted his wife but spoke to me. "The cops don't care
like I do. It's just another assault to them. It's Mandy to me, *my* wife,
*our* lives."

"Jude, I don't like the direction here. I don't like the way the
pace is picking up," I said.

67

"Yeah. You're right. Me either. I tried to play by the rules, that's why I hired you. Now we're changing the rules. And we're not playing anymore."

"They aren't either," I objected. "The stakes are too high here. Look at it: First they just came by, tossed around rakes, flipped on lights and windshield wipers. Then they graduated to breaking into the house, tossing around furniture, going after one of the horses."

"And killing the bird," Amanda added.

Jude didn't look like he cared much about a parakeet but he got behind the principle real easy. "Then Amanda," he said.

"Yes," I agreed. "Then Amanda."

"And that's when they went too far. Look, Kat, it's not that I don't trust the cops to do a good job, I got a buddy who's a deputy sheriff. Hell, it's because of him I know how overworked they are. They're going to do their best for Amanda, I know that, but they have a lot of other priorities. I don't. Just one. Just my wife." He picked up his glass of iced tea and drank half of it. "Just—my—wife." He set the glass down with a click.

"Here's what I'm thinking, Todd," he continued, ignoring me. "Run things as usual today and tomorrow. Tomorrow afternoon I toss a bag in the truck, kiss Mandy and take off for the airport. Business as usual."

"Jude, I—" Amanda began.

Jude winked at her. "I drive to the airport, park in long-term parking, walk in, have a cup of coffee, pick up the truck and come on home. I drop my truck off at Wade's and take his truck instead. Over to your place.

"When you come over tomorrow evening to help Amanda with the chores I'm in the truck bed, maybe me and Wade," he continued thoughtfully. "Under a tarp would work. You back the truck into the barn, we scramble off. You and Mandy finish the chores, and you take off. Wade and I sit around and drink iced tea, eat baloney sandwiches and wait for developments. Long as it takes, that's what I got. See anything wrong with it?"

"No." That was Todd.

"Yes." That was me. "There's a fairly long period of time when Amanda's all by herself. Your basic window of opportunity, Jude. And who's Wade?"

"We keep the phone lines open all the time between Mandy and Daisy. Todd's watching out. No one's going to get past us." The threat was heavy in his voice. "Wade's a friend of mine, lives close by."

"And if they do show?"

"Not *if,* when. And probably pretty soon. These boys seem antsy as all git out and more and more serious about it. When they arrive we have a little discussion."

"Discussion" was a euphemism. No kidding.

"You beat the crap out of them, that puts you in the wrong," I said stubbornly. "You hold them until the cops get here—"

"Yeah," Jude said flatly, "that's what I'll do. I'll ask those boys if they'd like to sit down with my family and friends and have milk and cookies while we wait for the cops to come. Then when the cops get here, charge them with trespassing and let them go, the problem will be settled and we'll just wave bye-bye real friendly like. Yeah, that's what I'll do. We got milk and cookies, sweetheart?"

Amanda stared at him helplessly.

"Ladies, if you'll excuse me, I got work to do." Jude stood, then leaned over to kiss Amanda, his kiss, his hand, lingering and affectionate. "Todd?"

So the guys left. Left us in a puddle of sticky silence. The day was heating up just like the people. Amanda got up and switched the air conditioner onto high.

I had quit, so there was no reason for me to be there.

Charity spoke first. "I think Jude's right, Kat."

Yes. Part of me did too. I certainly understood. He had to protect everything he held dear. I also understood that we didn't know enough here—who we were taking on, how big they and/or their organization was, how bad it could get. Too many unknown factors; too big a window of opportunity.

"Exactly how much and what kind of trouble did you stir up?" I was on shaky ground here and I knew it. "I'm not working for you anymore, Amanda, I'm asking as your friend."

Amanda got teary.

"All *right,* Kat." Charity whistled and clapped, egging me on.

"You're an advice columnist," I said glumly. "Shut up and quit giving lousy advice."

"Way to go, Kat," she said softly.

Charity knew as well as I that I couldn't just walk away. Who says P.I.s are tough? What the hell—she couldn't either. When I'd pulled Lindy off the streets and dropped her off at Charity's to keep her safe, Charity hadn't even blinked. Instead, she bought Lindy teenage clothes to replace hooker outfits, fed her and kept her busy and off the streets until I found her a real home. With my grandmother. Lindy was part of my life. Now it looked like Amanda Rose was too.

A detached and emotionally uninvolved attitude is the mark of a true professional.

"How much? What kind?" I reiterated as I sipped on my iced tea, watered down now by the melting ice.

"I've got everything here. I kept good notes and records."

An accountant would do that, I thought.

"Would you like to see them?"

"Yes. Please," I added on an afterthought. No need to let assault, attempted rape and vigilante action make me forget my manners.

We cleared away the largely untouched iced teas, wiped the sweat rings off the table and spread out the papers. It was quite a stack.

"This first batch is everything that I found out: photocopies and other documentation, all my notes, including a written record of all conversations, in person or on the phone.

"The second is copies of my correspondence with the Food and Drug Administration." That was a slim file.

"The third is letters I wrote to the people whose names I found in the first file."

"Those names are presumably patients, or relatives of deceased patients who had received defective heart valves?"

"Exactly. Names, medical data, dollar amounts, any information I could get. Not a lot," she added. "It was all entered into the records in a kind of corporate shorthand jargon. To hide things, of course, or to make them look and sound better. I guess it's the same as the military figuring that saying soldiers died in friendly fire sounds a lot better than saying, 'Hey, we messed up and one bunch of our guys shot up and killed another bunch.' That's what we have here, a whole lot of 'friendly fire' stuff."

"How many letters did you write?"

"Six. I hadn't gotten to the rest of the names but I will. I'm still working on it. I have twenty-eight names. And then I have a whole other list of people who received a Louden heart valve. That one's not long, certainly not complete. They shut me out of those files before I got very far. I don't know if these people have suffered any complications from their heart valves; I don't even know if they're living or dead. I want to find out but I really don't know how to pursue it just yet without leaving myself wide open legally. I don't want to do that, or do anything that would compromise what I'm trying to accomplish."

"I wonder," said Charity, "what would happen if someone wrote me a letter about defective heart valves and I published it. We couldn't use a company name without proof, of course, but we could suggest that those individuals with heart valves get medical advice."

"Publish it? In your *column?*" Amanda's eyes sparked with excitement.

"We could look into it."

Great. Now I had two troublemakers on my hands. Swell. Four, if I counted Jude and Todd, which, I thought glumly, I might just as well. Five, if I counted Wade. Terrific.

"So," I said, summing things up—it was rubbing off on me, being around an accountant—"the following are folks who might not be real happy with you: Louden management on every level—local, regional, and national; Louden employees who are worried about losing their

jobs due to diminished production or plant closure; people at the FDA
who will be reluctant to see their shortcomings made public, though
that seems a little far-fetched."

"Old news," Amanda agreed.

"And potentially everyone who has settled a lawsuit with Louden,
and their relatives and associates."

"Why?" Amanda was puzzled by that one.

Charity saw it immediately. "Your husband, the darling heart-
breaking apple of your eye, dies because of a faulty heart valve. You
are desperately grief-stricken but not so much that you don't sue and
then settle out of court for seventy-five thousand dollars, say. You also
agree not to reveal anything about it."

"That was invariably a condition of settlement, wasn't it?" I
asked.

"Yes." Amanda saw it. She got it. It was adding right up.

"And then," Charity continued, "someone comes along and
threatens to make public that seventy-five thousand dollars was the
price you put on your husband's life and that you agreed to keep quiet
knowing that the valve was still being marketed and that others,
equally innocent, could die."

The question was not who wanted to get Amanda but who didn't.
The last list was the short one.

"May I take all this with me?" I asked Amanda, scooping up the
files. "They probably shouldn't be here, anyway." I thought of fire, I
couldn't help it.

"Sure, I guess you can. But, Kat, you're not working for us now
and I can't ask you to—"

"You're not. Shall we say I'll hold it in safekeeping for you for a
while, and leave it at that?"

She thought it through. "All right. Thank you."

"Pierced ears," Charity said.

"Huh?" Amanda and I chorused, not immediately catching the
connection between defective heart valves and pierced ears.

"Let's go get your ears pierced and buy you some diamonds,"
Charity said to Amanda.

"Or pearls." Amanda was sparkling again.

"Both," Charity said grandly, "and a bikini."

Amanda blushed. "Me? A bikini? I can't possibly—"

"Yes." Charity was firm. "Jude will love it."

It was obvious from the way Amanda smiled that Jude would. It was obvious that they were once again going shopping. I was pleased that Amanda had found something that diverted her, that made her happy but . . . Okay, I considered stopping right there—if I went on I would be a wet blanket for sure. I sighed. Then I went on.

"Jude was right, Amanda."

Amanda and Charity stared at me blankly.

"You don't need new clothes or makeup to be beautiful. Beauty is an inside thing as much as it is—"

Charity snorted.

I whirled around, mad as a wet hen and a junkyard dog put together, mad as a—

"Don't be such a goody-two-shoes, Kat."

"It's *true!*" I was livid. I was outraged. I was a lot of things but not speechless. "It's—"

"Well, of course it's true," she said sensibly. "Nobody's denying that or arguing with you. Not for a minute. It's just that there's absolutely no reason why we can't have outer beauty as well as inner beauty. Is there?"

"No." I felt like a Grinch. "I just don't want Amanda to forget her real beauty." I looked at Amanda, spoke directly to her. "You used to look at yourself in the mirror and not be able to see it."

"I can now." Amanda spoke softly. "And I know you're right, Kat. I *know* you are, but oh! Oh, it's so lovely and wonderful to be pretty on the outside, too!"

She was radiant. Maybe I was right and that radiance had little to do with makeup and makeover, but I understood, too, that she had felt plain for a long time, that it would take time to change that.

"Thank you, Kat." Amanda's lips brushed my cheek. "You've helped a lot."

Charity slung her bag over her shoulder, tapped her foot and jingled her keys. She's not exactly famous for her patience or her subtlety. "Ready, Amanda?"

"Ready." Amanda smiled at me, then at Charity.

"Have fun," I said to them, "but be careful." I meant it.

Amanda shrugged it off with another sweet smile. She was going out with Charity; she was protected. And Jude was home now. Jude would keep her safe—he always had. My job? I'd just quit. Amanda? Apparently she had forgotten Karen Silkwood. She was focused on Cinderella.

"Be careful," I said again. "You're on an awful lot of shit lists."

I didn't say hit lists, but I could have.

# 10

Dear Charity,
   Is it ever OK to kill someone?

                                                    **Just Asking**

Dear Asking,
   I don't know about OK. It is legally justifiable, as
well as understandable, to kill in self-defense or to protect your family. Also to protect your dessert—particularly if it is chocolate.

                                                    **Charity**

~~~~~~~~~~~~~~~~~~~~~~~~~~~~~~~~~~~~~~~~~~~~~~~~~~~~~~

Her voice was very quiet and very scared. "Kat, please come. I'm so
afraid. I shouldn't ask you, I know, but I don't know what else to do,
where to turn."
   "What are you afraid of?"
   "Jude."
   The answer was simple, shocking. Had I expected it?
   "Why?" I asked.
   "I've never seen him like this. He won't listen to me. He won't try
to work this out in any other way but his. This will lead to violence, I

know it will. I don't want to be hurt, but I don't want someone else to get hurt either. Then it just goes on and on. I'm afraid it could be more than that, too. Kat, I've got to go. Please say— I'm so afraid, Kat."

"No, I won't be a part of that. You can come here anytime you want to, though. Or call the cops, Amanda." I'd said I'd help and I would, but I wouldn't collude in vigilante violence.

"The cops won't come until something happens, and then it'll be too late."

I was hoping I could sit tough. I was hoping she wouldn't ask again.

But she did.

And then she told me the rest.

"I'm on my way," I said. I gave in just like that. Anyone with the sense that God gave gravel would have. Tough, huh?

"Thank you," she breathed into the phone and hung up.

On my way over I passed a Raley's supermarket and, in a sudden impulse, pulled into the parking lot. Ten minutes and I was back on the road crawling along in the five-thirty rush-hour exodus headed out of Sacramento on 99 South. It was after six by the time I reached the Hudson place. Jude had thoughtfully left the chain off although the gate was closed. *No need to look for bolt-cutters, boys, c'mon in.* That Jude, what a host.

I parked the Bronco right in front of the house and climbed out carrying the large pink box. Amanda met me at the door. We walked into the kitchen where we had the best view of the yard and the barn. I put the pink offering on the counter. Neither one of us had spoken. I went first.

"Your earrings are beautiful, Amanda."

Quickly she touched sparkly stones in newly pierced ears and tried to smile. "Thank you. And thank you for coming."

"Any calls or threats? Anything out of the ordinary? Any anything?"

"Just Jude."

Just Jude. TV and movies have made it popular for good guys to act like bad guys. On the screen they get away with it. On the streets? Not usually. And they shouldn't. Jude had bought right into Hollywood's good-guys-acting-like-bad-guys concept. Jude, alias Dirty Harry, alias—

"He won't break cover?" I asked.

"They. Wade too. Do you remember Wade? Jude said you two met at the hospital after the car crash. No, they won't. Not for you, though Jude will be mad about it. He might after dark, though I doubt it. The yard lights light up everything. Shoot, you can practically read out there. He'll be especially pissed about your car, afraid it will warn off the guys."

"It might."

She didn't say anything.

"Let's figure it out, Amanda. Jude's right that we have to slow down or scare off these guys somehow. We can't ignore the seriousness of their threat after the last assault. They've got to get the message that they can't mess with you. I'd like the criminal justice system to deliver the message; Jude wants to do it himself."

Amanda was silent.

"Will he calm down if we postpone the confrontation?"

"Jude? No." She turned her head toward me and the stones in her ears sparkled and her eyes were dead pools that absorbed light and let nothing out.

"Then let's let it happen if it's going to—next time I might not be around. I'll move the Bronco behind the house."

"Okay." She spoke dully. She was terribly afraid. "I hate violence," she stammered. "I'm so small. Everyone could always pick on me, beat me up, run over me."

I agreed with her but I didn't say it out loud. What I liked even less was the sensation of being a sitting duck.

"Do you have a big mean dog, one who responds to commands?"

"Georgie's very protective and territorial and minds pretty well," she responded doubtfully.

"We want Georgie in here with us."

. . .

It was well after dark when the car pulled in. Two, maybe three doors slammed. All the lights in the house were out. The dogs barked, but they were shut up in the barn. *C'mon in, boys.* The front door wasn't locked. That's where they came in. *Welcome. How nice that you could drop in.* They weren't quiet, they weren't efficient, they sounded like dumb good old boys who'd been sitting in Bob's Bar all afternoon tanking up on liquid courage and waiting for it to get dark. One of them fumbled and swore, probably looking for a light and finding the switches taped down. *Hey, life's a challenge.* I listened, pretty sure there were only two, could be one more outside of course. They tromped through the house.

"*Fuck.* Nuthing, man. And no one in the bedrooms."

Two bulky silhouettes in the kitchen door. When the doorway framed both I hit the flashlight. It was a powerful big beam one, the kind cops use. Instinctively their hands went up to shield their eyes and faces. I didn't see any weapons. Two guys. I hate unfair fights, two men to take down a woman. And I loathe men who pick on women.

"Howdy, boys."

One of them growled and headed for the voice, for me.

"Bad idea." I said it pleasantly. "I've got a gun." He kept coming. I fired a shot into the ceiling.

Nothing. No movement. Not even a twitch. Probably have to pay these boys to get them to breathe in the next ten minutes.

"Juries love that," I said conversationally. "They'll be touched to know that even a terrified, defenseless woman shaking in her shoes and in fear for her life played fair and fired a warning shot before she blew away the intruders."

Sounds of swearing, whimpering.

Lousy losers. Swell. Another thing I hate.

Outside we heard scuffling sounds, a grunt, then a thud.

"Hit the light, Amanda, let's see what we have here."

She pulled a chain on the lamp we had placed on the sideboard.

"Well, well, isn't this special?" I recognized one as the guy in the coverall who had spit at Amanda in front of the Louden plant. Buck. There was a screwdriver in his pocket. Well, well. Later we'd check him for bad breath. "Know these boys, Amanda?"

"Yes." I could barely hear her. "They're from the plant."

Out of the corner of my eye I could see the doorknob turn. The back-up troops were finished outside and coming in here. We'd arranged all this through Todd when he came to do the chores. Okay, I'd arranged it. And threatened to blow the whistle, call the cops, whatever, if they didn't cooperate. So they had. But not graciously.

The dead bolt wasn't shot but the latch was on. It didn't matter, of course. Jude had a key. So he *kicked* the door in.

*Shit!*

Too much TV. Too many movies. Too much macho. *Yo, Dirty Harry!* Naturally it was at that point, when Jude kicked the door in and came roaring through like an explosion, that things got out of control. I backed up and stuck the gun in my waistband. Too many people too close together. And the dog. We'd kept Georgie quiet until this but now he was snarling and barking wildly. I stayed between Amanda and the action.

The guy behind Mr. Spit took off backwards and headed in the direction of the front door. Wade, right behind Jude, melted out of sight. Good for him. Too bad for the other one.

Spit had his screwdriver out and his eyes crossed. He was trying to look tough but he was in trouble and he knew it. Jude was one big bad mad mean mutherfucker. And that, right now, was his nice side.

Spit waved his screwdriver around. "Watch out," he squeaked. "You gonna get hurt."

Jude laughed. He didn't look scared. Then he swatted the screwdriver out of Spit's meaty hand with a short length of two-by-four, dropped the two-by-four and reached out for the man. First he smashed Spit in the face. *That's for Amanda, pal.* Then he picked him up by the neck and threw him, forty miles per hour or so, onto the kitchen table. That was when the table broke.

What the hell. It was only Formica.

Jude kicked him in the ribs hard enough to break a couple. *That's for Amanda too.* Nice. Now his ribs would match his teeth—both broken. The guy was moaning with spittle, snot, tears and blood all over his face. Amanda was weeping. Jude reached for his throat again.

So that was when I threw the pail of ice water I had sitting in the sink at Jude. He staggered back, then snarled and started to come toward me—his hands ready, his hatred up, his mind on automatic pilot and destroy.

"*Enough.* Back off, cowboy."

He shook his head dumbly, wiped the water out of his eyes and blinked.

"Amanda, call the cops," I said.

Jude growled at me.

"We've got them: illegal entry and armed assault. *Back off!* Amanda Rose, *call the cops!*"

She looked at Jude. He blinked again, then nodded. She ran out of the room. Wade clomped back in.

"Get him?" Jude demanded.

"Got him," Wade answered. "They're both trussed up out there."

Our boys were breathing hard but looking a whole lot better, and wetter in Jude's case, than the other boys. Of course, that's the way it's supposed to be with good guys and bad guys but so often life doesn't follow the script.

Most of the rest of the evening we followed the script. The cops arrived. We told our stories more than once—we were talking to cops, remember—and we got to watch the bad guys being hauled off to county accommodations and their car being towed away. All of which was satisfying. Very.

"Just as well," Wade commented as he watched the tow truck. He had a black eye he hadn't had when I'd met him at the hospital a week ago. "Damn thing wouldn't run without carburetor wires anyway."

Never underestimate a country boy. I used to, but I don't anymore, haven't since I was about eleven.

After the cops left, Amanda made coffee. *Coffee?* On a hot night
after a fight? Jude tossed the last kitchen table leg and assorted
Formica scraps out the back door.

"Beer, Kat?"

"Only if there's no wine or whiskey."

Jude found a small jug of white wine, not great but not swill.
After a night like this I wasn't real pushy about vintage or quality,
anyway. Quantity, maybe.

Jude and Wade were drinking beer, I had a glass of wine and
Amanda had a mug of coffee. I was balancing the pink bakery box on
my knees since there was no table. Jude was getting plates and forks;
we were past napkins. It was that kind of evening.

"C'mon, honey, let me make you a Kahlúa coffee with cream. You
like that."

Amanda shook her head. I unwrapped the big pink box. It was a
huge cake, chocolate of course, because I had bought it. CONGRATULA-
TIONS!!! was written in large letters in pink and blue.

"What's this?" Jude asked.

Wade didn't ask, he just held out his plate. "I reckon a big piece
would do for a start." He winked at me.

I smiled but didn't cut the cake. Not yet. "Amanda?"

She blushed.

"Tell him, Amanda Rose." She'd told me to get my help, to get
me over here so, by God, she could tell everyone else too. She could,
or I would, and it better be true. No. I didn't think she would lie about
it. I didn't think so, but I wasn't absolutely sure.

Amanda Rose stood tall for a tiny woman. Her voice was clear
and strong, as beautiful as she, and it had nothing to do with makeup.
"I just found out this morning, Jude. We're going to have a baby."

There were tears in his eyes. I saw them through mine before
Jude started testing her kiss-proof makeup again.

Wade got tired of waiting and cut the cake.

# 11

Dear Charity,

A bunch of us work at a defense plant. One guy keeps making a fuss about a part he says isn't up to specifications. He keeps this up, we could lose the contract and our jobs. I say we straighten him out. What do you say?

Needs The Bucks

Dear $$$,

He sounds pretty straight to me. Whatever happened to live and let live?

Charity

~~~~~~~~~~~~~~~~~~~~~~~~~~~~~~~~~~~~~~~~

Amanda called in sick again the next day, Wednesday. Thursday she went back to work in her new clothes, with her new attitude and her new life. Two new lives, really, one for her and one for the baby.

Jude drove her in, parked in the ABSOLUTELY NO PARKING AT ANY TIME! zone in front and walked her to her office. His knuckles were pretty badly scraped and banged up from the fight. Nobody missed it. He'd never gone to the plant before, never escorted his wife in before.

Nobody missed that either. Amanda's coworkers hadn't met him before; they knew him now. He was still looking and acting like one big bad mad mean (but handsome) mutherfucker. He still was.

On his way out he stopped at the plant manager's office.

"You can't see Mr. DeVito without an appointment," the secretary told him bravely, if foolishly.

"Watch me," he said.

And she did. And he did.

Jude wouldn't tell us what he'd said, just that he'd made his position clear.

I bet.

And the troubles stopped.

The problems and harassment at work were over. Amanda's coworkers, she reported happily, seemed to go out of their way to be nice, to be friendly. No one messed with her clothes and her wastebasket was empty, trashless, and pristine. She never had to make coffee, her cup was always full. There were flowers on her desk, smiles in her office, cheerful words flying giddily about, lots of *hi-how-are-yous*, *good-to-see-yous*, and *ain't life swells*. Altogether, it sounded like more fun than a hog-calling on a hot day at the state fair.

Management was a little cool but they left her alone; they left her to do her job. There were no problems, unusual occurrences, visitors, or unusual anything else at the Hudson place. No phone calls or threatening cards. Nothing.

It was almost too good to be true.

Amanda and Jude told me all this at dinner a week later. And I told them what I knew: "The boys are out on bail, but they'll stand trial on it. The D.A.'s office says it's a strong case. Have you seen any of them at work lately, Amanda?"

"No, but in the ordinary run of things I wouldn't. We work in different areas and our paths aren't likely to cross."

"Speaking of paths crossing, I decided to look up Buck Lassiter —the cutie-pie with the screwdriver—and have a little chat."

Jude looked at me and I flushed.

"Curiosity," I said.

He laughed. "And?"

And:

I had followed him home one day after work, followed him home and followed him in. The boy didn't look real good. His ribs had been broken in the little scuffle at the Hudson place. Buck Lassiter was going to remember Jude Hudson for a long time.

"Yo, fuckface," I said softly, as the door started to close behind him. He tried to slam the door but that was tough; I had my foot in it.

"Not a chance." I busted on through. Buck had strength and weight on his side, but that was it. I had guts, determination and ooomph.

He stumbled back, hands up and shielding his face and ribs. "No—" he moaned.

"I'm coming in, Buck. Invite me."

"Fuck off," he said.

I didn't think he had that much grit left. "Close enough." I moved in on him swinging things: arms, legs, purse, and all in the direction of his fractures, his pain.

"Who do you think you *are?*" he whined at me.

"The one with the gun, the big friends and the attitude, Buck. Who do you think?"

He whimpered. Guys like him make me want to puke.

"Who's at the bottom of this, Bucky-boy?"

His face got red. "I don't know what you're talking about."

Still whining. Swell. I swung my purse meaningfully. He winced, getting the message. I started to feel like a creep and a bully until I remembered his screwdriver action on Amanda. So I got over it—just like that.

"Start."

He shook his head.

It was a long strap purse, stuffed specially with some heavy items. I hit him square in the ribs with it. "That's just an opener," I said as he gasped for breath.

There were tears in his mean little eyes. "Nobody." He was still gasping.

"Bullshit. You're not smart enough to figure it out on your own, Buck. Your kind takes directions. It"—*it* for sure—"doesn't give them." I hefted my purse.

"The word came down." He hugged his belly protectively, not looking at me.

"What word?"

"I'm *telling* ya. Back off, for crying out loud!" He was whining again. It made me feel like puking again. "The word was Hudson was trouble and Hudson was fucking with jobs. So get the bitch—that's what the word was."

"And?"

"And nuthin'," Buck said sullenly.

I swung the purse meaningfully.

"*Fuck!* I'm telling you, ain't I?" he cried, aggrieved, innocent.

Oh, right. Yes. Sure. Give me a break.

"The word was, if somebody got the point across to Hudson, there'd be something in it for him. The word was—" He hesitated.

I tried to look benign.

He shrugged, a bad move with cracked ribs, and winced. "The word was: Anything goes. So, what the fuck? I signed on."

What a regular guy. "This was from management?"

"All I heard."

"How about the employees?"

"Nobody cares, nobody gives a shit. Not until the word comes down that it could be your job. So, yeah, once the word got out that the Hudson woman was threatening jobs, you got guys that is mad, you got guys that would do something on it. You got volunteers in these guys. Way it goes," Buck said, excusing base, venal, despicable behavior as though it were nothing but a burp.

A screwdriver attack? Three guys on a woman? His excuse

wasn't good enough. No kidding. His excuse wasn't even good enough for his grammar.

"What did you get out of it, Buck?"

"Fuck off."

"What?" I took a firm grip on my purse.

He cowered behind a La-Z-Boy. "Fuck off, fuck off, fuck off."

I could have gotten more; I could have beaten and terrorized him for it, but I didn't have the heart, or maybe, more accurately, I had too much heart. I left. His fuck offs got louder as I got farther away.

Beat that for courage.


I paused, looked at my plate, took a bite.

"Was he acting on his own, Kat?" Jude asked.

"No, Buck's not smart enough. What he is is dumb enough to get into trouble. They—someone in management, I'm sure—threw money and ideas his way, then set him loose with his buddies. He didn't do a great job, but not bad. He got to Amanda. He got to all of us. Not bad."

Jude growled. Beside him, Amanda looked pale and pensive.

Her wan look got to him. "It's over," Jude said firmly. "To hell with him, right?"

The answer wasn't simple. It was yes and no. To hell with him was yes. But was it over? I didn't think so but I didn't know why and I couldn't back it up. I didn't say it, but there it was anyway. I figured that was the no.

"Amanda, are you still writing letters?"

Her eyes flickered. "No," she said. She was lying and she crumpled when I glared. "Well, not to the people who settled with Louden. To the FDA, yes."

It still wasn't the whole truth. I gave her the third-degree stare.

"I can't just walk away from it, Kat, even after all this. I need to put together as much documentation as possible so there is no way the FDA can ignore it."

Talk about the boundless optimism of youth.

"And I filed a complaint with OSHA."

"Oh?" More boundless optimism.

"Yes, based on the fact that I was assigned to work in an area where safety training and safety equipment are mandatory, and I had neither."

I think that the words *Amanda Rose—Gadfly* were imprinted on Amanda's soul somewhere.

It was one of the things that made me respect and care for her. It was one of the things that worried me. It was one of the things that made me sure it wasn't over.

"Kat, would you pass the mashed potatoes, please?"

I would, I did. For Sunday dinner at the Hudsons' we were eating Jude's favorite meal, chicken and mashed potatoes and other heavy stuff and so what if it's a 108 August degrees outside (I am not kidding —this is California's Central Valley) and that's why we have air-conditioning. The new kitchen table was old-fashioned and pine and a big improvement over the Formica one, although almost anything is an improvement over Formica.

"More fried chicken, Kat? Amanda, honey, have some more."

"I'm only eating for two, Jude," she said mildly, "not five."

He grinned at her. "More milk, sweetheart?"

She shook her head, but she smiled. Me, too. They were a happy young couple in love with life and each other, expecting their first child and a happily-ever-after ending.

"When do we get to meet your guy, Kat?"

"Yes," Amanda agreed. "We want to meet Hank."

Hank is the Las Vegas police detective who is the man in my life. We met when I was in Vegas on a job and have been together for a while now.

"Soon, I hope. He's traveling a lot working on a case that crosses state lines. When it winds down, he'll take some time off."

"Good," said Jude, reaching for another chicken leg. "We'll plan something."

Yes.

Somewhere in this we had moved from P.I. and clients to friends. It was a move we were all content with.

When I drove home later that evening, a sweet Delta breeze ruffled through the trees and my hair and the evening smells hit me, water and newly mown hay or grass and the scent of roses. It was summer. Life was full of love and promise.

It was almost too good to be true.

# 12

Dear Charity,

Can you believe a company that would *knowingly* manufacture faulty medical devices, a surgeon who would *knowingly* put one in a patient, and a world where a darling baby who didn't have to die did? What can I do?

Mad As All Git-out

Dear Git-out,

Forget getting mad. Get even. Get everyone responsible. Get a lawyer. Payback works.

Charity

~~~~~~~~~~~~~~~~~~~~~~~~~~~~~~~~~~~~~~~~~~~~~~~~~~~~~~

We had lunch the next week—Charity, Amanda, and I. I thought it was a party, a celebration in honor of our success (so far, so okay), the baby, the fact that we'd all survived ten days of temperatures over 108°—today was a chilly 96°—and that the harassment of Amanda had stopped. That's what I thought, but I was wrong. Amanda had taken the day off and they had gone shopping.

That was good, I mused, and harmless. When I got there they were twittering away like an illustration of the classic Dumb Blonde stereotype. Talk about insensitivity. They waved as I pulled a chair out and sat down but didn't interrupt their conversation. Talk about manners.

I listened with half an ear and mind because the conversation was about fashion, skirt lengths, and maternity clothes. Their happy tone lulled me into complacency. Being an accountant, a mom-to-be, and newly pretty was enough to fill Amanda's life right now. More than enough, I imagined. Somewhere in the middle of our entrées they moved into discussion of the letter. That was when I found out how wrong I was.

"What letter?" I asked, sitting up.

"The letter in my column warning about the possible danger of artificial heart valves," Charity answered. Amanda beamed.

Uh oh.

"It will advise people to check with their doctor on the reliability of the medical devices used."

"Is that a good idea?" I made my voice worried, not hard, and decided to pitch an altruistic appeal first. "Won't it panic a lot of people needlessly?"

"It will, I know." Amanda's smile faded slightly. "But I don't see any way around that, Kat. This information has got to go out, and if Louden won't assume a responsible position, if the FDA won't do its job, then *I* will. *We* will." She smiled at Charity. Charity smiled back.

Yesterday Superman, today the Lone Ranger and Tonto.

"I think we ought to talk about this some more," I said firmly, a single voice of reason, or doom, or both.

They shook their heads.

"How long before it appears?" I demanded.

"Tomorrow."

"No! It doesn't happen that fast, I know it doesn't."

"We did it a while ago."

"Amanda—"

"Kat, don't worry so. There's nothing to connect the letter with me."

"You didn't use your name, or mention Louden Industries, or Sacramento?"

"No."

The pain in my chest eased. "How is the letter signed?"

Amanda blushed. The pain came back.

"Concerned in California."

I groaned.

"California's a *big* state," Amanda pointed out reasonably.

"Kat, if you're not going to finish your pasta, may I?" Charity inquired. "No sense in letting it go to waste."

I shoved the plate at her. "Charity, what happens after you publish a letter like that?"

Charity munched her way thoughtfully through some pasta with sun-dried tomatoes before answering. "The shit hits the fan," she said.

Exactly what I was afraid of. "Amanda, give it up. It's not just you anymore. You have your baby to consider."

"That's just why I can't, Kat, don't you see?"

I didn't, no, and I said so.

"Suppose *my* baby had a birth defect that was corrected with a defective device, and people knew about it and didn't act on the information, and my baby died."

*Hiyo, Silver.*

"And that *will* happen to someone. I couldn't live with myself if I let that happen. Anyway, I think you're exaggerating the danger. Everything has settled down since the police investigation. It will be fine, you'll see."

I wasn't convinced. Charity delicately speared a tomato and ate with relish.

"And here's the good news. I've saved the best for last." Amanda tossed her head and the new diamonds sparkled like her eyes. I hoped the baby got those eyes. "Our plant manager called me into his office yesterday. Mr. DeVito said he wanted to personally thank me for bringing to light a potential issue—which is pretty vague, true, and doesn't admit there's a problem, but what the heck, it's a start. He asked me to turn everything over to him. I said I had. He said, yes, but you have copies, and I said I didn't. Which is true." She grinned at us. "I don't. Of course Kat does."

That was a technicality. I shook my head.

"He didn't look like he believed me completely."

"I can't imagine why." I said it sarcastically and she ignored me.

"DeVito said the president of Louden is putting together an investigative team to look into it. He asked me to leave everything in their hands."

"And?" I asked.

"And I said I would. Then he said they were giving me a raise and new job assignments. No more troubleshooting, for one." She and Charity laughed. I didn't.

"A raise, do you think? Or a bribe?" she asked me.

No flies on Amanda Rose.

Amanda looked at her watch. "I'm late," she said blithely, "I've got to run." Hugs, a wave and a whisper of perfume, and she was gone. And then back. "When I said I'd leave it alone?"

Charity nodded. I just watched her.

"I lied." And gone again.

*Hiyo, Silver, awa-a-a-a-a-ay.*

I sat there in a funk.

"Shall we split a dessert?"

"No. Charity, I don't like this. I agree—"

"Please."

"Okay. Whatever you want," I answered before she asked. I wouldn't eat it anyway. It just made Charity feel less guilty about dessert.

"Amanda's absolutely right. It's got to be stopped." I paused while Charity ordered a modest confection consisting of chocolate, hazelnuts, whipped cream, strawberries, brandy and five layers of cake. "Somebody had to tell the truth; somebody has to watch over these guys. I just don't want it to be Amanda anymore."

"Who then?" Charity asked reasonably.

I didn't know.

"She is the only one with the information, the interest, and the guts." Charity's eyes got misty as her dessert approached.

"Mmmmmm." She had her fork at the ready but paused, politely wait-ing for my answer.

I didn't have one.

"I think you're making too much of this, Kat." Charity dove into her cake. "Life really isn't such cops-and-robbers stuff. Anyway, once Amanda sees that the investigative team is doing its job and that changes are made, she'll leave it alone. There are other people in-volved now—she's not in any danger."

No?

And would the investigative team do its job?

*Do pigs have wings?*

The waiter cleared our plates. I looked to see if there was a silver bullet on Amanda's side of the table.

There wasn't.

The investigative team; the raise; the boss who thought she was the best thing since sliced bread, dual carburetors, and panty hose . . .

It was almost too good to be true.

# 13

~~~~~~~~~~~~~~~~~~~~~~~~~~~~~~~~~~~~~~~~~~~

I read it in the paper two days later.

### ELK GROVE WOMAN DEAD

Amanda Hudson of Elk Grove died in an unusual accident at her
home Sunday evening. Hudson, 25, was apparently relaxing in
her outdoor spa when a string of lights broke loose from fasten-
ings, fell into the spa and electrocuted her. She was discovered
the next day by a neighbor who got worried when she didn't

answer her phone. Hudson is survived by her husband, Jude, who
was out of town on business at the time of the accident.

It was early morning. The sun was just up and the birds were singing
happily in the cool morning air. I was on the patio drinking coffee,
drinking in the fragrance of the roses and the lingering promise of
summer. I just made it to the bathroom in time, threw up until there
was nothing left in me. It didn't help. What was making me sick wasn't
something I could throw up. Not the sickness. Or the sadness. Or the
dread.

The phone rang.

*Was it murder?* I asked right away before I said *I'm sorry,* which
he knew anyway but which I was to say over and over in one way or
another in the days to come. Oh God! No way *sorry* covered it. *Was it
murder? Was it?*

"Kat—"

"Jude, I'm coming over. I just saw it in the paper. You should
have called sooner."

"Kat—" His voice cracked.

"Forty-five minutes. I'll be there. Hold on." My voice didn't
crack. My heart did, had, was. It was a full verb declension there.

Jude looked old, looked like someone who had given up a long time
ago and no way was anything changing his mind now. He sat at the
new kitchen table. A quart of orange juice was in front of him and he'd
been drinking it out of the carton. There was a spill on the table with a
fly buzzing it and a pink terry-cloth robe on his lap. His hands were
wrapped in the robe, clutching it. Georgie lay at his feet.

"I can still smell the soap she used." His voice was as dead as
his eyes.

"It was a girl, Kat, the baby. I lost my girls."

My eyes filled with tears.

"We wanted to call her Julie Rose." Jude stood, picked up the carton of orange juice, tipped his head back and drank in great gulps until it was gone, carefully set it down, then stepped over to the kitchen wall, pounded a hole in the dry wall with his fist and walked out the back door.

I let him go. He stumbled across the yard, Georgie at his heels and tail dragging, sat on the grass, his back against a huge sycamore tree. When he ran his fingers through his hair he left a smear of blood on his forehead. Georgie lay next to him, his head on Jude's knee.

It seemed an eternity as I stood and watched and the fly buzzed, but it couldn't have been more than a few minutes until Todd and Daisy drove up. They climbed out of the truck, stood motionless for a moment, then Daisy walked over to Jude. Georgie's tail raised in one pathetic wag, then subsided.

Daisy sat on the ground next to Jude and took his hand in hers. He tried to pull away but she wouldn't let him. She held his hand and then she turned his face around with her other hand and forced him to meet her eyes.

The hurt was only beginning.

Later we sat at the kitchen table. I had wiped up the orange juice, swept up the dry wall, made lemonade and was answering the phone, which rang constantly until Jude turned the ringer to off.

"Let me tell you about Amanda Rose," he said then.

It was a story. His voice had a once-upon-a-time quality to it.

"When we met I thought I was something. The girls fell all over me, a big, good-looking, successful guy. Yeah, I thought I was something. And, if I thought about it at all, I thought she was nothing much. I was a young arrogant asshole with a pretty face, a strong body, a small amount of charm, and the sensitivity of a lizard on a hot rock. And Mandy? She was just a plain little thing."

Pain walked across his face and stomped out the light in his eyes. Stomped and stomped and stomped.

"One night, when I had nothing better to do, I bumped into her and asked her out. Asked her out like I was doing her a big favor, asked her out knowing she would go—nobody ever turned me down."

He said it not with arrogance but as a statement of fact.

"They lined up for me, the girls did. And she said, 'Oh no, thanks, I've got to read *Consumer Reports* and pick out a new toaster.' And she laughed. Turned me down for a toaster and laughed!

"Later, when I learned how to ask, she taught me how to love and live, how to see things like she did. I was good-looking Jude and she was plain Amanda Rose, but she was the beautiful one, not me. I thought she was something else. In the morning she would drink her juice too fast, like she was eager for its sweetness and for the sweetness of a new day. Sometimes she'd get the hiccups, then come sit on my lap so I could pat her back. Oh God, I love her!"

Nobody spoke when Jude stopped. It was hard to move through the pain in the room. It was hard to breathe. A fly buzzed, the sound small and loud in the silence.

"The cops say it was an accident. They say it's one of those things that just happens. They're wrong."

Under the table Daisy's knee pressed against mine and she reached for my hand. Sympathy and concern. Maybe more. Maybe she thought that Jude was losing it. It was something to consider.

"I want you to come back to work for me again, Kat."

He told me, he didn't ask me. And my job description had been redefined. I wasn't muscle anymore, I'd graduated. I was brains. I was an investigator. I would do it, he didn't have to ask. I'd loved Amanda too.

"They killed her. Find out. It has to do with Louden. Prove it. And then we blow it out everywhere—press conferences, billboards, whatever it takes. Amanda Rose is not dying for nothing."

Silence again. Even the fly had stopped buzzing.

"The police do a good job, Jude, and they say it's an accident."

"They don't know what we know, Kat."

No. And they weren't blinded by emotion either.

"Just check it out."

"Yes." I heard tires on gravel outside. "How long had the lights been up?" Out back, the dogs started barking.

"The ones over the hot tub?"

"Yes."

"A year and a half, I think. The Christmas before last."

"The dogs? If someone came over, if it wasn't an accident"—I couldn't yet bring myself to say murder—"why weren't the dogs barking?" Like they are now, I thought. "Why wasn't Amanda aware of someone approaching? Why didn't she get out of the spa to investigate? The dogs were running loose, right?"

"No." Anger in Jude's voice. "They should have been but Mandy often puts them out behind the barn. She does that when they chase the chickens. It makes her mad. Georgie was loose but he wouldn't hurt a fly. Getting by him would be no big thing."

Outside, car doors slammed. There was the sound of voices that were hushed and subdued. Death, after all.

The house started filling up with family and friends. I stood to go.

"My girls," Jude told me. "Don't forget."

No.

I started with the cops. I would have preferred going over the patio and hot tub area but that would have to wait. There were too many people and, although death was on their minds, homicide wasn't.

I called Henley to see if he was in, then headed downtown to the Sheriff's Department at 7th and G, lucked out with a parking place on 7th. In the shade, too. A small thing, but something.

Henley okayed me, so they waved me through locked doors and on up to his office. I found it easily enough. I'd been there before.

"Knock, knock," I said, leaning on the doorjamb.

"Hey, Kat, c'mon in."

I looked with affection at the graying, balding man with dandruff (talk about a bummer, balding *and* dandruff!), a middle-aged paunch and a sharp mind. He was a nice guy, a good cop. We shook hands and he cleared off a chair, tossing a thick pile of papers on his overflowing desk.

I put a paper bag down on a stack of folders where it teetered, then balanced precariously. "I brought you some sweet rolls, Bill."

"Yeah? Good. Thanks. The guy whose turn it is to pick up doughnuts is on a health kick so all we get is muffins." Henley sneered as he drew the word *muffins* out. "The blueberry, cranberry nut, and chocolate chip move pretty fast. Time I got there this morning there was only bran, and, shi-i-it, those suckers will stay with you for a week."

I'd brought a coffee for him and a diet Dr Pepper for me.

Henley looked concerned. "You oughtta stop drinking that junk, Kat, it's bad for you."

I laughed in his face, the face he regularly stuffs with sugar, empty carbos and high-cholesterol fats. "Give me a break, Henley."

He grinned at me and tore into a sugary, empty carbo, high-cholesterol cinnamon roll with nuts and raisins. "What's up?"

"The Amanda Hudson death."

"She the one in the hot tub?"

I nodded, saddened that she was the hot tub death and not a name, not a person. Soon just a statistic.

"We didn't find anything. Neither did the coroner. It was ruled an accident."

"Drugs or alcohol?" I couldn't imagine it, I didn't believe it, I was just checking.

"I don't know. Lemme see if Zack's around. It was his case." He took a sweet roll with him and left, returned with Zack Taylor, who was a lean-muscled machine, and who declined a roll.

"No drugs or alcohol," Zack said after we shook hands and played catch-up, the wife was fine, the kids older, that sort of stuff. I hadn't seen him in a year or so, maybe not since a barbecue last summer. "Hudson'd eaten a light meal a few hours earlier, coroner says. She didn't drown, and there was no water in her lungs. No marks, no bruises, no signs of a struggle. Her body was contorted in a way consistent with electrocution."

I didn't ask, I didn't have to. I'd seen photos in a long-ago case and the images were still sharp, still violently etched in my mind. That image became Amanda before I could help it, before I could stop it, her arms bent at the elbow and extended, her fingers rigid, stretched out and bent like claws, her mouth in a startled moue, her eyes wide open, wondering, surprised, asking a question that would never be known. Or answered. Or understood. Something in me bunched up in a hard, hot pain.

"The spa area?" I asked finally.

"Same thing. No signs of a struggle. Nothing out of place, nothing out of the ordinary. It wasn't a crime scene, Kat, it was an accident. There are a lot of accidents involving pools and hot tubs. Too damn many, and all preventable, that's the shame of it."

"The lights?" I asked.

"They weren't put up properly, they were loose. I mean, it's the kind of thing you'd do, I'd do, anyone'd do, but it's not the right way, and it's not safe. When you're stringing up electrical like that you should use insulated staples." Zack made a U with his hand. "They've got sharp points on each end. You drive them in around the wire and that wire doesn't go anywhere."

"And that's not how they were put up?"

"No. Nails were hammered in and bent up. Works, but easy enough to dislodge the wire if someone pulls it, or the nail gets twisted. The wind can even do it. Nothing fancy, nothing premeditated, nothing murderous. Just stupid." *Just an accident.*

"Her husband thinks it's murder."

"Yeah, he told us. You working for him?"

"I'm a family friend. I said I'd look into it. He tell you the background?"

"Yeah, pretty much."

"Amanda was a crusader. Not just a person with a conscience but a passionate believer in right and wrong, in justice. She ran with the Superman/Lone Ranger/Joan of Arc crowd, Zack, and she stayed out on the front lines. No rear troop or backup support tactics for Amanda Rose."

"You know this from her, not her husband?" Zack asked.

"Yes." I told him about Amanda's trip to the Louden plant in Texas and her hell-raising there, the files she'd photocopied, the phone calls, the letters she'd written to Louden management, to the FDA, and to some of the patients/consumers involved with Louden products, faulty or not.

"I didn't know all that." Zack sounded thoughtful but unconvinced.

"I don't think Jude knew. Amanda didn't tell her husband much about the letters or let him know the full extent of her investigation. She didn't want to worry him."

Zack and Bill both nodded. It was not news to them, any more than to me, that husbands and wives did not always tell each other everything.

"You saw the assault report?" I asked.

"Yeah. Talked with the officer and the detective who handled it. They both did a good job, both said they thought that Hudson's harassment problem probably originated with management, but nobody at Louden was talking and they couldn't prove it."

I told them of my visit to Buck Lassiter.

"Speaking of the fucking Lone Ranger," Henley said sourly, reaching for the last sweet roll.

I ignored the comment.

Zack whistled. "Okay. But it's a long way from there to murder."

It was, yes, I agreed. And not the kind of distance you bridged with a rash assumption, especially if you were a cop.

Zack shook his head. "We got nothing to go on, Kat. Nothing at the scene indicates anything but an accident. We didn't find anything and we went over it. We looked. I'd need more than what you told me, a lot more, before I could move on it. You find something, I'll move. Until then—" He shrugged.

"You find something, you bring it to us," Bill said, not sounding like he thought I would.

And I had to admit that past experience tended to corroborate that assumption. I nodded affably in Henley's direction. Why not? It didn't cost anything. "Thanks, Zack. Let me know if you find out anything else, could you?"

"Sure. I'd be surprised, though. Good luck." He made his mouth move up slightly around the edges. Zack's a good cop but not one who smiles a lot. "One thing, Kat."

Something in his voice caught me. Even Bill raised an eyebrow.

"It wasn't the lights that killed her. I'm not sure they were powerful enough to do it, but they didn't. They were loose but not down."

"It was electrical, though?"

"Oh yeah. No question. What killed her was a portable CD player that had apparently been balanced on the side of the hot tub."

I thought that one over carefully. Cops, particularly in a homicide, often do not release all the information. They withhold a specific and crucial detail or details as a way to keep a killer's MO under wraps, to weed out false confessions and copycat killings. *Killer? Homicide? MO?* "So, you're wondering?"

"We always wonder." Zack's eyes were hard and speculative—cop's eyes.

"But nothing to hang it on?"

"No. Like I said."

I nodded my appreciation of the information and stood. "Thanks, Bill."

"Yeah. You're welcome."

I grinned at him. "Want me to let you know if you can help in any way?"

"Yeah. Thought you'd never ask. I'd'a brought it up myself but I'm too damn shy."

Zack snorted and left the room.

"See you, Bill."

He nodded, gnawed off another bite of sweet roll and went back to a three-inch folder open on his desk.

I saw myself out.

Accidents just happened. Murder didn't.

# 14

Dear Charity,

I think it's in extremely bad taste for people to carry on at funerals, don't you? Funerals should be quiet and dignified.

Sad But Silent

Dear S but S,

Death isn't always dignified. Why should funerals be?

Charity

~~~~~~~~~~~~~~~~~~~~~~~~~~~~~~~~~~~~~~~~~~

I called Zack the next day.

"Will you come to the memorial service?" I asked.

"Amanda Hudson's?"

"Yes."

Long silence. I was pushing my luck with him. I kept on pushing.

"Zack, I know you're busy—"

"What's the agenda, Kat?" Meaning: *What's* your *agenda, Kat?*

I was asking a favor of a busy cop so I didn't play dumb. I spit it right out. "If her death's not an accident, if I'm right on this, there is someone who knows it better than I do, someone who's complacent in the accident verdict. I'd like to see that complacency shaken. Please," I added, tossing the word in like a hat in the ring, or a penny in a wishing well. Couldn't hurt.

"Where?" Zack asked. "When?"

I told him.

"Be there if I can."

He hung up, but not before I tossed in a thank you. Couldn't hurt. Besides, I meant it. I like to see the pressure build. Cops do too.

I had to stop at a 7-Eleven for panty hose the next morning. I don't wear panty hose much at any time of the year and never in August, when the thermometer climbs over a hundred degrees. Never if I can help it. I decided today I couldn't. Then I decided to take some time off soon, go rafting on the American River, get my legs tan enough to skip panty hose. The 7-Eleven had nothing in my size. Naturally. I pushed through the entire stock and finally found an off-white small in the middle of the taupe Queen. Close enough—I was in yellow linen.

Amanda's service was to be held in the McKinley Rose Garden on H and Alhambra. The roses were profuse in cultivated splendor, brilliance and grandeur, heady with perfume and promise. It was a favorite spot for weddings; I had never been to a memorial service there before.

Tuesday. Ten o'clock. Eighty-two degrees and a lot of people. It was a quiet gathering. We were not celebrating life the way a bride and groom would, the way the roses were. A studio photograph of Amanda in a silver frame was placed on a freshly painted white wooden easel. Cut roses in all colors were tied with silver ribbons to the easel, the flowers ranging from tight elegant buds to full overblown blossoms starting to drop their petals. If it was symbolic, it was wrong. Amanda's flower had been a bud, cut off early.

The picture was one taken of the Amanda I had known when I first met her. She was prim and plain in pink and pearls. I turned away quickly, blinked hard.

I walked around, yellow linen, green eyes and a notebook. I made no attempt to play down the fact that I was looking, noting, writing. Play down? Okay, I tuned it in, amped it up, played it out. I was mourning Amanda in my own way.

Zack was there, was early as I was, and good-looking in slacks, a summer-weight jacket, white shirt and dark silk tie. His gun and badge weren't showing, he didn't have cop written on his forehead, but that was about it. He walked around with his shoulders square, his hands in his pockets, his eyes noticing and hard. He was as obvious as a cop in a *Dragnet* segment, only better dressed. I was impressed. We spoke briefly, each filling in a few blanks for the other, then separated.

It was getting warmer.

I already had a run in my new panty hose. Roses, after all.

A woman in a stunningly simple white suit walked through the murmuring crowd to stand beside Amanda's photograph, her hand on the easel for several minutes before the shushing and then the hush traveled through the crowd and settled into quiet. Then she spoke into silence drenched with the rich perfume of roses.

"Amanda loved roses, and here, in the midst of the flower she loved, we have gathered to say good-bye."

Someone, a woman, started crying softly.

"It is always difficult to say good-bye to someone who leaves us too soon, who dies too young. Our task today is doubly difficult, not one good-bye but two, not one life but two. Amanda and Jude were expecting a child."

There were audible gasps. Someone sighed out *no*. The crying woman cried harder. To my left a man sucked his breath in sharply, his face warped with emotion, then smoothed out in an instant, less than a second. If I hadn't caught it in that moment, I wouldn't have.

I stepped back and watched his polite, attentive, unreadable face. Nothing. He was dressed impeccably in navy slacks and coat, a pale blue shirt, and a contrasting, expensive tie in diagonal stripes of silver and medium blue. A bare head, a gold watch, a class act. Medium height, broad shoulders, narrow waist and hips, strong muscular thighs and legs, short black hair, brown skin, eyes hidden. Damn

105

dark glasses, anyway. He looked at me then, felt my stare. Our eyes would have met but for the glasses. I was wearing them too. We both looked away. I stepped back and drifted, holding my notebook.

*We cannot guess why God took these two flowers, plucked them from this garden so soon.*

But it wasn't God, I thought. God doesn't toss CD players into hot tubs to take someone out. That was a human, not a heavenly, action. And it was not—I was almost positive of it now—a foolish accident for which Amanda was responsible.

I was at the back and on the edge of the crowd. Jude stood at the front with his family and Amanda's. I had met some of them when I first arrived. Todd and Daisy were there, Wade and a pretty, freckled woman I assumed was his wife; many friends and neighbors, the men dressed semi-formally and often in western attire, the women in bright summer colors that went with the roses.

A tighter knot of twelve to fifteen people stood off to one side. They wore street clothes, jeans. A few were in coveralls. Most had arrived together, four or five to a car. Louden Industries had given paid time off to anyone who chose to attend. One token management-type figure was there in an ill-fitting gray suit, one that he had outgrown fifteen pounds and several lapel changes ago.

The good-looking guy startled by news of Amanda's pregnancy stood off to one side of the company group. He had come alone, I assumed, and was standing alone, his jaw working slightly.

An arm slipped into mine; I looked down into dark glasses and a face framed by blond hair and a floppy hat. The hand resting on my arm clutched a wadded-up lace handkerchief. Charity hiccuped.

"Will you do something for me?" I asked softly and her forehead wrinkled into a frown. I couldn't see her eyes. "We'll cry later. Right now I want you to pay attention. Look for anything that stands out, doesn't add up or make sense. See who's upset, who's crying, who's not."

The frown furrows smoothed out as she whispered back to me. "It's a cliché, isn't it, Kat, that the murderer always comes to the

funeral? I thought it only happened in books and movies. You know—
the beautiful unknown woman in black with a veil hiding her face,
though how we would know she's beautiful with a veil hiding her face
is beyond me. Anyway, there's no one here in a black veil. Oh, Kat,"
she whimpered and hiccuped and a tear slid out from under the dark
glasses. "I'm not making light of it, I'm *not.*"

"I know," I said gently. "Just look around, please. For Amanda."
I patted her hand and walked off.

*We all loved Amanda Rose in different ways. We will all say good-
bye in different ways.*

My eyes worked the crowd like a pickpocket, sneaking up on
people and emotions and stealing what they thought was theirs alone.
No privacy in a murder case. Briefly I caught Zack's eye. It twitched
in what could have been a wink on a less solemn occasion. He was
doing the same thing I was, working the crowd.

*Please feel free to share your memories of Amanda, your thoughts,
your farewells.*

I looked at Jude, tall and gorgeous, his face drawn into lines of
sorrow, pain, and ugliness. He looked old still, and hard. The word
*farewell* sang in the silence, swooped and floated and dove like a
butterfly on a hot summer day.

It was getting warmer.

The young woman who had been weeping throughout walked up
to the easel, took a scarlet rose and a silver ribbon. "I am Margaret,"
she told the crowd. "Amanda was my best friend in the seventh grade.
Mandy and Margie. We talked about everything. We even picked out
names for our babies. And now—" Tears finished her sentence.

Many people spoke. Some took roses, or touched the photograph,
or brought a flower up. There were many tears.

It was getting warmer as well as wetter.

Finally there was silence broken by birdcalls, the easy busy
drone of bees, the sound of traffic, of a car backfiring, and a siren in
the distance. It wasn't over. I didn't know what was to come, but I
knew it wasn't over. The knowledge that held me, hot now, sticky now

in the heat, held everyone else as well. We were in thrall to the heat, the moment, and an unknown.

Jude moved forward.

Of course. A ripple went through us all; collectively we wondered why we hadn't known. He stood by his wife's photograph, facing us, meeting people's eyes, seeing something we weren't privy to. When he spoke it was a single line.

"I will never say good-bye."

It wasn't an observation or a comment, it was a threat. It was a statement of unfinished business. No one missed it. A young child started to wail and was echoed by an infant. Even the baby got it. Then it was my turn to speak. I didn't plan it or think it out; I knew it only in that moment. I walked up and stood next to Jude.

"I don't know how many of you saw Amanda recently, her new haircut, sparkly earrings in her pierced ears, bright splashy summer colors and clothes. She was different—beautiful and happy. She could finally see what all of us had already seen, already knew: that she was as beautiful on the outside as she was on the inside."

A bird, close by, false started and then burbled into lush song, clear and lovely. Sounds hung in the air, dipped and climbed. As suddenly as it began, the song ceased. I spoke into the silence.

"It is appalling when an accident takes a dear and beautiful person from us. It is unspeakable when it may not have been an accident."

There was a gasp. I had spoken the unspeakable. Nobody else spoke; it was a tough act to follow. Something made me look at Jude; something in me saw it coming. He picked up Amanda's photo, swung and smashed it against the easel. Glass and frame exploded into the silence and summer. He pulled the picture from the debris and, ignoring the glass, tore it across again and again, then dropped the fragments.

I spoke the unspeakable; he acted it.

It pretty much broke up the occasion.

I stayed until most everyone had left. So did Zack, still looking like a cop, and Charity, looking like a Woman's Page reporter from thirty years ago with her big floppy hat, flowered dress, high heels and tears.

"You always so subtle?" Zack asked.

I ignored that and introduced him to Charity.

*"Dear Charity?* No kidding!"

Speaking of subtle. I left them trading compliments and wandered around. The man in blue had taken a white rose and left alone in a silver-gray Porsche immediately after Jude busted the picture. I got that tag but didn't bother with the other vehicle plates. Jude could put me in touch with family and friends, and the Louden employees were easily available through standard means.

Zack shook Charity's hand, raised a hand in salute to me and walked off. Charity started to walk over but stopped, then waved and discreetly headed for her car when she saw Jude approaching me. He had come out of nowhere. Anyone can be a phantom rising out of a foggy mist on a gray day, but it's tough to do on a clear summer afternoon. Not that Jude looked like a phantom.

"I behaved badly." His voice was ugly, contradicting the implied intention in his words.

"There is no bad and good when you've lost your wife and child. There aren't any rules." And that was true. No question. But his violence and the destruction of the photograph had shaken me. I asked about it. "Why?"

"I don't know." He shook his head like a big dumb zoo animal. "I guess I'm just mad at the whole fucking world."

I didn't like the answer.

"Come out to the house? The family's all going to be there."

"If I can. I may follow up on something first."

He nodded grimly and walked over to an anxious knot of people waiting for him.

It was hot now. It would get hotter.

.   .   .

I didn't loiter in the ABSOLUTELY NO PARKING AT ANY TIME! zone. I found an inconspicuous spot underneath a shade tree and parked, opened the windows and slumped down behind the wheel. The Louden contingent might have come right back or they might have gone out to lunch. I was hoping for the latter. I wanted another shot at attitudes and expressions, at fixing faces, especially while I still had their attire and demeanor from this morning fresh in my mind.

The clock in the Bronco told me that it was shortly before noon and that I had up to an hour's wait ahead of me. I wished I'd packed a Thermos or stopped for cold drinks. Talk is cheap and wishing is cheaper. I gasped in the heat, the yellow linen and I fading perceptibly and rapidly. First the panty hose, I wiggled out of them in no time. Pale bare legs looked better than a run. Then I stuffed my hair up into a Giants baseball cap that I wore with the bill backwards, pulled off my earrings and necklace. It was good enough for a head and shoulders glance.

At twelve o'clock the plant's main doors busted open and regurgitated a batch of people. Nobody I recognized. After that a steady trickle for the next ten minutes. Then nothing until shortly after twelve-thirty when the trickle reversed itself and started into the plant. I slid down a little farther. Not difficult, I was a puddle of sweat. First I saw cars, then faces I recognized from the morning. Most looked everyday, or what I assumed was everyday for them. Three women walked in, subdued and quiet and exchanging only monosyllables. Two guys in coveralls laughed, jostled each other, and exchanged high fives. For them, the funereal mood hadn't lasted long. I leaned my baseball cap, ears straining, out the window, but no dice—no incriminating words, no murder confessions, just laughter and gossip. At twelve fifty-five a familiar Porsche pulled in and parked; a familiar figure in navy slacks, blue shirt and striped tie climbed out and walked briskly into the plant.

Well, I'll be damned. I hadn't figured him working here. I rolled up the window, fired up the ignition, flipped the a/c up to blast and took off for the nearest cold drink. In the parking lot of Lulu's Cafe I pulled off my baseball cap and shook out my hair, then headed inside. Two and a half glasses of iced tea and a quick tuna salad on sourdough later, I headed out, jewelry back on, lipstick and makeup fresh (if you can call a dusting of powder and blush makeup), and back to Louden. I tried to smooth out the wrinkles in my linen dress, but that was pretty hopeless.

The manager's office was not difficult to find, though the manager was.

"Mr. DeVito should be right back," his secretary assured me after checking his schedule, frowning, and making an interoffice call. "I can't imagine— Did you want to wait?"

I did.

"Would you care for a cup of coffee?"

I wouldn't, thanks so much. I'd just managed to lower my body temperature a few degrees and wasn't in the mood to raise it again.

The secretary's office was the size of a small closet, her chair the only one. And she was a nervous worker, scuttling around, fussing in file cabinets, on the phone, and about her desk. I got in the way as much as humanly possible, then apologized profusely for my ineptness. Unasked, indeed unwanted, I bounced in to "help" her move a large box and knocked over a half-full can of Pepsi, apologizing profusely for my clumsiness. I darted across the room toward a box of tissue, "tripped" over a carton of papers and, with a little kick, sent them flying.

Not bad for someone with almost perfect balance.

Before I could start apologizing profusely again, the secretary caught me by the elbow and steered me toward her boss's office. Her thumb and forefinger bit into my elbow like tongs. "Perhaps you would care to wait in Mr. DeVito's office?" she said through tight straight lips, almost without moving her mouth. How did she do that?

"What a swell idea," I enthused, "and then I won't be in your way."

"Yes," she said, the annoyance in her voice still under control, but getting touch-and-go, I thought. The tongs didn't release me until I was safely inside DeVito's office. She exited without a word, pulled the door shut behind her. She would have slammed it—that was my bet—but it stuck, grated complainingly, sighed into place. There were two visitor's chairs there but I graced neither of them.

I started tossing the place.

# 15

Dear Charity,

I'm doing something at work that's not quite honest,
but what the hell? Everybody does it and it's not hurting anyone. What do you think?

Fudging

Dear Fudge,

I think there are a million excuses if you want to find
one. You found two and it's still wrong.

Charity

Time was a luxury I didn't have, a commodity I couldn't count on, and
confrontation was not a ring I wanted to step into. Hey, I'd just graduated up from muscle to brains.

I started with the desktop, my heart hammering like a carpenter
paid by the job. A letter from Louden's local lawyer regarding a trash
disposal complication and disagreement. I made a mental note of the
firm's name. A letter from the corporate counsel in the national office
in Houston asking for information "in re the Hudson situation," ending with a firm and not-so-subtle recommendation for action and a

swift resolution. The letter was dated nine days ago, would have been received two or three days later, putting it two or three days before Amanda's death. Sooner, if faxed.

A note on a four-by-six pad said:

Harry

Buck          Check "benefit" increase

Ray

A family photo complete with matronly woman (wife?), twenty-fiveish young woman (daughter?), and two children, one smiling, one drooling (grandchildren?), and that was it for DeVito's desktop.

Inside the desk I found a bunch of predictable stuff: letterhead paper, paper clips, stapler, memo and appointment book in elegant hand-tooled leather with elegant pristinely white pages, multiple copies of a company newsletter, one of which I snitched, folders filled with production and distribution data. I didn't have the time for them so I kept moving. No surprises.

Make that one surprise. I almost missed it. It looked like trash, a used tissue, except why keep a used tissue? Not a tissue, a cocktail napkin from the Paradise Inn with a bright carmine lipstick kiss smacked onto its liquor-stained surface. Beneath the kiss in heavy black ink was a heart carelessly and sloppily inked in, and beneath that: *Shelley.*

I glanced at the photo of the well-dressed man in the three-piece business suit with wife and family gathered around him. He was balding, graying, a little potbellied. I wondered if DeVito had a sports car, a little black book, a hair transplant and a male midlife crisis. He looked the perfect candidate for the whole package.

There were filing cabinets and a computer. I didn't bother with either. No time. The wastebasket was a dark green metal one, the kind I remembered none too fondly from grammar school. Underneath a doughnut box (half a dozen powdered), the sports page, and a lottery ticket were four crumpled pages from the memo pad on the desk. They had handwritten notes and doodles on them. I smiled again.

And snitched them. Finders keepers. I heard voices in the secretary's office, the thudding of my heart, and then the grate and scrunch of the door. When it opened I was in a visitor's chair gazing expectantly up at the door with my legs neatly crossed and a calm hokey little smile perched on my lips. And hardly sweating at all, honest.

DeVito walked in. I had not seen him at the memorial service. "How do you do, Miss Colorado. Sorry to keep you waiting." He didn't look sorry.

"Ms.," I corrected blandly, "and not at all. Thank you for seeing me, Mr. DeVito."

A quick false smile chased an even quicker, but sincere, frown off his chunky face. "How may I help you, Ms. Colorado?" He had moved to stand behind his desk, but not to be seated. Clearly I was not to delude myself into thinking that this was to be a long or intimate interview.

"I am a friend of the Hudsons. Jude Hudson asked me to act on his behalf and pick up his wife's personal effects. He is understandably unable to do so himself at this time."

DeVito nodded in what I assumed was meant to pass for warmth and/or sympathy.

"He also asked that I speak, if possible, with Amanda's friends and coworkers."

I said it with a face empty of expression, with just a hint of grief in my voice. DeVito sat down, picked up a paper clip and, with a vicious twist, turned it into a visual "statement."

"Amanda's death was so sudden, the grief so overwhelming that Hudson is, I think, grasping at anything for understanding, information, and consolation." My voice suggested that while reasonable people might not approach a situation in this manner, bereavement did not make one reasonable and, further, that it was only reasonable to understand this, only compassionate to comply.

DeVito destroyed another paper clip and picked up a third. "Uh-hhh—"

I whipped right through his hesitancy. "With your permission I would like to visit briefly with Amanda's coworkers. Or, if that would be too disruptive"—I waved my hand to indicate that disruption was the *last* thought on my mind—"then perhaps you would give me names and phone numbers and mention to people that I will be calling?"

Paper-clip skeletons were piling up in front of him now. I shuddered at the thought of his office supply bill. I had him, no question.

DeVito was well within his rights to refuse me access to Amanda's desk, to his employees, to any information about any of it. Well within. Securely within. But to do so would make him look like a jerk and a cretin. And refusing me access didn't mean I wouldn't pursue it anyway. Both notions had crossed his mind, I could tell. Another paper clip bit the dust.

"What beautiful children," I crooned. "Your grandchildren?"

He beamed at me. And beamed and beamed. "Yes. Well, uh, Miss, Ms. Colorado, I am happy"—he frowned—"to be able to cooperate with the Hudson family on behalf of Louden Industries." DeVito's expression told me that he thought the flowers the company sent, a large expensive arrangement I had seen at the ranch, were more than enough. "Naturally, happy as we are to do so, and sensitive as we are to the issues—"

Personally I thought sensitive was a strong and inaccurate exaggeration of his feelings. I watched him link the twisted, crumpled, deranged paper clips together. If this was a metaphor, it was not a good sign.

"—still, we really *cannot* afford to have our employees' workday unduly disrupted."

I wondered if he had taken a special class to learn to talk like that: BusinessSpeak 1A. "I can certainly sympathize"—sympathize was too strong a word, too—"with that, Mr. DeVito, and I will be brief, I assure you," I said, also in BusinessSpeak, and stood.

He followed suit, scattering paper clips and disinclination, both of which I ignored.

He sighed. "This way, please." We took off at a brisk pace.

I followed him past his thin-lipped secretary and down a rather bleak corridor that opened into a sunny, well-lit room decorated with plants, pleasant if bland pictures, wall art (sic), and four curious faces. The faces were behind desks in partially partitioned-off cubicles. All were turned toward us. All, I was sure, had been at this morning's service.

"This is Ms. Colorado," DeVito said gruffly, coming to a halt in the center of the room. "She is acting on behalf of Amanda Hudson's family. Please feel free to give her your attention and help. Annie, will you do the introductions?"

A perky brunette with spiked bangs bounced up obediently from her chair.

"Fifteen minutes or so, Ms. Colorado." DeVito said it as though it was a polite request. We both knew better.

"Thank you." I agreed to his terms.

He brushed his hands together several times, flipping his fingers slightly with the last washing motion as though he would be happy to be rid of me, then nodded abruptly and left the room. I turned to Annie.

She stuck out her hand. "Annie Williams." She introduced the others—Sally Murphy, Letty Thomas, Celia Evans—and then looked inquiringly at me. The ball was in my court. I served.

"Amanda's husband wanted to know about her last days, about anything she might have said or done, about anything special or perhaps unusual."

Four faces composed themselves in understanding, compassion, and pity, and then professed ignorance. Amanda, her coworkers told me, had been pleasant, even warm and friendly on occasion, but not particularly communicative about her life, thoughts or personal affairs. I saw a flicker in Annie's face at the word "affairs." On my request Annie showed me Amanda's desk and work areas and explained her job to me. There was nothing new. Last on my list was going through her desk. No hurry there. Management, somebody, would have cleaned out anything notable long ago, days earlier.

As I packed a coffee cup that said *Amanda,* a dried flower arrangement in a basket, six CDs and a paperweight into a shopping bag I'd brought with me, Annie started to get teary. The three other women glanced around, looked nervous and embarrassed, then started to slip back to their desks, their lives and a known place in the scheme of things. Letty's phone rang and she scampered off eagerly to answer it.

I put my hand on Annie's arm. "You cared about Amanda?" She nodded and sniffled. "Could we get together and talk sometime?" Another nod and then she bolted. I finished packing Amanda's things and then sat in her desk chair and looked around, tried to see the place, the setup with her eyes. It was just another workplace. No writing on the wall. No clues, no death threats. Nothing spoken or unspoken. Annie reappeared, her nose blown, her face tidied and dusted unevenly with powder. She handed me a slip of paper with her name and phone number on it. I gave her the business card that said consultant, not investigator.

"Annie, will you show me where Amanda was attacked?"

Her hands flew about nervously. "I, uh, I guess so. Mr. DeVito said to show you whatever you wanted."

On the way to the main part of the warehouse and the loading docks we passed a men's room.

"Is this where Amanda was locked up?"

"Huh? The men's room? Why would Amanda be there? The ladies' is just down the hall and I didn't hear of anyone ever getting locked in."

The Louden warehouse looked like any other warehouse I'd ever been in. It was big, big enough for someone to sneak up on you unnoticed and do serious damage before help could hear, would come. And it was noisy, forklifts and other equipment seemed to be in pretty steady operation in the center loading area and up aisles lined with metal shelving stacked with boxes. I walked around quickly. Annie tagged aimlessly behind like a dinghy in reluctant tow.

In the office building again, I started to say good-bye to Annie, then stopped. Now was as good a time as any to ask about her involuntary flicker when someone said Amanda was incommunicative about

118

her personal affairs. It was ridiculously easy to isolate the word that had made her nervous.

I spoke as though rash assumption were fact. "Annie, Amanda was having an affair, wasn't she?"

Her eyes widened. Her mouth started to shape itself into an O but she caught herself and said nothing.

"Who was it?"

"I . . . I don't . . ."

I held her eyes with mine and she stuttered to a stop. Then I stood there looking mean. The possibility of murder does not bring out the best in me.

"He was at the memorial service, wasn't he?"

She nodded miserably.

"Who?"

"I don't know for sure. I—"

"Who?" Nothing. "What does he look like?" Nothing. "What does he drive?"

"A Porsche." She gave in. "A silver one. He's— No, I—I don't know anything."

"Thanks, Annie." She nodded dumbly again.

I walked back to DeVito's office to thank him.

"You're welcome." He looked as though he was glad to be rid of me. It was the first honest and straightforward thing I'd noticed about him.

I hadn't seen Buck, or Harry, or Ray.

I would.


The sunflower-yellow linen sundress lay in a crumpled heap on the floor of my closet. I was wearing denim shorts, a baggy pink T-shirt with the short sleeves rolled up into cuffs, white Reeboks and socks and my Giants baseball cap. The cap was black with orange letters and looked pretty putrid with my pink shirt. So much for me and fashion statement.

This time, sitting in the Louden parking lot, I had a dash fan plugged into the cigarette lighter and a Thermos with icy lemonade. It's hotter at four o'clock in the afternoon than at noon. And it was shaping up to be a day when I did my fair share of sweating.

I hadn't planned to be here. I had planned to follow Amanda's footsteps, Amanda's trail, to check out the trouble she'd stirred up, the enemies she could have made, almost certainly had made in the last months of her life.

But here I was.

Call it a hunch.

Boyfriend?

Call it more than a hunch.

# 16

Dear Charity,

One of the big problems in this here country is people who dont follow the rules, like they marry someone whose a different color or religion. Alot of people agree with me but dont have the guts to say it.

Red, White And Blue Guts

Dear Guts,

You can't spell. Your grammar's shaky. You're missing the red, white, and blue point completely, and you're worried about rules? Please!

Charity

~~~~~~~~~~~~~~~~~~~~~~~~~~~~~~~~~~~~~~~~~~~~~~~~~~~~~~~~~~

I was very hot, very frazzled and damp, and my lemonade was almost gone before I spotted him. I was also wondering whether it was worth it. He had reacted—okay, overreacted—to the news of Amanda's baby, then quickly masked it. Did that make him guilty? I didn't know. That's why I was here.

It was after four. At three forty-five the next shift had started drifting in. That lasted until shortly before four. There was a brief hiatus and then the doors were punched open and workers spilled out into the heat and glare, briefly filling up the parking lot with moving cars, noise, radios, and joking—sometimes harsh—comments. Then silence again.

Five minutes later, the guy in blue walked out, pushed through the heat and climbed into his Porsche. I'd fired up the Bronco when I saw him stride through the plant doors, then headed out of the lot into the street. There I loitered between two parked vehicles, a bashed-up mustard-colored van and a slicked-up semi with silver silhouettes of nude buxom babes with gravity-defying breasts and nipples on its mud flaps. I pushed my Giants cap back and wiped off the sweat on my forehead. The a/c was starting to kick in. Starting didn't cut it.

The Porsche took a left instead of a right as I had done (to hang out discreetly behind the mud flap babes), then it proceeded sedately down the street and idled at the red stoplight. I waited until the light changed. Then I pulled out, made a quick U-turn, zipped through an orange light and picked him up in front of a white Camry with a distraught mother and a screeching child. The Camry was weaving all over the street as the woman tried to soothe her child. I gave her plenty of room—especially since at the next light she nearly rear-ended the Porsche. When the light changed he took off, putting distance between us. I pulled around the Camry, zigging as it zagged. Except for that brief burst of speed, he was a careful and cautious driver, not flashy at all. He paid attention to the road but otherwise seemed preoccupied. After half a mile or so I gave up on keeping cars in between us and trying to be totally inconspicuous and subtle. I'd save that one until it was needed.

We got on Highway 50 going back into town and then exited at Howe Avenue. At Fair Oaks we moved into the left lane and waited for the light to change. My skin was prickly now with goose bumps but I left the air conditioner on high. It felt good. The light changed and traffic crept over the bridge and on toward midtown. Where Fair Oaks splits and one fork becomes H Street, the other J Street, we moved into the right-hand fork and onto H. I dropped back a bit, though I didn't think he'd noticed. Most people don't, and there was still plenty of traffic around us.

We wandered through the beautiful, shady streets of River Park. The houses were ranch style on good-sized lots, wooden and brick face, even concrete block. Most dated back probably to the forties and fifties, but all were beautifully cared for in well-established and well-tended yards.

River Park is an older, solid middle-class area with a strong neighborhood feeling and a lot of personality and charm, but not a great deal of individuality or eccentricity. There were trees and camellia bushes everywhere. Sacramento, the Camellia City. The Porsche made a quick left, then right, then headed down a quiet street and parked in the middle of the block. I drove sedately past, eyes glued to the road. Then I made a U-turn and parked at the corner under a sycamore tree planted when Truman was still in diapers. As the driver of the Porsche got out of the car and went into the house I threw up my hands in a show of frustration and yanked a map out of the side pocket. It was a Tahoe map. Rats. I pawed through my collection but didn't find anything local. Mostly I use a Thomas Guide.

I was a fake, the props might as well be too. I spread the map out on the wheel and for the next five minutes turned it this way and that, folded and unfolded it, traced unknown Tahoe streets with my finger, pursed my lips, wrinkled my nose, puzzled up my forehead and peered clandestinely and myopically up the street from under lowered brows.

I sure as hell hoped someone was watching. It wasn't Oscar material maybe, but it was pretty damn good. I turned the a/c down and checked the time. I couldn't keep it up much longer. Map reading on the whole wasn't good for much more than five minutes. Ten, maybe, but that was max. After that, the normal person would fling herself upon the mercy of a greasy, pimply, insolent gas station attendant. (The normal *female* person—the normal male person would drive around aimlessly for hours until he figured it out by cosmic happenstance, accidentally arrived at his destination, or ran out of gas.)

Pretty soon I'd have to move on to the car phone routine. That was good for another ten minutes, easy. I don't have a cellular phone —I'd just as soon be a picnic for starving ants—just an inexpensive, and now broken, phone with a long cord that flopped around a bit, though I tried to keep it taped down between the bucket seats.

I was scratching my chin thoughtfully, about ready to pick up my "phone" and "dial," when the door to Porsche's house opened. After tailing him and hanging out in his vicinity I was feeling quite familiar, even friendly, and as though we should be on first-name terms. It was something dignified, I decided, and a little formal: Andrew, not Andy; Bernard, no, too stuffy; and Clarence was too old-fashioned; Drew, hmmmm, I liked that, dignified, a little unusual; Edward, Edwin, Elmer? No, no, no. While I was trying to think up an F he got into his silver car, looking fetching in white shorts against strong dark muscular legs, Hawaiian shirt and sneakers, and sped off.

I gave him travel time, then pulled up to the front of his house, a two-bedroom ranch with charm and a peppy new paint job, and parked. I reached into the back seat for the plastic bubble that said SID'S PIZZA and the empty pizza box I had stashed there. Not that I would ever in a million years eat a pizza made by a guy named Sid. The only Sid I'd known was a complete jerk who couldn't pour piss out of a boot if you put instructions on the heel.

Climbing out of the Bronco I adjusted my Giants cap to a jaunty angle, snapped the bubble on the car aerial, balanced the pizza box, professionally, I hoped, on the palm of one hand and loped up the concrete walkway to Porsche's front door. The door was set back, sheltered a bit both from the weather and prying eyes. Perfect.

With my shoulder blocking the view, I pushed up the lid of the metal mailbox to the right of the door and flipped through letters that I didn't actually remove. Tampering with the mail is a felony rap that only the postal service manages to dodge. So, even though I was standing insecurely on a technicality (*I didn't remove the mail, Your Honor, just looked, honest!*), it felt a lot better than courting a felony.

It was a pretty solid haul. A phone bill addressed to Clem Davis, a Radio Shack catalogue addressed to Clem Davis or Valued Occupant (that Radio Shack, always handy with a complimentary turn of phrase), a personal letter, a picture postcard and an advertising circular. Yeah, I read it, and I know, I know. But it wasn't a *personal* postcard, just a goofy little character with a big toothbrush reciting his list:

1. EAT YOUR VEGETABLES!
2. DON'T GET YOUR FEET WET!!
3. BRUSH AND FLOSS YOUR TEETH!!!

On the flip side the hired minion of a local dentist reminded Clem it was time to get his teeth cleaned.

Clem. I liked the name; it seemed to fit him. I pushed the doorbell, hoping belatedly that Clem's elderly mother didn't live with him. No answer. If she did, Mom didn't care to answer the door. Pizza box aloft, I pushed off the porch and over to the nearest neighbor. No answer there. Or at the next one. This *was* a quiet neighborhood.

I was on my third house, across the street and kitty-corner from Clem's, before I scored. I knew I would going in. I'd seen the flutter of the dingy, transparent curtain and then the flash of inquisitive eyes and metal rollers.

"Yes?"

The eyes peered and snapped at me through a half-open door on which the paint was peeling ever so slightly. They were eyes faded long ago with malice and discontent, set in a shrunken ugly head that had wisps of thin yellowed hair wound tightly in the rollers. The head sat on a skinny little neck that disappeared into a shapeless housedress, a style that I had, up to now, thought had blessedly gone out in the fifties.

"What do you want? I didn't order a pizza, young lady." She looked disapprovingly at my baseball cap. "Young lady" was merely a courtesy term. Obviously, a *real* young lady would never wear a baseball cap. Or deliver pizza.

"Maybe they gave me the wrong address, I dunno," I said, verbally confirming her low assessment of me, "but I can't find 'em. I thought it was—" I stabbed a thumb at Clem Davis's house.

"Ha!" she said.

"It was a girl who ordered but no one seems to be there."

"He has a girlfriend, a *white* girl," she emphasized with nasty disapproval. "And he's a *black* one."

"I don't see any cars. Is—"

She cut through that. This woman didn't care about my questions and I probably didn't have to bother asking them. Her pump was already primed with racism, small-mindedness and vindictiveness. The whole thing made me sad. Then I remembered I was telling lies to elicit information. If I was to rot in Investigator Hell for telling fibs, I might as well pay attention. Sad would have to wait.

"Cars? Oh my, yes. She's got a big one, yes indeed. She's just a little bitty thing but she drives a big old white Cadillac. Imagine." She wrinkled her nose so it, like her heart, was shriveled up in disapproval.

"Well, thank you, ma'am." I bounced the empty pizza box on my fingers in sporty fashion.

And congratulated myself on a nice piece of detective work.

And then that, of course, went right to my head and made me complacent. From there it was a pretty short, and familiar, hop to foolish and/or foolhardy. They are different but often, in my case, pretty much the same. No point in leaving, I thought (sic), without taking another little run up to Clem's porch and checking out what kind of locks he had. For later. For just in case.

A couple of clean-cut kids with weird hair meandered down the street arguing lethargically and paddling along on their skateboards. I gave the pizza box a happy, peppy, nonchalant twirl, headed up the path and rang the bell for the sole benefit of the nasty hag across the street. The skateboards banged and clattered behind me. I heard a dog bark, too. Nice neighborhood, I mused, as I leaned forward slightly to inspect the locks.

"Good, solid, double-keyed dead bolts," a pleasant voice said behind me.

Uh oh.

"Funny. I don't remember ordering pizza."

"No?" That *was* odd. "I guess it wasn't you, then. I'm having a *heck* of a time finding out who did. *So* sorry to bother you, sir." I started to tap dance and sidle. Trouble was, he was going to have to move or I couldn't get by.

He didn't.

I couldn't.

Shit happens.

He smiled at me, but only with his mouth, his eyes were hard. Then he flicked the pizza box with his forefinger and it tipped rakishly before I caught it. Damn. Of course empty boxes don't have much stability.

"First a yellow dress, then shorts, a baseball cap and a pizza that isn't a pizza." He reached out, took my baseball cap off, handed it to me.

Rats. I tucked the box under my arm, took the hat, shook out my hair and ran my fingers through tousled curls and possibilities. He was on to me so I didn't have a lot of options left. Maybe honesty? It's a last resort in a situation like this but we were fast approaching last-resort territory. I considered shouldering past him, but only briefly. I'm strong and in good shape but no match for a well-built muscled male in his late twenties.

"Well?"

"It's a long story," I said. And it was and it wasn't.

He nodded. "Would you care to come in?"

I nodded back—though I did and I didn't—and it was an invitation that was and wasn't. I decided not to test the wasn't, not yet. Anyway, I had the neighborhood snoop, eyes bulging, mouth agape no doubt, all agog and monitoring the situation closely. I'd seen the curtains flutter.

Clem Davis opened the (double-keyed, dead-bolted) door and motioned me to precede him. I did. Grace under pressure.

"Please sit down," he invited (demanded?) and walked to the phone, picked it up and punched buttons. I stayed on my feet and did a quick mental review. There was nothing the cops could get me on, I was sure of it. I hadn't taken any mail; there's no law against walking around with an empty pizza box draped over your arm like an invitation. There wasn't anything, but it would be annoying. And Davis was still between me and the door.

"What do you like?"

"What?" I asked stupidly, still trying to come up with stories to tell cops.

"On your pizza. That damn thing"—he jerked his head at the box —"has made me hungry."

"Oh." Relief flooded through me. I soaked it up as though it were rain on California farmland in a drought year. "Anything—except anchovies."

He nodded and spoke into the phone.

"And pineapple. I like pineapple." I looked around the front room, picked a chair and sat. Davis wasn't going to turn me in to the cops, he was going to feed me. So far, so okay. I checked out the room. Clear, clean, modern lines, a thick pile rug, two matching couches in off-white, color accents in pillows, a small Chinese rug under a glass-topped coffee table and modern paintings on the wall. A baby grand, polished and sleek, with sheet music out.

Not my taste, but taste. Definitely. And bucks.

Davis got off the phone. He picked up the brown paper bag he'd carried in, pulled out a six-pack and detached two frosty bottles.

My mouth started to water. "Please," I said when he held one up in an unspoken question.

He twisted the top off and handed it to me. "You're drinking my beer, you're going to eat my pizza, you cased my house—"

*Followed him, lurked about in his neighborhood, tried to read his mail, chatted up his neighbors, the list could go on for a while.*

"I should know your name."

"Kat Colorado," I said as I stood to meet him in a handshake. "I'm an investigator." Honesty had prevailed. Or pragmatism, since he'd recognized me from this morning.

"It's Amanda's death, clearly. You said as much this morning."

"You don't seem surprised."

He shrugged, brown eyes on me. "People have a hard time accepting what happens, especially if it's painful or unexpected. That's natural. You're private. I guess the cops didn't find anything so I would assume there's nothing much to find. It's either a money issue or someone having a difficult time accepting reality. Someone willing to shell out to support that illusion."

Okay, I was the surprised one. He'd given me a long answer to a simple question. But he hadn't addressed my comment. I thought I'd try again. "You don't seem surprised."

"I didn't figure you were taking a poll."

0 for 2. I could have gone for three rejections but twice was enough for me. "You cared about Amanda."

"I liked her," he corrected me firmly, and took a long pull of his beer. "I liked her and respected her; almost everybody did."

"What do you do, Mr. Davis?"

His eyes narrowed.

I reached for a specific. "Are you an accountant as well?"

His face cleared. "No. I'm in advertising and marketing. I put together, produce, and package infomercials for our sales reps to use in presenting our products to hospitals, clinics and other businesses. I conferred frequently with Amanda. At first, she just provided me with the facts and figures, the stats I needed. Later she became interested and involved in the creative end of it. She had a good eye. I found her input helpful."

I reflected on how different that was from what Jude did. And how appealing Amanda must have found it.

The doorbell rang. Ha. They never deliver pizza that fast in *my* neighborhood. Davis put his beer down to answer it. In a moment he reappeared with a pizza box, then with paper plates and napkins. The pizza wasn't Sid's, thank God.

"Let's eat, we can talk later."

"You're the boss."

We chowed in silence for a while, me making an all-out effort not to drop anything on the white couch or rug.

"What do you think about Will Clark?" Clem asked.

"Huh? What? Who?"

"Will Clark. The Giants' first baseman. The one who pulled the last game out. I guess wearing a Giants cap doesn't make you a fan, does it?"

It didn't, not by a long shot. So we ate pizza. Then he told me about a production of *As You Like It* that he'd seen at "Shakespeare in the Park" and we talked about rafting on the American River, where the water level in this drought year was so low and sluggish that it was hardly worth it. I'd have to get tan someplace else, I thought. And ate pizza. And talked politics. And ate pizza. I was stuffed. Davis closed the box, piled plates and napkins on top of it, then took it all into the kitchen, returning with a couple more cold beers.

"Well?" he asked.

I had eaten.

It was time to sing for my supper.

# 17

Dear Charity,

Is it OK to have an affair with a married man? We're *really* HOT for this.

In Love With A Married Man

Dear In,

Depends on who you ask. You think it's OK. Your married man thinks it's OK. Divorce lawyers think it's OK. But I bet the wife doesn't.

Charity

~~~~~~~~~~~~~~~~~~~~~~~~~~~~~~~~~~~~~~~~~~~~~

"Jude doesn't think Amanda's death was an accident."

"I'd heard that around the plant and you said as much this morning at the memorial service." *Old news*, he meant. "So Jude hired you?"

"In a manner of speaking. I'm a family friend."

"What do the cops say?"

"Accidental death."

Brown eyes met mine in a long clear gaze. There was gray in his hair at the temples, in his mustache, a streak in his right eyebrow. He was *very* good-looking. Amanda Rose knew how to pick them, no question.

"As her husband, he is understandably upset. I doubt that his judgment is at its best now."

It was a compassionate and temperate assessment of someone who had lost it as violently as Jude had at that morning's service and we both knew it.

"How well did you know Amanda?"

"Not well—in passing, really. As I said, our jobs brought us into a fair amount of contact and we worked together frequently. Amanda seemed a pleasant and friendly person but she rarely spoke much about herself. She seemed a private person, as am *I*." There was no mistaking the emphasis on the last pronoun. "As I said, I liked and respected her. Certainly I am saddened at her death." His eyes were sad but clear, guileless. "Ms. Colorado, if you will excuse me—"

"I know," I said.

He threw back his head and laughed, then took a long drink of beer that probably wasn't very cold anymore. "What do you know, Ms. Colorado?" he asked casually.

"I know you and Amanda were having an affair." I had known when I heard the sharp intake of breath, seen his face at the news that Amanda was pregnant, but that kind of knowing didn't, wouldn't cut it with anyone. "I can prove it, too. Your neighbors can identify both Amanda and her car in her visits here."

His eyes never left mine. "Ms. Colorado, if you will excuse me—"

One minute I was sitting in his living room drinking beer, the next I was standing on the porch staring at the closed front door and listening to the dead bolt shoot home. He had taken the beer bottle from my hand and with his hand on my elbow gently steered me outside, Giants cap, pizza box and all. *Bye Kat. See ya.*

Clem wasn't Buck. I couldn't scare or bully him. I sighed, stuck a business card in the door and walked out to the Bronco. Across the street the curtain fluttered. I waved at it. I would have waved at Clem too, but why bother? He wasn't watching. He had tossed me out; he figured he was done with me.

I decided to sharpen up on the Giants or quit wearing my baseball cap. Will Clark? Okay. My feet dragged a little as I walked.

Damn.

I was glad, I guess, that Amanda had known such a man, and known the love that I was certain was there too. Davis hadn't let me see it; nor had Amanda. Not a clue, not a whisper. And who could blame them? They had reasons for their silence. Good ones. Adultery is always a good one.

Correction: I was glad—if he had had nothing to do with her death.

But even in the innocence of murder, there was the absence of innocence in adultery. I deal in deceit. It should not startle me, should not amaze me, but it does—in good people especially. And how to work it out when deceit and love were a package deal? I have a hard time with it. Amanda had apparently loved both Jude and Clem. I understand how this happens—it had happened to me once—but I still have a hard time with it.

Damn.

I wondered if the Giants were playing this weekend. Maybe Charity would want to leave the relentless heat of the valley and drive to San Francisco. We could sit in smog and traffic and then freeze our toes off in Candlestick Park in the wind and fog and ocean smells and breezes.

I considered how I would get by Clem Davis's defenses. Facts, I thought. Concrete evidence. I'd have to slam him with that.

Soon.

I hadn't thanked him for the pizza.

Later.


When I got home the message light on my phone machine was blinking. I ignored it. I called Zack instead. It was late, it was after hours, but homicide cops don't work nine to five. I got lucky; Zack was not only there, he was answering his phone.

"What did you think about the memorial service?"

"Different." There was a scuffling sound on Zack's end of the line and then his voice got muffled. "That lab work back yet? No? Call them first thing in the morning. Let's get it moving. Kat, where were we?"

"The service."

"Yeah. Right. So?"

I sighed. Nothing I dislike more than a gabby cop. "Anything strike you?"

"Yes and no."

"Zack!"

He relented. "Kat, people often behave very oddly at funerals and services. And it's not murderous impulses, bad consciences, or anything complicated; it's because they're torn up with grief, out of their minds with it sometimes. I saw a woman—a young woman who had lost her nine-month-old daughter—pull the baby out of the coffin, then try to leave the church with the corpse. She kept screaming, 'She's mine, you can't take her away, you can't, you can't!' It took three guys, big guys, to get that baby away from her."

"Geez." I often sound stupid when I'm overwhelmed, when I don't know what to say.

"The woman?" I asked, my heart still in a clutch.

"She's okay. It took a while, but they have a new baby now."

It was something in his voice. "Zack?"

"Yeah. She's my cousin."

I pushed that around in my mind, like a lump in a bowl of oatmeal. "Were you one of the three guys?"

"Yeah. We were close as kids. I've always loved her and I hardly recognized her face that day. Grief and madness."

I thought about Lear on the moor. "Jude?" I asked.

There was a silence. He was shrugging his shoulders. I knew it though I couldn't see it.

"What are you asking?" he said finally.

"I don't know, I'm not sure." And I wasn't, but this morning—with its additional evidence of Jude's violence—had shaken me.

"Kat, the man just lost his wife, whom he obviously loved very deeply, and their unborn baby. One day he had a family and a future, the next he's got nothing. A lot of guys, and I'd bet Hudson's one of them, don't handle grief well. They go silent or withdrawn, or angry. Sometimes they get violent."

*Jude pounding a hole in the dry wall of his home. Jude busting up Amanda's photo. Jude driving too hard and sloppy and daring, taunting fate to fuck with him. Jude drinking too much. Jude never crying.*

"Sometimes people turn their anger in—into depression, drinking, drugs. Into nightmares and self-blame. Men would be better off if we cried, I guess, but we don't, not most of us. That answer your question?"

"No."

He laughed, sounding weary.

"Maybe Hudson's angry at the world, mad as hell at anything that crosses his path. Maybe it's the only way right now that he knows to get the grief out. His behavior was odd, yeah, but it doesn't make him a murderer."

Grief and madness.

"Anything else?"

Silence while he shrugged and I pictured it. "Not particularly."

"I made it pretty clear I was poking around."

"I noticed," Zack said drily.

"Stir things up, see what hits the fan. Zack, what do you think about going out to the plant, asking a few questions, backing me up with apparent police interest?"

Silence. No shrug, though. Then: "I might be able to do that. I'll try to find the time."

"Thanks."

"Yeah."

"Did you guys find anything at the scene, tire tracks, or . . ."

My voice trailed off. Tire tracks in the dusty bone-dry dirt of a California summer? Yeah. Right. "Reports of unfamiliar people or vehicles in the area?"

"Nothing. Not that it's surprising. Places are spread out in that area. Neighbors keep an eye on things, yeah, but you can't watch what you don't see."

"Nothing?"

"One. One small thing."

"Hmmmm?"

"A cut rose was found by the hot tub. It wasn't from one of the Hudsons' bushes, nothing even close to it."

"And?"

"Someone could have given it to her at work, she could have picked it up on her way home, any number of possibilities."

"Or someone could have brought it over that evening before killing her."

"Long shot."

"Possible."

He grunted. I didn't blame him.

"What color was it?"

"The rose? Yellow. One of those real deep yellow ones with red on the edges of the petals. Pretty."

Red. Like blood, only there had been no blood, just a lethal jolt of electricity. In the background someone hollered Zack's name.

"Kat, I gotta go. Look, we lost a child three years ago, our first. Crib death. Afterwards I took my daughter's bed out in the backyard and busted it up until what was left wouldn't have made a meal for a hungry termite. It's hard." Long pause. "Catch you later," he said abruptly, and hung up.

I stared at the phone for a while. Nothing. No answers, no explanations, no human or philosophical disclosures. I punched the message retrieval button on my answering machine: Jude's voice, harsh, hoarse, demanding. "Kat, get out here!" No *please*. No *could you? would you?*

Grief and madness. But murder?

. . .

On the drive out I heard birds calling, heard a peacock squawk and then the quiet coos of doves, heard the *snick snick* of the sprinklers, felt the Delta breezes. A beautiful summer evening, only Amanda was dead.

Jude had left the gate closed but unlocked. All four dogs were running loose. They knew me now but still barked, not long and continuously as they would for a stranger, but briefly and in a friendly fashion, enough to tell Jude that I was here, that it was okay. Then they escorted the Bronco in, tails high or wagging, tongues lolling, ears alert and cocked. They looked better and happier than either Jude or I did, for sure.

Jude came out onto the front porch and watched me park. His arms were folded across his chest. No smile. No sign of welcome. There were no other vehicles there, just the Bronco, Jude's truck, Amanda's wrecked and burned-out Cadillac. I walked up to the porch and stood at the bottom of the steps where Jude towered over me.

"I thought there would be people here," I said. "Family, friends. If I'd known you were by yourself I would have come out sooner."

"I told everyone to get the hell out. I wanted to be alone."

He'd been drinking; heavily, I thought. "You called me."

"Yeah. I don't want people moping around and feeling sorry for me. I can't stand the crying and carrying on. I want someone who's doing something." Jude's knuckles were taped and gauze was loosely and clumsily wrapped around his hand.

I looked at it, at him. "What did you bust up this time?"

"Fuck you." Then he smiled wearily and gestured toward the Cadillac. "Mandy's car. I tried to put my fist through the windshield."

"Through the *windshield?*" That was tough, impossible, I would have thought. "We've got to figure this out before you're completely busted up and no good."

"Yeah." He nodded, still tired, still busted up. "I found something, and something happened. C'mon in."

I followed him in. He was walking pretty straight, maintaining pretty well. Of course it would take a lot of booze to topple a guy Jude's size and weight. A bottle of Jack Daniel's sat on the kitchen table, one third down.

"You want a drink?"

"Not that. Got anything else?" I looked around at the mountains of food that had been left out. "Jude?"

He followed my glance. "I behaved badly. They wanted to help. I couldn't handle it."

I didn't say anything. I started putting food away.

"Kat."

"First things first," I said gently. "Did you eat any of this?"

"I don't think so."

"Go for it. I'll have some too." I filled up two plates, found a bottle of wine and a glass, and we ate. Ten minutes, a pound and a half of food later, and Jude looked almost human. He helped me clean up, fixed another drink, then brought out his display: a square hard-plastic dirt-smeared compact disc case, the kind they call a jewel box in record stores. According to the label it was Scott Joplin ragtime piano tunes. But, except for the label, the case was empty.

Big fucking deal.

I looked at him in puzzlement. Even with all that bourbon I thought he'd be slicker than this.

He saw my look. "Hang in there, Kat."

Okay. Good. Maybe I was missing something.

"It's not ours."

I waited for more. I'm quick, I'm a detective—but that wasn't enough for me to get it.

"If it's not ours, somebody had to bring it here, somebody who didn't belong, maybe her killer."

Or Amanda borrowed the CD from a friend, or bought it and Jude didn't know, or any number of things.

"Mandy hated piano music, Kat. She liked almost all kinds of music—classical, jazz, Dixieland, rock, even country, which is mostly what I listen to. But not piano. She wouldn't listen to piano stuff. Organs she wasn't wild about but she'd tolerate. It was only piano."

"Why?"

"She said because of piano lessons when she was a kid. She said— But it wasn't that simple, Kat."

No. It never is.

"She loves"—he groaned—"*loved* music but she had no musical sense or ability, so trying to play anything made her feel dumb. Somehow she tied that into feeling inferior. There was no real reason for it but it got much bigger than the piano."

I nodded. I had it now. I was up to speed. I thought about the gleaming baby grand piano in Clem Davis's living room, the scattered sheet music propped up on it. Maybe Jude was right, maybe it was something. "How did she die, Jude? Exactly. I know it was electricity." I knew more. Did Jude?

The pain that crossed Jude's face made me turn away. I stared out the kitchen window blindly, waited for an answer. Waited for an eternity or two.

"I thought at first it was those damn lights over the hot tub. They were half down, half up when I saw them and the cops made a big deal out of it. They asked me about CD players, too, but I didn't connect it up, not until this." His bandaged hand gestured toward the compact disc box.

"You have only one CD player?"

"Two. One in the house, part of the stereo system, the other a portable. Mandy used the portable a lot. She used to take it to work with her, especially when she was out of town on business."

"Both still here?"

"The portable's missing."

"Where did you find this?" I pointed to the case.

"Way out back, fifty feet or more from the spa area in tall grass. Only reason I found it was I was out whacking weeds after Mandy died, trying to stay connected." He splashed bourbon into his glass and onto the table. I resisted the impulse to suggest that he go whack some weeds.

"What did kill her?" I was still on that. I had to know what Jude knew.

"I thought it was the lights until the cops started asking about the CD."

"Did you ask them?"

"Yeah, they didn't tell me shit, just that they were still investigating. As for our missing CD player? Sometimes Mandy forgot and left it at work. Maybe someone stole it. Fuck! You don't like to think that way about people but—" He jerked his face out of his glass and looked at me, then smashed a fist on the table.

I didn't have the same problem with it that he did. Grave robbers systematically looted the pyramids and Mayan tombs; passersby steal jewelry and wallets from accident victims; there was undoubtedly someone out there who would steal the pennies off a dead man's eyes. Stealing Amanda's CD player wasn't improbable, it just hadn't happened that way; the cops had it, neatly tagged and stashed as evidence in her increasingly untidy death.

"Does Scott Joplin or ragtime music mean anything to you, suggest anyone?"

"No." He started to reach out for the case.

I caught his hand by the wrist. "Put this in a plastic bag and give it to the cops. Don't get any more prints on it."

It took him a moment to figure it through the liquor fog. Then he pulled his hand away. He didn't touch the case.

"Was there anyone at Amanda's memorial service you didn't know or recognize, except for the group that was obviously from the plant?"

"Yeah." No hesitation, no thinking it over. "I meant to talk to them, to thank them and see how they knew Mandy. I meant to, but then I lost it . . ."

"No idea how they knew her?"

"None."

"How many people didn't you know? What did they look like? Age? Sex? Anything?"

"I dunno, Kat." He rubbed the back of his hand over his eyes. "Ask me tomorrow, okay?"

"Okay. What else, Jude?"

"The letters." He got up, went into the living room, came back with three or four envelopes that had been torn open. "Mandy's dead, but she still gets mail. How about that?" He tossed the envelopes onto the kitchen table, then slumped into his chair. "There's one to me, too. Read it last."

I skimmed through the top three. All were responses to Amanda's inquiries about the Louden heart valve. None threatened to murder her. "May I take these?"

Jude nodded, then drank more bourbon.

I turned to the last letter, read it through quickly, read it through slowly.

"Sucks, doesn't it?" Jude's voice was dull and heavy, his assessment accurate.

It did, yes. No question.

# 18

~~~~~~~~~~~~~~~~~~~~~~~~~~~~~~~~~~~~~~~~~~~

*Dear Sir,*

The letter began affably enough but looked like a kindergarten effort, with printed block capital letters and clippings pasted on to three sheets of creased and smudged paper.

*Did you realize that one of the greatest threats to healthy young adults is the possibility of accidents?*

*In the home:*

A newspaper clipping had been pasted beneath it. It began:

ELK GROVE WOMAN DEAD
Amanda Hudson died in an unusual

I didn't read the rest; I knew what it said.

*While traveling:*

Three clippings were pasted here. The first was about a high-speed chase in which the speeder, a man, died in a fiery collision; the second about a plane that was blown up en route from the Middle East; the third about a woman and child killed in a hit-and-run. The police were still looking for an unidentified drunken driver.

*You just never know!*

This statement was followed by another batch of pasted-on clippings. I skimmed the headlines: Child, 3, Falls in Well and Drowns; 13 Stricken with Food Poisoning at Four Star Restaurant; Father and Son Killed in Driveby Shooting; Minimart Clerk Stabbed in Holdup Attempt; Bereaved Husband Kills Self.

The background paper around the last one was covered with red lines boxing in the clipping; stars, little exclamation marks, and little round red circle faces with frowns instead of smiles were in abundance.

YOU CAN'T BE TOO CAREFUL!

the next to the last line urged, all in caps, and then:

CAREFUL PEOPLE DON'T ASK QUESTIONS!

it told us. It was signed:

*a friend*

all in lower-case letters. And finally:

P.S. KURIOSITY KILLED THE KAT!

I hate anonymous letters.

I reread the letter, then said, "First thing we do—"

Jude looked up from flexing his hands and checking out his damaged knuckles. He did a few in-place shoulder rolls and bulged his biceps. It looked good, but not, of course, against hit-and-run cars, bombs, and random attacks by numbers of people, especially insane or deranged people.

"—is beef up our life insurance."

Jude let his breath out in a snort of exasperation.

"Hey, cowboy"—I grinned at him—"don't let them get you down."

"Yeah," he muttered. "Yeah."

He slammed his fist on the kitchen table and hardly even winced. I marveled at the regenerative and staying power of a young male body. He poured himself another three or four ounces of bourbon. Hmmmm. Or the deadening power of alcohol.

"Second thing we do is show this to the cops."

He snorted.

"Who knows, it might pique their interest. Third thing—"

What? I thought. Where to start?

1. *Stay out of hot tubs.*
2. *Stay away from CD players.*
3. *Ditto speeding cars, bombs, etc.*
4. *Don't take candy from strangers.*
5. *Change your socks every day.*
6. *Eat a well-balanced diet.*
7. *Watch out for—*

"Third thing?" Jude and his bourbon asked impatiently.

"We circle the wagons. Safety in numbers. Get somebody out here with you. Several somebodies, maybe." I didn't bother to suggest he leave, although I thought about it. Amanda hadn't left; Jude wasn't going to either.

He considered it. "Yeah. Okay. When you coming out?"

I shook my head. I didn't want a twenty-four-hour job. I wanted to go home and leave this case behind me some part of each day. KURIOSITY. I wasn't just an investigator, I was a person, I had a life. KILLS. I had cared deeply about Amanda; I cared, too, about Jude; about the possible heart valve victims, about a lot of things, but I couldn't—I wouldn't—stop my life, focus everything on this. THE KAT.

KURIOSITY KILLS THE KAT. KILLS, KILLS, KILLS. What the heck, I'd give it a try. "Tomorrow," I said. "I'll be here tomorrow." I'd overlooked something: I had to retrace my steps first. Jude could take care of himself for twenty-four hours.

"Thanks, Kat."

For a moment I saw a scared little boy in the back of his drunken eyes, a boy frightened of things he couldn't beat up or pound down or understand.

Feeling like Methuselah, I got up. "Will you be okay tonight?"

"Yes." He dismissed the thought and flexed his muscles. As though muscle could stop evil.

I let it go but I thought I should try to pound some sense into him. And soon. "I've got a full day tomorrow. See you late afternoon or early evening."

"Thanks, Kat." He held out his left hand, the one he wasn't trying to turn into hamburger, and took mine.

"Quit beating yourself up, Jude. Save it for the bad guys." I wondered about the signature on this glued and pasted letter and on the anonymous condolence card addressed to Amanda. A friend. The same friend? I didn't know. Signing a letter with the word "friend" was not exactly a new concept in the anonymous letter business. I'd compare the two soon.

I stuck the letters in my purse, gave Jude a quick hug and then he and the dogs walked me out to the Bronco. He rode with me to the gate, the dogs running behind, and padlocked it after me.

I cried on the way home. Fighting to find Amanda's killer and keep Jude safe hadn't left me much time for mourning. I got onto 99 North and then onto 50, wishing the whole time that I had tissue in the car. Alma, my grandmother, was right, I should carry a handkerchief. After I cried, I thought things over.

Theoretically it's relatively easy to follow someone's trail. Most of us are creatures of habit and routine, and it's amazing how many things we do every day at the same time and place. Other things are consistent and predictable by the week—working out at the gym Mon-

day/Wednesday/Friday, visiting Mom on Tuesday, bowling on Thurs-
day—or by the month, or by the season.

Theoretically.

Of course life isn't theory and that's where it all breaks down.
Amanda, like all of us, was predictable in most things: her work
schedule, her home life, chores at the ranch, interaction with neighbors, friends, and relatives. That was easily seen and I'd gone over it
all, found nothing remarkable.

Clem Davis was the wild card in Amanda's otherwise predictable
life.

Domestic disturbances are volatile and dangerous. Police hate
those calls. A boyfriend. A husband. This woman had one too many
men. Murder was certainly solidly within the realm of probability, at
least statistically.

I yawned and watched a guy in a Trans Am who thought his car
was his personality—or maybe just his masculinity and he wouldn't
bother with a personality—weave in and out of traffic looking cool
with slicked-back hair, bare tanned chest and prominent guy-on-the-
loose attitude. He slugged down something in a can—an adult bever-
age, I bet—and narrowly missed clipping a Sable packed to the dash
with mom and the kids. Don't underestimate a guy-on-the-loose attitude, I thought. Jude Hudson was a loose cannon, one loaded with
powder, alcohol, and grief. Clem Davis was an unknown, but he too
could be loose.

Wild cards. Jokers?

I yawned again and passed the Sable. Mom was yelling at the
kids, who were squabbling over something that changed hands a lot.
On the radio Credence Clearwater Revival was stuck in Lodi again
and then the Supremes gushed on about Ooooooooooh!! Baby Love.
Mom seemed largely unaware of the road, hadn't even noticed the
Trans Am or contemplated losing a fender or a child. And unaware-
ness leads to danger. Danger; sometimes death.

The other wild card in Amanda's life, the big one, was the investigation she had single-handedly launched at Louden. That was the

place to start looking first because that was where the trouble had started. That, of course, was also where Amanda was unpredictable, where she had stepped out of everyday, where she had left her routine. I exited Highway 50 at Sunrise going north into Fair Oaks, one last glimpse of the Sable, kids still fighting, mom still yelling and oblivious, and followed Sunrise to Madison, then cut over to my part of Orangevale.

The hard evidence? The attacks on Amanda at home and work, the harassment at the office and the vandalism on the ranch all pointed to Louden. Or, in Buck and the boys' case, were directly connected.

Hard evidence.

All right. I had the paper trail Amanda had given me for safe-keeping shortly before her death. I drove past a shopping area with doughnuts, Italian, Chinese and frozen yogurt and wondered whether there was any food at home, then decided that there had to be— although that could be hopeless optimism—and that I was too tired to stop anyway.

The paper trail.

I'd follow up on Buck and his buddies, on the Louden plant and specifics I could dig up there, on what had happened to Amanda and why and by whom. Yes. But it was time, past time almost, to dig into her records, her notes. It was time to start dogging her footsteps, to see if I could see what she had seen. See what she had seen, then perhaps done. See what could have gotten her murdered. Look, Jane. See Spot. Watch Dick kill.

I yawned one last time as I pulled into the dirt driveway, then smiled as I looked at my two-bedroom white with blue trim wooden house in the middle of a large lot that was covered with trees and roses and flowers and everything that had ever caught my fancy at the nursery. Ranger barked twice sharply to welcome me and then whined and whimpered in excitement. Most of the lot is fenced. He was behind it and I called out to him. He yipped once more, then raced off to the back door to wait for me.

I locked the door to the Bronco, then nearly stumbled, tired and hungry and grumpy, as I walked up the path, climbed the porch steps to my house. The kitten stood up, stretched, mewed at me.

"What are you doing here, little one? You're supposed to be in the backyard." He yawned and arched his back against my hand, put his front paws on my arm, his way of commanding *pick me up.*

I did, but it was a reflex. I was looking at the Fed Ex envelope lying on the mat where the kitten had been curled. I didn't pick it up. It looked all right but it wasn't. Federal Express won't leave anything without authorization or a waiver, and I hadn't given either.

I unlocked the door, stepped over the envelope, snapped on lights as I walked through the house to the back door. Ranger charged in and did quick laps around us, the kitten and I frozen in place until he calmed down. It was that or be knocked over by seventy pounds of Australian shepherd. Seven laps later I fed them, latched the back screen door and poured a glass of cool white wine. There was a breeze through the house with both the front and back doors open and it felt wonderful.

I sipped my wine and walked back out to the front porch, picked up the envelope. No TO, no FROM. It was a genuine red, white and blue Fed Ex envelope but it had been hand-delivered—there were no shipping cards or address labels on it. I headed back into the house, latching the front screen door behind me. Outside, car tires squealed nearby and I heard the sound of a backfire, shivered before I could catch myself. Backfires sound so much like gunfire. Too much.

I tossed the envelope on the kitchen table and went through the fridge. Didn't take me long. Neither did the cupboards. Egg salad, that was the best I could come up with. I boiled eggs and made a sandwich with slightly stale sourdough bread, giving the animals the leftovers. They fell all over themselves in anticipation, in joy and ecstasy. Four-legged is simpler, no question.

I poured a second glass of wine, ate my sandwich and stared at the envelope propped up against a jug of wilting flowers. I opened it, but only after I swallowed the last bite. Good thing.

It was a thirty-two-page report on sexual crimes and mutilation. Single-spaced.

With pictures.

Throughout the text—in the margins, and on pictures of deeply mutilated and violated female bodies—someone had scrawled in red felt pen: *KURIOSITY KILLS THE KAT; DEAD KATS TELL NO TALES; KILL KILL KILL; WATCH YOUR PUSSY, KAT; KATS DON'T HAVE 9 LIVES.* There were crude sketches of cats that had been even more crudely dismembered. Drops of blood were drawn in. *KILL KILL KILL* everywhere.

Amanda had done the right thing and gotten—not accolades and thank-yous—but hate and anger. And death? It had come her way; now it was coming mine. I had another glass of wine before I went to bed.

Circle the wagons was right.

I dreamt of mutilated, torn, ripped, bloody bodies.

I woke up full of hate.

# 19

Dear Charity,

I consider myself a warm, kind, helpful person who is correct more often than not. I point this out to others and am amazed that they do not appreciate my help. Why is this?

Almost A Saint

Dear Almost,

Righteousness is not appreciated. Thoughtfulness is.

Charity

~~~~~~~~~~~~~~~~~~~~~~~~~~~~~~~~~~~~~~~~~~~~~~~~~~

Using the word murder too freely is the kind of thing that can keep you awake at night. So are thoughts of death and mutilation. I'd woken up hot and sticky at three a.m., then sat up in bed, stretched to reach the cord that would turn the ceiling fan onto high. I kicked off the sheet, flopped back on the pillows, listened to the fan pushing air and waited for the breeze to cool me down.

Was that what I was doing too? Pushing air? But saying the word murder is not a good way to push air around. The cops didn't think it was murder. Accidents happen, even to careful people. And accidents kill. I sighed and got up, tripped over the sneakers I'd kicked off and left in the middle of the rug, bashed my thumb catching myself, then stubbed my toe. Well, shit. And I *never* kick my shoes off and leave them in the middle of the rug because I *always* trip over them when I get up. I never do, but I had.

And maybe Amanda had too. Not sneakers on the rug but a portable CD player on the edge of the hot tub. Maybe it wasn't murder. Harassment and nasty intimidation, but not murder. I got to the kitchen without further mishap, poured a glass of water from the bottle in the refrigerator, stood at the counter chugging it. Everyone was up now. The kitten was crunching on the biscuits in his bowl; he has a might-as-well-eat-as-long-as-I'm-up philosophy about life. Ranger lay watching me, head on his crossed paws, blue and brown eyes on me, waiting to see what would happen next.

I finished my water and felt more awake, not less, so I poured a glass of white wine and headed out onto the patio, the pet parade in close attendance. Outside it was cool, breezy and quiet. The stars were faded out by the relentless realities of a three million voltage urban existence, but the moon was high, sort of full and beautiful.

Maybe it wasn't murder.

I was stuck in a groove like an old 78.

Maybe Amanda had done with her portable CD player what I had done with my sneakers. Just that once she'd broken a rule and set the player on the edge of the spa. Maybe Clem had brought over the Scott Joplin to try to get her to like it and she'd played it after he left, hated it, and in annoyance reached out and Frisbeed the CD case into the weeds, then accidentally knocked the player into the tub, electrocuted herself. Maybe.

But maybe not. Yeah, this was fun. This beat sleeping. Sure. The breeze and drink had cooled me off outside but I couldn't calm down inside. I needed to know more. Before I could establish who or why, I needed to know what had happened. Accident or murder. I needed to feel sure in my own mind.

I fell asleep finally, cooler but not wiser.

In the morning I hit the paper trail, spread it out on the kitchen table to figure out what was what. It broke down into three general categories.

The first file held company records, photocopies and other documentations, Amanda's notes on the documents and written records of other observations and conversations. It was a large file that also included data on available Louden stock and inventory as well as data on what inventory had gone out over the last two years. It didn't take a statistician to add it up. Common sense worked fine. Louden had shipped a lot of potentially flawed stock. Even more was still available, was neatly packaged and boxed and warehoused, waiting for shipment. Quantity of stock × production cost × warehousing cost = Big Bucks Investment. Big Bucks Investment = Major Commitment to Status Quo. Amanda was the negative number there. I hadn't realized until I saw the figures just how high the stakes were.

High enough that it could make a woman's life seem like a necessary expedient, even small change.

The second, a slim file, held copies of Amanda's unanswered correspondence with the Food and Drug Administration, the federal watchdog agency that Louden was answerable to. I put it aside. The third file started off with two lists. I flipped back to the first file; it was all information pulled from the company records. The first list was the longer: close to sixty names, some with addresses, most without; dates of surgical procedure in some cases but not all; very scanty medical data. Amanda's handwritten note indicated that this information all came from direct contact by the patient or his/her doctor with Louden. The company kept no records of who had received their medical devices and had no procedure for identifying or contacting recipients of a faulty product.

The second list in this third file was shorter. This, apparently, was the liability list. The deceased patient's name was given, as was the name and address of the litigant. The list was followed by photocopies of the correspondence Amanda had had with the litigant. Some of the names had phone numbers jotted next to them.

In the margins were neat notations: dates of contact or attempted contact, occasional reference to a longer appended note that followed. The second list seemed the most promising by far, but the first bore the earliest dates so I started there.

Investigation is largely methodical plodding, not flash and spark and on-target intuitive jumps. Not like TV.

The first phone number—I looked up the area code—was in Nebraska. Jeanne-Marie Johansen. Jeanne-Marie Johansen sounded like oats and corn and barley and unending midwest plains, with Wholesome branded deeply in its consciousness. I picked up the phone and punched numbers. A voice as smooth and rich as cream and wild honey answered on the third ring and I asked for Jeanne-Marie.

"She's still in school and afterwards she has cheerleading practice. May I help you?"

"This is Kat Colorado. I'm an associate of Amanda Hudson and we're doing a follow-up study of recipients of the Louden heart valve. Are you Jeanne-Marie's mother?"

"Yes." The cream had curdled, the honey was gone.

"Has my associate been in touch with you?"

"I told that woman not ever to call again! After all the worry and pain we've been through and now she's fine, she's *perfect*, that's what the doctor said. It's cruel of you to make us worry and wonder, to make us go through all that again. She's fine. She's fine, she's *just* fine!" Jeanne-Marie's mother hung up on that shrill mantra. I hoped she was right. Unfortunately denial is not the best insurance policy.

Albert Smith in New Mexico was next. He caught it on the first bounce.

"Hello!" he hollered.

I moved the phone two inches from my ear.

"Albert Smith, please."

"You got him!"

Add another two inches in distance. "Mr. Smith, I'm calling from California. My associate, Amanda Hudson, and I are—"

"I remember her, purty voice. Sounded like a real purty little thing."

"Yes."

"Well, dearie, what can I do for ya?"

"It's about the heart valve, Mr. Smith."

He chuckled in my ear. "Your associate tell you what an old coot I am?"

"No."

Another chuckle. "She was a sweetie, she was, trying to get me all worried and fired up about this here valve thing. Well now, I appreciate the concern, I surely do, but I got to tell you it's given me four more years, and for an old fart that ain't too shabby. I'm going to see eighty-three next week."

"Happy birthday, Mr.—"

"And eighty-three is plenty, dearie. More'd be nice but even so the good Lord can take me any time, any time atall. I seen my kids and grandkids grow and prosper and I seen the world turn around a lot of times and that's a sight more'n most kin say. Don't worry now, miss, I'm blessed and God bless you too."

Albert Smith hung up and I sat limp and wrung out, older already by far than before. How had Amanda done this?

I called three more names and got anger, fear and a hang up. One more, I told myself, and I would stop for the day. I mused about how difficult it was to face death or even the possibility of it. Easier to be angry or in denial or in ignorance. Easier to hope than know. Easier not to know.

I made my last call and regretted it instantly. "Fuck you," the man said in a harsh ugly voice, when I identified myself. "Fuck you, fuck you, fuck you. Are you some kind of a morbid fucking ambulance fucking chaser? Fuck you. You think I—"

I hung up. I would never ask him anything again, would never know, did not want to know anything more about him or his heart or his life. I was trembling violently. I could feel the hate fill me up, threatening to spew out of me in ugly vomit and bile as it had out of him.

Amanda had tried to throw lifelines of information, hope and help to all these people, to build a safety net of love and concern. Instead it had become a web sticky with hatred and viciousness, anger and greed. Maybe with murder. But, and I wondered with hate in my heart, had she really tried to build it with love? Righteousness is not love. Righteousness is meritorious and commendable—in theory—but not endearing, not loving. Narrow-minded righteousness is the kind of thing that gets people hated, that gets people killed.

I didn't want to make any more phone calls to anyone on a list. I was tired of being a nice guy, tired of being beat up. Better to beat up on someone else.

I was caught in the web. That's what hate does.

I didn't see it.

I just looked for someone to beat up on. It didn't take me long to find him.

# 20

Dear Charity,
   Are flowers always appropriate and in good taste?
                                          Ever-bloomin'

Dear Bloomin',
   Well, I wouldn't send them to a diva who forgot her
aria or a defendant sentenced to die. Otherwise, yes,
though I prefer chocolates myself.

                                          Charity

~~~~~~~~~~~~~~~~~~~~~~~~~~~~~~~~~~~~~~~~~~~~~

Okay, I wasn't bright and perky like a cartoon character should be,
but I dressed like one anyway in khaki shorts and matching trail or
camp shirt or whatever they're called. Charity had bought them at the
Banana Republic and given them to me as a present. It's a store where
I never shop; it's too easy there for your individuality to get trampled
out by yuppiness. That said, I admit that this outfit is one of my best
disguises.

   I pulled on white socks, brown work boots (steel toes and all),
stuck a plastic pencil/pen holder in one of the forty-six or so pockets
in my shirt, filled it up with pencils, pens, a calculator. I clipped on a

laminated picture I.D. with my picture and someone else's name under the company name, Sacramento Public Utilities District (SPUD). There is no such thing, although there is a Sacramento Municipal Utilities District (SMUD). I tucked a clipboard with a stack of official-looking forms on it under my arm to complete the ensemble.

I gazed at myself in the mirror and smiled in satisfaction. Good. Ooops. I pulled my hair back in a tight ponytail at the nape of my neck, then clipped a can of (empty) dog spray on my (khaki) belt. Perfect.

Like a kid on Halloween, I was all dressed up.

All dressed up to snoop.


Clem's dwelling looked familiar and friendly to me. After an evening of beer and pizza, why not? The silver Porsche was nowhere in sight, was presumably in the lot of Louden Industries. I parked just past his house in an empty stretch, then hopped out, clipboard in hand and pencil behind my ear. It's hard to overdo this kind of stuff; the way you get caught is not by overdoing it but by acting unsure and as though you don't belong. Then you stick out and people wonder. They do that long enough, they call the cops. With a purposeful, confident air you're just another working stiff doing your job. You're background.

I strode around to the side of the house and stopped at the meter there. I looked at it, made a few notes on my clipboard, then shook my head, *tsk*ed audibly and walked to the back of the house, professional purpose oozing, I hoped, from every pore. There I blew it, stopping dead in my tracks, gasping in surprise, letting my mouth drop open and, in general, stepping out of character. I had never seen anything like it.

The yard was a small paradise of roses. A pebbled path led to a white gazebo covered with climbing roses. There was no lawn, just pebbled paths wandering through beds with roses of every color and size, roses rich and heavy with blooms and fragrance. The scent was incredible, indescribable.

Finally I shut my mouth and moved. There were three or four

157

yellows but only one that fit Zack's description of the rose found near Amanda's body. The bush was redolent, lush with blossoms. I pulled out a small pair of scissors from one of my too many pockets and cut off three, one a bud, one partially opened, one in full glorious bloom. There was nothing in the gazebo but a small table circled by built-in benches. An out-of-place and half-full beer bottle stood on the table. I kept moving. The windows in the back of the house, bedrooms probably, were curtained and impenetrable.

I took the roses I had picked (okay, stolen) from Clem's bushes and left, hopped in the Bronco, snapped the lock button, wrapped the flowers in a dampened towel I'd brought with me and drove off. I didn't peel rubber but I moved along at a brisk pace. It was the virtual certainty that these roses and the rose found at a crime scene (okay, alleged crime scene) were identical that impelled me. I drove from East Sac to Freeport Boulevard and the Capital Nursery there. Wet towel in hand, I trundled in and threw myself on the mercy of a certified nursery person. Together we combed through books of roses.

"Here," she said, after a long silence broken only by the flip of pages. "This looks like it. I haven't seen anything else that's close."

"Is it readily available?"

"Let me check." She left books for computer and scrolled through data. "No, it's a special order and fairly expensive."

I thanked her, took the roses and was off again. I considered calling the Sheriff's Department and, if I caught up with Zack, running the roses past him. I considered it, but not for long. He wouldn't just say yes, no, maybe so, and see you, Kat. He'd ply me, cop fashion, with a bunch of nosy questions. I pulled the elastic out of my hair and shook my ponytail loose. Then I went back to the office to change out of my meter reader outfit, admire Clem's roses, look up Clem's number, and think.

At four-thirty I started calling Clem Davis at home. At four-fifty he picked up the phone. What a deep pleasant voice he had. I hadn't particularly noticed it yesterday with his good looks seducing my vision, his words misleading my mind, his hands pushing me out the door. Not like a murderer's voice at all, I mused.

"Mr. Davis, Kat Colorado."

"Ms. Colorado." His voice was still pleasant, but definitely cool. "I thought I made my position clear."

"Step two."

"What?" He dropped cool; I could hear puzzlement now.

"I thought we could talk about horticulture and coincidence."

"Ms. Colorado—"

"Specifically about a yellow rose tipped and streaked with scarlet. It's an unusual rose and not readily available. That's the horticulture. The coincidence is that the cops found a rose like that on the ground near Amanda's body and—"

He hung up on me. Futile, but who could blame him? I disconnected, punched the redial button, got his answering machine.

"You didn't wait for the rest of the coincidence," I said pleasantly. "The part where I say that I noticed you have a rose bush just like that in your backyard, and then we exclaim in surprise and wonder and clap each other metaphorically on the back and say, 'Oh my gosh, small world for sure.'

"Here's the deal, Clem Davis." I let my voice go from gossipy to hard. "I will be sitting on a park bench in McKinley Park feeding the ducks in half an hour. You can talk to me, or you can talk to the cops. That's my next stop if you don't show.

"Did you know—" My voice slipped back to chatty and cheerful. From my midtown office I could see two tanned young women walking by, making animated gestures, smiling, laughing, pretty in pastel colors. *"And then he said . . . And then I said . . ."* Their cheerfulness, unlike mine, was real. I felt a twinge of sadness.

"It's amazing what they can do in police labs today. They can compare the chemical composition, trace amounts of fertilizer, soil makeup and so on, of different plant specimens and tell if they came from the same parent plant."

I crossed my fingers just in case I was telling a whopper, but I didn't think so. I thought that was standard and easy stuff. I thought I remembered a conviction because of a match-up of soil samples on a man's boot with soil from a crime scene forty miles away.

159

"I took samples, Clem. And pictures, too." That *was* a whopper and I forgot to cross my fingers. "Don't bother to dig up the yellow rose. Half an hour." My turn to hang up.

On my way to the park I stopped at a neighborhood convenience store, picked up two cold cans of soda, a bag of chips, a jar of extra hot chunky salsa and a loaf of bread. Whole wheat, naturally, to build strong little duck bodies.

I found a parking place and a bench, both in the shade. Still, I didn't generalize and assume that fate was running in my direction. Not yet. In the park I unpacked my goodies and flattened the brown paper bag, placing it in the middle of the bench like a tablecloth with a soda at each end and the chips and salsa in the middle. I admired my handiwork but didn't assume I could be a housewife. I was pretty sure there was more to it than that.

I ripped open the whole wheat bread wrapper. Before I had the first crust out I had a whole flock, or whatever ducks assemble in, gathered on my edge of the pond. I fed them a few slices, then opened up a soda and the chips to feed me. My mouth was full—naturally, that's how life works—when Davis arrived.

He didn't look thrilled to see me. I waved at him and at the spot on the bench next to the soda. It was a Dr Pepper. "I got you regular, you obviously don't need diet." I was drinking diet. I didn't need it either, but would soon if I drank regular.

He hesitated, then sat down and popped open the soda, had a few chips. I passed him the loaf of whole wheat and the ducks went into a simulated or practice feeding frenzy at the sight of a bread wrapper in motion.

"Mr. Davis—"

"Kat, now that we've become such pals, what with you snooping around my house, stealing my roses, threatening me and feeding me, don't you think we've progressed to a first name basis?"

I nodded, wincing a little. Words like "snoop," "steal," and "threaten" do that to me, especially when it's an accurate description of my behavior.

"Look, Clem—"

And that was when a duck flew into his face—a blind duck, I guess, as the bread was in Clem's hand—ricocheted off his upper body and then crapped on his knee.

Clem was not amused.

# 21

Dear Charity,
   Is it ever acceptable to make a judgment about a person based on color?

                              Minding My Ps And Qs

Dear P and Q,
   Yes. Absolutely. A red-faced person is mad or embarrassed. A blue one, cold. A gray one, dead.

                              Charity

~~~~~~~~~~~~~~~~~~~~~~~~~~~~~~~~~~~~~~~~~~~~~~~~~

Clem swatted the duck away, then scared the pinfeathers off the rest of them by jumping, hollering, and flapping his arms. Scared the booties off a tot in a stroller behind us, too.

   *"Really,"* said the kid's mom, over the kid's yowling, and in the kind of tone that implied that only total slimebugs would scare birdies and babies. Clem was oblivious as he heaved the rest of the loaf out into the pond.

   "Sweet," I commented. "Generous, too, although most people take the wrapper off first."

"Hope the damn ducks choke." Clem looked at his soiled knee, stomped around some more, sat down, then glanced over at me with a charming and disarming type smile. "Hey, sorry."

I wasn't charmed, I wasn't disarmed. What I was was interested in the display of temper, in the sudden hot flare. I didn't address that, though. I went in for the big stuff.

"How about I just ask you what was with you and Amanda and the circumstances of your visit out there the night she died? And how about you just answer? That way we can skip my explanations, your protests and justifications—"

"I don't think so," he said.

I ignored it. I looked up into the trees and sky. I love watching the leaves flicker in their endless green breezy dance, love seeing the sky change shape and pattern. The blue was clear and brilliant, as though the clouds had been banished to a faraway space, marshmallows on some other heavenly confection. Flickering green leaves are better even than the red and gold of autumn ones. And you don't have to rake them, just watch them. I turned back to Davis.

"That way I won't have to bother you with details. Like, although you were discreet at work, you were not discreet enough. I won't have to tell you about the beans your neighbors readily spilled, the dirt they dished; about Amanda's journal"—an outright, outrageous lie—"and, of course, about the roses." I looked at him then. His were eyes clear and steady, not flickering like the leaves.

"What Amanda and I had is private."

"Nothing is private in murder."

"You say murder. The cops haven't. If they do, let them ask me." He was acting tough but he was on the defensive.

"All right, we can do it that way," I said agreeably. "I'll turn this over to them, see if they feel there's enough to open a murder investigation."

I ate a couple of chips and waited for his move. The ducks had managed to get most of the bread out of the wrapper, had gobbled it

163

up, maybe the wrapper too, and were swimming off looking for another sucker with supplies.

"You're prying into someone's life, trying to cause trouble, threatening me. That's wrong."

My threat had worked, but only because it wasn't a bluff, because I had the facts to back it up.

"A man who committed adultery and was at a murder scene is telling me what's wrong?" I inquired politely.

His eyes narrowed into kind of mean-looking slits.

"I cared about Amanda too," I told him.

A sharp intake of breath, like at the service when he found out about Amanda's pregnancy. Which reminded me.

"You didn't know about the baby?"

"No." His jaw was working, his arm muscles bulging, then relaxing, his hands opening and closing. Like the ducks, Clem was in nervous motion. I had made him jumpy. Very.

"Was it yours?" I listened to ducks squawk and squabble, saw some furious paddling, watched a few iridescent feathers fly and settle. Clem was paddling furiously too, I thought, wondering whether to risk my going to the cops or to tell me something and try to shut me up. He decided on the latter.

"No, it couldn't have been. We were very careful. Amanda was married to Jude, not to me. She would not have had a child with anyone but her husband. She was very clear about that. Sometimes I was amazed that we were having an affair, amazed that I got to see the side of her that I did."

"Why were you?"

"Having an affair?"

"Yes."

"Well, now," Clem's voice slowed, then jumped off the edge of civility and into a rough ugly drawl. "You know how black likes to slide into white pussy." His eyes, like his voice, were mean and hard.

I met the eyes, didn't wince. "I didn't say that, or imply it. Aren't you overreacting?"

"First you accuse me of murder, then you say I'm overreacting."

And exaggerating, I thought, but I let it go. "All right. Why?" I asked again.

"We cared."

It was one of those simple easy answers that was totally complicated. I sighed. "Clem—just tell me so I don't have to look at scraggly ducks and try to worm it out of you, eat chips and pretend I'm entertained for too much longer. I understand," I added lamely, trying to soften the last comment. But did I? Could I? "I'm here for one reason. Because Jude and I loved Amanda too, and if it was murder—"

I let "murder" hang in the air. It's an ugly graceless word and, like a kite with no tail, doesn't fly well. It did the trick, or maybe his own love for Amanda did.

"It started innocently enough."

Had there ever been an illicit lover who hadn't said that?

"But everyone probably says that."

"It doesn't make it less true." I spoke words I didn't necessarily believe.

"We worked together and one day decided to continue our discussion over lunch. It was only business. I found her smart and efficient, but a little cold and aloof, not personally attractive at all. As we left the plant that day someone made a stupid and insensitive remark."

I thought of all the stupid and insensitive remarks I'd ever heard. Too many to count. Too many to guess at, though I had a notion. He wasn't spitting it right out so I asked.

"What?"

" 'Now, *that's* hard up,' " he said, after a silence broken by quacking and roller skates.

I winced.

"Yeah," said Clem. "We got in my car and I noticed that there were tears in her eyes. It isn't as though I'm not used to shit like that. I said something about ignoring it. She blushed and stuttered something, started stammering and throwing words and feelings around."

He stopped. The quacks and skates didn't. A radio played in the distance—"Moon Over Miami."

"It took me a minute to figure it out," he said finally. "Mandy was apologizing for embarrassing *me*. This redneck honky asshole is making a crack that *she* must be hard up to eat lunch with an African-American and she takes it"—he shook his head in disbelief—"that this dumb cracker means *I'm* hard up, because to her mind it's a good-looking guy going out with a plain woman. She's not thinking black and white.

"Kat, I thought she was pulling my leg or just being nice or something. It took me a minute to figure out that she wasn't. So then I figured that she was impossibly naïve, but nice at least. And," he added, "she had feelings. She wasn't just a cold professional. That was what brought us together."

"What?" I asked. He'd enumerated too many things: feelings, sympathy, business—

"The knowledge that we were both out of the loop. You don't really understand it, you can't unless you experience it." It was like an echo of Amanda: *You can't understand it, you're beautiful.*

"An African-American male in a racist society, a plain woman in a society that values beauty?"

"You got it."

Yes.

"Yeah, and here's something else that everyone says." Clem laughed, a laugh with hard edges and no mirth. "Her husband didn't understand."

I smiled, but not because it was funny. And no, Jude didn't, wouldn't, couldn't. Jude saw Amanda as beautiful and he thought that was all that mattered. He couldn't comprehend that what he thought didn't necessarily affect how Amanda felt, or what her eyes saw every day in the mirror.

"And you did understand?"

"Some. Sure. I'm used to being judged by what's on the outside. Amanda never did that. She looked at me as a person, first as a colleague, then as a friend, then a man. Amanda didn't do it, though I did, at first. I judged her the way I blame white society for judging me." His voice dared me to blame him.

"How?" I asked neutrally.

"I saw her as cold, plain, business-like. I looked at the surface and assumed that was all there was to it." He frowned as a duck paddled by in desultory fashion. I couldn't tell if the frown was for the comment or the bird. Then he tore his attention away from the bird and gave it, slightly tattered, to me.

"Murder isn't something you want to think about, much less connect up to someone you love, even if—" He broke off that sentence like I would snap a twig.

"Even if you have doubts, suspicions," I finished.

"Yes."

"Murder isn't something anyone accepts easily, even when it's indisputable. And, if it's not—" Uh oh, how to put this tactfully?

"It has to be rammed down your throat." Clem opted for truth not tact. "You've pretty much done that, rammed home my suspicions. And, except for one thing, I think you're right. You're accusing me, but I had nothing to do with it."

*Speaking of things everybody says.*

"What made you suspicious?" I asked.

"The paper said she was electrocuted. How? Mandy was smart, careful and methodical, the last person in the world to balance an electrical appliance on the edge of a hot tub. She would *know* what an accident could mean. She would never do something like that."

"You were out there that night."

"Yes," he agreed, the reluctance heavy, thick and sludgy on his tongue like motor oil after ten thousand miles.

"In the hot tub?"

"Not the hot tub. We visited in the house, then walked outside. I rarely went there, you know, she usually came to me. Black stands out in Elk Grove, and neither of us wanted that. Nor did I care to be in her husband's house. She had asked me out to say good-bye, to call it off." There was no pain in his voice and eyes.

I wondered at it and asked. "It was a mutual decision?"

"No."

"Why?" I wondered if he would tell me to go to hell or mind my own business, but he was into talking, maybe into easing pain through words.

"I wanted her to leave her husband, not to leave me."

"To marry?"

"Whatever she wanted was okay with me."

"You talked about it?"

"I did. She didn't. She said she loved Jude and she wouldn't leave him. End of discussion. I understand it now."

Because of the baby, I thought. "Why was she having an affair with you if she loved him?"

He shrugged. "She didn't mean to get involved any more than I did. We just liked each other and then it got out of hand."

*It got out of hand.* I replayed the words. *It did, they didn't.* Interesting.

"I appreciated that she looked at me as a person, that she listened to me and liked me, found me interesting and attractive."

"And Amanda?"

"I listened and appreciated too. Her husband and I are very different. He kicks ass, butts heads or blows up. He doesn't exactly listen or work out quieter, more reasonable alternatives."

I thought that covered it pretty well, yeah, but I didn't say so, out of loyalty and other considerations.

"Amanda really liked to talk, to discuss things. She liked gentleness, sensitivity. In everything," he added.

*He means in bed, too,* I thought. "How long were you there that night?"

"I arrived about nine and stayed for a couple of hours."

"You drove up to the house?"

He nodded. "Mandy left the gate unlocked. I was to lock it when I left."

"And you did?"

"I did," he agreed, without expression.

"Did you see an electrical appliance of any kind in the spa area —a radio, TV, hair dryer, tape recorder, portable lights, anything?"

"No."

"Did you notice the string of outdoor lights?"

"So that's it." He thought it through before answering. "I noticed, but I didn't pay attention, if that makes sense."

"Were any falling down, coming loose?"

"I don't think so. I would have noticed if they were because I notice things like that. The fact that I didn't means that they were okay. At least," he amended, "not falling down or hanging. I wouldn't have noticed if the staples were loose, although it stretches probability, even credulity, to think they all suddenly came loose."

It did, stretched it way too far.

"Where was Amanda when you left?"

"In the driveway. *Alive.*" He threw the word at me, spat it in my face, dared me to question it.

But I didn't. I'd seen what he could do angry.

A duck waddled by on the walkway, eyed us malevolently and squawked. Clem clenched a fist, looked at me, relaxed it slowly.

# 22

Dear Charity,

I just found lipstick (not my color!!!) on my husband's shirt and panty hose (not my size!!!) in his glove compartment. Is this a clue?

Hot And Bothered

Dear Hot,

No. It's lipstick and panty hose. If you want a clue, talk to your husband. I'd make him do his own laundry, too—lipstick stains are *tough!*

Charity

~~~~~~~~~~~~~~~~~~~~~~~~~~~~~~~~~~~~~~~~~~~

I spent the night at home—Jude wanted space, he said. He was rude, he swore and then he hung up on me. Way to go.

It gets better.

I came home to a pile of stuff sitting on the front porch under a rock. On top was the cover of a *Soldier of Fortune* magazine along with a bunch of pages that had been ripped out of it. Guys with bulging muscles, hot hard testicles, and blacked-out eyes glared at me. Three covers from true crime books in black and white and blood red had been raggedly torn off. There were pictures of guns and knives and

machetes. And more mutilated bodies. Female. I tried to make myself
fill up with hate but I couldn't.

All I could feel was fear. And it filled me up.


I got to the ranch early the next morning. When I called at six-thirty
Jude said he'd unlock the gate for me. The way he said it I was sure
the gate was already open, that it had been unlocked all night and that
Jude had been daring someone to come by, to mess with him. He
might just as well put up a sign: *C'MON, MAKE MY DAY.*

I honked when I drove up. Jude sauntered out of the barn, waved
at me as I got out of the car, then headed back to finish his chores. I
walked around behind the house and over to the hot tub. I was relieved, somewhat surprised to see that Jude hadn't taken a hammer to
it and sent it to Hot Tub Heaven.

"What are you doing?" he asked me fifteen minutes later as I sat
on a bench in the hot tub, leaning back, relaxing.

"Thinking."

"You look stupid."

Grief does things to people's manners, I've noticed it before. He
didn't look hung-over, which was a nice change.

"How long has this been empty?"

"I pulled the plug as soon as I got home."

I nodded. No explanation necessary there. "Have the lights been
hanging like this for a while?" I pointed at the string dangling above
us in the gazebo.

"No. I would have fixed them first thing. You don't want loose
electrical around water, Kat."

No.

Jude glared at me, then scuffed at the dirt with his boot. "I'm
sorry about last night. I know I asked you to stay out here but I just
needed to be alone."

"Anyone fall for it and come by?"

He shoved his hands in his pockets. "What do you mean?"

I didn't dignify his question with an answer.

"No," he admitted gruffly. "I was hoping— I just wanted to pound the shit out of someone, Kat."

"Look, cowboy, I thought we were working together, that our agreement was if we found something, the cops would handle it."

He let out his breath in an angry hiss. "Yeah. Right. Sorry. What are you doing in there?"

I climbed out of the spa, dry and dusty, and we headed indoors. "Looking. Trying to see something, find something the cops missed. Trying to figure it out."

"Did you?"

"No." I hadn't really expected to, cops don't miss much, but I was still disappointed. "Did they go over the house?"

"The cops? I don't think they went over it real close, but I don't know. According to Daisy they sort of looked around."

"That's what we're going to do."

"Why? What are we looking for?"

"I'm not sure. Anything that doesn't belong."

"I wouldn't notice that kind of stuff, Kat."

"Start." Disappointment makes me crabby.

"And people have been in and out of the house the last few days."

Yes. And it had been trashed before that too. It was a problem, no question, and it would be an easy and logical explanation for anything odd or out of place.

"After the cops went through that night, did you notice anything?"

"No, but Kat, I wasn't in great shape, I might not have. Anything like what?"

"Any evidence of company? Dishes, food left out, say a plate of leftover crackers and cheese, some article of clothing that didn't belong—"

"Like sunglasses?"

"Yes." Bingo. "Where did you find them?"

"On the coffee table. I don't know where they are now." He looked around the living room. I sat on the arm of the well-worn couch and waited. "Here." The sunglasses were on a haphazard stack of books on a shelf. We looked at the Ray-Bans.

"Not Amanda's?"

"No. These are expensive, aren't they? Mandy wore sunglasses but she got them at the drugstore."

They were expensive. Suppose someone had come over when it was light but not left until it was dark? It would be easy to forget sunglasses then. I did it all the time. Easy especially if you were in a hurry to leave a murder scene.

We walked through the house and I tried to jog Jude's memory with questions: *Was the bed rumpled?* "Dunno." *Did Amanda hang her towel up like this?* "I guess." *What was in the refrigerator?* "The usual stuff, I think." *Is this ashtray always out? You and Amanda don't smoke.* "Not always. Sometimes for guests." *How about— Is this— Why—* And then I hit it, gold or fool's gold, no telling. *What's this?* I pointed at an earring on the bedroom bureau.

"Mandy's, I guess. I found it in the hot tub when I emptied it."

"Could it have been there long?"

"No, I'd just cleaned and filled the tub the day before, after Georgie jumped in and muddied it."

"Was anyone else in the tub after you cleaned it?"

"Not that evening or the next day. I left to go out of town and Mandy went to work."

"Are you sure?"

"Positive. What's the big deal, Kat? It looks exactly like the kind of earring Mandy would wear."

It did—simple, understated, plain. The seed pearl with a small gold bead on either side hung from a delicate gold wire. "May I keep this?" I pointed at the earring.

"Sure. What of it?"

It was another something, and the somethings were adding up, were pointing away from an accident. The hunches were adding up too. Time to get out of here. Time to make a few phone calls. Time to pay another visit to good ole Buck.

In tune with my thought the phone rang. Life throws me when it takes on a soap opera-like quality. I looked at Jude, who looked at me.

"Get it, would you?"

So I did.

"Kat, you're there, good. How's Jude? May I come over for a visit this evening?"

"It's Charity," I told him, since I was the designated middleman. "Can she come over this evening?"

"I have something for him," Charity said into one ear and, dutifully, I repeated it.

"Okay," said Jude into the other, dubiously.

Dubious, I thought, was on the money. I wondered what Charity had for show and tell.

"Seven o'clock," Charity said and hung up.

That was hours away. I said my good-byes and headed for my office, stopping for a sandwich and a diet Dr Pepper on the way. Late breakfast, early lunch, snack, something like that.

I'd just finished my sandwich, wiped the mayo off my chin and my desk and was wishing I'd listened to impulse instead of reason and bought a large chocolate chip pecan cookie when the phone rang.

"Kat Colorado, Investigations." Drat, there was mayo on the phone. I looked around, vainly, for a tissue.

"Clem Davis," Clem said chattily.

I waited for more, waited for a while, wiped the mayonnaise on my jeans and decided that remembering to buy tissue made more sense than constantly washing my clothes.

"There's something I didn't say yesterday. I'd like to say it now."

"Okay."

"I didn't kill her."

"Okay."

There was a fairly long silence which I waited out with equanimity, giving Clem plenty of space to fill up with (I hoped) rashly spoken words. It was something I'd learned listening to cops.

174

"Another thing—"

"Okay."

"I didn't say this yesterday either. I loved her. I would never have hurt her. You don't hurt people you love."

Wrong. People did all the time. I remembered the expression on his face at the lake. It was the expression of a man who could hurt. It was the expression of a man who would have punted, drop-kicked, slam-dunked, or wrung the neck of a duck. Cheerfully. Without remorse, regret or reservation. With enthusiasm.

"You brought her the rose?" I asked. He hadn't said that either.

Another pause. It was like playing chess, which I didn't have the patience for.

"Yes. She loved roses."

"You mentioned you'd seen a side of Amanda you hadn't imagined. What was it?" I expected him to tell me to buzz off. I was right.

"The hell with that. What Amanda and I had was private."

Hadn't we been through this before? We had. Hadn't I explained there was no privacy in a case like this? I had. I waited for his brain cells to catch up.

"Okay," I said, when he didn't speak. It wasn't acquiescence, it was a threat, the same threat I'd made the other night: *You can play ball with me or with the cops. Take your choice.* And it wasn't a real choice. My rules weren't as tough to play by as the cops' were. For now I was the better option.

Clem slugged through the silence for about a week and a half before speaking. "She had a wild side," he said.

"Wild side," I repeated.

"Something in her that was real crazy, passionate, fun."

"Crazy? Passionate? Fun?" I repeated, as though it were Berlitz class and English a second language for me.

"We went away for a weekend once, when Jude was out of town. To San Diego. She bought a sexy, low-cut cocktail dress. We danced all night, drank too much, made love on the beach, watched the sun come up. She called herself Rosita that weekend."

*A sexy cocktail dress? Love on the beach? Rosita?*

175

I wondered what else I didn't know about Amanda Rose. What else? How much? I thought her death was the puzzle. Her life, which had seemed so clear, was becoming one too.

"And you're forgetting something."

"What?"

"Black and white. That's not exactly everyday around here."

No. It wasn't. That was true.

"I called you for two reasons, Kat. One I've already told you: I loved Amanda. If this is murder, I'll help you in any way I can. The second is that she trusted you, so I'm going to, too."

His voice told me that he wasn't convinced yet, that I had yet to earn that trust. That in turn told me that there was more, that he'd given me what he had to satisfy my curiosity, to end my questions, maybe to stop it here. Only I wasn't sated and I was still curious.

"I've told you what was private between Amanda and me. I'm trusting you to keep it there."

I gave him my assurance. I hoped I could stick to it.

When he hung up I turned to the pile on my desk: the lists I couldn't face for now; the three letters addressed to Amanda that Jude had given me; the anonymous letter and note; and the newsletter I had snitched from DeVito's desk at the plant. I was comparing the signatures, A Friend, on the anonymous letter to Jude and the note to Amanda when the phone rang again.

"Katy."

For the second time that day my heart started beating wildly.

# 23

Dear Charity,

I want to write a note to a friend and tell her what she's doing wrong and I don't want to sign my name. Is that okay just this once?

Anonymous

Dear Anon,

Sure. Of course, the only people I know of who write anonymous letters are pond scum, gutter slime or trash. But suit yourself.

Charity

~~~~~~~~~~~~~~~~~~~~~~~~~~~~~~~~~~~~~~~~~~

"Hank, where are you?" He sounded so close, as though I could reach out, touch him, meet him for lunch. Or, even better—

"Indianapolis."

"Indianapolis?" I didn't get it. Hank was a detective with the Las Vegas police. I knew he was traveling on his current case, but still—Indianapolis?

"I've been to hell and gone on this case and it's not over yet. Not real close even."

Indianapolis. Shoot. That meant lunch was out. Lunch and everything else. Definitely. Rats.

"How are you, Katy?"

"Fine. Good. Busy. I miss you. Any idea when this case will be
wrapped up?"

"No. It's already taken longer than I expected. After that, though,
I've got a week coming. Can you get away?"

"Yes." I didn't even have to think it over.

"Good. What do you want to do?"

"Hawaii," I said, again without thinking. And, when I stopped to
think it over, it still sounded right. August was the off-season in
Hawaii. It would be hot and sticky there but hot and sticky was nothing new to those of us who lived in Sacramento and Vegas. And
beaches were.

He laughed. "Buy a new bikini. Start packing."

We hung up on the kind of noises and words that sound great to
lovers and foolish to anyone else. We were both smiling.

When I could let go of thoughts about Hank, I switched to
thoughts about Annie, Amanda's coworker at Louden. She was young.
She had liked Amanda enough to be upset, to cry over her death. She
wasn't a blabbermouth. I'd seen her eyes flicker over something I'd
said, seen her bite her tongue and file it under Later.

Good enough for me to take a risk.

She'd given me both her numbers. I assumed the obvious on a
weekday morning and punched out her business number.

"Accounting. This is Annie. How may I help you?"

She spoke in swift, polite tones with the words slightly run together, *howmayIhelpyou.* It reminded me of a doll I'd had as a child
where you pulled a ring attached to a string in its back and it spoke
like that. I had taken an immediate dislike to the doll.

"Annie, it's Kat Colorado. Amanda's friend."

"Oh." Anxiety crept into the polite voice.

"Can you talk?"

"Just for a minute, a *short* minute."

"Can we keep this between us?"

"Of course." Indignant now.

I smiled. "Amanda was attacked at the plant, as you know." She made affirmative sounds. "And at home, too. Her husband was there that time so she wasn't hurt. Buck, Ray and Harry were the guys who came out to her house. They work at Louden. Is there any way you can find out for me where they hang out after work?" Not to mention if.

"Yes, ma'am." She spoke in formal tones now. "I do not have those figures and that data immediately at hand but— ifyouwillgivemeyournumber—I will look it up and get back to you. Willyoubeavailablelaterthisafternoon?"

"Yes. Thanks, Annie, you're a peach." I gave her the number.

Someone pulled her string and wound her up again. "You'reverywelcome."

I hung up pleased. Two in a row. I went for three and struck out. Surprise.

"Doctor Wilder is not available," the brisk but sympathetic (wasn't that a contradiction in terms?) voice informed me. "If you will leave your number I will see that the doctor gets the message." Her tone indicated that although she would (briskly, no doubt) see to it, she *personally* did not care one way or the other.

I left a message for Merry, no, Meredith now. When she moved up into the exalted (sic) medical ranks of surgery she'd dropped the Merry in favor of the more formal Meredith. She'd told me, giggling over champagne one night as we admired her brand-new degree, that Merry Wilder didn't sound dignified enough for a surgeon. Too much joie de vivre, I guess.

From Merry to anonymous letters. A comedown. I reached across my desk with reluctance. I didn't want to touch them, read them or take them seriously. But I did.

And I didn't come up with anything definitive.

Maybe it was the same person, maybe not. The sympathy card had words lined out and added in black ink, ballpoint, with capital letters that were uniform, consistent and nondistinctive. The printed letter with pasted clippings was signed in blue ballpoint mostly in lowercase unremarkable letters. The fact that they were both signed "a friend" meant nothing. "Friends" were rampant in the anonymous letter, phone call and threat business. An expert could tell, perhaps; I couldn't. I put them aside.

I looked at the clock, impatient, curious: twelve-fifteen. Annie was probably at lunch. I swallowed the impatience, not caring much for the taste. It was not quite twelve-thirty when the phone rang.

There was considerable background noise, the hum of a number of conversations blurred together and an occasional voice that stood out, though still indistinguishable.

"Hullo. Hullo?" said the one clear voice.

"Annie?"

"Hi. Look, here it is— Hey, you won't believe how I got it."

"How?"

"We're having hamburgers, see, a bunch of us from work, and kind of joking around and I said I didn't think guys knew how to have fun and they said, ha, howsabout girls, they just did their hair and nails and went shopping, and I said, yeah *that's* fun." I winced. "And what did they do that was so much better and *they* said— Uh oh," her voice picked up speed and urgency. "So, anyway, it's a pool hall and bar, the Blue Pocket, anytime after work to midnight—"

"Annie, c'mon, we'll be *late*," someone in the background hollered.

"Hey, Charlie, gotta go," she said gaily to me. "See you tonight then." She blew a kiss into the phone and hung up. I grinned. If I ever needed an assistant with ham acting ability, I'd look up Annie.

The Blue Pocket. Okay. Good. I knew what I was doing later tonight.

Rereading the letters addressed to Amanda gave me a jolt. They made her passion and naïveté come alive again. Two were brusque and short, one was longer and much more informative. I tackled the short ones first. The handwritten one said *mind your own business and leave me alone* without wasting the writer's words or the reader's time. The typed one said essentially the same thing with an added threat to call in a lawyer if Amanda didn't heed the "request."

The longest one was much more intriguing.

Dear Ms. Hudson:

I am amazed, really, that you would write to me and interfere in a situation that doesn't concern you at all. The death of my child was a devastating personal loss, one that has been difficult for me, as it is for any parent, to recover from. Your interference has not made that process any easier. In fact, it has made it all the more difficult. I struggle to put the past behind me, to get over my loss and continue with my life.

You mentioned that you wished to pursue some of the points made in our phone conversation. But I do not.

How can you imagine that someone would knowingly profit from the death of a child? I think that idea and you are beneath contempt.

I insist that you leave me alone.

The letter was signed, but, as the signature was illegible and there was no name typed below, it was something of a moot point. There was no return address on the envelope. I looked at the postmark. Carmichael, CA. It was a start.

I jumped at the sound of shouts and the noise of in-line skates outside my office window. *Hey, race you to the corner, loser buys lunch.* The sounds of jumped skates landing on the pavement. *I'm going to have a double goat-cheese soy nut burger.* Goat-cheese soy nut burger? In Sacramento? Do people eat that kind of thing here? Anywhere? When the phone rang again I jumped again. Rhythm. I had it, no problem.

Meredith's voice was strong and cheerful, one reason why we had called her Merry, one reason why I still did sometimes.

"Katy, it's been too long. What are you doing? Can you get away? Let's grab lunch."

"Okay. What?" I asked, goat-cheese soy nut burgers on my mind still. "Where?"

"Anything. Anywhere. Greta's, Celestine's, Paragary's, you name it."

"Greta's. Fifteen minutes?"

"See you!"

Greta's is on 19th and Capitol, not a long walk from my midtown office. Even on a hot day it's a pleasant stroll, the sidewalks shaded by the huge trees, sycamores, elms and liquidambars that flourish in Sacramento. It's practicality, aesthetics and heat control. Such a deal. Many of the houses, especially the Victorians, have been refurbished, tarted up again in the Easter egg colors they once sported. The sidewalks are clean and flowers pop up in yards and shout out in colorful summer delight. Every time I walk down streets I've driven dozens, hundreds of times before, I see something new, something to enchant me. I stepped off a curb and over a cigarette butt, a condom wrapper and a smashed Pepsi can. Reality check. Enchantment is, sadly, a short-lived thing.

Greta's was packed, as it always is at lunchtime. The food is great and reasonably priced, the atmosphere pleasant and informal and dominated by the long deli cases full of irresistible delights and goodies. We found a table by the window and ordered immediately.

"I've got the menu memorized," Meredith said cheerfully, as she rattled off her choices. I ordered a bowl of gazpacho and an iced tea.

"Tell all!" Merry commanded and we gabbed about jobs, vacations, friends and life. I'd finished my soup and Merry was considering dessert by the time we'd caught up. We were laughing at everything. It was when I told her about the Louden case that we stopped laughing. Just like that. Reality check.

"It happens, Katy." Her face had lost all its light and humor.

"Often?"

"More often than the public is generally aware of. More often maybe even than the medical community is aware of. Not only does it happen, but such incidents tend to continue indefinitely. It often takes a scandal, a public outcry, or a lawsuit to stop it. Sadly, many companies in the medical arena find financial profit more compelling than patient health." She shook her head, sighed deeply.

"Aren't we, as consumers, protected by the FDA?"

"Theoretically, yes. But in reality the FDA, like most watchdog departments, is greatly overworked and seriously understaffed. Any time you have that combination, even assuming the best will in the world and the aggressive support of the administration—" She broke off and we looked at each other. That was, with the recently past Republican years, a big assumption and we both knew it. "Even assuming that, there are a lot of loopholes and cracks. A lot of stuff falls through. Often the FDA follows up something only when it has been called to their attention some other way."

"Lawsuits, magazine or newspaper coverage, *60 Minutes?*"

"Something like that," she agreed.

"You're not surprised by what I told you?"

"I'm not surprised," she agreed. "I wish I were, but I'm not."

"Had you heard it before?"

"Louden? No. I'll listen up now. I'll let you know."

Merry didn't have dessert and we parted on a quiet, almost somber note. Gambling with death does that to you. Life is a gamble of course and we're all playing, but we're not all playing with a stacked deck. The name on this deck was Louden.

Had Amanda lost the last deal?

# 24

Dear Charity,

Is it true that smart people play Scrabble, obnoxious people play bridge, lowlifes play pool, and everyone plays around?

JoJo

Dear JoJo,

No. Why do you ask?

Charity

~~~~~~~~~~~~~~~~~~~~~~~~~~~~~~~~~~~~~~

Rafe answered on the seventh ring as I was starting to give up hope. "Yo."

"Let's play pool," I said after hi-how-are-you.

"For money?"

He kept the question low-key, as though he were asking a stranger—someone who hadn't known him for years, someone who didn't know he was a pool shark without a conscience and with a custom-built pool cue. My grandmother, Alma, is the only one I know who will play Rafe for money and we all know she refuses to pay up so she doesn't count.

"Get real," I answered.

He chuckled. "Where?"

"The Blue Pocket."

"*Where?*"

"It's a divey bar and pool hall in Rancho."

"Why? Let's go to the Eight Ball or Sammy's." He named pool halls where we often play.

"The Blue Pocket," I repeated. "And don't bring your custom pool cue, okay?"

"Oh, we're not playing pool then, we're just playing."

"You're playing; I'm working."

"Got it."

"And dress down. Well, not too down." Rafe's already so informal I don't like to encourage him unduly. "Dress divey bar."

"No problem."

True. That was pretty close to how he usually dressed.

"What time?"

"Eight."

"Pick you up? You're on the way."

"Good."

I opened the door a couple of hours later to Rafe's impossibly gorgeous large and muscled frame. Dark glasses hid dark blue eyes and his blond hair was cut short sides and top and was longer and curly in back. The glasses came off fast when he caught sight of me.

"Don't like it, babe. It's different but it's not you. Or," he said thoughtfully, "if it's you, you've changed and I don't think I care much for it." He winked.

I was wearing tight—poured-on, actually—black jeans, a black tank, also tight, and a ripped-up Corona T-shirt with tears and holes in strategic places showing the tank and the curves in my body. My hair was moussed and fluffed and I had on tons of makeup—pancake, blush, eye shadow and bright red lipstick. Also wild gimmicky jewelry to match.

I didn't look like me. Not to me, to Rafe or, I hoped, to Buck Lassiter. A good friend could have passed me in the mall, thought I looked vaguely familiar but not recognized me. And not just because it's almost unknown for me to go to the mall either.

"Also"—Rafe leaned over to peer at my eyes—"I don't think you're supposed to have gummy black lumps on your eyelashes."

"Shut up," I said crossly. "Makeup isn't my strong suit and it isn't Kathi's either."

"Who's Kathi?"

"That's me tonight."

"Yeah? Well, Kathi, you ready to shoot some pool?"

I was ready to shoot some pool. And to shoot a couple of ducks out of water.

"I'm your cousin, okay, not a date or a girlfriend. No, maybe not even a cousin. A neighbor or something. We're *not* romantically involved."

"That ought to be easy."

I ignored his grin and stuck my wallet in my back jeans pocket—not a piece of cake, it took two shoves, the jeans were that tight—locked the door and we headed for Rafe's Corvette. We're old buddies and I'm the only woman I've ever known who is immune to Rafe's sexy good looks and charm. I don't have to resist, I'm immune. I'm also the only woman friend he has besides Alma, who is eighty-two. Everyone else tumbles in instant love/lust/longing for him and becomes limp and senseless with passion. It's not only ridiculous and boring, it's a pathetic commentary on members of my sex.

We had an uneventful fifteen-minute drive to the bar. I'm not counting the two red lights we ran, the bicyclist (a death-defying daredevil without lights or reflectors) we just missed, the twelve lane changes in two blocks at 10 mph over the speed limit or the kitty who lost two or three feline lives to stark terror. I'm not counting because Rafe always drives that way. Also because halfway there I closed my eyes. The only time Rafe drives like he's straight is when he's drinking. Then he tries to act and drive like a normal sober person. It's the only way to tell that he's drunk.

The Blue Pocket wasn't unique. It stuck out only in its conformity. From the outside it looked dingy and dirty and the inside immediately and inevitably corroborated your worst suspicions.

You know, even before walking in, that it will be dark. No windows, or very few and those tightly curtained, no lightbulbs over forty watts except for the one at the register. Sometimes there are pictures, old and dark and dirty like the rest of the place, beer signs, old-fashioned neon; sometimes not. Always there are beer bottles and dirty glasses sitting around with cigarette stubs floating in disgusting liquid. Always there are hopes gone up in smoke like the cigarettes.

Those are the sights. Then there are the smells. Spilled liquor, stale beer, cigarette smoke from last year, last week, yesterday. Smokers at the bar. Worst of all is the rank, raunchy, rotten smell of promise, prospect, and illusion drowned and now bloating, decaying in alcohol. Hanging over everything is the smell of disinfectant. After a few breaths you forget that it's there. You forget what it means: Disinfectant is to mask the stench of what wasn't cleaned up, of piss and vomit, of decay, dead dreams and worse. Clean places never smell of disinfectant.

I never come to places like this unless I'm on a job.

I never like it.

The sounds are better than the sights or the smells. The banging of beer bottles and drinks on the bar, the dull sound of a banked shot, then the click of pool balls, the shout of triumph as one slides into a pocket. Quarters chuck into the jukebox, the cash register rings and people talk and laugh. If you don't listen to the laughter too closely, or look at the faces, it sounds okay.

I ordered a beer, bottle, no glass. I won't drink out of glasses in a place like this. Rafe was behind me and grinning—I was watching in the mirror. Putting him in a place like this is like sticking a pig in mud. Everything I hated about it he loved. Already he was wallowing. He ordered a double and I paid, then looked around. No Buck, though I thought I recognized one of his buddies looking fetching in greasy styled hair and a stained T-shirt under a sports shirt he'd unbuttoned, sort of an urban-Tarzan-gone-to-seed look.

I put my hands at my sides, my wrists a little behind me. "Hold me back," I muttered and Rafe grinned. "You know the drill," I said, standing tough, changing the subject, trying to hold Rafe to it.

*"No problemo,* babe." Rafe spoke to me but his eyes were wandering.

I knew what they'd land on, I'd already looked the place over. I dropped a hand on his arm as he saw her and started to get up off the bar stool. "Hold it, Tiger."

He winked at her across the room and she stuck her 42D's out an inch farther in mute acknowledgment. How she could see him wink in the dull smoky haze was beyond me. Maybe it was pheromones.

"You know the drill."

"Yeah." He grinned at her.

"Tell me." I didn't trust women with bouffant teased hairdos (unless they were in a fifties movie), or 42D bustlines climbing out of a red lace bustier. I didn't trust bars like this, I didn't trust Rafe, and I sure as hell didn't trust pheromones.

"Huh?"

I rest my case. "The drill, Rafe," I said snappishly.

"You're my neighbor. You're here to play pool." He was too, but that was before bosoms and pheromones called his name. "I'm to stay out of your way, talk up the locals, find out what I can about the guys you point out to me."

The bouffant babe's mouth pouted, then pulled into a fake yawn. With a becoming little wiggle she stretched her arms overhead in time with the yawn. She was a synchronized babe. Her nipples bobbed up. Rafe's head bobbed along. She beckoned. So did her nipples. How did she make them stick out like that in warm weather?

"And stay out of trouble," I said.

"Yeah."

"Quit thinking with your pants, Rafe."

"Yeah."

She gave a little sideways stretch and all the curves and bumps on her body danced around, unlike her hair, which was sprayed into a helmet, shining and immobile as concrete.

"Yeah," Rafe said again, although I hadn't said anything. " 'Scuse me, got to go talk up a local."

He got up. Bouffant babe smiled at me in triumph. Briefly I wondered how she could enjoy the triumph over a man who was staring at her nipples, not into her eyes. Briefly. Then the front door opened and Buck and Ray sauntered in. I turned away from male lust, bosoms and pheromones to contemplate a possible triumph of my own.

Correction: I turned away from male lust and pheromones to more male lust and pheromones. Dive bars are fertile breeding grounds for these attributes.

"Hi." A smoky, beery breath hit my cheek.

I didn't wince. Good, huh? "Hi." I picked up my bottle of Bud Light and walked to a pool table trailing a parade of guys, male lust and the ever-present charged-up hormones. Hot dog. Just got here and already I was Queen of the Prom, head of the parade.

I plunked a quarter down on the edge of the table. "Game?" I asked the air and three guys tripped over their beers, words and shoelaces jockeying to get into place. A young stud beat Buck out. Damn. Ah well, maybe Buck would stand on the sidelines and brag about attempted murder to gather in my attention and spark my lust. Guys thinking with their crotch do things like that. Speaking of crotch, I looked around for Rafe and the babe. Nowhere in sight. Well, shit. Good thing I had insisted on holding the Vette keys.

I racked up the balls, then spent quite a bit of time picking up cue sticks, sighting along their length, putting them back. I stuck my chest out a bit, pouted my lips. It worked for 42D, I was betting it would work for me. It was a bet I could have put money on and won. Finally, satisfied with my pool cue, I smiled and came back to the table. I'd racked them up so Studly broke. It was a good clean break, balls all over the place. Studly sank two balls, would have gotten at least another one except I lounged on, then off the table and distracted him until he blew his shot.

Out of the corner of my eye I saw Rafe go to the bar and order drinks. Good, he was still here. I was playing pool; he was playing pussy. Same old Rafe, same old game. I'd seen him bored—at a symphony, say—but never if he was around liquor, women and pool tables.

I chalked up my cue, took an easy shot and sank the three ball. The next one was harder but not a challenge. The third was a long shot, a tough bank. I sank it, stopped to chalk my cue again. The boys weren't looking at my bustline anymore and their macho dander was up. They were watching me play and they didn't cotton to being beaten by a "girl."

"Hey, guys, not bad, eh?" I said, setting myself up. Then I blew a shot. Deliberately.

"Not bad," someone said. *For a girl,* he meant, but it was unspoken. There were a bunch of half smiles when I blew it. I pouted, tugged at my tank top strap and swore girlishly (*aw shit! damn it anyway!*). The smiles got bigger. One more good shot and then I blew the rest of the game. They hid their grins and patted me on the shoulder. Studly bought me a beer when he won. I thanked him for the game, then put my quarter up on another table.

"Who wants to beat me now?" I trilled gaily, then tipped my beer back and chugged several swallows. Lowering the bottle, I looked around, caught Buck's eyes and smiled. He smiled back. Not a glimmer of recognition. I held my smile and his eyes just a shade too long and hoped Rafe would stick around in case I needed help bailing.

"Well, why the he-e-ell not!" Buck said and racked up the balls.

I broke, sank my first shot, then gave away the next. I wanted to play well enough to draw out the game and the conversation but not beat the pants off him. I'm a decent pool player and I could have wiped up the table with Buck but, except for the satisfaction, it wouldn't have done me any good, so I didn't bother.

"You look familiar." He squinted at me and flapped fat beefy lips around dumb words. I was repelled but not worried. Kathi looked and sounded like Kat the way Tina Turner and Jackie O. look like sisters.

I swallowed the repulsion and held on to the smile. "Yeah, you too. You ever play at the Corner Pocket or the Eight Ball? No? Well, gosh, I don't know then." Buck missed a shot and I chalked up.

"What's your name?"

"Kathi."

"You with anybody?"

"Naw. I drove over with a friend, that's all. What's your name?" Like I didn't know. Like I cared.

"Buck Lassiter. Where you work?"

"I'm an auto parts runner. You?"

"I drive forklift."

"Oooooh," I said, hoping I wasn't overdoing the girlish ooze. "I *love* guys who work with their muscles." He lapped it up. Actually, although you can overdo girlish ooze pretty easily it rarely matters because guys don't think it's overdone, they think it's Reality.

"Yeah. I work with muscle all right, in more ways than one." He said it suggestively and winked and leered.

I played pool so I wouldn't have to look at him, sank the five and seven, bounced the eight ball around a little.

*I work with muscle in more ways than one.*

Sure as cold beer in August this bozo wasn't talking about using the muscle between his ears. That left the one between his legs (a wildly original guy thought) or putting the muscle on someone. Or both.

"Ooooh," I said. "Like what? Like how?" I missed a shot and looked at him sideways, looked at him flexing his muscles. *Ooooh.* Like gag me with a pool cue.

"At work I'm the kind of guy they call in to *fix* a situation." He smiled.

"Fix?" I asked, hoping we could speed this up. I can't maintain girlish all that long.

"Yeah. Fix. You ever have a problem with an ex-boyfriend or something you let me know and I'll fix it."

"Fix it? Like—?" I pretended to be searching my limited brain cells for words.

"Like no more problem. It's gone."

"Gone? *He's* gone?"

Beefy lips smiled at me. "G-O-N-E, gone," he said. Aretha Franklin didn't have a thing on Buck.

"For good?"

He winked. "For good," he repeated, and sank his last ball, then the eight ball. "Buy you a beer?" He put his hand on my arm.

My flesh crawled, wanted to git G-O-N-E gone. I looked for Rafe. He was still at the bar with the babe. She was tucking pretzels into her ample cleavage and he was licking them out with his tongue, sucking at them with his lips. I mean *for godssake!* It wasn't that late, he wasn't drunk, it was too goddamn much. *Really.* Even for Rafe, which was saying something. He is the perfect example of a man who needs to be on a short leash. Make that a choke chain. Buck and I staked out stools at the bar, then I walked over.

"Talk to you for a minute, Rafe?"

"No." He had finished with the pretzels and was licking her breast. Buxom had closed her eyes and was whimpering slightly.

It was disgusting.

When the fight broke out I was almost pleased.

# 25

Dear Charity,
  I say that it is perfectly OK to take as many prescription drugs as you need to kill either physical or mental pain. My friend says no. What do you say?

                                                          Painless

Dear Painless,
  I think that there are a lot of dead people who agree with you.

                                                          Charity

~~~~~~~~~~~~~~~~~~~~~~~~~~~~~~~~~~~~~~~~~~~~~~~~~~~~~~~

Rafe stood up to watch. Fighting used to be a participatory, not a spectator sport with him, and he still maintains a semiprofessional interest. He moved down the bar so he was between the action and me, took my hand briefly, squeezed it, let it go. I was covered and I stayed where I was. For sure.

Dive bar stuff. Some guys wanted to prove they had huevos. Okay. I wanted to stay out of the way. Bar brawls can get nasty fast. It had started off with two guys, I think, but four or five were involved now. I watched Buck. He stayed on the sidelines darting in every now and then and jabbing with his pool cue. He connected with a groin, a kidney and an Adam's apple, so right there I knew he didn't play by the Marquis of Queensberry's Rules. Surprise. He managed to do a considerable amount of damage and not get hurt. His little piggy eyes and fleshy smiling lips told me he was enjoying himself. Love to see a guy who likes his work. Sure.

With an offhand backhand he hit a guy hard across the throat with his pool cue, watched him go down like wet cement, then cracked the knuckles of another. He was the only one not fighting with his hands. Nice, huh? It broke up the melee though. All things considered, I decided Buck could kill—if he played by his rules, didn't fight fair, and went up against an unarmed and weaker opponent.

Like a woman. Like Amanda.

*G-O-N-E.*

I grabbed Rafe by the elbow. "We're out of here," I hollered over the uproar.

He nodded, then turned back to Buxom Babe, reached out and touched her left (erect) nipple gently with the tip of his finger. She smiled. *What was the matter with her?* Obviously she had no sense of decorum, and, God knows, Rafe doesn't. *Didn't she have any pride?* She licked her lips provocatively, just the tip of her tongue protruding. Guess not.

"I am *never* taking you anywhere again," I announced as the bar door swung shut behind us. Behind the closed door, chairs and beer bottles smashed. Rafe grinned. Vette keys in hand, I opened the door and climbed in the driver's seat. I was driving, I'd had enough excitement for one evening. "That was disgusting and," I added snippily, "if you'd slipped and bounced off her hairdo it would have whiplashed you into next week."

He was still grinning. "Want to know what I found out?"

"What? Exactly how much cheap perfume—Harlot's Revenge, no doubt—she uses? A bottle a week? A day?"

"Katy?"

"*What?*" I said, still snippy but only because I hate to see Rafe make such a fool of himself. "What?" I asked again in a normal voice.

194

"Buck and the boys run a little muscle-for-hire business, have for a year or so now."

"How serious?"

"Would they murder, you mean? I don't know. They rough up people and property. As for the rest, these guys didn't know or wouldn't say."

"He told me he could 'fix' problems, 'take care of situations,' 'git people gone.' Truth or bravado?"

"Could be either. Could be a little bit of both. You win at pool?"

"I threw it. Rafe, would you have slept with her?"

"Her?" He looked genuinely shocked. "Katy, I'm a fucking fool, but not a crazy fucking fool. No way."

Well, *thank goodness,* the man had some sense.

"Without AIDS, of course, it'd'a been a different story."

But not much. "Rafe, how did she make her nipples stick out like that?"

He yawned. "Don't know, I wondered about it myself. Next time, Katy, let's shoot pool, not suckers."

"Okay."

We could, that was fine, but I was glad to know about the suckers too. Or maybe suckers was too nice a word? I pulled the Vette up in front of my house, tossed the keys into Rafe's lap. He leaned over to kiss me good night but I averted my cheek.

"Wash those lips with Lysol first."

He laughed. "No kidding."

No kidding.


When I got out to the Hudson place the lights blazed inside and out. Jude was up—trying to bash nightmares senseless maybe, which I knew from experience was as useless as trying to build a snowman on a hot August day.

"Kat, you look like hell."

Snide comments. Swell. And a damn good reason not to have a roommate. He's stressed, I told myself. Ignore it. Of course I'd forgotten how I was dressed, moussed, and made-up, forgotten I *did* look like hell.

"How was Charity? I'm sorry I missed her."

"She canceled."

"Oh . . . How was your evening?"

"Shitty."

I liked snide better than this. "Quiet?"

"Dead, if you don't count a bunch of hang-up calls."

*Dead.* We avoided each other's eyes. "Shit." He put his head in his hands and just sat.

I went to the refrigerator to get a glass of wine. "Jude, it's going to be hard for a while, no way around it. I don't suppose you'd consider slacking off on the tough-guy routine and crying?"

"Go to hell." It was muffled. Like words through a mouthful of coffee and doughnut, not through tears.

"Why did Charity cancel?"

"I don't know. I didn't pay attention. She's coming by in the morning."

I sat down at the kitchen table with my wine.

"Do you ever get over it, Kat?"

"A death?"

"Yeah."

"No. Not over it, past it."

"You got to live long enough to get past it. You got to want to." It wasn't a threat, it was a statement, a statement I didn't like the sound of. He laughed a fun-house laugh with fun-house edges and distortions, echoes and mirrors. It gave me the fun-house shivers. "I found something today that changed things for me."

The TV was on in the next room. *Darling,* a woman's voice cooed. *What's the matter? Why are you looking at me like that?* Her voice changed, stopped cooing. *Darling? What in the world—*

Then the TV screaming started.

Jude's face swung toward me. It was handsome and cold. He was loaded but not drunk out of his mind.

*What's your choice for a pain reliever?* a charming male voice asked dead air in the next room. *For muscle pain, a headache that won't quit, a—* A heartache, I thought. Was there a pain reliever for heartache?

"What I found today got me over the death, over Amanda, over everything."

*Don't suffer needlessly when help is at hand. Reach for—*

Everything? No. I figured he was still in denial. "Did you bust up anything?"

"No."

Okay, good. I relaxed. It couldn't be that bad, and denial is understandable, especially at first.

*Do dirty floors get you down?* the TV screamed.

"Only two things to bust up. One's dead, the other I haven't found. Yet."

Things? Dead? Bust up? Yet? Uh oh.

*Does your floor wax let you down?*

"What are you talking about?" I wasn't relaxed anymore.

He pointed to a snapshot lying face-down on the kitchen table. "I found that in Mandy's things, her drawer. I was just going through her stuff trying to hold onto the memory, the smell, the feel of her, and I found it."

I picked up the snap.

"Who's the guy?" he asked me.

*Clem. Clem Davis and Amanda Rose (Rosita?) leaning, laughing into each other and the camera. Mandy's face was half-turned to Clem's, her hand on his cheek, her lips parted and eager. Lovers, no question.*

"Who the *fuck* is he?"

"I don't know."

"I'll kill him." His voice was toneless.

The TV guffawed, then Arsenio said something I couldn't quite catch through the smash of Jude's fist on the table and the TV laughed again.

"I'll fucking kill him," he said. Jude, not Arsenio. Arsenio was making a joke.

I decided to lie. Well, keep on lying, actually. "So she had a boyfriend before you. So, big deal." I took Arsenio as my role model and said it with a shrug and a smile. He does it better, I know, but I gave it my best shot.

"Look again," Jude said in the same evil, ugly monotone. "She's wearing *my* rings, Kat. Or read the fucking date on the back of the fucking picture."

My best shot hadn't been good enough. I stared at the rings that stood out dramatically against Clem's dark cheek. The wide gold band. The sparkling diamond. The TV told a politician joke and then another one. Cheap shots. Easy shots. Laughter. Jude pounded the table, new sturdy pine, not the old Formica. Good thing. I looked at the date on the back of the picture. Three months ago.

"You're wrong, Kat. I see it now. You get over death with hate. You know, before I met Mandy I dated a lot of beautiful women. Knockouts. Drop fucking dead knockouts. And I got tired of it. They were so caught up in themselves, in their beauty and the power it gave them. They were beautiful outside but often not inside. Amanda was nothing like them and I loved that about her. I even loved it that she wasn't pretty, that I was the only one who could see her beauty. I thought that made her mine."

The TV laughed, laughter with an insane edge, or was that in my mind?

I thought that though Jude was a nice guy, he was also a selfish bastard.

"Stupid, huh? I thought she was my wife and special and really she was just another goddamn fucking whore."

Arsenio promised *we'll be right back.*

Amanda silently laughed with Clem.

I said nothing.

Jude stared at the photograph. "Deader than a doornail," he said and walked out of the house, letting the screen door slam behind him.

Georgie padded to the screen and stared out, whimpered to follow. I got up and opened the door for the dog.

What was deader than a doornail? Amanda? Jude's love for her? Clem?

I thought about following Jude but decided against it. I was sick of male violence. The bar fight, Buck, Jude, even Rafe's wandering hands and eyes.

*Fucking. Kill. Whore. Dead as a doornail. Dead. Kill, kill, kill.*

I heard the pickup door slam, then the screen door was wrenched open, slammed shut as Jude stomped past me. Swearing. Surprise. I was, by now, fed up with obscenities. Big-time fed up.

"You seen my goddamn motherfucking keys, Kat?"

"Goddamn motherfucking no," I said loudly enough to be heard over his slamming around and the TV.

He walked back into the kitchen, hands at his side, no fists. Finally. "I'm sorry," he said.

"Yeah. Sit down, okay? Let's talk."

"I can't. I got to move, got to—"

"Bust up things? Pick a fight? Kill someone? What?"

"Whatever." At the screen door Georgie whined, on the wrong side of the slam again.

The TV screamed at us: *It's the sale of the year. You want a car, you need a car. Hey, we got you a car. Come and get it. Today! Not tomorrow. Not the next day. Today!*

"No matter how many things or people you bust up, Jude, the pain will still be there."

He stared at the hole he'd smashed in the wall a couple of days ago, picked up a loose piece of dry wall, tossed it at an exposed two-by-four, missed.

"Hate's easy and simple. It just doesn't solve anything."

*Dial 1-800-555-1234 and this amazing Whiz-o-matic can be yours for only $19.95. Act now!*

I got up and turned off the TV. "You can love more than one person at a time and in more than one way."

"No. Not Mandy."

"Amanda loved you."

"No. Not if— No. A man doesn't think that way about his wife."

I stared at him in disbelief. It's all in the perspective, I guess. "Men do it all the time, Jude, only it's usually the other way around. It's the man who has the affair. Then it's multiple choice, pick (a), (b), or (c). It can't hurt/she doesn't know/I'm not taking anything from her or the marriage." I spoke into silence that was really a four-letter word. "Tell me you haven't been there."

He didn't. He couldn't.

"I've been there, but never with Mandy." He let the dog in, got a bottle of Bud from the refrigerator. "I didn't, I wouldn't have. I travel a lot, so before we were married there were girls I saw in other towns. It didn't mean anything, Kat." He peeled a corner of the beer label back. "But Mandy went to someone else. I wasn't enough. What we had—" He chugged his beer. "I'm going for a walk." He got another beer out of the refrigerator, held the door open for the dog, got out this time without slamming the screen. Progress?

I peeled off my clothes and took a shower. The mousse and makeup came right off, the smell of smoke and beer washed away. It was only the wisps of lust, anger, and hatred that seemed to cling still.

I went to bed in the guest room, dreamt bad dreams, tossed and turned.

It's never too late to change jobs.

# 26

Dear Charity,

I really want to get ahead. Some of the most success-ful people I know bend the rules and cut corners. So?

Going Places

Dear Going,

It depends on where you want to go. Chuck Colson, Ivan Boesky, and Michael Millken went to jail. Mother Teresa is going to Heaven.

Charity

~~~~~~~~~~~~~~~~~~~~~~~~~~~~~~~~~~~~~~~~~~~~~~~~~~~

We were on our third cup of coffee and Jude had just told me that "Love is no fucking—oops, sorry, Kat—picnic, and I'm not signing on again" when we heard a car. Cars, actually, though I didn't know it was plural until I walked outside. Charity's Beamer was first. The hazy outline of a little white car choking along in Charity's dust followed.

I walked out to meet her, Jude stayed inside. Charity climbed out of her Beamer with a shopping bag in hand.

"Katy!" She gave me a big hug. "Hi! How's everything?"

"Fine," I said absently and incorrectly. "Who's that?" We both looked at the small white car, a VW Rabbit that had emerged from the dust cloud and parked next to Jude's truck.

"Not a clue." Charity shrugged. "When I was unlatching the gate she drove past, then stopped and asked me if this was the Hudson ranch. I said yes and she followed me in."

A young woman wearing short shorts, the kind that barely covered her butt, and a tank top one size too small climbed out of the VW. She clutched a bunch of slightly wilted flowers and a bottle of tequila and ambled over to us on gorgeous tan legs that were about a quarter mile long. Her lips, fingernails and toenails were all painted an explicit shade of Wanton Red.

"Hi," she said as she walked across the dirt driveway to us. "I'm Lynda, with a y." She smiled, showing even white teeth with a gap between the top two. "Is Jude here?"

I nodded. "Inside."

*Who the hell was Lynda and what was she doing here?* I started to wonder about it, then stopped. Jude had long ago overloaded my wonder and worry circuits with talk of murder, death, killing, jealousy, rage and busting up. I couldn't work up much interest in Lynda, even with a y.

We headed up to the house, the dogs sniffing at Charity's clothing and the animal smells there and at Lynda's miles of legs. I opened the door and walked in.

"Hi," Lynda said brightly. Then she tripped over the threshold, bounced off a wall trying and failing to catch herself, plummeted into Jude's arms, her head nestling against his chest, the flowers and tequila sandwiched tightly between them. "Ohmagosh!"

I think that's what she said. It was pretty muffled.

Jude straight-armed her away from his body, holding her by the elbow at arm's length. "You okay?" he asked. She nodded. "Good." He let go. She backed up and tripped over a kitchen chair. Jude caught her elbow again, righted her, pulled out a chair and helped her into it.

Her face was crimson as she stopped biting her lips long enough to stammer out a profuse, largely unintelligible apology. Lynda was, I noticed, very pretty; even prettier when blushing.

"I'm Lynda," Lynda said to Jude, "with a y. We met a long time ago. I heard about . . . about . . . about your troubles and I wanted to say I was sorry and see if I could help or something. I brought you this." She pushed the flowers and tequila across the table toward Jude. "I'm your neighbor. Sort of . . ." Her voice drifted off.

I glanced at Charity, who rolled her eyes up to the ceiling, then sat down at the table clutching her shopping bag.

"Thank you," Jude said. "I appreciate it." He looked at Lynda, nodded—almost in dismissal—then looked away.

We waited for Lynda to leave. She didn't. It occurred to me that it might be a long wait. I looked at her thoughtfully. For sure she wasn't my idea of an old-fashioned, consoling neighbor. Charity's eyes caught mine. Hers, either, I could tell.

Jude carried on as though his kitchen wasn't cluttered up with silent females and poured himself a cup of coffee. I followed his example and got the milk and sugar out. Jude sat down. I watched Lynda out of the corner of my eye still thinking she would leave. No. Apparently sensitivity wasn't her strong suit. So I poured her a cup of coffee too. She smiled her thanks brightly. Jude stared at his coffee. Charity fidgeted like a little kid who had to go to the bathroom.

Charity broke first and rattled her cup. And cleared her throat. And commanded our attention with the tissue-wrapped items that she took out of the bag and placed on the table. "I wanted you to have these." A bright brave smile was draped on her face.

Jude stared at her dumbly. I had no idea what was coming, Charity is unpredictable. Lynda managed to finish her cup of coffee without falling out of her chair, breaking her cup, or creating some form of unnatural disaster.

"Open them, go ahead," Charity urged Jude.

He eyed the packages with all the eagerness of a vegetarian at an All-You-Can-Eat!!!Prime-Rib-Dinner.

Charity's enthusiasm got the better of her finally and she started tugging tissue paper off. Amanda's face gazed up at us, radiant, laughing, alive with excitement and happiness. You could see, practically count, the sparkles in her eyes. The photographs were remarkable.

"I took them when she stayed with me after her new haircut, after our shopping trip. Aren't they wonderful? I had them enlarged and framed."

I watched Jude staring at them wordlessly as Charity, unheeding, unnoticing, arranged them on the table in front of him, a mosaic of laughing, smiling, brilliantly alive Amandas, a repetitive photographic counterpoint to death. I held my breath, anticipating the inevitable explosion.

Charity's twittering receded into the background of my mind until all I could hear was Jude's ragged breathing. I felt like a resident in a war-torn country who had heard the planes scream by overhead. Next the bombs would fall.

Jude's face and eyes were shuttered up like an already-bombed house. I didn't try to read his expression. Finally, silently, he stood, carefully slid back his chair, and walked out the screen door without slamming it.

I started breathing again.

No explosion.

Or maybe he was heading outside to let off steam, to bust up stuff, wring a chicken's neck, mug a cow, ride and spur a horse into a near-fatal lather.

"Oh no, no," Charity wailed on an annoyingly high note. "Did I do wrong? What's the matter? I meant it for the best."

"It was a thoughtful thing to do, a lovely thing," I said truthfully. "Perhaps it's just too soon. Would it be all right if I put these away for a while until Jude is ready?" She agreed to it mournfully and I began to return the pictures to their wrappings (shrouds?).

"People react to death so differently." Lynda announced the obvious with the solemnity of a Philosopher/King handing down Truth big-time. "One just never knows, but of course if it's not one thing, it's another."

I stopped wrapping to gape at her.

"Live and learn" was the next *bon mot* she popped out.

I continued to gape but at least remembered to shut my mouth.

The woman could hardly walk. Or talk. Damn good thing she was beautiful. I glanced sideways at Charity; she rolled her eyes. I wished again that Lynda would leave and, again, I was disappointed.

"You can't make an omelet without breaking eggs," she chirped at us.

I got up to put away the photographs. Charity got up to pour more coffee. The screen door banged. Jude walked back in, stood there at the door like the Grim Reaper come to call. Weren't we having fun?

"I'm sorry," he said stiffly. "I didn't mean to be rude. Thank you very much, Charity. They're great, really great. I guess that I . . ."

The sentence hung there uselessly like the dropped tailgate on the back of a rusted-out pickup.

As always, Charity was gracious. "It's all right," she assured him, "I understand. And you're very welcome."

"Time heals all wounds," Lynda twittered as she reached for the sugar, knocked over her coffee, jumped up and out of the way of the spreading hot liquid, tumbled over her chair, fell back, tripped, tipped to one side, then fell into Jude's angry grip.

It was like the Marx Brothers, only not nearly as funny. So I guess it wasn't like the Marx Brothers. I decided to go look for bad guys, I'd had enough fun here. My good-byes went unanswered, my departure was barely noted. Whether Lynda had come here with an agenda, just to be neighborly, or to unload dinosaurs of the Cliché Kingdom, she now securely occupied center stage.

"Bye," I said again. No answer. Charity was mopping up coffee. Lynda was holding on to Jude. "See you," I called.

Georgie wagged his tail.

That was as good as I got.


I headed downtown toward the State Capitol and its legislative offices —always a swell place to find bad guys. Today I had a specific agenda, though. I wasn't just randomly cruising the halls for civil servants swilling at the public trough, lobbyists with dirty money to lob around, or assorted fat cats. They were there, but I had other things in mind.

I forgot it for a while at first, I always do. It's the approach. The street is lined with palm trees which border the wide green lawns and the flower beds surrounding the Capitol. There are trees everywhere in the park, as there are all over Sacramento. I walked up the broad steps and onto the marble and mosaic tile, under the high ceilings and grandeur, walked through the halls, footsteps echoing, then stood in the rotunda and looked up at the dome.

*Eureka*—I have found it—is the motto of my state. Here gold, dreams, and loves have been found and lost countless times. And would be again. I walked past the old offices of yesteryear's governors, secretaries of state, attorneys general, and treasurers. Museum displays now, the offices are splendid and serious in carved wooden appointments, heavy desks and cushioned chairs, Oriental rugs and thick draperies. The rooms were pristine in their display. The dirt and dust, lust and greed that had once trafficked there was gone now. The action was on the floors above.

I headed for the basement. The information I wanted was, if anywhere, in the legislative bill room. I tried to think like a legislator, a stretch for me.

The bill room was empty. A long, old-fashioned wooden counter faced me. I leaned on it and said, "Hullo," and then "Yo!" and was considering venturing into the back when I heard a rustling and rumbling. An impeccably-dressed and impeccably-earnest male yuppie emerged. He peered at me through wire-rimmed glasses. "May I help you?" His diction was as flawless as his attire.

"Is there an index to current legislation?" I asked, knowing there had to be. Hit and miss, blind luck, even inspired guessing could not cut a path unaided through the maze of proposed legislation. Not for me, not for anyone.

"Indeed there is." He handed me two slim paperbound volumes: *The Legislative Index, A–L* and *M–Z.*

"And if I find a bill I am interested in, may I get a copy of it from you?"

"Absolutely." He beamed at me. Democracy at work.

I beamed back, thanked him, took my loot and headed down the hall to the Capitol restaurant where I appropriated an iced tea and an empty table. I had a notion what I was looking for. Most likely it was a bill that was general and broad in application, i.e. addressing the whole area of defective products and/or environmental hazards. If I was lucky, it would also include the issue of court settlements and/or secrecy agreements, maybe the protection of whistle-blowers as well.

I struck out on *defective products* or *products, defective.* Also on *settlement(s); confidential agreement(s), personal injury, wrongful death.* Bummer.

I bought another iced tea, took a deep breath.

My first score was under *DEATH—wrongful death, see DAM-AGES.* I saw *DAMAGES* and found: *personal injury actions—confidentiality agreements, etc.,* and *wrongful death actions—confidentiality agreements, etc.* Both had the same senate bill number. Eureka.

I scored again under *ENVIRONMENTAL CONTROL—hazard, action re environmental: confidentiality agreements, etc.* And again under *FRAUD—confidentiality agreements, etc.* All four references had the same bill number. Eureka.

I looked at the clock. An hour and a half, two iced teas. I headed back to the bill room, made my request, and was promptly handed a small newsprint pamphlet. The bill was only six pages but it took me quite a while to read it, and even longer to understand it since it was not written in English, but in legislative legalese.

This wasn't just a score, this was a home run, bases loaded. The name of the senator who introduces a piece of legislation is at the top of the bill. I looked up his/her office number. Was I on a roll? Would I find the senator in? I took the elevator upstairs to see.

Yes and no.

"The legislature is out of session and the senator is in district office today. Could someone else help you?" The middle-aged secretary pushed her wire-rimmed glasses down her nose, peered over them and spoke kindly.

"Yes, thank you," I said, not foolish enough to turn down an offer of informed assistance. "I am interested in this bill." I held up the pamphlet: Show and tell. She peered nearsightedly at it. "Perhaps I could talk to one of the senator's aides or someone else who worked on it?"

"Ah," she said, "that would be Alec. Let me see if he's free." With perfect timing a man burdened down by an armload of files staggered through the outer office. "Alec, do you have time—?" She broke off meaningfully and gestured at me.

"I can give you ten minutes if that will help?" He looked overworked; he sounded friendly. I agreed that it would help. "If you'd care to sit in the library there." Alec shrugged a shoulder in the direction of a combination library/conference room. "I'll join you in a moment."

He was back in less than a moment. We shook hands, introduced ourselves, and I told him what I was after. "Interesting bill." He pinched his chin and looked thoughtfully at the ceiling. "Interesting history. You know, it's been dubbed the Sunshine in the Courts bill. Are you familiar with its provisions?"

I nodded and recited what I had learned. "It confronts the issue of secrecy agreements. Currently companies settle with claimants injured by dangerous products or hazardous materials on condition that court records of the proceedings are permanently sealed. Critical safety information is therefore kept from the public and, as a result, more people are injured and killed." I took a deep breath. He nodded approvingly. I plunged on.

"If I understand it correctly, this bill allows secrecy only where a constitutional right to privacy is involved, for the legitimate protection of trade secrets, and for the protection of whistle-blowers. It prohibits secrecy agreements merely to cover up product liability, fraud, and so on?" I ended on a question mark meaning: Did I get it right?

Alec nodded cheerfully in answer to my implied question. "You got it."

"Who supports it?"

"Interesting you should ask." He grinned. "Ralph Nader on down through just about every consumer, environmental and safety, health, public interest and victim group."

"And opposed?" I asked, though it was obvious how it was stacking up. "Companies with something to lose?"

"You got it. We have huge files in there filled with letters from individual companies or corporations who are in very strong opposition. You're welcome to look at them here—they can't leave the office."

"Is the opposition expressed in blatant terms of self-interest?"

"Rarely that directly. Generally opposition takes one of two forms. Either as a threat, i.e.: We employ a lot of people in this state and we'll pack up and leave if the business climate is unfavorable, or —and this is my favorite—public concern. You know: Litigants will lose fundamental rights." He snorted. "Or: The courts will become too clogged. Et cetera."

"I am assuming that in most of these cases the company involved in the secrecy agreement knew of the defect and continued to market the defective product. It's more cost-effective to settle an occasional lawsuit than to correct the problem."

"Yes," Alec agreed cheerfully. "That's it. And the public loses many times over. Government regulators don't see data that could help protect consumers. Current victims are denied evidence of the defects; potential victims are completely unaware of the risks. And manufacturers have little or no incentive to change harmful products."

"And the FDA?"

"The FDA does not adequately protect the consumer." His answer was terse.

"What about other states?"

"Texas, Florida and New York have enacted similar legislation; currently it is under consideration in a number of states." He glanced at his watch. My ten minutes was up. "I'm running late, I'm afraid."

"What are the chances of this bill being passed?"

He sighed. "It has been defeated several times. Things are better now, though; things are changing. The current political climate is more receptive. Maybe this time it has a chance."

"If I were to mention that I am currently investigating a local company marketing a faulty medical device—?"

"And can prove it?"

"Getting closer."

"That could be the shot in the arm and the publicity that this bill needs." He grinned, then frowned. "It would also make that particular company, and you, real unpopular in the business community." He stood up abruptly, then leaned forward toward me, palms down on the table. His eyes were grim. "Be careful. I'm not sure you realize how much is at stake here, how rough some of these companies can play. Call me if I can help. I'll ask Adele to pull those files for you."

I pushed my luck with one last question. "Do whistle-blowers have anything in common?"

He stopped abruptly. "Is that what started your investigation, a whistle-blower?"

"Yes."

"He get into trouble?"

"Yes."

He held my gaze for a moment, then said, "A whistle-blower can be anyone—housewife, CEO, scientist—and you're right, they have something in common."

He listed the somethings for me.

"They have a strong, often single-minded sense of justice; they don't back down or off when told to; they are shocked at being blamed for doing the right thing, at being persecuted for telling the truth." Alec drew a deep breath. "While all this is very admirable, it also makes them very vulnerable. You, too, if you're involved in it. Good luck." He waved at me and walked out.

I spent the rest of the afternoon with the files. Most, as Alec had said, were letters on corporate stationery in opposition to the bill. The letterheads formed a veritable who's who of major medical, chemical, petroleum and biotechnical products and insurance companies.

Louden Industries was there, vehemently opposed.

Surprise.

Later, on my way back to the car, I forgot to notice the beauty of the Eureka mosaic, the marble, the carved wood, the murals. I didn't see the palms or the flowers.

I was focused on greed.

# 27

Dear Charity,

What is the best way to get over the sorrow of losing a loved one? Prayer? Exercise? A new project? A new loved one? I am so sad.

Crying All The Time

Dear Crying,

I'm sorry you're sad. All of the things you mentioned are good. So is time. And chocolate.

Charity

~~~~~~~~~~~~~~~~~~~~~~~~~~~~~~~~~~~~~~~~~~~~

I called before I went back out to the ranch.

"Yeah." Jude didn't sound exactly welcoming.

"It's Kat. Do we need anything? Shall I pick up Kentucky Fried or subs?" I was still dazed by corporate subterfuge; I didn't feel like coping with dinner.

"No. Look, Kat, do me a favor and don't come out. I need some time and space."

"All right." Good thing I'd called. No kidding. "Jude, did Amanda have files or anything like that at home? I saw a desk that looked like hers but there wasn't much in it." It was a lovely antique that held receipts, canceled checks, current bills and two small drawers with stamps, paper clips, a small box with spare car and house keys, and the like.

"In the closet in the spare bedroom there's a file cabinet. I don't know what's in it exactly. Mandy took care of most of our bills and stuff. You can go through it anytime."

"Did she keep—"

"Look, I'm busy, I gotta go."

And he hung up.

Son of a bitch.

I tried to write it off to stress and grief but I was getting tired of making allowances. I slammed the phone down with about ten pounds too much pressure. Speaking of making allowances.

Ranger and Kitty were glad to see me. I did a bunch of chores under their close supervision and then we had tuna melts for dinner. Okay, I spoil my pets now and again. I still hadn't named Kitty. I thought it would bother me but it didn't. He was elusive, chimeric, and so, obviously, was his name. Time would tell. There is a season for everything. A name is only a name but— I caught myself and stopped. I guess there are worse things than sounding like Lynda, though, to be honest, I couldn't think of any offhand.

I poured a glass of wine and took it out onto the patio. There is a fountain there now. Water bubbles up unseen and flows and splashes over rocks and into a small pool where shimmery goldfish and a small delicate water lily live. Hank and I built it last summer because I love the sound of running water so.

Ranger immediately wandered off to inspect every square inch of the backyard, which is the way dogs get their news updates, and Kitty wantonly attacked a trailing vine on an ivy geranium, dispatching it in no time flat to the Great Nursery in the Sky. I sat swinging in the loveseat glider and thought how nice, how perfect it would be if Hank called.

He didn't.

And I didn't know where he was and couldn't call him.

Life is not perfect.

I went to bed early. Images of Amanda and Clem, then Jude, then mutilated bodies floated through my mind before I could slam the door shut. After the slam I opened another door onto flowers and sunshine, waves and beaches and Hank, and then I must have slid into a dreamless sleep.

I got up early. Mornings before the heat are precious. I watered the tomatoes and squash, the peppers and roses, fed the fish and put out fresh water for the animals. Seven o'clock. A quick shower, two cups of caffeine, a hasty glance at the headlines and I was ready to go. On my way out I picked some yellow dahlias, a red rose, and blue salvia. For Jude. Why not? Seven-thirty.

There were bullets strewn around in the driveway. I picked them up and hefted them. Bullets, not shell cases. Six of them. *Dead kats tell no tales.* The message was clear. I climbed in the Bronco, then saw that the aerial had been bent double. Swell. Nice way to start the day.

I hit some traffic going into Sacramento, but going out of town toward Elk Grove it was clear sailing. The Hudson gate was latched but not chained. The dogs picked me up halfway down the drive, they knew me now, wagged and yipped but didn't bark. I parked next to Jude's truck and a white VW Rabbit. Convertible. I looked over at the barn expecting to see Jude and a wave. Nothing. Eight-fifteen.

I had the key Jude had given me but I didn't need it. The door was open, the screen closed but not latched. I knocked. Georgie was whining on the kitchen side of the screen. I opened the door to let him out, then stepped in.

Something was wrong.

The house was tidy and picked up and it smelled of roses, I thought. And perfume. Or perfumes. Names flitted through my mind like demented fairies: Obsession, Madness, Ecstasy, Desire, Passion. The flowers I'd picked were in my hand still and I put them into a glass of water. I thought about the VW Rabbit as I glanced into the front room, investigative habit I guess, because really I knew. A pink camisole was tossed rakishly onto the wing chair, a matching bra floated on the chaste depths of a Chinese rug. I didn't see the (matching, no doubt) panties but I got the drift, no problem. I was on my way out when a half-naked man walked in.

Jude. Yeah, well duh.

I kept walking.

"Kat!"

I didn't answer; I didn't look; I picked up the pace. Almost to the screen door, almost clear, almost free of this.

"People get over things in their own way."

I stopped, I didn't turn. "That's not getting over, you've got your verbs wrong." I started to walk again.

"Give me ten minutes," Jude said. "I'm asking you."

I walked out. For ten minutes I stood in the freshness of the early morning, life a wanton summer celebration all around me, and had bitter mean thoughts. Lynda walked out and headed quickly over to her car saying nothing to me. It was wrong, I knew; it was way out of line, I knew; but I headed over to the Rabbit too.

"Why?" I asked.

"He needed me." She licked her lips. "Love is never having to say you're sorry." *Love?* "Anyway," she said with some spunk, "who are you to ask?"

Who indeed?

Lynda climbed into her Rabbit on that parting shot. "It's okay," she said. "Really. Don't sweat it." Second parting shot. "I met him way back when and I always *always* wanted to sleep with him, so I did." Third and final parting shot.

Georgie and I watched her drive off. I was still trying to decide whether to leave or wait when Jude came up behind me.

"Kat."

"Good job," I said. "You showed her. That will really teach her. Hey, Amanda, payback's a bitch."

"Kat." His voice was funny. I swung around to look at him. There were tears in his eyes. Maybe. I shut my mouth, trying to swallow hate, contempt, rage. Trying, because Lynda was right: Who was I to ask, to sit in judgment? And why was I being so much harder on Jude than I had been on Amanda? We walked back to the house.

Jude held the screen door open for me. "Coffee?" he asked and then stumbled around the kitchen. He was barefoot and his T-shirt was on backwards and inside out.

"Okay," I said, although I didn't think I'd drink it. My mouth was still full of bile.

"Kat, first I lost Amanda and my baby—our baby. Now I've lost my marriage. I didn't know the woman I was married to. The woman wasn't what I thought she was. The marriage wasn't what I thought it was."

Not Amanda; the woman.

The coffee was ready. Jude stared at it. I didn't care one way or the other.

The woman.

"I don't think I've ever hated so much in all my life. First I hated the guy, but what the hell, he was just taking what was offered. What was she doing? What was she wanting and getting from him? Why didn't she come to me?"

The lack of expression in his voice frightened me more than if he were drinking, or shouting, or punching in a wall. Just to be doing something, I got down two coffee mugs and poured. He didn't notice. The coffee was thick and black, too strong. I added milk to mine though I drink my coffee black.

"She lived a lie. She wasn't the person I thought I knew."

"She was, Jude. She was all that and more, more that you hadn't seen or known yet. That doesn't mean—"

"Slut. Liar and cheat."

The rage and contempt had long since drained out of me. I couldn't sustain it in the face of Jude's loathing. And I didn't want to be what I saw in him.

"Jude, Amanda—"

He shook his head. "Don't even try."

So I didn't.

"Maybe it wasn't my baby." He ran his fingers through thick blond curls. "You're mad at me. You have a right. I'm not defending my behavior but, by God, *I* didn't break my marriage vows. Ever. The ring on my hand meant something."

It wasn't there now. The hand he held up was bare, though it was branded still by a band of white flesh against the deep brown of his tanned skin.

"The woman last night meant nothing. I didn't invite her. I told her to get the hell out, I had nothing for her. She can't walk without tripping, or talk without saying stupid things, but she can fuck. I took what she offered. It maybe kept me from killing something last night."

Killing. Too many deaths: a woman, a child, a marriage, a dream.

"It wasn't making love, I don't know what it was. She wanted a hard-on so I fucked her. I came but there was no pleasure, no release, no feeling. There was no love in me, no desire—just hate. I fucked because if I stopped I was going to kill something. I may still."

He left the room. I was frozen in silence and in the circle of hatred. I didn't know how to get out of it. Sounds in the background, a closet door opening. Footsteps.

Guns. A shotgun, a handgun, a rifle. He unloaded them and put them on the table.

"Take these, Kat. I don't trust myself. Take them and get the hell out of here."

"I'm not going."

"You're going. I want to be alone."

I took the guns.

I went.

The radio was on a country station. The songs: "She Took Everything But My Heart"; "Why Not Me?"; " 'Til I'm Over You"; "Lonesome Standard Time." I punched the button for the oldies station: Ray Charles singing "Crying Time." Was there no end to it?

Do you get over love with hatred? I didn't think so. You could bury it, for sure, but it would still be there and, after a while, it would be rank, festering, foul. It could explode. It could be as dangerous as guns.

The Stones came on singing "Time Is On My Side." I wasn't sure it was on mine.

I made a mental list as I drove back, not the fun or usual kind of list, a wish list, or shopping, or even things-to-do. A suspect list. Amanda had not died accidentally, she had been murdered, I was certain of it, and everywhere I went in search of answers I was engulfed in anger and violence. They swirled around Amanda, foamed and frothed. It scared me.

The list.

I started counting:

1. Alec saying: *I'm not sure you realize how much is at stake here, how rough some of these companies can play.* Amanda had been a big problem for Louden. Had they played rough?

2. She had been a problem, too, for a number of the employees and their job security. Buck saying: *You got a problem? I can get it gone. G-O-N-E.* And Amanda was gone.

3. Jude. He was a man capable of killing. I had seen his violence. I had seen him out of control. He had given me his guns, afraid of what he might do. Had Jude known about Clem before this? Had he hidden that knowledge, murdered Amanda and only then "found out"? It was a possibility.

4. Clem was looking pretty good too. He was capable of rage and violence. Of murder? I didn't know. He was a boyfriend who had wanted to be a husband. *I would have married her, done whatever she wanted.* Even if capable of murder, would he kill the woman he said he loved because she left him? It didn't seem likely. Unlikely? It happened all the time.

5. And the names Amanda found, the names of the heart valve victims.

Fun list, huh?

Who else? I thought of the letters and phone calls, the replies
Amanda had received on her queries to those who had made cash
settlements and agreed to secrecy agreements with Louden. The responses to her queries had ranged from dismissive to blatantly hostile.
And the anonymous letter. I needed to get onto that. And I needed to
call Jack, a lawyer I knew. I was pretty sure he handled personal
injury cases like those brought against Louden.

As I drove I thought about how to play it. Hard, heavy, and
violent, like everyone else? Polite, low-key, subtle, with implied
threats if necessary? That, too, could work.

I remembered Amanda's eyes, wide and frightened, as we waited
for Buck and the boys that night in her kitchen. *I hate violence. I'm so
little and it has always scared me.* Amanda had fought back even
though she was terrified.

I pulled into the Louden parking lot.

Ready to go.

Ready for a fight.

# 28

Dear Charity,

My husband's favorite saying is *First things first.*
First is making money. Second is racing motorcycles.
Third is drinking beer. Fourth is football. I'm fifth.
Maybe. Do you think this is right? What *is* first? I think
I should be first.

Me First

Dear MeMe,

You pays your money and you takes your choice.
Your husband thinks he's first. You want to be first. I
think love and respect should be first.

Charity

---

"Kat Colorado," I said in a pleasant voice to Miss Hatchet-Face, the
secretary. "Here to see Mr. DeVito. I was here the other—"

"I know who you are." Her tone was sour. "Don't move, don't
touch anything. I will see if Mr. DeVito is free."

"Thank you," I said, and faked a sneeze. She glared at me.
"Sorry. I have to breathe," I added in a reasonable tone.

She *hrummphed* at me, tugged on the manager's door, and disappeared inside. I tried to read the papers on her desk. Give me a month
and a half and I can read an upside-down letter, no problem. If it's

short, that is. I didn't read it—I didn't have a month and a half, the secretary was back in no time at all.

"Mr. DeVito will see you," she said, still sour but clearly triumphant at getting me out of her office. I "tripped" over her wastebasket on the way out. It was small of me, but there you go, gloating never brings out the best in a person.

DeVito was speaking on the phone and shuffling papers as I walked in. He did not bother to look up. "Yeah. Yeah. I understand but I want it resolved. Get on it. Yeah." He hung up. No good-bye. His dark eyes flicked over me. No hello. Miss Manners would not have approved of any of this. I was with Miss Manners.

"Well, well, Ms. Colorado, I did *not* expect to see you again." *Did not expect to, do not want to.* "I am quite busy." He scowled. "Make it short." Notice he had not asked me to sit down?

"A few things have come up. I'd like to interview a couple of your employees."

"No." Mr. Helpful. Mr. Agreeable.

"All right, then. I'll go to the police."

"Do it." He sneered at me, trying for Elvis, I think, but missing badly. I liked his answer, though. In real life hardly anyone ever folds just because you say you're going to the cops. That only works in the movies. In real life these guys know what you know: If you had enough to go to the cops, you'd be there.

DeVito called my bluff, so I raised him.

First I sat down in the visitor's chair, made myself comfortable. Then I examined my fingernails. Nothing to see. Wait a minute! I looked more closely. Was that the beginning of a hangnail? Shoot!

"Get out of here." He dropped any pretense at a sneer and moved right on to a snarl.

"I know about Buck Lassiter's little sideline business. I know he hires out. I know what he hires out to do. I know how he does it and for whom."

"What an employee does on his own time is of no concern to me."

"Not unless you hired him," I agreed.

"Nonsense," he sputtered. From a sneer to a snarl to a sputter. I had him.

I leaned forward in my chair, keeping my voice pleasant. "Suppose I could connect you—actually, you and Louden—to Buck. To Buck and his after-hours visit to the Hudsons'. As you know, Buck and his pals are going to stand trial for breaking into Amanda's house and threatening her. They claim it was personal. I don't think so. Let's suppose I can prove that."

He blanched slightly.

"I'm sure the cops would be interested in this information, especially in the light of new evidence that makes it clear that Amanda Hudson's death was no accident." I spoke in a light, clear, confident and unconcerned tone—this is important if you are lying—then settled back nonchalantly in my chair.

"Information?"

"Information," I agreed. "I can tie Buck to Louden. I can show his attempted attack on Amanda wasn't personal at all. I can show that you hired Buck to 'take care of the problem,' 'to take Hudson out of the picture.' "

"No. It wasn't that at all. They were—" He broke off, but it was too late. I didn't know it for sure before but I did now. I shook my head sadly. No bottom to him. I hoped DeVito didn't play poker. Although if he did, I'd be happy to get in on the game.

"The police—" I began.

"What do you want?" he croaked, all the fight gone, DeVito nothing but a flat tire now.

"I want to talk to the foreman on the loading dock and a couple of other guys."

"Who?" I raised an eyebrow. "All right, but this conversation, this information doesn't go any further."

I shook my head in disbelief. First he admits guilt, then he reenforces it. Here was a guy who needed to watch more cops-and-robbers shows on TV, get the hang of it. Or maybe he should just get out of the bad guy and nefarious dealings business.

"You have my word," I said, lying through my teeth. He looked at me suspiciously and I smiled in a wholesome, benign fashion. I stood, he followed suit, and we walked out through Miss Hatchet-Face's office. I walked a little too close to her desk and started to stumble, reaching out to the desk for support. She lunged wildly for her Pepsi and knocked it over. Then I caught myself in mid-stumble without ever touching her desk. That's life for you. She made a rude noise and glared at me.

I smiled back sweetly. "Oh, *too* bad," I said. It was a full can, too. Way to go.

"This way," DeVito said, and marched along, so I marched along behind him and on down to the shipping and receiving area of the warehouse. There was a large open space down the middle of the long warehouse with aisles perpendicular to the center. Along these aisles shelves and scaffolding were heaped with merchandise. The loading dock was at the far end of the building. In the center area two forklifts were idle, one partially loaded and running. DeVito skirted several stacks of boxes and walked up to a man standing by the partially loaded forklift.

"Ms. Colorado, this is my foreman, Sam Coleman." A stocky man in his early to mid-forties looked up from a clipboard with a shipping order on it.

"Sam, this is *Ms.* Colorado. She has a few questions for you, for some of the other guys too. Help her out."

DeVito was back to snarling, Miss Manners please take note, but the foreman ignored it and smiled in an affable way.

"Sure, Mr. DeVito, glad to," Sam said. DeVito stomped off. The foreman pushed his hard hat back with one hand, leaving a red, slightly sweaty band where the hat had rested, gestured with the other hand in a friendly way. "How can I help you?"

"I'm an investigator. I was hired by Amanda Hudson's husband."

He rubbed his hand across his forehead. "That, huh?"

"That, yes."

"Her accident?"

"Her death. What do you know about it?"

"Only what I heard, that she died at home in her hot tub." He frowned, furrows tightening across his forehead, his lips in a hard line. "Not a good way to go. Helluva accident."

"There's talk it wasn't an accident."

"I heard it." His voice was noncommittal. Sam was going to cooperate, he wasn't going to spill his guts.

I changed tactics. "Amanda was looking into something here at the plant. She found what she thought was a faulty product Louden was shipping out regularly."

"I heard that, yeah."

"What happens in a situation like that? A faulty medical device could kill people."

Sam pushed his hard hat back again, rubbed his forehead, said nothing.

"Did kill people," I added.

He glanced around. We were alone. "Look, between you, me and the forklift, Amanda Hudson was right. If there's a problem, you pull the product and freeze the inventory, figure out what the hell is going on.

"But, and here's the deal, we don't *know* there's a bad product. You start pulling products, you not only hurt the company, you hurt the people who work for the company. Like me. I'm just a regular guy, miss. I got a wife who's not perfect, but what the hell, neither am I. We got two kids. The wife, she don't run up charge cards or serve steak every night. We push to meet the mortgage, pay the bills, make ends meet. We're saving to take the kids to Disneyland next Easter, God willing and nothing goes wrong."

Sam looked at me to see if I was paying attention. I was. "Here's the deal. The product the Hudson gal was making a fuss over is one of the biggest moneymakers Louden has. We pull that, there are a lot of jobs, maybe mine, gone. I lose my job, where the hell am I going to find another one in this economy? I lose my job, we lose the house and the family goes hungry. Look, I have to choose between my kids and a stranger, I go with my kids every time. I don't feel bad about it, that's life. Amanda Hudson was making things look pretty bad to some of us here."

I was silent. I figured he had more to say. I was right.

"You asked me about her death. Okay, I don't think anyone here particularly liked her or what she was doing. But I don't think anyone here killed her. That's crazy. We'll fight for our jobs but we're not killers. None of us. No way."

I thought about Buck and was not as sure about that as Sam was.

"I'd agree with that," a male voice said. I turned around.

"This here's Pete." Sam introduced us. We didn't shake hands. Pete had his hands in his pockets and looked like a mad little guy with a Napoleon complex. He got right in my face. "What the world don't need is more meddling, troublemaking, interfering folks."

Pete jerked a hand out of his pocket and shook a finger under my nose. "You heard the saying: If it ain't broke, don't fix it? Well, I guess Amanda Hudson there meant for the best but it wasn't broke. Nobody showed us or proved it was broke so there was no call to go around fixing things. Maybe *she* could afford to holler broke and lose her job, she a married lady and all, but I sure as hell couldn't. I got a family."

His voice was loud and the decibels kept climbing. Guys had drifted in closer, six or seven around us now, nodding, agreeing.

"Yeah."

"She had no call to—"

"That's right."

"Nigger-lover," someone snarled in a low voice.

"Yeah. You said it."

"She didn't speak for no one here, that's for sure."

"She spoke outta turn." It was a high, shrill voice, almost feminine. I turned. The speaker was a scrawny, nerdy, intense man with thick glasses that made his eyes look pig-like. Somebody snorted behind me and the pack started to drift off. "The Scriptures tell us that it is God's Will that Woman be subject to Man."

He spoke in capitals and with emphasis. I listened in resignation. His coworkers thought he was a nut. I could tell by the instant and mass drift.

Sam waved a hand at me. "Lemme know you need anything else, I'll be around. Phil"—Sam spoke to the nut—"make it short and get back to work."

"Woman," Phil hissed, pig-eyed attention concentrated on me, "came of Adam's Rib and is rightly Servant to Man and Man's Desire. That Hudson woman was a troublemaker serving neither God nor Man. And she was Struck Down, yea, even so, and by the Sword, the Instrument of God's Will. For all the Faithful are the Instruments, the Swords of the Almighty Righteous Lord."

He had body odor. I stepped back but it followed me, as persistent as his whine, as dogged as his faith.

"Are you one of the faithful, an instrument of the Lord?" I asked, a glutton for punishment.

"I am!" Phil slashed his arm down in a sword-like movement and walked away, leaving a miasma of body odor behind.

Avenging pseudo-angel with a trumped-up cause, a reason to hate and be hateful. A reason to kill? People like Phil make me sick. Also scared and nervous.

"She was E-vil," he hissed into my ear. "Evil, evil, evil!"

I jumped, then chided myself. He'd snuck up on me. I know better than to turn my back on a whining wienie like that. They play by their own rules, play dirty. Play dirty, yes, but murder?

"*Evil!*"

"Go fly a kite, Phil."

"E-*vil.*" His little piggy eyes glittered at me. Hate, malevolence and ugliness spilled out. I was glad I didn't believe in his god, a deity of darkness and hatred. He opened his mouth to say, I assumed, the same word again.

"Fuck off, Phil."

I left him standing there, mouth open, and headed back to the office area of the plant, waving good-bye and hollering my thanks to Sam. On a second thought I walked back and handed the foreman a business card. "I'd be glad to talk to you or anyone else about this."

The card almost disappeared under his big thumb. He looked at it, then at me. "I had a lot of admiration for Amanda. She was gutsy. She stood up for what she believed. I think that ain't easy either. I'm sorry for what happened."

"She was my friend."

"I'm sorry for you too, then. That's a big loss."

"Did you know that she was going to have a baby?"

I saw it in his eyes—the wife, the kids, the dreams of Disneyland. ABC's and Sunday school and the senior prom and hopes for tomorrow.

"I'm sorry," Sam said. He turned and walked away.

I stood for a moment, then shrugged. I wasn't going to get anything else here. The guys had confessed to having a lot to lose, to anger, resentment, fear, maybe even more than that. But not murder, not by a long shot. And I wasn't going to get that no matter how long I stayed.

I headed out with the possibilities.

Louden, too, had a lot to lose if any of this became public. A key product would be revealed as fatally flawed; their careful, expensive cover-up would be out in the open. This publicity would be as well-timed for the Sunshine in the Courts bill as it would be badly timed for Louden Industries. There would be more lawsuits and settlements. A lot more.

High stakes.

High enough for murder?

The guys at the plant? Men and women had died on picket lines fighting for jobs, on rangelands fighting for homesteads, on farms fighting over water rights. They had died fighting not over a legal technicality but for their lives and livelihoods, for the well-being of their families and children.

Jobs were tight now. Many hardworking families were only an

emergency and six months away from foreclosure, no medical insurance, life on the streets.

Murder? Maybe.


Back at my office I pulled out Amanda's files, the ones I had taken from her for safekeeping. Also the file I had opened on the case. I wanted to go over the letters Amanda had received again and the names and addresses of the people she had contacted. I wanted matchups.

Amanda had planned to contact everyone she could who had settled out-of-court in a secrecy agreement with Louden. There were twenty-eight names and addresses in her file and she had written six letters to people on that list, phoned some of them. I started there, looking at the list and speculating how I would have approached it in Amanda's shoes. Three likely possibilities occurred to me: numerical order, chronological order, geographic proximity. I checked the filed copies of the letters Amanda had sent.

Bingo.

Geographic proximity. There were four western states represented; three names in California—one in Los Angeles, one in San Francisco, one in the Sacramento area.

Bingo.

I struck out in L.A. No such name at that address, no new phone listing in that name in the L.A. area. I tried San Francisco, although by now I wondered if I was wasting my time on this angle. Long shots pay off just often enough so I can't ignore them and not quite often enough to keep me in business.

A gentle feminine voice answered the San Francisco number. Young, I thought. I asked to speak to Dr. or Mrs. Ruskin.

"They're out of the country. May I help you?"

"Oh, dear." I tried to sound devastated. "How long will they be gone?"

"Until the end of the year. Dr. Ruskin took a year off to work in Switzerland on a project that interested him."

Was she, I asked politely, family? Oh no, she had replied, she was house-sitting. Perhaps I could speak to their son? Oh no, she said. There was a gentle note of regret in her voice. David died last year. It was shortly after his death that the Ruskins had decided to go to Switzerland. I made sympathetic noises and thanked her, then we hung up and I eliminated that name.

I looked at the third name and address: Roberta Heald, Carmichael, California. Carmichael is an upscale unincorporated area in Sacramento County just a few miles from me. I looked up Heald in the phone book. Heald, R., followed by an upscale, even for Carmichael, address. One of the replies to Amanda's inquiries had been postmarked in Carmichael.

Eureka.

I picked up the phone.

# 29

Dear Charity,

I think the most important thing we can do for our children is to teach them not to trust *anyone* and to be *suspicious* of *everyone*. That way they'll be safe. Don't you agree?

Scared Out Of My Wits

Dear Out of Your Wits,

No. They'll probably be alone but alone is not safe either. Teach them what is good and what is bad. Teach them to be cautious.

Charity

~~~~~~~~~~~~~~~~~~~~~~~~~~~~~~~~~~~~~~~~~~~

"What's up?" Chandra caught the phone on the first ring. "How's the murder and mayhem business?" she inquired.

I skipped over the questions. "Do something for me?"

"If it's fast. I'm slammed right now." She said it cheerfully.

Chandra was a journalist who worked at the *Sacramento Bee.* "I need you to run a name through your files: marriages, births, deaths, news mention or society coverage. Is that fast?"

"You bet. God bless computers. Where are you? Give me your number so I don't have to look it up. What's the name?"

"Roberta Heald." I spelled it.

"Taking ten," she said, and hung up.

It was closer to twenty but it didn't matter.

"You know how to pick them," she said, as though our conversation had never ended. "I've got stats all over the place. How detailed do you want it?"

"Big picture first."

"Hmmmm. Okay. Info on Heald and family for the last six years only. She's thirty-four. Was married. Husband: Nicholas James Heald, died two years ago, age thirty-two. No mention of cause of death. Two children: Nicholas Jr., six; Emily Ann who died a year ago at age two. Real estate transaction six months ago in Roberta's name only. No news items with the exception of a paid announcement that Heald had been taken on as a broker at Rafferty, Schmidt & High Associates."

Interesting indeed.

"Numerous recent mentions of Ms. Roberta Heald in community, charity and social functions and fund-raisers. Heald was involved with the symphony and the Crocker Museum. Also gallery openings for local artists, the Help a Child Today Foundation. All the events are money and high-roll, the kind the best people patronize." Chandra put a spin on *best*. "No indigent elderly, homeless, poor, or drug addicts cluttering up this charitable scene. Ooops, I mean economically-deprived and chronologically-challenged, temporarily-undomiciled, financially-challenged, chemically-dependent and/or aligned."

I grinned. "You're swell, Chandra."

"Yeah. Like I said, thank goodness for computers. That do for now?"

"That'll do. Call you for lunch."

"Looking forward to it." The line went dead.

Chandra is not big on hellos and good-byes. She told me once that if you never said good-bye, you would never lose a person. I saw the loss in her eyes when she said it and then, quickly, it was gone and she laughed. Is it ever possible to leave the long-ago hurts behind? I had thought then, as I did now, of my little sister. The phone whined at me to *please hang up the receiver now.* I disconnected, then dialed again.

I struck out at home and at the office. I scored with the car phone. "Charity."

"Hi, Katy, what's new? Did you—"

"Update later, all right? I need your help."

"Okay, shoot."

"Roberta Heald. Do you know her? Have you heard of her?"

"No. Should I have?"

"Not should, but I thought you might. She's a player in social, charitable, and art circles." I rattled off names. "You are too, aren't you?"

"Sure. I don't get very involved but I do send money and lend them my name, so they love me. What's with Roberta Heald?"

"She's one of the names on Amanda's short list."

*"Shit! Nice use of the turn signal, pal. Just got out of driver training, huh?"* A horn blared. *"Go back for a refresher course!* Katy? Sorry about that. How can I help?"

"I want to talk to her. And I definitely don't want to get into Amanda's angle. Kiss of death there, judging from Heald's response to Amanda's letter and phone call."

"Hmmmm."

"Yes. Can you call her? Play up your name and position? Sling around references to the glitter names you know in the best circles, particularly art, music, and charity? Ask her, as a favor, to talk to me. Well, not to Kat, but to—" I paused to think of a plausible name.

"Claire. Claire La Lune," Charity decided. "What's her phone number?"

I gave her both home and work. "And Charity, Claire's okay but not La Lune for Pete's sake—"

She laughed. "It should appeal to her classical side. I'll get back to you." And she hung up. No good-bye. Like Chandra. Miss Manners, please note.

Ten minutes later, my phone rang.

"Damn, I'm good," Charity said.

No hello.

"Well, that's an exaggeration. As soon as Roberta Heald heard my name she fell all over herself. She's the kind of person who's impressed by fame and name. Bleaaah," said Charity, who is not that kind of person, and who then made a series of inspired rude noises to punctuate her point.

"She agreed to see you, no problem. Please dress up a bit for the interview, Katy. Be calm and stoic and reveal an occasional slice of wild sorrow. You know, a bit of distraught mourner. I told her you lost a child and needed someone to talk to."

I winced at the melodrama. Thank God Charity's got a ruthless editor.

"That's what'll work with her. I told her to expect you but not when. *Ooops!*" Brakes squealed and tires screeched and Charity screamed, *"Hey, your mother wears combat boots!* Life's such a crapshoot," Charity said cheerfully, presumably to me. "Keep me posted."

Another hang-up with no good-bye.

I disconnected and dialed Roberta Heald's home number. A child's voice answered.

"May I speak to your mom or dad, please?"

"I don't have a dad." He was matter-of-fact.

"May I speak to your mom then?"

"Okay," he said agreeably and thunked the phone down. "Mo-o-o-o-mmmm! Tele*phone!*"

While I waited I listened to a rhythmic thumping that sounded like a ball being bounced, and to a loud children's TV show with a lot of excited and enthusiastic voices and songs. It took mom a minute and a half to get to the phone, and she arrived out of breath.

"Yes? Hello?"

"Roberta Heald?"

"Yes."

I thought I heard disappointment in her voice. Mine wasn't the call she was expecting?

"This is Tri-Star Photography Studio and we have a family portrait special this month for only—"

"Oh. No, no thank you."

She hung up.

I changed my clothes, put on makeup and jewelry, even perfume —what I could find of the above commodities in the slim pickings at my house.

Then I picked up my car keys. Time to roll. I made pretty good time to Carmichael, though I wasn't paying a lot of attention driving over. I was rehearsing my lines—read: making up lies and stories. And working out a deeply affecting emotional appeal—read: Go for the heart, forget the mind. And trying to hit just the right note of pathos and sincerity—read: more lies and dissembling. It wasn't the sort of task that made me feel real good about myself or my job.

I pulled up in front of a stately edifice. Not a mansion exactly, but not Sears mail order either. A lot of masons, bricklayers and carpenters had once roughed up their hands here. There was special detailing in the wood trim, a slate roof, and stained glass and leaded work in many of the windows.

Summer flowers grew in wanton profusion in curved delicate weeded beds strewn around the house. Carnations, lobelia, dahlias and ordered and bordered roses were in full bloom. These were not ecstatic heavenly roses like Clem's but docile and obedient ones, blooming because it was summer and they had been placed there. I could hear the TV through the screened windows.

I took a deep breath, walked up the steps and rang, the bell.

"Mo-o-o-ommm." I heard a child's voice holler. "It's the do-o-or." Then the uneven thump of small sneakered feet, and the door swung open.

"Oh," the boy said, surprised. He looked about six, I thought— though I'm not great on children's ages—with an open, engaging face and smile. His skin was golden, his eyes big and brown. Straight brown hair tumbled over them like fringe and he pushed at it frequently in a reflexive action. His left leg was in a metal brace and he favored it.

"Who are *you*, anyway?" he demanded, looking up at me—his small hand on the doorknob still.

"My name is Claire." Lie number one. "Is your mommy here?"

"Yes. But who *are* you? Mo-o-o-ommm! Do you want to come in? I'm watching a movie. You can watch it with me."

I listened to him, appalled. "No, thank you. You mustn't invite people in if you don't know them," I said earnestly. "It's not safe. I mean *I'm* safe" (oh shit, lie number two. I wasn't a threat to the child, God knows, but I wasn't safe either) "but—"

"I know you," the child said reasonably. "Your name is Claire. It's a good movie. I can make popcorn, too. I do it in the microwave and it's easy. It has butter and everything. I like watching a movie with someone. I never do, though. Come on, *do.*"

"I'll wait here for your mom," I said primly.

He frowned. *"Mo-o-o-ommm!"* Nothing wrong with his lungs.

I heard the quick clatter of high heels, felt the rush of air and was ambushed by the scent of her perfume before I saw her.

"Teddy! Teddy, you're early and I wasn't dressed—" She sailed around a corner and skidded to a stop, as much as you can skid wearing high heels. I had the distinct impression she would have flung herself at Teddy. She glared at me. "You're not Ted."

No. Hard to argue with that one.

"She's Claire," the child announced. "She wants to watch TV with me and have popcorn *and* ice cream," he added hopefully, in case we were on a roll here. *"With* chocolate sauce and marshmallows."

"No." I shook my head. "I—"

"Never mind," she said. "He says that about everyone."

Looking at Roberta Heald, my heart tightened in sympathetic loneliness for the child. She was dressed in a short white dress with gold open-toed fuck-me sandals, gold jewelry and a glittery bag she now tossed carelessly on the hall table. I didn't think she was wearing panty hose and she didn't need to. Her skin was a deep, even, golden tan. Her tan shoulders set off the pure white of the dress; a thick gold bracelet was clasped on her slim upper arm.

Her hair was blond with dark roots. Straight, like her son's, it swung in long even waves just brushing her shoulders. She was stunning, although not beautiful. Had she left her hair its natural color she could have gone for the Cleopatra effect. Her gold earrings were large hoops, a snake biting its tail. A gold toe tapped suddenly, almost viciously.

"Well?" Her voice was as impatient as her toe. "Well!"

"Claire La Lune," I said, trying not to wince. Damn Charity anyway. "Charity Collins was in touch with you, was she not?" I put a polite look of inquiry on my face and held it there for a beat or two. "Have I got the time wrong? Perhaps this is not, after all, convenient . . . ?" Lies number three and four, the numbers still climbing.

"Oh." Her face cleared. "You're Claire, yes. Charity, of course. Such a *dear* person, we *do* go back."

About an hour and fifteen minutes. So I wasn't the only one lying. The boy tugged at his mother's dress in the gesture of a much younger child trying to get attention.

"Nicky, dear"—the words and sounds were sweet—"go watch TV and let Mommy—" He sniffled, she peered down at him. "Well," she said briskly to both of us, "let's go into the kitchen, shall we? I'll just make Nicky a snack before the baby-sitter comes. I'm going out soon. I must have misunderstood Charity or—" She looked at me.

Or I had. Or I was lying. *Or* was right on the nail in either case.

"Shall I come back at a more convenient time?"

I glided in a bit, closed the distance slightly. Nicky smiled at me and picked his nose. I smiled back and looked away, looked at mom. She swept the frown off her face, like a jock dismissing an idea, and *click-click*ed off to the kitchen, beckoning us to follow. Nicky trotted along, uneven but steady on his feet, fast. And grinning.

Roberta wordlessly pointed me in the direction of a stool at the built-in counter, then got down two wineglasses and yanked a bottle of Chardonnay out of the refrigerator. She cocked an eyebrow at me. I nodded. Lying is always easier with alcohol. I sipped white wine and watched her peer at the open refrigerator.

"What do you want, Nicky?"

"Pizza."

She closed the refrigerator and checked the freezer, took out a frozen pizza, placed it on the counter and turned on the oven.

"Well?" she asked me and dove back into the refrigerator, reemerging with raw carrots, celery, and a red apple.

"I want peas, please, Mom," Nicky piped up. "Peas please, peas please, please peas peas please please." He tugged at her skirt again.

Deftly she disengaged his hand, brushed at her white skirt, looked at me. "Well?"

"I'm sorry, I hope this isn't too personal." Up to about my fifth lie now, the numbers still climbing. "I lost my baby . . . Charity said that you . . . that you had had a similar experience. It's so hard. You know that, I know. It's just that how do you ever—" I looked at her helplessly. "How do you go on?" I picked up my wineglass, set it down, picked it up again and sipped.

"I had a little sister," Nicky said into thick heavy silence. "Her name was Emily. Like my gramma. We didn't lose her but I got lost once in a big store because I didn't mind my mommy." His bright eyes peeked at her through thick lashes. "Emily didn't get lost, she died. I miss Emily a lot. Where did you lose your little sister?"

Mom frowned. The golden toe tapped. "Nicky, go watch TV. Go *on*," she said to his reluctant *Mo-o-omm.*

"Can't I stay out here and . . . and visit?" Hard to miss the plaintive note in his voice.

"No," she said firmly. "Scoot. I'll call you when your dinner's ready." They'd had this discussion before. He'd lost before. He left with bad grace, sticking his tongue out at his mother's back to make up for the defeat.

I took another sip of wine. Liquid courage. "How did you get over it? It's so devastating."

It wasn't all lies. I hadn't lost a child but, like Nicky, a sibling. It was a long time ago, but my little sister and her death were with me still.

She fussed with the vegetables, cutting them up into child-sized portions. "I work a lot."

"What do you do?"

"I'm a broker."

"Stocks?"

"Yes. I do charity work, too. For the symphony, the Crocker Art Museum, for abused and neglected children. Free time is the most difficult time"—she shrugged tan shoulders—"so I fill it up."

I thought of Nicky alone in the family room with no one to share his movies and popcorn, his dinner and the memories of his sister. Charity evidently did not begin at home here.

"How did it happen? Is it all right if I ask? Do you mind?"

She frowned and looked away. "It was a heart problem."

"Oh. How sad. And I thought they could surgically correct almost everything these days. I know it's amazing what they can do . . ."

"Yes, that's true. Emily had three operations. We thought everything would be all right and then she died one night in her sleep. I . . ."

Roberta stood there with the frozen pizza in her hand, staring at it, at the floor. I don't think she was seeing either one.

"Just like that we lost her. I wasn't even worried. I didn't know that there was anything to worry about. I thought our worries were over. I didn't get to say good-bye. My baby girl . . ." She was silent for a heartbeat. Then she shook her golden head fiercely, stalked over to the oven and stuck the pizza in. She shut the oven door too hard and winced, then walked over to the sink and started peeling carrots.

"All the clichés are true." The peeler gouged deeply, relentlessly into the carrot. "Life goes on. You get over it. Sort of. People are cruel, though. I guess they don't mean to be, but they are. They say horrible things like *It was God's will* or *You're young, you can have another child.* As if another child could replace Emily. They even said *Maybe it's better this way.* How could it be better? Emily is *dead!*"

There were deep pools of black anger in her eyes.

"One woman kept after me and after me." There was despair in her voice. "She kept saying that something was wrong in the medical procedure, with the heart valve. She said over and over that I would let my baby die in vain if I didn't tell everything about it, that it would be my fault if—"

My heart was heavy. It sounded an awful lot like Amanda. Amanda, the avenging angel, the passionate, one-tracked, one-sided, obsessed avenging angel.

Roberta flung the peeler into the sink with violence and grabbed for her wine, drinking most of it in several desperate gulps. The eyes that looked at me finally were filled with anguish, with tears.

"I'm only human," she whispered. "I just wanted to cry for my baby—my Emily—my Emily." Her voice became a croon, the words a lullaby for the dead child. She put the wineglass down unsteadily, placed her hands on the counter, slipped out of her golden sandals, put her head down on her arms and wept in deep, almost soundless sobs. I stared at the delicate shoes, her vulnerable bare feet, her heaving shoulders.

"Roberta." I touched a shoulder gently.

"She didn't know, that woman, she hadn't lost a baby. How *dared* she? I couldn't do what she asked, I'm not perfect. I just needed to go on, not think about it all the time. It was tearing me apart and she was blaming me. She—"

The doorbell chimed.

"I'll get it, Mommy. It's Ted, it's Ted, it's Ted." Uneven running feet, excited voice, sounds of a door opening and closing and a male voice. "She's in the kitchen, Ted," Nicky said.

Roberta knocked over her wineglass as she straightened up. It shattered on the ceramic tile. We stared at each other.

"She's making my dinner." Nicky again.

Measured steps, steps with weight behind them. A big, heavy, double-chinned blond man walked into the kitchen. He was nice-looking in a way that money made the most of.

"Robbie?" he asked.

"She lost a baby too. We were just talking and I—" She broke off and stared at her knuckles.

Ted crossed the kitchen quickly and put his arms around her, kissed her, looked at me, then back to her. "Would you like to wash your face?" he asked in a tender voice. "I'll finish Nicky's dinner."

She nodded, then pulled out of his arms, started out of the kitchen, still barefoot. "I'm sorry," she said to me, "I meant to listen to you. I wanted to help you. Come back later if you wish." She reached out and brushed her cheek with mine, soft skin and perfume. "Thank you for listening to me." The words floated on a cloud of perfume toward me, then she slipped away. Quick footsteps ran up the stairs.

Ted spoke first.

"It's been a year but it's very hard for her. Still." It was hard on him too, I could see it, could hear it. "Emily was a wonderful child." He saw the question in my eyes and shook his head. "Not my child, no, but I loved Emily too. We all did." His voice was kind and gentle toward me but protective also of Roberta and her family.

The doorbell rang again.

"The baby-sitter," Ted said, and started to walk me out and welcome the sitter in. The girl at the door looked like someone who would watch TV and eat popcorn and sundaes with Nicky. I hoped so.

"Claire? Claire, could you please come upstairs for a moment?" Roberta's voice.

I put a foot on the heavy wooden staircase, a hand on the ornate carved banister. Ted stepped in front of me, body-blocked me. I raised my eyebrows. "It's her house," I reminded him politely.

He flushed, then stepped back. "Baby-sitter's here, Robbie," he called up the stairs.

"Okay." Her voice was musical and light. No tears, no mourning now. "Claire?"

"Yes," I answered. "Coming."

"In here," she trilled as I neared the top of the stairs. "In the bathroom."

The notes floated and bobbed around me like soap bubbles, iridescent in the sunshine. I caught a glimpse of a boy's bedroom, sports equipment, many toys and books; a guest room with a brass four-poster, a pristine white coverlet and a folded quilt in an early American pattern. The master bedroom was a symphony of pale and medium blues accented with lemon yellow and rose. Chinese rugs covered the hardwood floors. I could hear piano music in the background, cool, clean syncopated jazz.

I followed her voice into the master bathroom, white tile with gold faucets and fixtures and emerald green towels and accents. Lace curtains threaded with green covered the window. Sunlight spilled through the lace.

Roberta sat at a built-in vanity at least five feet in length. Her tanned face smiled at me from the large mirror ringed in lights that stretched the full length of the vanity.

"Tears," she said cheerfully. "They really do a job on your makeup, don't they?" The bubbling cheerfulness in her voice wasn't reflected in her face. She dabbed carefully at her eyes with a wash-cloth, opened them wide and surveyed them critically.

"I apologize," Roberta said, eyes on her reflection.

"You needn't."

She fumbled with makeup in expensive brushed gold containers. There was no Cover Girl, Maybelline, or Mary Kay in sight, trust me on this. She picked up a double strand of pearls, put them down, fingered a heavy gold necklace and earrings, pushed them aside. The top of the vanity was littered with jewelry, gold, pearls, emeralds, amethysts. It all looked real to me.

"They're beautiful," I said admiringly.

"Robbie?" Below, Ted sounded impatient. I swallowed my dislike of his attitude.

"I've been promising him an evening out for ever so long," Roberta told me, watching her face in the mirror, applying mascara carefully. "Just us two. It's so hard with children, finding a good baby-sitter and all." She squinted at her reflection, then added more blush.

"Robbie!"

"I wanted to talk to you, to help you, Claire. You know."

"It doesn't matter."

"It does."

"Later, then." I smiled. I liked her very much, even though I found her mercurial mood changes puzzling. There was something of a child—a little girl—in her still, I thought.

"Robbie!"

"Almost," she trilled.

I waved at her pretty reflection. In the mirror, she waved back.

"Later," Roberta said, making it a promise with her smile.

I slipped downstairs and outside. The door closed on me and Nicky calling to his baby-sitter, Ted laughing, and the TV. It was a happy family scene.

I walked to my car and thought harsh thoughts. I hadn't come with an open mind, I'd dragged along a lot of preconceptions, most of them of the garden variety unflattering kind. Roberta Heald's cool elegance and gold fuck-me shoes had buttressed those assumptions nicely, made me sure, even arrogant in my smugness. I climbed in the Bronco and rolled down the windows. There was a breeze now, the heat of the day behind us.

People dealt with grief in many ways. Lynda spouted clichés, Jude pounded dry wall into dust and tried to punch out windshields. Roberta had thrown herself into her work and charity endeavors. Nicky could probably have used more of his mother's attention but he was by no stretch of the imagination a neglected child. He had comforts and love.

Work and charity efforts. My mother drank herself to death and neglected my little sister, who died of pneumonia. I took a deep breath. Back to reality. It was time. I had been too quick to jump to conclusions, conclusions based on Amanda's naïve words, answers, and assumptions. Were they sacred now that she was dead? Of course not. Conclusions based on money, gold shoes and sophistication.

I was wrong.

The tears, the sorrow and the hurt had been real. So, too, was the offer to help me in the future. Roberta was well-dressed and rich, and she was nice, she was generous.

"Robbie?" a voice within the house called.

"Coming!" Her voice was lilting.

I started the Bronco, mad at myself and at Amanda. She had simplified things into black and white and I had bought right into it. I remembered the jumbo box of crayons we had as children, more colors than our fingers and toes. Life isn't black and white.

I was starting to hate this whole mess, and then I hated myself for hating it. The hate circle again. I tried to remember how Amanda had acted out of a sense of love, a sense of what was right. And that Jude and I loved Amanda.

But the hate was stronger.

# 30

Dear Charity,

When do the ends justify the means? Bad guys do bad things to get good guys, but then good guys do bad things to get bad guys. I don't get it. Is that ever OK?

Confused

Dear Con,

No, it's not really OK. Unfortunately hardly anyone plays by the rules these days. You are not the only one who is confused.

Charity

~~~~~~~~~~~~~~~~~~~~~~~~~~~~~~~~~~~~~~~~~~~~~~~~~~~

Ranger didn't greet me.

Huh?

I have a fenced-in yard and Ranger should be in it. I didn't see him. No barking either, though he would only bark briefly in greeting. He knows the sound of the car, of my step. I whistled and thought I heard a whimper.

Not Ranger, he doesn't whimper.

I headed for the backyard. It was Ranger. He was whimpering; there wasn't a whole lot else he could do and thank God he could do that. I dropped everything in my hands and ran. He was on a choke chain tied to a rope and strung up on the rope to a tree limb. No slack. The dog's head was up in the air, his neck out straight. He was on his toes. When he collapsed in exhaustion, he would strangle. It was close now. He wobbled as I ran, then fell, tried to scramble back up on his feet, moaned deep in his throat.

Sixty-three and a half pounds of dog, and I picked him up. First try. Had that chain off in a second. I carried the dog, staggering slightly, to the house. The back door was unlocked, as it often is. Ordinarily no one can get past Ranger. He was licking my face, wagging his tail feebly and making happy dog noises. Understandable. I put him on the floor. He struggled to get up as I filled the water bowl with fresh water. I went back out, shutting the door behind me.

The kitten was still unaccounted for, that's why. I don't ever worry about him either. To get to him someone, something, would have to get past Ranger. Not likely. Not ordinarily.

I found the kitten after checking all his favorite hiding and play spots. This spot was a new one to me. He was tucked into an over-turned clay pot with dirt on his head, cobwebs in his whiskers and fear in his eyes. How long had he been listening to Ranger cry and struggle to stay on his feet, to stay alive? He squeaked as I approached and scrambled out, tripping over a dirt clod.

Ranger wouldn't eat, although he drank a bathtub or so of fresh water. I ran my fingers over his body, found a hard lump on his side that was tender to my touch. A tranquilizer dart? Or was that only in the zoo, on PBS nature specials and in bad movies? I'd call the vet tomorrow and ask. Kitten ate enough for a growing family of four, washed his face, licked Ranger's nose for a while, then stretched and curled up in the curve of the dog's belly, purring deep in his little body.

I sat on the floor with them and thought how easily it could have gone the other way. Then I brought the phone down on the floor with us and called Charity, who else? I take her all my waifs.

"I am bringing Ranger and Kitty out to the ranch tomorrow."

"Okay, why?"

I told her and waited for the explosion. Not a long wait. Ten minutes later she finished thinking it through.

"Kat, you come too. If it's not safe enough there for the animals, it sure as all git out isn't safe enough for you."

No. Maybe not. Of course Ranger wasn't expecting the unexpected and couldn't handle a .380. I was and could. That kind of detail evened out the odds. The kitten stretched lazily and sleepily batted a paw at Ranger. I said good-bye to Charity and went outside to look for the choke chain. Not that I thought checking it out was likely to get me anywhere—they were as common as dirt. It wasn't mine—I wouldn't put one on an animal.

I couldn't see a thing. The moon wasn't out yet and the yard light wasn't on. The light was a mercury-vapor lamp, common enough in rural areas and on farms. A photoelectric cell automatically tripped the light at dusk and cut it at dawn. We were way past dusk. I didn't think it was the bulb, but I got a flashlight and checked. It was and it wasn't. One of those things. It had been shot out, small caliber, I thought. I got a ladder, replaced the bulb, then found the choke chain. It told me nothing, but I tossed it in the garden shed along with the shot-up bulb.

It is not clear to me what kind of a sicko will harm animals to get a message to people, but the fact that this was a message was very clear. Whose message? Did this incident and the ones at the Hudson farm have the same source? That was probably close to both a working assumption and a certainty.

I wanted to be doing something, so I called Jack's office and left a message on the machine asking if he could please fit me into tomorrow's schedule. Jack is an attorney who handles personal injury and public-hazard lawsuits.

Then I called Shelley Garner. According to the copy of the Louden newsletter I had filched from DeVito's office, Garner was the editor. She was in. Swell. I jumped on the situation, madder than I was tactful. So I wasn't subtle, I just hit her with it. Call it the pie-in-the-face approach of investigative technique.

"Ms. Garner, Kat Colorado. I've been around the plant on several occasions looking into the circumstances of Amanda Hudson's death. Perhaps you heard that?"

"Yes," she said. *Who cares?* She didn't say it but it was there.

"I want your help."

"So?"

Translation: *People in hell want ice water, the drowning want a life preserver, and a starving person wants a cheeseburger, large fries, and a Coke but what's it to me? Nothing. Not a thing.* Translation: *Fuck you.*

"You have information I need."

"So? I'm busy now. See ya."

"And I have information you don't want out." Silence. I waited her out. I had guilt and fear going for me. She would bite. They always do.

"What?" The hard edge was gone, her voice had a querulous waver in it.

"Mark DeVito, the Paradise Inn, the Apple Tree, Best Western. Shall I go on?"

"Well, *shit!* How do you—? I mean . . . I mean, I did not!"

But she had. I had the company newsletter. Mark DeVito's photo was in it as company manager; Shelley Garner's photo was at the head of her news and gossip column. I'd taken the newsletter around to several of the motels near the Paradise Inn cocktail lounge. It was the cocktail napkin with the lipstick smear from the Paradise Inn that got me started. Not only *had* she, they were regulars. I'd gotten confirmation on that from three sources.

"I did *not,*" she repeated, trying to beat up truth with denial. "I did *not!*"

"Great bluff, Shelley."

"Go to hell!"

"I'm an investigator. Finding out this kind of thing is what I do."

"Well, shit!"

Exactly.

"What do you want?"

"To talk to you."

Long silence. There weren't a lot of choices here and she knew it. "Would you tell?"

"Yes."

That was a lie. Probably. Tell who? Who would care? Half the world, though not my half, I hoped, seemed to slip around these days. Of course there was Amanda and she was in my half so maybe it was all of us? My heart tightened up. Not me. Not Hank—

"You're a shit."

First a sneak, now a blackmailer. Yeah, I was; Shelley was right. I thought about Amanda and the jolt of electricity that had killed her. I was now well into ends-justifying-means territory, a dangerous place, as I know from experience. I was a shit, but one who cared about Amanda. If Shelley was this scared about what I'd said, there had to be more. So I'd play on that too. I was a shit, yeah.

"I want to talk to you. Tonight. I'll meet you wherever you say."

She didn't say anything for a while and when she spoke it was sullen. "You'll have to come to the house. I got a sick kid and I can't get a baby-sitter."

"Where?"

She gave me an address in Roseville.

"Thirty minutes."

"No, I—"

"Forty-five," I said in the spirit of compromise. I hung up, let Ranger out, then put him back in the house, closed most of the windows, turned on the cooler and all the fans in the house that weren't on, locked the doors. I grabbed a flashlight and walked my place, looking for anything or anybody wrong. Okay. So far.

I took my time getting there, parked down the street from Shelley's house, got out to walk it. It was an older area of Roseville. Most of the houses were two- or three-bedroom homes built back in the days when Roseville was a railroad town. There are houses, many of them, built on Southern Pacific railroad ties with wooden walls that had been the insides of boxcars. The houses were, mostly, neat and well-kept with small but carefully tended yards. The streets were quiet now, the raw power and drive of a growing and voracious railroad town dead long ago.

You could still hear the trains occasionally but not often. You could still find that unpolished eagerness, the surge of joy and rush to build, to succeed and grow, but mostly in the old photographs, photographs in the museums or historical records or in the old railroad bars like the West House. Not in the new faces. Roseville isn't a railroad town anymore. It's a bedroom community for Sacramento.

A kid walking a dog sauntered by me snapping his gum. The spell of the old days was long broken, the gum snapped me to attention. I walked around the block and back to Shelley's house.

It was shabbier than most of her neighbors', in need of painting and basic carpentry. A tricycle was tipped over on the front lawn, a red balloon still tied to its handle but deflated and dead on the dried-out patchy Bermuda grass lawn. A dog was barking hoarsely inside as if he'd been barking for days without stopping and the porch light automatically flicked on as I walked up two steps. A hand pulled back dirty white or beige net curtains in the door and Shelley Garner stared at me, unwelcoming, unsmiling. Who could blame her?

I didn't recognize her immediately. She seemed perkier in the Louden corporate photo I had. She didn't recognize me at all. I held a business card up to the glass panel in the door.

She glanced at it, opened up.

The inside of the house was not a surprise. It matched the outside—shabby overstuffed furniture, kids' toys tossed around, the lingering smell of greasy hamburgers and that indefinable but definite something that tells you that small children and animals are in residence.

We faced each other across a coffee table cluttered with a mass of Tinkertoys and scattered crayons. The dog was old and a little mangy. He had stopped barking and scratched fleas disconsolately on the floor at Shelley's feet.

I led with a hard right. "A woman died, Shelley. Was murdered.

I'm sorry about this invasion of your privacy but murder excuses a lot." I softened it. "Even if, to your mind, it doesn't justify it."

The expression on her face lightened, though not by much. "Sit down."

I sat on the couch—the cushions had been a lot springier in the Eisenhower Administration—narrowly missing a half-eaten Hoho which I retrieved and put on the coffee table.

"Would you like something? Lemonade?"

I looked at the coffee table, the Hoho, a tipped-over Coke can, a coffee cup with cigarette butts floating in dregs and a crumbled graham cracker.

"No, thanks."

She sat in a chair opposite me, her shorts and T-shirt a wrinkled cotton that had faded with repeated washings. Her legs were crossed and a scuffed sandal dangled from one foot. Her toenails were painted and the polish chipped. There was a charm bracelet on her left wrist. "You want something from me, and if you get it you won't tell. Is that it?"

"That's it." Or almost. I might not have the heart to tell even if I didn't get the information. I was talking tough on a maybe empty bluff. But maybe not. "Why are you so afraid of it coming out? Surely—"

"It's not such a big deal?" She finished the sentence for me, making it a question.

I shrugged.

"It's not that simple. It's his wife. You see, she doesn't understand Mark. He doesn't love her but he has to stay for now, for the family's sake. He's waiting for the right time and then he'll tell her, he'll leave her and we can be together, we can get married. If she found out now she'd be really upset. She'd make the divorce hard, take Mark to the cleaners. I don't know why else she'd fight it. She doesn't love him. They never even have sex."

I looked at Shelley's face, open and trusting, though her demeanor was still tinged with the sullen. She believes it, I thought, all of it. Hook, line and sinker.

"What's your job?"

"Office manager."

Often a corporate euphemism for secretary. "DeVito has a secretary."

"Yes. Gloria handles Mark's immediate business and letters. I coordinate everything throughout the plant, oversee it, make sure it gets to the right place, gets handled, that sort of thing."

"Everything goes through you?"

"Pretty much and generally twice, coming and going." Her face had relaxed now. She was on sure ground and speaking of something she knew well, did well. She was almost vivacious, almost smiling. I could see where she would be pretty.

"I want access to the files on out-of-court settlements, product liability, company strategies and related activities."

Her face went white and pinched up. Fear.

"Shit!"

Her vocabulary needed work. No kidding.

"You're not supposed to know this. How did you? I can't, I *can't can't can't*," she wailed. In the back of the house somewhere a child cried briefly, sleepily, then abruptly stopped. "I can't," she whispered.

I shrugged. Heartless. Hard as nails.

"Please."

"Make copies of everything. You have two days."

"No." The despair was heavy in her voice. "Someone would see. It's impossible, *absolutely* impossible. Even if you tell . . . I can't do it. Besides, none of that stuff is at the plant."

"Where is it?"

"I don't know."

Something flickered in her eyes. She looked at me quickly and then began picking at a scab on her sunburned knee. She was lying. Her eyes flicked up at me to see if I was buying it. Then she dashed recklessly into the silence.

"All that kind of stuff would be at corporate headquarters. In Texas. We're just a branch office, shipping and receiving. We wouldn't handle product liability or strategy or legal. We *wouldn't*. Corporate would. Does. *Sorry."*

She shrugged her shoulders slightly, lifting her hands in an I-can't-help-you-there gesture. Her eyes slid around again. She was lying or there was more to it. Something.

"That it?" There was relief in her voice. It was lighter, happier. I shook my head. It had clicked in now.

"No? What?" She picked off the rest of the scab and tossed it on the rug. Going barefoot in this house would be a definite health hazard.

"Paul Lowell."

"Uh . . . wha . . . what? Who?" She stuttered it out.

Lowell's photo had been in the newsletter too, along with a chatty piece identifying him as an executive from corporate headquarters, here for the purpose of doing the "annual plant evaluation." All employees were instructed to cooperate fully with Mr. Lowell. His title was not given. The areas of interest or evaluation were not specified.

"What are you talking about?" Shelley's voice was tight and nervous again.

"Corporate sent Lowell out. Why? Assessment, damage control, cleanup?" All of the above?

"I don't know." She was stuttering again.

"What's his title?"

"I don't know."

"Shelley!" There was a threat in my tone, no question.

"Corporate counsel," she said sulkily.

Bingo.

"Does he have an office at the plant?"

"No-o-o-o. No. He uses Mark's whenever he wants to, needs to."

"Does he keep records, files, papers there?"

"I don't know."

Probably not. He was looking into the situation, the problem. The answers and policy would come from him or higher up. I doubted

Lowell would leave his accounts around the plant, allowing others access to them. I sighed. It had to be checked out, though.

"Where's he staying?"

"Who-o-o?"

"Pay attention, Shelley. We're still talking about Paul Lowell, not the Easter Bunny, not the Tooth Fairy."

"I d-don't know."

I snorted.

"Oh, all *right*. At the Madison."

"The Madison?"

"Off Highway Fifty not far from the Sheraton."

"Sunrise exit in Rancho Cordova?"

"I guess."

"I want access to DeVito's office, the file cabinets, everything."

Shelley sucked in her breath with a sharp hiss. "I *can't. Really.* I just *can't.*" She wrapped her arms around herself in a protective hug.

"Sometimes things get accidentally left out overnight. No harm done and nothing missing, though naturally you would want to put it all away first thing in the morning."

Shelley thought that over. "Yes," she said. "All right. And that's all? You won't ask me to— You won't ask anything else of me?"

"No. I'll call you and tell you what night. Then you leave the files open and the copy machine on. I need Lowell's phone number and room number at the hotel, too. That's it, that's all."

"All right." Some of her natural color was back, the pinch of fear easing.

"Shelley, he won't ever do it." I stood, narrowly missing a crayon and an Oreo already ground into the carpet.

"Who? What?"

"DeVito. Married men say those things, they don't do them. He won't tell her, he won't leave, he won't marry you. They never do."

Her face went white and pinched in instant replay.

I let myself out.

# 31

Dear Charity,

What do you think takes the most courage: bungee jumping, high-speed auto racing, Russian roulette or facing a firing squad?

Daredevil Danny

Dear D.D.,

Please. All those are a piece of cake compared to living life honestly and well.

Charity

~~~~~~~~~~~~~~~~~~~~~~~~~~~~~~~~~~~~~~~~~~~~~~~~~

I woke up with a bad taste in my mouth and an emotional hangover. This investigation, more than any I could remember, was full of ugliness. The nastiness at the Hudsons', Buck and his boys, the events at the Louden plant. I was an ever-increasing part of it—lying to Roberta, bullying Shelley—and the nastiness was coming to me.

I got up. Wallowing in ugliness, recrimination and regret was not as appealing as a hot shower, juice and caffeine. Wet and yawning with Ranger—slow-moving but better—at my heels, I walked out onto the front porch to start my morning search for the paper. I have never met my carrier. He comes and goes in the dark of the early morning, but his approach to paper placement is creative. It hits the porch twice a month, tops, the rest of the time it's a hunt. Maybe he's from a broken home.

Ranger started growling, hackles up, tail out. This growl is his meanest sound. It didn't seem to be directed in any particular direction but it was there. Still only half-awake, I sat down on the porch step and looked around.

Like that day at Amanda's house, it took me a moment to take it in.

*What's wrong with this picture?*

*Can you fix it?*

Some of it I couldn't fix. Not the ceramic planter which had held a Martha Washington geranium that was smashed on the edge of the lawn. I'm not wild about geraniums, but still. Not the hose that was neatly severed, then just as neatly coiled back in place. Not the marigolds that had been pulled out by the roots, then laid in tidy wilting rows. Not the cheap plastic outdoor thermometer that had been snapped in half.

The dog growled, the kitten tried to scramble in my lap. I stood, saw that there were more things wrong on the edges of this picture. Surprise, surprise. Landscaping rocks had been moved and a trowel I had carelessly left out had been stabbed into a flower bed. I found cigarette butts, a crumpled beer can and the empty plastic wrapper for a bag of salted peanuts.

It was a deliberate, ordered viciousness, a quiet, mincing menace. It was silent, sneaky, sly moves in the dark. I hadn't heard. No surprise there. Ranger hadn't either, still in a heavy, exhausted place from yesterday's ugly experience.

*While you slept, while you thought you were safe and secure, I was here. Back off. I could come again. I could get you any time.* I stooped to pick up the wilted geranium. *I could smash you just like this.* The message was clear.

The feeling started dancing in the pit of my stomach, high-heeled shoes with sharp-pointed toes punching at me from the inside. I was getting closer. I was also getting mad. No, madder. I ate, dropped the animals off at Charity's ranch and headed downtown.

I never did find the paper.


Jack has an office in a high-rise on Capitol Mall, a building that proclaims *Money! Success!* in a loud, clear, tastefully well-modulated tone. The murmur of possible pretense and lies is there too, but it's muted in the presence of such conspicuous consumption and indulgence. Fountains, mosaics, elegant furniture, veldt-like carpeting and original, nonrepresentational art abounded there in the lobby. The elevator glided up to the fifth floor, taking me with it. The language spoken on the fifth floor was also money. This is undoubtedly why lawyer jokes are so popular. Bottom line, we know where all this money comes from: our pockets.

I passed several law offices before arriving at Jack's. He is an executive partner in his firm, successful, hardworking and well-off. And—keeping in mind that he is a lawyer—honest. We go back a number of years. Jack is one of the few lawyers I'll work for; I'm one of the few private investigators he'll call.

His secretary—wearing three months of wages in knock-off couturier—greeted me with a smile, showed me in. I threaded my way past lush ficuses and an aggressive palm that swiped at me as I slipped past.

"Yo, Jack."

"Katy, how are you?" He came out from behind his quarter-acre desk to hug me.

"Puzzled, but well. How's Holly?"

His handsome face clouded over, the lines and wrinkles suddenly more prominent. Jack and Holly have been married for over twenty years; four or five years ago she was diagnosed with MS. "Good. She'll be happy to hear news of you. Pepsi?" It was nine-thirty but Jack is a cold caffeine addict.

I nodded. Me too. We settled down to sodas and business.

"What's up, Kat?"

"I'm working an investigation that involves a defective medical device. There are a number of settlements to victims, some of them considerable, I suspect, and all of them in out-of-court agreements with secrecy as a condition. My angle concerns a whistle-blower trying to pull this out of the closet and make it public information and a public concern."

"Should I ask for specifics?"

"Not yet."

He nodded, pressing his fingertips together.

"There have been threats involved, both verbal and physical. There is no question that the threats are connected with this, although that of course will be tough to prove. Harassment too. Some minor, some major." Like murder. Murder was major. "I need an understanding of what goes on here from a legal standpoint."

"The big picture?"

I nodded. I love the way Jack will talk about legal issues in English and without condescension.

"The history on this is long and growing. A number of cases have come to public attention: General Motors fuel tanks, Bic lighters, Pfizer heart valves, Dow Corning silicone breast implants that leak, widely prescribed painkillers causing life-threatening allergic reactions, faulty Pap smears. That's unfortunately just a partial list." He sipped on his Pepsi, then leaned back in his chair, making it creak slightly as he rocked it.

"Many companies have chosen to settle claims confidentially. There are, from a corporate point of view, a number of advantages to this. It gets that particular monkey off the company's back; it does not draw attention to an allegedly defective product or public hazard; it's cost-effective."

"It's cheaper to settle than correct the defective product?"

"Yes, or at least as long as the numbers, number of cases and dollar amounts, stay small. That's where the secrecy, the confidential agreements come in. Because of this secrecy, information is greatly restricted. Other victims, consumers, and potential victims are—and

257

the company hopes they will remain—unaware, uninformed of the hazards."

"And the defective product?"

"Does it stay on the market, you mean?"

"Yes."

"Frequently. In some cases a decision is made to pull or revise a faulty product. In many cases, probably most, no such decision is made until, or unless, there is public disclosure, *60 Minutes*, say, and public outcry. Then the product is no longer cost-effective, so it gets modified or scrapped. Also, the perception on the part of the public of blatant corporate callousness can be extremely damaging to a company, to other corporate products and services, and so on."

"How does disclosure come about?"

"Many times through just the process you mentioned, a concerned citizen or worker, someone willing to blow the lid off a cover-up."

"Does that work?"

"Sometimes." He nodded. "Especially if the whistle-blower can get media attention, involvement and commitment. The answer to your question also depends on what you mean by work."

"On the one hand there aren't any more exploding Pinto gas tanks, and on the other Karen Silkwood is dead?"

"Yes."

*And Amanda Hudson.*

"At what point does a whistle-blower come to a lawyer?"

"Frequently they don't."

Astonishment must have registered on my face.

"Surprised? Whistle-blowers tend to be idealistic, to have a strong sense of what is right. Or wrong. They believe in justice and they usually believe, somewhat naïvely, that justice will be done if only they can call the attention of the appropriate person to the problem. These people don't generally consult attorneys. If they do, it's not until much later in the game. Not until they lose, or are faced with the loss of their job, or become victims of intimidation and harassment."

"Does that happen often?"

"Loss of job, intimidation and harassment? Yes."

"And the victims—do they understand what's involved in a confidential agreement?"

"It's spelled out quite clearly. Terms of the settlement restrict communications regarding, let's say, the defect, the product history, the amount of settlement and so on."

"How could anyone make that choice, enter into such an agreement?"

My voice sounded harsh and angry. *Anyone* of course included Jack as the attorney representing a client. He'd walk away with a hefty percentage of that silencing settlement as a fee.

"It's not that simple, Kat."

It wasn't, no; it never is. And it's all too easy to judge from the outside.

"Plaintifs must choose between their individual interest and the public good. That can be a terrible choice."

I thought it over, thought that sometimes the choice must be a foregone conclusion. "If the primary provider dies and the family is struggling to survive there might be very little choice?"

"Exactly. If you are desperate to feed your family, pay your bills —often huge medical bills—and to find the space to grieve and the courage to go on, it is difficult, or even impossible, to make the general public interest your personal and immediate priority."

Yes.

"And that, too, can become a burden. They know, signing the agreement, that this is information the public should have, information that would save lives."

"Information they can't share, things they can't say."

"Yes. There is no question that the enormity of the problem has been obscured by secret court settlements. None at all. The issue is a tough one: Where do you draw the line between private rights and the public interest?"

"Are you familiar with the Sunshine in the Courts bill?"

"Yes."

"And?"

"Do I favor it? Absolutely. The legislation would protect individual rights; it would protect the public; it would protect legitimate corporate trade secrets. It also removes from the victim that unspeakable burden of choosing between what is best or even essential for them in the present, and what is best for everyone in the long run."

A picture—the picture?—was becoming more and more clear in my mind. "Tell me what this process does to an individual."

Jack looked at me steadily. "I'll do better than that, Kat. I'll introduce you to a friend of ours. Holly met Jeanette last year in a workshop on grieving and coping. Holly was trying to come to terms with the MS and Jeanette with her loss. You free for lunch?" I nodded. "Let me see if I can set it up." He reached for the phone, spoke briefly, then turned back to me. "Not lunch, but Jeanette will meet you in the lobby of the Crocker at five-fifteen, okay?"

"Yes."

He confirmed it, said good-bye into the phone and hung up. Then he glanced at his watch. "I've got another appointment waiting. Call me if I can help with anything else."

"Yes. Thank you. I know someone who should go to a workshop like the one Holly went to."

"She leads them now." He smiled, love and pride in his eyes. "Call her anytime."


Crocker is Sacramento's art museum on 3rd and O. It's not far from Old Sacramento, and the former home of one of Sacramento and California's prominent and pioneering families. Judge Edwin Crocker made his money as legal counsel for the Central Pacific Railroad. He was a great art lover and collector and amassed a collection of seven hundred paintings, one of the largest private collections in the country at that time. After his death, his wife Margaret emerged as a civic and social leader and philanthropist. In 1885 she presented the Crocker Art Gallery and the majority of the collection to the city of Sacramento, a gift of that pride and heritage, that California pioneer spirit, to the city she and her late husband loved.

I stood in the entryway of the Crockers' former home, a magnificent Victorian masterpiece. The floor was tiled in earth brown, tan and gray mosaic. Magnificently carved banisters and stairways curved up to the second floor. On the stairway above nail-studded copper treads were statues in clear cold clean marble and paintings that were framed and grandiose flights of artistic imagination. Ahead I could see the ballroom with its ornately carved ceilings and moldings. Trompe l'oeil, arches, columns and pilasters, rosettes and palmettes beckoned to me.

I was a few minutes early but Jeanette was right on time. She was younger than I had expected, mid-twenties with about fourteen pounds of glorious, curling chestnut hair rioting down her back. The sides were caught up in combs, opening up her face with its beautiful hazel eyes, heavy thick lashes. She wore no jewelry and she didn't need it. A straight delicate nose slid attention away from her lovely eyes and toward a mouth and smile that the Mona Lisa couldn't match. It was enough to tear your heart out.

"Kat Colorado?" She walked toward me and, when I acknowledged it, held out her hand, took mine in a cool firm grip. We walked past the desk, Jeanette holding up a membership card that looked worn and tattered but admitted us both without difficulty.

"You know my story?" It was more of a statement than a question.

"No. Nothing. I don't even know your last name."

She laughed. Her laughter was as rich and warm and lush as biscuits hot out of the oven dripping with butter and jam and whipped cream for extra.

"I hope you don't mind meeting here. I come to the museum all the time." She gripped her hands together tightly, looked at them, then back at me. "I felt so dead and ugly inside for a long time and this was the only thing, the only place that helped. I tried going to parks and the zoo but I couldn't bear the life and the beauty all happening, growing, changing there. The beauty and life is here too. But here it's —it's frozen in time. Somehow, I can bear it here."

She smiled vividly at me as if to make up for the darkness of her

261

words, and I felt the sadness at the back of her heart and maybe mine soon, too. We walked to the left, past the Crocker family gallery room, furnished as it had been when they lived here, now roped off, past the heaviness and solemnity of nineteenth-century German paintings, then upstairs.

"I'll tell you my story, Kat, shall I? I tell it all the time to try to help others, and I know that's why you're here."

She had, I thought, told her story so many times now that she could keep the pain and tears out, at bay somewhere. Upstairs we walked past the sculpture gallery, statues of human figures looking tortured and alienated—one headless, one with something indescribable and rectangular where its head should have been—then into the gallery over the ballroom. American landscapes—Yosemite Valley, Soda Springs and the Sierra Nevada Mountains. Jeanette walked to a bench and sat. I followed.

"I was twenty-three when it started, discomfort and pain— woman's problems. I went to my doctor many times. He did all the tests and they all came back normal. Later," she said, her eyes dark, "you think: Oh, why didn't I get a second opinion? I didn't. I trusted him. He said that some girls had these problems and that my emotional response was just making it worse. I believed him."

Someone walked into the room where we sat, looked at Jeanette, at her dark eyes, unsmiling mouth and pain, and walked out again. Anyone would have.

"One day, waiting to get my hair cut, I was reading an article in a magazine. The symptoms described in the article were my symptoms. Exactly. The article was about cervical cancer. Then"—bitterness— "then I went to another doctor and got a second, even third opinion. The pap smears did not come back normal. How could they? I had an advanced case of cervical cancer. I had to have a radical hysterectomy. And I'm lucky, I'm alive with no recurrence of cancer."

She took a deep breath. Her fingers were playing and fidgeting like little wild things in the folds of her multicolored cotton skirt.

"It turned out," she said, "that particular lab had a big problem with inaccuracies in pap smears." Then: "It turned out that my doctor was part owner of the lab."

I looked at Yosemite instead of the pain in her eyes.

"I have a boyfriend now, though I didn't at the time. We talk about marriage. We talk about children, too, because we both love children. It's very hard to know that you can never have a child of your own. Sometimes I can't bear it when I see a pregnant woman or a baby. I want to tell them how lucky, how blessed they are, how they must never, never take it for granted."

I looked at this woman who was heart-stoppingly beautiful, who had genes that begged to be passed on. Beautiful or looking like twelve miles of bad road, the choice should have been hers. Should have been and wasn't.

"I took it for granted."

"We all do sometimes. You were young, healthy and under a doctor's regular care."

"Yes. That should have been enough but it wasn't. If they had caught it at the beginning, with the first symptoms, I could still have . . ." She left her sentence unfinished.

Later I asked her: "Did you file suit?"

She nodded. "I wanted them to pay. Even though I knew that no amount of money would be enough, that no price could be set on what I had lost."

"And you won?"

She shook her head. "Yes," she said, and then "no" and nodded. There was confusion here, in her actions, in her mind.

"We settled out of court. At first I thought that I'd won. Then I realized that I'd lost. Again. Only this time it was different. I wasn't just hating someone else. I hated *me*."

I wanted to say something, but I caught her eye and didn't, couldn't. Not yet.

# 32

Dear Charity,

I was brought up to believe that you should always do what is right and speak out against what is wrong. I was too afraid to do that. Now I can't sleep.

Tossing And Turning

Dear Tossing,

You had the courage to recognize the truth; maybe next time you will have the courage to speak out. Try warm milk at bedtime.

Charity

~~~~~~~~~~~~~~~~~~~~~~~~~~~~~~~~~~~~~~~~~~~

"Why?"

"Oh." She smiled, but with her mouth, not her eyes. "Well, that's simple. They paid me a ton of money to settle and I thought I'd gotten to them, gotten back at them. But really I just became another cog in their wheel. An expensive cog, granted, but the way I settled made it possible for my doctor and others like him to keep on doing exactly what they had been doing. I helped make it possible for more women to be misdiagnosed like I was. Some of them will have cancer; some of them will have to have hysterectomies; some will die."

She was a small woman, five feet three or four. She was dragging
a lot of baggage around.

"Kat, what did they call the Jews who cooperated with Nazis?
Collaborators? I am a collaborator."

"You are too hard on yourself."

"Am I?"

The words were soft, the question hard.

"You were very young."

"Yes. You're right. I was. I've thought of all the reasons I can to
excuse myself. Shall I tell you?" Her eyes glittered and her hands
were restless and wild.

"I was only twenty-three. I'd been through an operation that was
traumatic physically and emotionally. I'd lost my job because you
can't work for months after an operation like that. I had no job, plenty
of bills, no savings. It was a lot of money. I wasn't hurting anyone.
You're only responsible for yourself. The case had dragged on into the
third year when I finally settled, and I was exhausted. I desperately
wanted it to be behind me. I wanted to get on with my life. I felt I had
no choice." She paused for breath. "But that's wrong."

"All the reasons you gave are correct, are good reasons. Even if
they weren't, even if they were wrong, even if you made a mistake, you
must not hate yourself."

True. And easy for me to say.

"You do see how easy it is for you to say, don't you?" She asked
reasonably, but there was anger there, hatred.

I answered it. "I killed a man once. I shot him in self-defense
before he could kill me. You do what you have to do and then you live
with it." I met her eyes, wide now, different now.

"Oh . . . Well, you know, then." Her hands fell to her sides.

"Yes." I knew. We looked at each other in silence.

She broke it. "Now I wish desperately that I hadn't settled. I wish
I had fought it out. Especially I wish that I hadn't agreed to secrecy. I
don't want to be part of their ugly secret, but I am."

"You can work against it in other ways."

"I know. I do. It helps. But I still have regrets."

"It's a difficult process, and I imagine that they made it as difficult as possible on you."

"They went out of their way, I think, to make it bad. The questions. The depositions. There is some connection with cervical cancer and sexual patterns. So what? The point is not how or why I got cancer, but that I had it and they repeatedly misdiagnosed the lab test. But they didn't focus on that.

"Instead it was: How many sexual partners did you have? When? How often? What did you do? Describe your actions please. More, please. More. More . . . It was always men asking, too.

"They call it discovery, but what they really wanted to do was to embarrass and humiliate me, to degrade me, wear me down and make me give up. They were always very polite, very formal, very careful never to harass me in any legally liable way. Nevertheless, I believe that was their intention. And it worked."

"It worked for a while," I said. "It's not working now."

"Cemeteries and museums." She spoke with the same awful smile. "No one talks, no one judges, no one cares."

"Except you."

"Yes." The pain chased across her face. "Except me. I'm trying to get over it."

"To live in the present instead of the past?"

"Yes. Why do you say that?"

"After I killed, I played the scene over and over again in my mind. What if I had done this? Or said that? Or thought of the other? What if? I woke on it. I ate, drank, lived, slept on it. What if? It almost got me."

"But it didn't?"

"No."

"How?"

I thought for a moment before I answered her. "I accepted what was, including the kind of person he was, and his actions as well as mine. I accepted that I couldn't change his death and my part in it and that I had done the absolute best I could. Then I made a decision to live in the present, not the past, not what if."

"Do you have what you came for?" Her voice was harsh, not matching the tears in her eyes.

"Yes. Thank you."

"I wanted to kill someone, you know—only who?—and where to put the blame? For a while I thought I'd kill myself."

"And now?"

"Now . . . I don't know. May I call you sometime?"

"Yes." I gave her my card.

"Maybe the zoo," she said softly.

I left her there on the bench staring into painted eyes that didn't see or care. I turned at the door and watched her for a moment. She didn't move, didn't turn. Still lost.


I called Jack when I got back to the office. "One question," I said, "I forgot."

"Shoot."

"How do you feel settling a case?"

"You want the best for your client, Kat, a client who is often desperate and injured, broke and exhausted. It's very gratifying to get a good settlement for them. It's a good feeling. I'm representing a person, remember that, not an abstract public interest."

A cartoon figure of a pathetic waif looking like the little match girl of the fairy tale and labeled "public interest" drifted through my mind. "Yes, I understand." I let the remark dangle.

The silence lasted so long I wondered if Jack would break it.

"It's seductive, Kat. All my training is in getting to the bottom of things, discovering the facts, discerning the truth, and here they are offering it to you. All that information is yours and all you have to do is agree not to tell what they've done. What you've done. Incredibly seductive. It's like sleeping with a woman because she's beautiful, irresistible, sexy. It makes sense to you at the time, but afterwards . . . in the morning . . . in the light of a new day, the questions start."

Afterwards, questions, seduction. They rarely come in that order.

267

"Thanks, Jack."

"All right," he said, sounding a little mad, and hung up. Mad at me maybe because I had made him mad at himself. Another angry person in this case.

Swell.

What was the score now? Jude, Clem, Buck and the boys at the plant, plant management, Roberta, Jeanette, Jack, even me. Our reasons differed but the emotion was the same. And anger was one of the reasons people killed.

It was almost six-thirty and I figured I'd head on out to the Hudson place. Jude should be there. I needed to talk to him and I figured that at seven in the evening I was pretty sure to find him. Pretty sure to find everybody dressed and with their underwear on. No guarantees, of course.

Jude was doing chores when I drove in. No VW Rabbit in sight. Good so far. He heard the dogs, looked up and saw the Bronco. He didn't bother to acknowledge me. I went into the house for a Pepsi, then sat down on the front porch step and waited for my number to come up on his screen, hoped it wasn't more than a one or two Pepsi wait.

"The hell you want?" he bellowed at me at last as he walked the path from the barn to the house. "Huh?" he asked, belligerent, mean, mad when I didn't answer immediately.

"I came out to say hello, see if you'd busted up anything else."

I smiled. It was a little hard to smile at him right now but I did it. Good for me. If Alma was right—that doing difficult things built character—I was up to about the fourth floor and climbing rapidly. Yessiree.

"And drink *my* fucking soda."

"Yeah. I got nothing better to do on a nice summer evening than drive a half hour in the wrong direction for a free can of soda and listen to some guy swear at me."

"Fuck!"

I took a last slug of the soda, crumpled up the can and tossed it into the yard, maybe making a statement about trash, aluminum or human.

"You know, Jude, except when Mandy was there, you were often like this—rude, crude and ignorant. It ain't cute; it ain't pretty; it ain't country boy." I thought for a moment. "Country asshole, maybe, and it gets old real damn fast. Five minutes, I figure, and you're way over that now. Way over. Of course you've got other reasons—grief, pain— and they're good reasons, no question about it. Just not good enough to act like a full-time asshole."

Georgie bumped his head on my knee and stuck his wet nose in my hand. The hard words made him uneasy. I patted him, looked at streaks of pink in the blue-gray sky, listened to the breeze in the leaves of the sycamore and to a faraway low-pitched almost tuneless whistle.

The sky got a little pinker, then orange. Too bad the beauty couldn't touch Jude's battered, dented, busted-up heart. Silence for a week or two while the sun slid down the sky chute.

"You eaten, Kat? You want a sandwich?"

"That would be nice."

Jude pulled the screen door open and stomped inside. He didn't hold the screen door; he didn't look at me; he didn't even sound like he wanted me to stay, but he was trying. It was enough.

He had the refrigerator open and his head in it. "Ham and cheese okay? Want a beer? You like pickles? Mustard or mayo?"

"I like ham and cheese, pickles and mayo. No mustard. Is there wine?"

"Maybe." He emerged with his hands full. "Go ahead and look."

The sandwich was good, huge but good. Jude had cut slabs of ham and cheese to fit a mouth his size. I have more trouble with a three-inch sandwich but I managed.

"You know who the guy is, don't you? You're such a hot fucking damn investigator, you should."

I didn't say anything. I had a bite of sandwich, a bite of pickle, I wiped mayo off my mouth. Then I reached for my wine. You'd think I hadn't eaten in days, I was that concentrated.

"Kat?" He sounded sane and reasonable but I wasn't fooled. I'd seen the fallout and debris too many times.

"Yes. I know who he is. I'm not telling, so don't even bother with it."

"You met him?"

"I'm not getting sucked into a conversation on this, Jude."

"Be reasonable, Kat. I'm just trying to understand what my wife was doing with another guy."

Be reasonable. I love that kind of stuff, especially coming from a guy like Jude whose idea of reasonable is pounding the crap out of something or someone. I *was* reasonable. I also valued life and health: Jude's, mine, Clem's, other people's.

"Remember how you, Wade, and Todd set it up that night and beat the crap out of Buck and his gang? How you said that was your way and nothing was going to change your mind?

"Yeah." Just-try-to-fuck-with-*me* tone.

"Well, I'm not talking. That's my way and I'm not changing my mind." Same tone as his. Jude got up for another beer.

"Kat, I don't get it. I just don't fucking get it. It's not that I thought that things were perfect between Amanda and me. Well, shit, that never happens and I know it, but I thought they were good." He slammed a fist on the table. "Goddamn mutherfucking—"

"Maybe that was part of it." I spoke quietly. He had to lower his voice and quit punctuating his syllables with fist-pounding to hear me —which, after all, was the point.

"What? What the hell you talking about?"

"Amanda was a quiet person. She didn't like shouting, swearing, pounding. She was terrified of violence. She hated it when you did things like that."

"Don't fuck with me, Kat." He flipped me a dangerous look, like a mean jock tossing a mean Frisbee.

"I don't have to, Jude. You're doing fine on your own."

"That's crap—"

*See. I rest my case.*

"Maybe Mandy sought out someone who didn't swear all the time, someone who shared that gentle, quiet side with her, or at least tried to understand—"

"I did." Mean. Forceful. Words driving into the air like spikes into timber.

"Did you?"

Our eyes met and held. I played stand-off and chicken and bet-you-can't and, to my surprise, won. "Amanda didn't want fists flying and things busting up around her. She had no choice at work—she took on that fight as a matter of principle. Maybe dealing with it at home too was too much."

Maybe? Probably not much maybe there. Wouldn't have been for me.

I watched muscles bulge and tense and tighten, sinews and veins stand out in stark relief, red and white, coming and going in an ugly ebb and flow of blood and hate. This is not my idea of fun. Shoot, I don't watch Rambo movies for precisely this reason. Clint Eastwood either or—

"What should I have done, Kat?"

It was another one of the four billion and twelve things that didn't have an easy answer, that wasn't black and white, that I didn't know. "I'm just trying to understand what might have been. You asked," I added finally, in my defense, watching his face contort. I swallowed hard and then yawned, couldn't stifle it, couldn't help it. I was stumbling, knee-walking tired.

"Yeah. Well, who cares, it's too damn late anyway."

Was it? I didn't know about that either. Yes and no. It was always too late for some things, but not for others. I yawned again. Bone-tired. Noise, dust. I could hear the car approach from some distance away. Tires on dirt road spitting gravel, dogs barking. I heard a rooster sound off. It's not true that roosters only crow at daybreak.

Jude gave no indication that he'd taken it in, just grabbed for another beer. My mind veered off then in a tired spiraling segue, remembered the last hop fields in California, maybe in the United

271

States, off Highway 16 past Sloughhouse. First just poles and wires and smallish plants, later everything covered in green vines, in hops. Jude slugged down his beer. The fields were gone. All imported now, I guess.

Tires spun on gravel in the yard, then the engine cut. The dogs were barking frantically, but away, not close—they'd been locked up. The visitor was expected? I stood and walked to the window. A white VW Rabbit. Surprise.

"Thanks for the sandwich." I threw the words over my shoulder.

"Yeah. Sure."

He wanted to say more about love, about Mandy, about the man/ woman thing, about whether it was too late, but Lynda's impending presence pretty much shut that one down. Neither of us thought the answer was in clichés. God, I was tired.

A car door slammed. Lynda, the walking, talking cliché, was on her way. So was I, and we were going in opposite directions.

"You ask her over this time?"

He didn't answer. His eyes seemed sad, though. Or maybe not. He could have sent her away if he wanted to talk more. Could have but didn't. I walked toward the front door so our paths wouldn't cross. Jude's back was to that room, to me. I was in the front room when I heard Lynda's voice at the back door.

"Hey, good-lookin', what's a nice guy like you doing in a frown like that? Gimme a smile, huh?"

I kid you not. You had to hear it to believe it, but once was enough. Once was plenty. Once was too much. I left.

The newspaper was on the front porch when I got home. Go figure. I had a shower, then skimmed the news as I drank a glass of lemonade. I even read the editorial page for a change.

## SUNSHINE IN THE COURTS BILL

*Caveat Emptor*—let the buyer beware—is alive and well. The following are all commonplace: artificial heart values that fracture in midbeat; all-terrain vehicles that tip over and crush their drivers; gas tanks that explode in high-speed crashes; cigarette lighters that blow up; breast implants that "bleed"; a painkiller that causes deaths and life-threatening allergic reactions; daily exposure of workers to toxic, even carcinogenic materials, without warnings or protections.

*Let the buyer beware.* How? Marketing considerations have been allowed to outweigh issues of public safety. Information that would alert and protect the consumer is sealed in court records. In 1914 Justice Louis Brandeis said: "Publicity is justly recommended as a remedy for social and industrial disease. Sunlight is said to be the best of disinfectants, electric light the most effective of policemen."

Legislative action is long overdue. The Sunshine in the Courts bill protects trade secrets as well as consumers. It deserves our full support.

Timing. The pace was picking up, the temperature rising. Good. It would be something if I could hand over, dish up, deal out a hot dog example of why the passage of this bill was so relevant, timely and essential.

I yawned. Time for bed.

# 33

Dear Charity,

Reading the newspaper and watching TV is scary these days. Is everything for sale? Does everyone have a price?

Disillusioned

Dear Dis,

Everything doesn't have a price. Everything isn't for sale. But too much is, that's for sure. Try to watch less TV.

Charity

~~~~~~~~~~~~~~~~~~~~~~~~~~~~~~~~~~~~~~~~~~~~~~~~~~~

When the phone rang, every cell in my body cried, *Don't answer!* In three-part harmony with choral backup and symphonic string treatment. I looked at the clock. Nine-thirty.

No rest for the wicked. For the angry. I picked up the phone and snarled into it.

"Ms. Colorado? It's Sam Coleman, from the plant. I wonder, could I talk to you? Could you meet me?"

"Okay," I said, the symphonic chorus of *no way*s in my head almost drowning out the word.

"Where?"

"Where are you?"

"Rancho."

"The sports bar on Sunrise and Fair Oaks."

"Fifteen minutes," he said and hung up.

I sighed and went into the bathroom, stared at my reflection for a long time before brushing my teeth. I ran a comb through my hair and dusted some blush on for that Still Awake and Alive look that is so attractive and appealing. There wasn't much I could do about the circles under my eyes.

I beat Sam, staked out a table and watched TV. In a sports bar you have no choice. Baseball. I ordered a beer, the sports mentality getting to me, and watched bats and butts wriggle, tobacco juice arc across the screen. Sam arrived before my beer did.

"Evening," he said and pulled out a chair. He looked at the waitress, not at me. "Draft and a shot of Beam." He didn't look happy about being here. "What's the score?" he asked finally.

I shrugged.

"Yeah. Look, I wanted to talk to you about Amanda Hudson. You know how I feel and that hasn't changed. I admired her in a way but I didn't like what she was doing and I'm glad it stopped. Hell, just about everybody is. But to kill her?" He shook his head. "Goddamn. That bothers me a lot."

The waitress brought our drinks. Sam tossed the shot down and chased it with beer. "Goddamn."

I waited it out.

"I'm saying this once. I won't repeat it or back you up on it. I won't talk about it again."

He looked at me and I nodded that I understood. The batter hit a pop fly that sailed into the first baseman's glove. Three outs. The field swarmed briefly with ballplayers, settled down again. Sam hitched up his chair, then pushed it back.

"After you came by the other day the guys started talking. Was her death an accident or not, that kind of talk. One of the guys said she had it coming and who cared. If someone hadn't killed her they damn well should have. Hell, he would've, he said, in a minute, why the hell not?"

The batter swung. Strike one.

"I said something about the baby and this guy said, well, tough shit, she coulda thought of that before, and she shoulda kept her nose out of our business."

Strike two.

"Another guy laughed, not like he thought it was funny but nervous-like and said, 'So, you kill her or what?' . . . I can't believe this is guys I work with every day, you know?"

The batter scratched his crotch, adjusted his hat, rolled his shoulders, then went into a batting crouch.

"Did he answer the question?"

"He laughed. Then he said no one ought to screw around with him and he walked off."

The batter swung. Strike three.

"I didn't like it. Nobody did. It wasn't just like guys joking around. It was— *Shit*, I don't know." He drained his beer, looked down into the glass. "If I'd lost my wife and my baby—"

The waitress started over, stopped when Sam shook his head.

"You got a pencil?" He was pulling a scrap of paper from the pocket of his T-shirt. I took out a pen, pulled a bar napkin toward me. "Name's Ace Belten. Want the address and phone number?" I did. Sam gave it to me. "He drinks almost every night at the Zephyr. Know it?" I didn't. "Little hole-in-the-wall hangout on J Street, J and Twenty-seventh or so. Ace is a bad drunk."

"What's he look like?"

"Tall and skinny, dirty blond hair. His eyes aren't good, he wears sunglasses a lot, pockmarks on his face. He looks mean and he is mean. No telling which came first. Works hard, though. Always puts in a good day." He said this ungrudgingly.

"What's he drink?" It was the question of an ex-bartender. Bartenders often identify people by drink.

"Don't know. I won't go drinking with him. Hey, I got to go."

"Thanks, Sam."

He reached for his wallet. The catcher dropped the ball. I said I'd get the drinks, then watched him walk out. He was a decent guy and I thought he was telling me the truth. The Zephyr. I sighed. Midtown. I sighed again, put money on the table and left.

Three strikes: You're out.

Four balls: You walk.


Streets like Fair Oaks, Jackson, and Auburn got their names because at one time they were the main route from Sacramento to the communities of Fair Oaks or Jackson or Auburn. Before freeways. I was in Fair Oaks on Fair Oaks Boulevard so I followed it into town. Fifteen miles or so later I cruised down J Street through midtown looking for the Zephyr. And found it easily enough, resplendent in neon: the name, the traditional martini glass with olive, and a tipped beer bottle with drops running up and down. Very nice. I've always liked neon. Unfortunately, that was the only thing I was to like about the Zephyr.

It was very dark. That was a plus, I guess. That way you couldn't see the dirt, the tawdriness, the lost cases. I picked out Ace right away, even though he wasn't wearing sunglasses. There were about four guys at the bar, several quiet couples in booths. Ace was at the end of the bar closest to the door. I climbed on a bar stool two seats down from him. He was staring steadily at me and making no attempt to hide it. I ordered a Miller Lite and took out a five-dollar bill.

"I'll get that," Ace said as the bartender put my drink down in front of me.

"Thanks." I tipped my beer bottle slightly in his direction.

"My pleasure."

He slid over two bar stools and settled in next to me. Yuck. This is what happens in bars if you let a slimeball buy you a drink. His elbow was about a quarter of an inch from mine. Shyness was a recessive gene in Ace.

"What's up with you, pretty lady?"

So was snappy repartee.

"Just relaxing after a long day at work."

"Ain't it the truth. Where you work?"

"I waitress at Denny's." I shuddered inwardly at the thought.

"Yeah? Where?"

Where? Uh oh, where *was* the nearest Denny's?

"Down the street?" He jerked his head in a question and I nodded in relief.

"Where do you work?" Challenging chitchat for sure.

"Plant called Louden."

"Didn't I see something about that in the paper? Didn't a girl who worked there die?"

His face darkened and he blinked rapidly four or five times. "Yeah."

"What happened?"

"It wasn't at work. She fried in her hot tub or something."

"Oh, too bad. Was she nice?"

"Naw, she wasn't. She was a meddling, interfering fucking bitch who kept sticking her nose where it didn't belong." He scowled. "And then she got it, she got what was coming to her all right." The scowl changed to a grin.

"Got it? What do you mean, got it? I thought it was an accident?"

"Yeah, well, now they're saying maybe someone killed her."

"Oh, wow! Who would do that?"

"Someone who hated her, I guess. Someone who hated her fucking guts and interfering ways." A grimace twisted his skinny, malevolent face. "Someone who had the guts to take care of a problem."

He was sounding like Buck and I was feeling sick to my stomach. "Do you do that, take care of stuff?" I asked casually.

"Yeah," he said, "I do," and he raised his glass and clicked it against my beer bottle. I didn't drink with him. "Yeah, I fucking well do. Hey, enough about her. I don't want to talk about some bitch who got what she had coming to her. How about you? Let's talk about you. Let's see that you get what you got comin' to you." Translation: *Let's see that you get me, Ace, the stud muffin.*

"Okay." Translation: *In your dreams.*

He grinned. "What's your name?"

"Lucy." The song "Lucy in the Sky with Diamonds" was playing on the radio. Ace didn't notice the borrow.

"Well, Lucy, drink up, I'll buy you another."

His elbow was touching mine now. I reached up and fluffed my hair, then put my arms down again on the bar and away from him.

"What the hell, maybe you and me could have a little fun?"

Naw. We'd had about all the fun we were going to have.

"What do you like to do for fun?" I asked.

"I like to win. I'm a real lousy loser." He leered and moved his elbow up on me again. "Makes me kinda mad to lose. Also, I like a pretty girl who don't talk much. How 'bout you?"

I looked at the clock. "Uh oh, I got to call my baby-sitter. I'm late." I stood and picked up my purse. We were through talking about Amanda and I was out of here, although not necessarily through with Ace.

"Phone's down there." Ace swung around on his bar stool and pointed. His arms didn't match. The left one was shorter, deformed somehow.

"I got to get her number. It's in the car." I smiled at him.

His eyes narrowed. "You're not walking out on me, are you?" His eyes blinked rapidly. There was no hiding the hate in them. Not that he tried. The good arm rested protectively on the other.

I smiled, picked up my half-full beer bottle and set it down on the five I'd tried to buy my drink with earlier. "Be right back. Don't miss me now." As I walked out he was ordering another round.

Someone would drink it. Someone always did.

On the way home I thought about his warped mind and deformed arm, wondered if they were connected.


That was the night someone tried to torch Jude's ranch and left thirteen mousetraps on my front porch. Only one had been sprung. There was a dead mouse in it.

*Watch your step. Dead Kats don't tell tales.*

# 34

Dear Charity,

I am totally FED UP with the way things are in the insurance company where I work. I want to get a gun and blow everyone away!

Pissed Off In Peoria

Dear P.O.P.,

Please. We have enough of that in post offices without starting it in insurance companies. Follow your employee grievance policy.

Charity

~~~~~~~~~~~~~~~~~~~~~~~~~~~~~~~~~~~~~~~~~~

I woke up on my own, no kitten scrambling on the bed, no Ranger making little cough barks meaning time-to-go-out. They were still in Charity's safekeeping. I missed both. No four-footers to trip over in the kitchen as I made coffee, and I missed that too. Still in the T-shirt of Hank's that I wear to bed, I pulled on a pair of shorts and headed out for the morning find-the-paper challenge.

I didn't get far.

It wasn't because of the paper.

And the mousetraps weren't the only thing.

Using a black felt-tipped marker, someone had printed YOU ARE BEING WATCHED on a piece of white paper. A ketchup bottle with an unbroken seal had been smashed on one corner of the paper, then tossed on the porch. It was crude and unimaginative, like a little kid playing at being bad, a kid who figured that ketchup would look like blood and scare someone. Simplistic and stupid, but impossible to ignore. More flowers and branches had been torn off and tossed around the lawn. I sucked in my breath on a hateful thought, stepped over the mousetraps, the glass and tomato goo and picked up the flowers to put them in water.

Inside, the kettle was whistling in cheery oblivion of the morning's first ominous announcements. I made coffee before looking for others.

*What's wrong with this picture?*

The padlock had been jimmied on the toolshed and tools tossed around in the backyard. A hoe dared me to step on its sharp edge, a rake smiled in garish toothy abandon. Nothing seemed to be missing, to be stolen, just in disarray. The bird feeder had been tipped, its seed emptied on the ground. The bright red hummingbird syrup had been splashed out, the animals' water bowls overturned. Heart in my mouth, I counted the goldfish. All five okay. I fed them lightly, then took the fish food inside. Fish will eat until they die if overfed and this joker was obviously not an animal lover.

There was fecal matter on the front lawn. Ranger never uses the front yard and I have a six-foot fence surrounding the property.

*How many things can you find?*

The newspaper was on the roof. There was another note in the mailbox. I'm in a rural area and the box is on a post next to the street, no sidewalks, so the mailman can drive up to it. WATCH OUT! the note said. A red rose in gorgeous full bloom had been cut with a six-inch stem, then its petals pulled off.

I could feel the rage inside me.

Like Jude I wanted to pound the shit out of something. Unlike Jude, I didn't. I got the aluminum extension ladder out and retrieved the paper from the roof, then went inside and poured coffee. Still mad, I gulped it down. So of course I burned my mouth and got even madder.

I wasn't in a good mood—no kidding!—when the phone rang. It was Jude, swearing. I hung up. It rang again. I answered again.

"Dammit, Kat! Goddamn motherfucking—"

I hung up.

The third time it rang I picked up, no hello, and said, "Straighten out or don't call. I'm sick of this."

"They tried to burn my place down, Kat." No goddamns, no motherfucks.

"What?" I asked, stumbling over to the coffee and then to a chair. "They *what?*"

"Last night about three o'clock I half-woke up, you know the way you do when something's wrong but you're not sure what?"

*What's wrong with this picture?*

"Then I heard it again, a bottle rocket. I'm thinking it's pretty goddamned late at night for that, not to mention a little late in the summer—I mean, we're way past the Fourth of July—when the animals start to go crazy. Not just the dogs, the horses. They're screaming, running wild, kicking. I can hear the sharp cracks of hooves connecting to wood."

I got a sick feeling in the pit of my stomach. That kind of animal craziness in the middle of the night probably meant only one thing.

Jude echoed my thought. "One thing that means. Fire. I didn't even stop to pull my pants on. No rain since March and it's tinder dry out there—a spark'd do it, never mind a bottle rocket. I jump in my shorts and boots and I'm there. I mean I fucking break the record for the hundred-meter dash and in cowboy boots too."

My mouth is hot and dry. Like dust, like ashes, like after fire has run across dry California valley grassland in late summer. "The animals?" I choke the question out.

"Okay. I opened the corral, set the horses loose, fucking two-year-old gelding knocked me over, almost got me, dogs okay too, lost a couple of chickens. Not that I care about chickens, it's just that Mandy—"

"The barn?" I was going for essentials, not memories.

"Yeah. Touch and go. Lost a bunch of hay, bales not far from the barn. I'm tossing it around like a madman trying to get it away from the barn, out of wind and spark distance. Barn caught in a couple of places but the fire department got there in time, doused everything up good."

I could see Jude in my mind, a crazed blond giant in cowboy boots and shorts—jockey or boxer, I wondered—tearing around in the flames, the light bouncing, glistening off the sweat on taut, straining muscles. Jude would fight it until he got it. Or dropped.

*What's wrong with this picture?*

"Lynda?" I wasn't asking if she was okay. Jude would have said. And he knew what I was asking.

A silence before the answer. "Mandy would've been out there in her nightie giving it everything she had, Kat, chasing stock, hosing the roof, pounding out sparks with a shovel. Lynda? Well, she called the fire department, that was a help. Then she watched from the porch and afterwards she asked if I wanted a glass of iced tea she'd made for me."

I didn't say anything. Not a lot to say.

"I asked her to leave, told her not to ever come out again without calling first."

Amanda and Lynda. Not a tough choice, not a tough call anyway you looked at it.

"Iced tea tasted good, though." He laughed.

What a day. I looked at the clock. Only eight-thirty. "I'll be out there in forty-five minutes."

"Yeah. Good." He started to hang up.

"Jude, you wear jockeys or boxers?"

"Huh? What the hell—?" I was silent. He laughed, maybe seeing the same firelit picture I was. "Boxers." He hung up.

So I finished the picture in my mind, the firelight dancing on

Jude's sweaty, soot-streaked, boxer-clad body. It fit. Easy. Then I switched gears. I didn't like this at all. I added it up as I got dressed, added and muttered, which—Charity tells me—is a bad sign.

This was the second fire. The first one, in the Hudsons' Cadillac —the one that brought me on the case—hadn't been predictable and/ or inevitable. An involuntary tremble hit me, zinged unpleasantly through my body. Fire. I hate fire. I shuddered again, then shook myself. There were numerous matching points in harassment tactics at both scenes. I ticked them off. At the ranch and here, animals had been threatened (the parakeet killed), garden implements tossed around and menacing notes left.

Someone had broken into the ranch house and done—too nice a word, true—things there; here it was outside. Excrement had appeared at three scenes, here, the ranch, and the plant. Ditto threatening communications. Amanda had been physically attacked at home and at the office. Jude was too big for them to mess with directly, and it wasn't clear whether the car sabotage was aimed at him or at Amanda. Probably the latter. I had been threatened but not attacked.

Bunches of dead flowers. *Curiosity kills the Kat.*

It didn't seem a big jump to conclude that the perps in each case were the same. That connected up Amanda's investigation, her death and my investigation. Bingo. Full house. Hole in one. Home run.

I finished tying my sneakers, grabbed a diet Dr Pepper and looked around for my keys. I was on my way out when the phone rang. More bad news? My heart sank. What now?

"Claire?"

A wrong number. Great! My heart bounced up like a basketball player. *Wrong number,* I almost replied, just remembering in time that *I* was Claire.

"Yes?"

"It's Roberta Heald. I called to apologize. I feel pretty awful about your visit."

"Oh—"

"No, please let me finish. You came to me for help and solace.

Not only was I no help, I cried on your shoulder. I just wanted you to know that I'm sorry, that I can be a good listener. Really. If you ever want to talk again, please call, please come by."

Did I feel like a heel or what?

"I want to hear your story and talk to you. I know how hard it is and I hope I can help."

I felt like a heel. No *or what* about it.

"You have to grieve before you can really put it behind you, before you can get over it. I learned that. Otherwise, what happens is that you fill up with hate and sadness and it spills over onto every-thing, even people and things you love."

"Thanks for the offer," I mumbled, messing up some consonants and stumbling through the hate and anger in my own heart.

"Yes, you're welcome. I'll let you go now, but please call, please come by again." The phone clicked gently in my ear.

I frowned at myself in the hall mirror. A heel? No question. But maybe I wasn't a heel if I could help put a stop to secrecy agreements and the production of products that resulted in the death of people like Roberta's little daughter.

It wasn't just Amanda's death anymore.

It had stopped being that a while ago.

Do ends justify means?

I headed out the door, headed out to the ranch.


"Well?"

Jude shrugged.

"You find anything?"

"I think I know what happened but I can't prove anything."

"Arson?"

"Yeah. Bottle rockets, and the intent was arson. That's what I think. The fire department guy says it was probably kids. Plenty of dumb-as-shit kids, after all, and nobody to prove a fucking thing with what we got here."

"And?"

"And too many bottle rockets landing in one goddamned place on top of too many other goddamned things in the same goddamned place."

Yes. That's what I thought too, minus a few goddamns.

"Hey, where you going?"

I flipped him a backwards wave. I had what I'd come for. Now I was out of here.

*What's wrong with this picture?*

I climbed into the Bronco, pushed Jude out of my mind, focused on Amanda instead.

I was holding my breath, I realized, as I unlocked my office door and walked in. It was quiet, clean—well, dusty of course—but fine. Everything was okay. I let my breath out in a whoosh, feeling sweaty little tingles of relief run through me. I don't know what I expected exactly, but there had been too much lately that was both unexpected and nasty. I sighed, sank into my desk chair, relaxed. I had a small amount of essential business to do. And phone calls—as I had things in mind that required preplanning and organization. Two things.

I was looking forward to both of them.

Of course, in my business you can't plan for everything. I heard a truck pull up outside, park. Heavy, brisk footsteps down the hall. United Parcel Service walked in, brown uniform, pleasant smile. I'm a regular on his route. He put a neatly wrapped and addressed package on my desk. I signed for it, waved at the UPS guy and finished my paperwork before opening the package.

I had relaxed too soon.

# 35

Dear Charity,
   I think crime pays PRETTY DAMN WELL. What do you think?

                                                    Considering It

Dear It,
   Sometimes it does. Sometimes it doesn't. Just in case, how do you feel about handcuffs, steel bars, boring meals and a single change of clothing?

                                                    Charity

~~~~~~~~~~~~~~~~~~~~~~~~~~~~~~~~~~~~~~~~~~~~~~~~~~~~~~~~~

The smell hit me first, the smell of death, a smell that had clobbered me again and again in this investigation. I didn't have to ask what was wrong.
   I knew.
   It was a rat. Very large and very dead. With a wide red ribbon tied around its neck and a .22 through its brain. It came with a note: *DO KATS HAVE 9 LIVES?* I read it twice before I walked it and the rat out to the dumpster in the back of the building. Hallmark does it better, no doubt about it.

Annie answered her phone on the second ring. "Louden Industries, howmayIhelpyouplease?"

"Hi, Annie. Kat Colorado."

"Hi!" she said brightly. "How's it going?" Her voice was a
whisper by the time she reached the last syllable. She'd be wanting a
secret decoder ring any day now. "Any more clues? You need help
with anything?" Still whispering. Always a great way to appear inconspicuous, especially in a standard office setting.

"Annie, what's the name of the janitor?"

"Barry?"

Why was that a question? "Are there several?"

"No."

"Is Barry security, too?"

"Well, sorta. He comes on at four and works till midnight. Then
we've got a watchman from twelve to eight. Why?"

"Could you get me his number and address?"

"I guess. Sure. Why?"

"Thanks. That'd be great."

"Hold, okay?" I held in silence that I much preferred to Muzak
and thought about how repulsive and disgusting rats are. Alive, dead,
either way they had zip for appeal. A red ribbon didn't help.

*DO KATS HAVE 9 LIVES?*

No.

"Hello? Still there?"

"Yes."

"Here it is." She rattled off numbers. "Oh, hey, there," she said
in an unnaturally high tone to someone in the office and then it was
back to me. "Willtherebeanythingelsema'am?"

"Thanks, Annie, you're a peach."

She giggled, said, "You'rewelcome," and hung up.

I dialed Barry's number. A man's voice answered. "Hi," I said,
"is Louie there?"

"Wrong number," he said pleasantly. I apologized and we disconnected.

. . .

He didn't speak right away and, when he spoke, his voice was not welcoming. "What can I do for you?" he asked with reluctance, with a sour look on his face. He knows who I am, I thought, but I identified myself anyway. He knew who I was, but no way he expected to see me on his porch.

"I know," he went on before I could answer. "What do you want?" He didn't invite me in. The heat was at my back and cool inside air leaked out past his bulky body—spread-eagled and protective in the door frame. His face was furrowed with years and worry, and sported a salt and pepper five o'clock shadow.

"You were Amanda's friend." I said it gently. "She told me, told me you showed her pictures of your grandkids."

"Yes." His voice softened somewhat. His stance didn't.

"She was murdered." I said it hard.

"It was an accident." Startled, less wary.

"No. It was murder."

He didn't ask me how I knew but he did ask me in. It was dark and cool inside, and I smelled bacon grease from many breakfasts over many years. Family photographs, especially of the grandkids, covered the walls of the entry hall.

"I need help."

"What?"

"I need to get in the plant. At night. Just to look around."

"No."

"I won't take anything. I won't disturb anything."

"No."

Not a lot of encouraging forward progress here.

"Amanda believed it was wrong to sell defective heart valves. People could die. They did die. She tried to stop it, to make Louden do what was right. Maybe she died because of that. Everywhere I go the trail leads back to Louden."

"Murder?" His voice was shocked. "You sure? Sure?"

"Yes."

"Murder."

I saw opportunity building and jumped on it. "Suppose you thought you heard a loud noise in the parking lot late at night, you'd check it out, I'm sure."

He cracked his knuckles, but said nothing.

"Suppose you stepped outside briefly to investigate, leaving the door ajar. Suppose someone slipped in without your seeing, then slipped out twenty or thirty minutes later, no one the wiser."

"That's a lot of supposing."

"Not so much. Not compared to—"

Not compared to murder. I left it there. I didn't offer him money —it would have been an insult. He was honest; he had liked Amanda and she had liked him. He was going to have to choose.

He was absolutely still as he thought it over. "When do you suppose this could happen?" he asked softly, his eyes on the photograph of a pretty smiling young woman and two small children which hung on the wall.

"Ten-thirty tonight." I'd gone beyond suppose and into definite plan. I think he had too.

"Murder?" he asked.

I nodded. He nodded. I left.

"Tonight," I said to Shelley twenty minutes later on the phone. "Tell me where the files are. Leave the copy machine on."

She stuttered as she told me. I repeated it back to her for confirmation. "Off the main corridor, second door on left, copy machine on in your office. Thanks, Shelley."

"Get a life," she snarled. "Stay outta mine."

Who could blame her?


Smooth. Like a vanilla milk shake on a hot day, it went down fast and easy. At ten-thirty Barry walked out the main entrance leaving the door ajar and swinging a flashlight around the parking lot. The light carved out bright ephemeral slashes in the dark summer air but not across me. I slipped in. Twenty-five minutes later I'd cruised the files.

Smooth.

Except that I found nothing that was third cousin, not even second cousin to relevant. Shipping, receiving, accounting, payroll and daily operations records—that's what I found. No legal, no indications of product failure or liability, no records of complaints, never mind million-dollar settlements. No nothing. I hadn't really expected to find it here—after all, corporate headquarters was in Texas—but it was still disappointing.

I put the folders back where I found them and looked around DeVito's office. A quick toss—what the hell? His desk was clean and cleared except for some paper-clip carcasses and a newspaper neatly folded open to the editorial supporting the Sunshine in the Courts bill. That explained the paper clips. A red light blinked on the phone, indicating there was a message to be picked up.

I punched the button. Why not? Snooping 101. *Nine o'clock. Houston. Where's the final report? I don't like what I'm hearing. I don't like what I'm not hearing. Wrap it up.* The caller didn't sound like a nice guy and it wasn't a nice message. I smiled. Smooth. I reset the machine.

Then the banging started.

And my smiling stopped.

I hit the lights, glanced out into the corridor. Still dark. Barry was scurrying toward the door and looking around nervously. Understandable. I slid into the hall and into the next office over.

"Mr. DeVito, what are you— Working late, huh?"

"Forgot something." DeVito was terse and tense.

Barry was voluble and tense. He chatted along in the background until DeVito told him to buzz off. I was silent and tense. DeVito banged around in his office for a while, then it got quiet. The phone light came on. Line two. I crossed over to a desk, bumped a wastebasket, cursed under my breath, waited for a three count, then punched line two and picked up the phone. Might as well add eavesdropping to my growing list of misdemeanors.

"Stop that woman—the detective. Put it to bed. Now."

*That woman?* Me.

Not as smooth as I thought.

I got out of there shortly after DeVito left. Smooth. Easy. Barry had aged—he was too old for cops and robbers. And right now I was too tired. Time to go home.

*Stop that woman.*

Not a lot of ambiguity there.

# 36

Dear Charity,

How do you tell the good guys from the bad guys? It's getting really tough these days.

Puzzled

Dear Puzzled,

Forget about what they say. Forget about how they dress. Forget about where they live and work. Watch very carefully what they do.

Charity

~~~~~~~~~~~~~~~~~~~~~~~~~~~~~~~~~~~~~~~~~~~

*What's wrong with this picture?*

I picked it up as I was coming down the block. Ace detective, or what? The yard light was out again. Shot, not burned. I'd just put in a new bulb and they last about a year.

*What's wrong?*

Plenty.

The pickup was older now but had once been a white and sharp and dazzling Cinderella-at-the-auto-mall-ball, but that was yesterday. Someone still cared—it was buffed up but not out. Older white Ford pickup? Common as dirt in this part of California. It was the stickers that gave it away. Harley-Davidson. Norton Cycle. A couple from hard rock radio stations and one that stated that this vehicle was Insured by Smith and Wesson. The personalized license plate holder told me that Pipe Fitters Screw Tighter.

I recognized it. Not too tough. The truck didn't belong on my block but it had fit right in at the Blue Pocket the other night. It takes a week and a half to describe it, but no time at all to add it up. Clue no. 2.

The next beat took me past the house. I didn't look. I didn't slow down. I sailed by and around the block. Pass no. 2 and I was revving up and getting in the mood for it. Yessiree.

*Stop that woman. Put it to bed.*

Here comes your chance, boys. I popped the glove compartment, retrieved my .380 and stuck it in my belt. Speaking of getting in the mood. Speaking of insurance.

My block again. Boy howdy, here we come. I picked it up to about forty-five, then hit the brakes, laid rubber all over the road, the screech of tires all over the neighborhood, stopped just short of my property. At the apex of the screech I leaned out the window and thumped—I mean *THUMPED*—on the car door a couple of times, then once again in the dead quiet of eleven forty-five p.m. in my country neighborhood. Sitting in the car, I opened and slammed my door twice in close succession.

"Ha-a-arry, you hit it. You shouldna oughta had that last beer, I *tolt* you so." I leaned out the window and said it in a high shrill voice with a whine in it. It carried well in the quiet night air.

"C'mon, let's git." Harry's voice was as low as I could do, not exactly testosterone-laden, but okay. "*C'mon.*"

"Harry, we oughtta find out who owns the truck or sumpin, *Harry.*"

I made like Harry and growled and cursed. Didn't want to keep it up too long, of course, and get caught at it.

"*C'mon,* Mabel," Harry said.

A couple more noisy car door slams, a quick U and more peeling rubber. Hello, Goodyear. Halfway down the block I doused the lights, slid over to the side of the road, turned around to watch a guy walking around the white pickup. Bingo. After a while he melted back into the shadows around my yard. Bingo. The Stop-That-Woman crew was on the job tonight.

I drove around the block again, opposite direction for a change of pace, parked a hundred feet off and hoofed it. Popped the loose board in the back fence corner and climbed through. It was a warm evening, zip for breeze. I smelled the cigarette smoke long before I saw the red glow. One. More? Another cigarette. Voices that were a low mutter, indistinguishable. Two voices. And zip for professionalism. Good thing for these boys that this line of work wasn't their primary source of income.

No yard light, no moon. I closed in on them, picking up a couple of smooth round river rocks from the path. They were snug in my hands, the gun snug in my belt, the smile smug on my face. It felt good to be hitting back. The cigarettes danced again, then separated, one floating up onto the porch, the other staying in the side yard. I headed for the porch.

I heard it coming seconds away, a car with serious muffler problems, and sped up to synchronize with it. Perfect. I tossed the first stone in the bushes at the edge of the front yard. It bounced and hit the fence, bringing the porch man out of my glider (lazy son of a bitch) to lean over the rail. With the muffler growl covering me, I swung up over the side of the porch and moved in.

A little guy.

I kicked him in the back of the knees and punched him in the kidneys, hard. He moaned, jackknifed, smacked his head on the railing, then slumped forward. I grabbed his legs and tossed him over into the rock garden below. This didn't make much noise, but I was betting it would bring his buddy.

I got off the porch the same way I got on.

"What in Sam Hill—?"

The guy I tossed was moaning and carrying on in the rock garden, the other one chewing him out. The second guy was big. No visible weapon.

"What the hell's the matter with you, stupid? I leave you alone for a minute and you fall off the goddamn porch."

"I didn't fall" (*dint*—for those of you who appreciate sophisticated dialogue). "She *pushed* me."

"Huh? The gal? Who? She here? How'd she do that? C'mon now, *c'mon.*"

"She did." The little guy sounded aggrieved.

"I did," I said, stepping out of the shadows.

The big guy's head snapped around to me. "You the one tossed my buddy off here?"

"I'm the one," I agreed.

"She is, yeah, Joe," the other one whined. "Hey, how'd you do that, huh?"

"You the one lives here?"

"I'm the one."

"How? I didn't even see you. How? Huh?"

"Correspondence course. I was sitting in a bar one day reading a matchbook and there it was. Looked good so I enrolled."

"Yeah? Man, I sit in a lot of bars and I *never* seen any good stuff like that. Maybe I go to the wrong bars, you suppose? How much it cost?"

"Len, she's pulling your chain," the other one—Joe—said.

"Yeah?" Little Len, aggrieved again. I had the feeling he was aggrieved a lot.

I laughed.

"Well, *hey,* that ain't nice. You got no call to be making fun of me."

That one cracked me up; I couldn't help it. Okay. I didn't even try. I think it was something about a thug chiding me for my manners.

"You the one lives here, huh," the one I hadn't tossed said. He started toward me. "We're going to have us a little chat."

"Be better if you stayed there."

I reached behind me for the four-foot length of two-by-two lean-ing there. Sounds like a lucky coincidence until you realize that there's quite a bit of stuff like that around my yard. I think this one was supposed to brace a tree that I never got around to putting in.

I looked the two guys over in the minimal light. I didn't recognize them from the plant. Most of them were not like this—they were just decent guys running scared. That's pulling out Buck and a couple of other obvious scumballs, of course. These guys were part of Buck's muscle-for-hire program, I'd put money on it.

One more rock left. I turned slightly and pitched. I played soft-ball, mostly shortstop, for years as a kid. Still do for fun. I can throw to miss or throw to hit. The river rock was the size of a softball. It caught Joe in the solar plexus. Bull's-eye. The big guy went down like a dangling preposition with an "unnnhhhh!" that was immensely satisfy-ing. I didn't need the two-by-two. I didn't need the .380.

"See," his little buddy said. "See. I told you she's like that." Len had started to move in but stopped when his big buddy went down and stayed down. He wouldn't go it alone. Bullies don't have much bottom.

"You, Len—that your name?" I took the silence for an assent. "I ever catch you around here again, you're not walking away, maybe not even crawling."

I was tired. I was mean. I hated it when I felt that way, talked that way. And I was lying. I don't bust heads without a lot of provoca-tion.

The guy on the ground started moving stealthily, surreptitiously.

"You make any move at all I'm going to kick you in the nuts, Joe, bust you in the chops or break your head. Maybe all three. Go ahead, make my day."

Aw, shit, Jude's approach was rubbing off on me. Still, I have a way of saying things like that, all interested and excited—like it's such fun that I can't decide what I want to do next. And it stops them. I don't look like that kind of person, but maybe I am. What do they know?

"I want you boys to hang out right here, make yourselves comfortable and all, while I go call the cops."

They wouldn't, I knew that. They'd scram. What they didn't know was that I'd pulled their spark plug wires. Joe and Len went anywhere tonight, they were walking.

I called it in as a burglary in progress. The cops roll pretty fast on that one. A burglary compounded by assault; perps dangerous, assumed armed. Cops roll even faster on that. Then I got a glass of lemonade and sat down on the dark porch to watch. It was open and shut. I'd called in descriptions of both guys, description and tag of the truck.

Open and shut. Over like that.

In the white pickup the cops found drugs and a handgun with the serial numbers filed off. They impounded the vehicle.

Muscle-for-hire. Jell-O for brains.


The phone rang at two-thirty. Doesn't anyone pay attention to Miss Manners anymore? The adrenaline slammed and danced through my body like Last Chance at the Racetrack of Life.

First try I swatted the clock off the stand and dropped the receiver. Second time I caught it.

It was Clem Davis. Drunk. Hammered. Nailed. Gonzo.

"I never should have left her that day, Kat. If I'd stayed they never would have got her." The words slurred and slipped.

"If you'd stayed, nobody would have tried."

"We never should have had an affair."

"Amanda wasn't killed because you were lovers."

I crossed my fingers like a superstitious kid. God, I hoped it was true. *Pleasepleaseplease* I chanted to myself, knowing it was foolish but feeling slightly comforted. Please. Because if Amanda had died because of their affair, that meant either Clem or Jude. I thought suddenly, sadly, that Jude was a name filled with heaviness and sorrow. Evil as well?

298

"Are you home, Clem?"

"Yeah. I was at the 2 Me."

The Club 2 Me on J Street with cheap drinks and reckless people. It would be easy to get hammered there. On liquor and emotion both. That was no way unusual, never mind any kind of a challenge, at the 2 Me.

"Clem, go to bed, okay? We can talk tomorrow."

"I thought nothing could hurt as bad as losing her when she ended it. I was wrong." He hung up.

Guilt. About what, exactly? And Jude? Why was Jude sleeping with someone so soon? Loneliness? Grief? Anger?

In the morning I found the goldfish, scooped out and left to die.

Rage filled me. Red-hot and wild at first, then tempered into something burning white, focused and horrible.

I buried the goldfish. No tears.

Too many bodies. Too much hatred.

# 37

Dear Charity,

My mom's always telling me to wear the "right" clothes. I think this is stupid. Clothes don't make the woman, do they?

Rebelling In Reno

Dear Reb,

Clothes are just clothes. They don't make anything *but* they are extraordinarily useful. And not just to keep you warm.

Charity

~~~~~~~~~~~~~~~~~~~~~~~~~~~~~~~~~~~~~~~~~~~

I was up early. I hadn't slept well. Hatred, like straw, makes for a lumpy mattress. I had a long To-Do list but Zack was number one. I called his office at seven-thirty and got him.

"Buy you lunch."

He laughed. "Not that you're not great company, Kat, but what's up? What's on your mind?"

"I've got information I think you should have."

Silence. Then: "Where?" He was too smart to accept it at face value but he went along.

"Felicia's? Twenty-seventh and Q. They've got great huevos rancheros. Twelve o'clock?"

"Twelve-thirty." He hung up.

I didn't smile, although ordinarily I would have. I love it when things work out the way I plan. This one had me a little jumpy, though. It was because I had to produce the goods and I didn't have them, that's why. I didn't have the goods, but Paul Lowell, corporate counsel for Louden, did.

I'd called up Shelley and bullied her but—except for making me feel small—it hadn't worked very well.

"I dunno," she whined. "I don't. Nobody told me Mr. Lowell's room number at the hotel. There's no reason for me to know it. There's *not*. All's I have is the phone number and I already gave you *that*. *Look,* you *promised* you wouldn't bother me anymore and—"

"Okay, okay," I said, tired of her whining, tired of feeling small. I disconnected, looked up a number and punched it out.

"Madison Hotel. How may I help you?"

"Hi," I said in a breathy, happy voice. "My husband is a guest at your hotel. Would you give me his room number, please? The name is Lowell. Paul Lowell."

"Just a minute, ma'am, and I'll connect you."

"No, oh *no,*" I squeaked, slathering an edge of panicky on top of the breathy. "*Please* don't do *that.* I want to surprise him, you see. It's our anniversary, our very first, and I want to show up with champagne and ummmm . . ." I giggled—suggestively, I hoped. "—and stuff. *Please* understand. It's *got* to be a surprise."

The clerk sounded young, but even so I figured my chances were 70/30 tops, maybe only 80/20 or 90/10. Personnel in a first-class hotel are trained not to give out room numbers. Or much of anything else.

"I'm sorry, ma'am. It's against hotel policy to give out a guest's room number."

*Damn!*

"Oh, *puhleeeze,*" I begged prettily. "Our *first* anniversary. You *do* understand, I *know* you do."

"Well—" He was weakening.

"I'll never tell. *Never.* Wild horses couldn't drag it out of me." I gave my the-honeymoon-isn't-over giggle again.

"1218." He blurted it out.

*Hot damn!*

"Thank you," I sighed. "Thank you thank you thank you." No kidding. Now I wouldn't have to stake out Lowell, probably by once again camping out on the hot summer asphalt of Louden's parking lot, waiting for him to leave, then following him around until he finally returned to his room—or I lost him and had to start over.

"You're welcome," the clerk said formally, but with a shade of regret in his voice—rules triumphing once again over compassion, probably.

I hung up and punched the redial button, getting a different front desk clerk. Good. I wouldn't have to disguise my voice. I asked for room 1218.

"Yes." A stolid male voice answered after one peal. The name Lowell has a New England ring to it but he didn't have the accent.

"Mr. Lowell?" I inquired in nasal tones.

"Yes." Short. Brusque. Business-like.

"It's about the suit we had cleaned for you, sir. I understand that you were not pleased with the results and I want to assure you that your satisfaction is—"

"I didn't have a suit cleaned. I don't know what you're talking about."

"Oh?"

"No."

"Oh, well, I'm so sorry to bother you—"

"Yes," he said and hung up. Not a loquacious type, our Lowell.

But I had confirmed his room number. I also knew he was due at the plant for a ten-o'clock meeting. Shelley had, unwillingly, coughed that up.

I phoned the front desk of the Madison again, quite the regular. I got a young woman this time.

"I'll need a room for one night, please," I announced in my querulous little old lady voice, "and I would like room 1218. I think of it as *my* room, you know, dear, and I always try to stay there when I visit you." Make that querulous *and* eccentric.

"Let me check that for you, please." Sounds of a computer clicking in the background. "I'm sorry, ma'am, that room is not available. May I—"

"Oh!" I made myself sound crushed. *"Oh!"* I spared a moment of sympathy for the nonsense and nuisance desk clerks have to endure. Then I sighed, a frail, elderly, on-the-edge-of-the-grave sigh. "May I have 1217 or 1219 then?" That in a thin, weak, bitterly disappointed tone.

More clicking. "Surely. 1217 is available."

"Will I have to wait in the lobby for my room to be cleaned?" I whined. "I do hate waiting for my room. You haven't become one of those hotels that doesn't allow guests to check in until some ungodly hour, have you? Because I do want to check in this morning and—"

The reservationist jumped in. "1217 will be ready for you when you check in," she replied, a note of exasperation in her voice.

"Thank you," I said primly and gave my name as Mrs. Katherine Merryfield Colorado, my time of arrival as ten and my Visa card as collateral.

I dressed quickly in IBM style: dark gray business suit, cream silk shell, pearls, low-heeled black pumps, then packed a couple of changes of clothing and the tools of my trade in an overnight bag. Also four beach towels in a garment bag just for heft, respectability and show. Then off like a prom dress.

I arrived at the Madison at nine-forty and checked in in a leisurely fashion, all the while scanning the lobby for the departing form of Paul Lowell. I saw several men who ballpark-qualified but without more information on height and build it was impossible to tell. I declined the services of the bellman—the fewer people who noticed me, the better—and made my way up to 1217. There was a maid's cart in the hall and an open door not far from it. Perfect.

I let myself into my room, tossed my bags onto the bed and called 1218 just to be sure Lowell had left. I let it ring seven times. No answer. Then I stuck my room key, a hard plastic computer card, into my suit pocket and, wallet in hand, marched out the door and down the hall. The door thunked loudly behind me as I walked away.

Ninety seconds later I was back. Standing in front of room 1218 with a cold can of diet Pepsi tucked under my arm, I rummaged furiously through my wallet. Out of the corner of my eye I saw the maid emerge from 1220.

"Well, for Pete's sake," I said crossly and very distinctly. I looked up and around, looked finally at the maid, who was looking at me. Naturally. I'd been loud enough to attract her attention. *"Oh!"* Relief flooded my voice. "Oh, thank goodness! Will you let me in my room, please? I locked myself out." I held up the soda. "I was *sure* I had my key with me." I smiled and walked toward her.

She smiled back but shook her head. "I'm sorry, I can't do that. Front desk will be glad to help you."

"Oh, *no!"* I wailed and started to look at my wrist, remembering just in time that I wasn't wearing a watch. "I'll be late for my meeting. *Please!"*

She shook her head. "I can't. It's a security regulation." Her eyes wavered when I slid a ten partway out of my wallet.

I gestured casually. "For your trouble."

Her eyes were glued to the bill. She shook her head again, eyes immobile in the moving head and never leaving the green. Hard to do. I slipped another ten out to join the first one. Her eyes slid away from the money, then up and down the halls, then briefly landed on my lapels. Looking for hidden tape recorders and/or Mike Wallace and the *60 Minutes* camera crew, I guess. I tried to look innocent. I definitely didn't look like Mike Wallace.

"No, oh no," she breathed out on a sigh and scurried off, away from temptation and back to her cart.

Well, *goddamn*, *60 Minutes* has really screwed things up for nefarious low-lifes who want to sneak into other people's hotel rooms. And for maids who break the rules. *Goddamn.*

Okay, I was flexible. I had planned for this. On to Plan B.

The maid disappeared into the room she was cleaning, 1220; I ducked back into the one I was occupying. I pulled the curtains, opened the balcony door and stepped out. Hot. No breeze. I checked the connecting door to 1218. Locked.

Quickly I changed into Spandex bicycle shorts and leotard. I was vibrant—electrical, even—in hot pink, lime green and lemon yellow. I pulled on hot pink socks and white Reeboks. Then I moussed, spiked and sprayed my hair, slathered on blush, eye shadow and mascara, stretched a matching pink sweatband around my forehead. I stuck my room key in my shoe and my head out the door. The door to 1218 was open, the maid's cart parked in front of it. Perfect. (I know, I know. I said that before and I was wrong.)

I stepped out into the hall, took a deep breath, let it go and sucked in my stomach. *Move over, Jane Fonda!* Then I traipsed down the hall. As I passed 1218 I saw, out of the corner of my eye, the flash of an arm and a flying towel. The maid was still in the bathroom. Too soon, but not by much. I sauntered down the hall toward the ice machine and elevator bank. Since I had the place to myself, I loitered there for a minute and a half, then headed back. The maid was in the bedroom/sitting room area with her back to me and vacuuming. 1218 was laid out in a mirror reflection of my room—entry, bathroom to the right, closet to the left, bed/sitting area ahead with glass patio doors and a balcony at the far end.

I stepped into the entry and nipped into the bathroom. It was tidy and pristine. She was done in here. Good. The vacuum hummed away like a busy little hive of bees droning in contentment. I considered humming in contentment myself. The shower curtain, like mine, had been pulled closed. I pulled it open, slipped in and closed it again. It was an opaque cloth curtain with a plastic lining. Swell. Now all I had to do was hang out inconspicuously in the tub and hope that the maid was as speedy as she was honest. No problem.

First my nose started to itch, then my leg threatened to cramp. Soon three hundred and three distinctly separate places on my body were in active physical rebellion. I leaned against the cool tile wall and sucked in a deep breath. Uh oh. Perfumed-soap air. I fought back a sneeze. I longed, yearned, lusted after the cold diet Pepsi waiting for me next door. Just thinking about that made me want to go to the bathroom. I groaned inwardly. My other leg felt slightly crampy now, my nose itched in a different place and my stomach demanded food AT ONCE. *God,* I am such a baby.

The vacuum stopped. I held my breath and scrunched over a little. Squeaking wheels rolled by. I let my breath out. Phew. Safe.

The bathroom light flicked on and the shower curtain twitched partially open. A brown hand with a MedicAlert bracelet on its wrist adjusted the towels on the rack at the end of the tub and added a short stack of washcloths. I was frozen under the shower head, not planning to breathe or move for a week or three, easy.

This could get a little tricky, could be tough to talk my way out of. My lies flashed before my eyes. *Hi, I was on my way to the gym and I think maybe I took a wrong turn.* Or *Plumbing maintenance here. This shower head has got to go.* No, I should have a wrench or something. Maybe a girlish squeal and an *Oooooh! You found me. Now you're IT.* Maybe a trip downtown, escorted first by hotel security and then by sheriff's deputies? I winced. Maybe free overnight accommodations courtesy of the county? My stomach knotted up. I gave myself a mental raise, a big one. On second thought, I assigned myself a long vacation in a tropical paradise: stress leave.

The hand disappeared. The shower curtain twitched shut. The bathroom light flicked off. I didn't breathe, move or relax. I'd fallen for this once already. The carpet deadened any sound of footsteps coming or going but the loud thunk of the room door was clearly audible.

I still didn't breathe, move or relax. No need to rush. We're talking about someone who has seen the accommodations at the Sacramento County Jail. No telephone. No room service. No complimentary fruit baskets. Nothing like the Madison.

After another minute of dead silence I slipped out, closed the curtain behind me, slammed the dead bolt on the room door and released the dead bolt on the connecting door between this room and mine. I'd left the door on my side open. I cannot even begin to tell you how happy this connecting door made me. The alternative was scrambling from one balcony to the other. *On the twelfth floor.* We're talking about someone who has also seen the accommodations at the Sacramento County Morgue.

I was covered now.

I started tossing Lowell's room.

No filing cabinets, no computer diskettes or files. No reams and piles of data. Just two slim manila folders stuffed pretty solid, sitting on the small desk next to the telephone. I started flipping through.

Names. Dates. Specifics on product failure and dollar amounts paid out. Court results. I whistled. This is an investigator's wildest dream come true: solid, irrefutable documentation.

I walked the folders next door to my room, unpacked the portable Fax machine in my overnight bag. Ten thirty-five. I figured I had thirty minutes easy. Probably all day, but why push it? The orange jumpsuits you wear in jail are unbelievably ugly, unbelievably unflattering. And orange has never been my color, anyway.

You can Fax a lot in thirty minutes.

I did.

It would all be waiting for me when I got back to my office. Technology is swell. I tidied up the folders, left them exactly as, and where, I had found them. Checked the bathroom and wiped up the Reebok prints in the tub. Remembered to take the dead bolt off Lowell's front door, set the lock on the connecting door and, just like Alice, stepped back into my hotel room and another reality.

I packed up the Fax machine, the IBM outfit and the going-to-the-gym outfit, and jumped into jeans and a hot pink T-shirt that matched my socks perfectly. Then I scraped off a little of the makeup so Zack would recognize me. So *I* would recognize me.

Back to the everyday work grind.

And off to lunch.

# 38

Dear Charity,

The woman down our block died suddenly after hardly being sick at all. My husband is *very* suspicious. He is sure her husband killed her and there's a big insurance policy or something and we should definitely look into it. What do you say?

Nervous Neighbor

Dear Nervy,

I think your husband should mind his own business. We do authorize people to look into suspicious circumstances but they are called police officers, not neighbors.

Charity

~~~~~~~~~~~~~~~~~~~~~~~~~~~~~~~~~~~~~~~~~~~~~~~~~~~~

My mouth watered at the thought of chips and salsa. I was headed into town trying to keep my speed under seventy-five.

I considered my plan, still a little jumpy about it. Not that it was a bad plan, it wasn't. It was a great plan. It was also heartless, thoughtless, mean and inconsiderate. I was dropping a dime on everyone I could think of. Not just random hit-or-miss dropping either, dropping to a homicide cop. Trying to make trouble, stir things up, see what happened. This is not a refined technique. In investigative work it is roughly analogous to throwing a bunch of shit around and seeing what hits the fan.

I thought of my goldfish, their dead, cold little bodies. They had names: Who, What, Where, When and Why. I could tell them apart. They even had rudimentary personalities. Had. Hatred rampaged around some more. Again. And the goldfish damage was nothing to the people damage in this case.

I beat Zack to Felicia's and was drinking iced tea with extra lemon and dunking hot fresh chips into salsa chunky with fresh tomatoes, onions and cilantro. *Very* hot. My favorite.

"Kat," Zack said somewhat formally, as he pulled out a chair and sat down, gorgeous in black slacks, a black shirt and jacket, a white tie.

"Hi, Zack. Hey, you a good guy or a bad guy? You look like a mafioso. Been going to a lot of movies lately?"

He laughed at that, ordered coffee. "Won't all those chips spoil your appetite?"

"Never," I said cheerfully. "Have some. Great salsa. Well?"

"Good guy, Kat. How about you?"

Uh oh. I was still wallowing in ethical ambiguity, so I thought it best to dodge that one. Dodge and start dropping my dimes.

"Amanda Hudson, right?" He beat me to it.

"Right."

"What have you got?"

"You know about the boyfriend?"

"Tell me."

I could see by the real interested look on his face he didn't. *Ding. The sound of a dime dropping.* I told him, tossed in the rose and everything, spilled my mind into the airwaves between us.

"You check up on the husband at all?" *Ding.* "See if he came home on the flight he said. Or, assuming he did take that flight, check to see if he had flown in before Amanda died, then out again. There were flights available to fit in with that scenario, I checked. And Jude is a jealous man. He knows about the boyfriend but claims he didn't find out until after his wife died." I said this deadpan, as in: What husband in his right mind would admit to anything else?

The police hadn't checked. Not that that was a surprise in a situation like this. After all, the coroner had ruled it an accidental death. I looked at Zack's face. They might check now, though.

"You're working for the husband?" he asked after watching that dime bounce around.

"Yes and no. He and Amanda both hired me. Then Jude asked me to work on Amanda's death/murder. That's what I'm doing."

"You ready to order?"

I ordered huevos rancheros. Zack picked up the menu, then tossed it down and ordered the same thing.

"Zack, there's been a lot of harassment, intimidation and violence around this. Three instances that I know of have been reported to the police: the attack and attempted rape of Amanda at the Louden plant; the break-in and assault at her home; the assault attempt on me at my home last night."

Zack didn't ask. He'd let me finish, fill in as many blanks as I could before he picked it up. He was eating chips and salsa now, though. Steadily. A white tie, too. Silk. I was impressed at his bravery.

"Others haven't been reported. Anonymous letters and phone calls; trespassing and vandalism; a probable arson attempt at the Hudson ranch. And a lot of this can be traced back or tied into the plant and Buck Lassiter." *Ding.* I told Zack what I found out at the Blue Pocket about the muscle-for-hire business. "I think most, if not all of the above, stems from Louden management policy and direction. It will be hard to prove, though, and Louden probably won't take a fall on it."

Zack reached for another chip and said nothing.

"They've got their eye on me, too. I've been making waves they don't like."

"How do you know?"

"Everything I've already mentioned and several very specific confidential memos and communications that recently came to my attention."

"Ah," he said, finishing up the salsa.

"Here you go," the waitress said, cheerfully. "Hot plates. Be careful." We dove into our food.

"And there's no reason to be after me except for my involvement in the Hudson investigation."

"You working anything else now?"

"Paperwork."

"What kind of waves have you been making?"

I shrugged. "I'm keeping busy."

Zack grimaced. "Why do I bother to ask, huh? Anything else?"

"One more angle on why there's a lot at stake for Louden." One more dime to drop.

Zack piled rice, beans, and salsa on a flour tortilla, bit, chewed thoughtfully.

"There's legislative action pending now that would deal with the issues that Amanda was involved in, was so upset about. It's been dubbed the Sunshine in the Courts bill and would, among other things, prevent secrecy agreements. Companies with a defective product would find it much harder, or impossible, to keep the knowledge of that defect from other victims, potential victims, the public eye in general."

"Wide-ranging repercussions?"

"Yes. Particularly financial. This could cost some companies more than a Third World debt. This is a bill with solid consumer appeal. Corporate America, not surprisingly, is equally solid against it. Suppose it all came out now? Consider the timing."

Zack looked at me.

"The bill is pending. I'm trying to tie in the charges of harassment and intimidation, maybe the murder of someone who opposed secrecy agreements, to a huge corporation with a defective product that's been making them millions. There's a paper trail of dropped lawsuits; a lot of people have been paid a lot of money not to mention the fact that the Louden heart valve not only doesn't always work, it sometimes kills."

Zack chewed thoughtfully.

"I spoke with a local woman whose daughter died because of a defective Louden product. Amanda had found her and started to follow up on that and on other, similar cases. She is not the only victim."

"You know this from the woman?"

"No. She can't speak of it with any specifics, can't finger Louden. That's the point of secrecy agreements."

"She could confirm the general outline, the overall picture?"

"Yes."

"What's her name?"

I told him.

"How much did Roberta Heald get, do you know?"

I did. This information was one of the things that had made my raid on Lowell's hotel room so worthwhile. "A million and a quarter."

Zack stared at me for a beat . . . two . . . three. I was dropping heavy-duty dimes now. He whistled. "No shit?"

"No. That's how much is at stake. That's why murder is a possibility and not a far-fetched one either. Details on that heart valve defect and exactly what it was worth are not information that Louden wanted circulating. Here." I slid a paper across the table. "Data."

Zack folded his napkin and pushed back his chair. "Thanks for lunch, Kat."

"You're welcome. And—?"

"And I'll look into it." He stuck the folded paper in the pocket of his black suit jacket.

I watched him leave as I nibbled a chip pensively. Half a dozen dimes. I was going to get mileage out of my sixty cents, no problem, no question.

Cops do this kind of stuff a whole lot better than I do.


I headed for the office. Zack would rattle some cages. Understatement. I figured the fur would start flying, the shit would hit the fan soon. Understatement. I figured I'd be ready. That was the plan.

Clem was first. He walked in without knocking. No *Hi-how-are-you?* No *What's-up?*

"Look, Kat."

I looked and saw an angry African-American male striding around my office using up all the available space, oxygen and patience.

"Hey, Clem, how's it going?" Courteous in the face of turmoil, that's me. Probably Girl Scout leader material right there. "What's new?"

"Screw you, Kat. A cop called this afternoon. He wanted to talk about my relationship with Amanda, about her death, about where I'd been at the time, about roses, about a whole lot of things I didn't want to talk about and he shouldn't have known."

"Shouldn't?"

"That's right, shouldn't. Wouldn't have but for you."

I shook my head. "Let me put it to you again, Clem. You seem to have missed it. Watch my lips now." I enunciated with exaggerated care. "M-U-R-D-E-R. You with me so far? Not illness or an accident. Murder. That's why the cops are on it. That's why I'm cooperating. Still with me?"

He snarled.

Jude walked in. "What the fuck is going on, Colorado?"

I sighed. This was going to be today's theme, today's big question, I could tell. Talking with a cop can be a lousy way to start off a day. Talking with a homicide cop about a current homicide investigation is, by all accounts, much worse.

"Sorry," Jude said. Not to me, of course. To Clem. "Didn't mean to interrupt. Look, Kat, I gotta talk to you. When?"

"Hi, Jude. Fine, thanks. How are you? This is Clem Davis," I said, courteous in the face of blatant discourtesy. "Clem, Jude Hudson."

Jude and Clem were both in range. I had my eye on Clem. When the impact of Jude's presence hit, his eyes narrowed, then went back to normal. There was an almost imperceptible hand movement, a low grunt. Jude caught it, caught something, and he swung around to look closely at Clem.

The two men measured each other.

I watched with interest.

"Davis," Jude said in roughly the same tone he would use in commenting that there was cow shit on his dress cowboy boots.

This was one dime I hadn't meant to drop. Certainly not in my office. I have an expensive computer and a number of other things that I am rather fond of and don't want busted up. Jude knew the score. He should. He had found the photo in Amanda's underwear drawer and studied it long enough. Rage slowed him down at first, but he was up to speed now.

"You're the one." Short and hard.

"I'm the one," Clem agreed. *Want to make something of it?*

Macho flowed. Testosterone oozed. They eyed each other, still measuring maybe; counting, adding it up, subtracting the irrelevant; each wondering *What did she see in him? What's he got that I don't? How could she be with him when she loved me?*

I held my breath. They were doing the guy staring thing now. I counted to six thousand and three. Slowly. Pleasant experience. No wavering, no back down, lots of ongoing ever-growing macho. I started over. Two thousand and ten this time. Still holding my breath.

The phone rang.

I silently blessed Ma Bell.

"I'm leaving," Clem said. His eyes were mean and hard, his tone soft and dangerous. "I'll be back." It was a promise, maybe a threat, maybe both. Maybe to both of us. Jude scowled. We both watched Clem leave.

I let out my breath, let the phone ring.

Jude kicked a chair out so he could sit in it and pounded a fist on his knee. "Son of a bitch."

I held my breath again. Some habit. Some fun.

"Why, Kat?" Pound. Pound.

"Why what?"

"Why a black guy?" He slammed my desk for a change of pace.

"African-American," I said automatically. "How come you didn't start pounding and busting things up?" My question was punctuated by the rhythmical thud of his fist on his knee.

314

"When I was a kid I always fought, wrecked things. I thought if I smashed it, it'd go away, be over, done with. But it doesn't work. I've seen that since Amanda died. Saw it didn't work with her, saw what I lost and why. You made me see that." He looked at me and he looked mad, not grateful, so I didn't feel much like taking credit or even saying thank you.

"There's always something you can't smash. There's too much to destroy, no matter how hard you try. I'm trying to figure out something else, but sometimes that seems even harder."

It was a start, I guess, but he had a long way to go. Gandhi had left him in the philosophical dust on this one, no question.

"Why a bl—an African-American, Kat?"

"That's racist. Not to mention stupid." I was never considered for Miss Congeniality.

"No, it's not. Hey, there are plenty of white guys who—"

I got to a thousand this count. "Yeah, you're right," he said tonelessly. "It's racist, it's stupid."

"Amanda picked Clem for a friend because of the qualities he had that she appreciated and admired. I don't imagine that color was a factor in her choice."

"No," said Jude. He had stopped pounding but had a dumb dazed-horse look on his face. "I don't get it, Kat. Fuck, I just don't get it. Amanda was the only woman for me. I wanted to be the only man for her. It's not too much to ask, is it?"

"It takes more than asking, Jude." I wasn't a great loss to the diplomatic corps, either.

He clenched a fist, then slowly relaxed it. "I hate him because he was with my wife. There's nothing fucking racist about that. I don't care what the fuck color he is, I hate his guts for being with Mandy."

He stomped out without saying good-bye.

The rest of the afternoon was surprisingly quiet, if you don't count the voice on the phone that growled YOU ARE BEING WATCHED! followed by a phone slam. Too bad. I could have used some kind of positive diversion. I tried to feel good about myself and my job but it was getting tougher and tougher these days.

Dropped dimes hit hard sometimes.

The chickens were coming home to roost and some of them were pretty scraggly-looking. The chicken I really needed, fine feathers and plumage and all, was loose. Still. The bait was out. Still.

Federal Express arrived at four-thirty with a package from Kansas. Another chicken come to roost. It pretty much made my day. I made a few phone calls. Running out of roosting room, no question about it.

Dead rats, dimes and chickens.

I hoped I was onto something.

# 39

Dear Charity,

I know a woman who says she wants to hire someone to kill her ex-husband, his new girlfriend and their baby. What do you think of that for problem-solving?

Wide-eyed And wondering

Dear WEAW,

I think her problems are just beginning.

Charity

~~~~~~~~~~~~~~~~~~~~~~~~~~~~~~~~~~~~~

I read the Fed Ex through twice, then made a couple of local calls. Interesting. My stomach growled, but dinner was going to be way down the line.

Then I called Clem.

"Hell with you."

Great. Clem and Jude were starting to sound alike.

"You take a Scott Joplin CD out to the Hudson ranch the night Amanda was killed?"

"Huh?"

317

"This is a yes or no question, not a true/false, not a multiple choice, not a huh."

"I gave it to her, but not that night. Earlier. She didn't care for piano music. I love it. I wanted her to listen, to learn to appreciate it."

"You wear Ray-Bans?"

"No."

I hung up. I forgot to thank him. Six-thirty. I called Roberta.

"Hello, this is Claire."

"Oh, *hi!* How are you? Okay? I was just thinking about you. I'm glad you called."

Two inches. That's how high I felt. And shrinking fast.

"Roberta, I need to tell you something."

"Of course. Anything."

I paused in the silence. Not too late to change my mind, I thought. But it was. "My name isn't Claire. It's Kat Colorado. I'm a private investigator. I was a good friend of Amanda Hudson and I—"

*"Oh!* You *lied.* How *could* you?" She hung up.

I called back. The phone rang sixteen times before Nicky answered in an excited voice.

"Hi, Nicky, would you write something down and give it to your mommy?"

He thought about it. "Okay."

"It's numbers. Can you write numbers?"

"Yes." Scornfully. "Only *babies* can't write numbers."

I gave him my office number, then asked him to repeat it back to me. He was number perfect.

"Will you give your mom that message and tell her that Kat called and it's real important?"

"Cat? Like kitty cat?"

"Yes. And it's real important, okay?"

"Okay."

The receiver thumped down, disconnecting us. I waited until nine-thirty, the phone smirking in silence the whole time, and then I left. My stomach was growling again.

By arrangement with the owner I often park my car in an alley not far from my office. In midtown there are a number of alleys running between the letter streets. Backyards or driveways face the alley, houses/offices face the street. Midtown, day or night, is never that wild. Cars and people coming and going, not too many at nine-thirty. Most legitimate, some walking the line or over the edge. I didn't see or hear anything unusual.

*It came out of nowhere.* That's what hapless bystanders always say.

*No lights, no warning.* They say that too.

I heard the acceleration, but by then it was too late. By then I was in front of the Bronco heading for the driver's side. The vehicle was coming at me from the driveway across the alley. Not that fast, but fast enough—there wasn't a lot of distance to cross. It was a pickup with a wide high steel bumper across the front. Perfect to smash me up against the Bronco. I wasn't the only one to think of this; it had undoubtedly occurred to the guy standing on the accelerator too. Swell technique for rearranging 83 percent of the bones in my body. That, too, had occurred to him. The noise of the truck engine was loud in my ears; the fan belt squealed slightly.

Steel bumpers and a bad guy. I had two choices, only one out.

I took the out.

I ran at the pickup, leapt and dove onto the hood of the speeding vehicle, fingers and toes scrabbling, pushing, grabbing for purchase on the slick metal.

Then slipping—sliding—as the truck slammed into the Bronco. I heard the crush of metal, the twisted squeal of protest. My car but not my body. Big difference.

My feet slammed onto the bumper bars; my fingers, hooked in the crevice in front of the windshield, almost ripped out, but held. Pain plowed through my body. The truck roared into reverse, veered into the street, then lurched forward, back, forward, back.

Trying to shake me. Son of a bitch.

I was a limpet. I wasn't getting off until we got to my stop or it was a whole lot safer. I sure as hell wasn't getting off to get run over or to try to escape in a vehicle that might not be drivable. That last pickup maneuver could have punched a hole in my radiator. Or this clown could have disconnected the spark plug wires. Two can play that game.

I picked my head up and peered through dusty, grimy, bug-smeared glass. Well, knock me down and clutch the pearls—a familiar face. A bug among bugs.

"God*damn,*" Buck snarled and started trying to swat at me, to swat me off the hood. Speaking of bugs. I shimmied and scooted over a bit.

"Hey!" someone out of my limited peripheral vision yelled. "What's going on? Hey, *you!*"

Buck hit the gas. Tires squealed. I hung on. He was looking a little scared and nervous now. I snarled, then stuck my tongue out at him. The feeling was almost gone in my hands. Something hard hit my cheek with numbing force. Buck. The truck veered, overcorrected twice, then straightened out. A shudder ran through its metal body. Buck was never going to make it to the Indiana 500. I heard the blast of horns. Where was a do-gooder motorist with a car phone and a finger itching to dial 9-1-1 when you needed one?

The truck took a corner on a right turn too fast, then a left, also too fast. Still trying to shake me. I was holding my breath again. Hadn't I been doing a lot of that lately? My eyes were tearing up, my fingers hurt like hell and my muscles were strung out, tense and jumpy. My brain was working overtime and speeding but not getting me out of this.

Buck slowed. I picked up my head and looked around. We were at about E and 26th. Uh oh. The freeway wasn't faraway. I didn't think I'd last long on the freeway. We had slowed down but even so were doing about 30. Rolling didn't seem like a good bet. Hitting the pavement at 30 mph didn't seem like a great idea.

Neither did a jaunt down the freeway. How long before I got too tired? Before the muscles in my arms and legs gave out? Before my fingers lost their grip? Not that soon, but not that long, either.

Buck was leering in a scummy way at me, licking his lips as though I were the next course. Road kill. Freeway platter. He picked up speed, leered harder. He had to shake me fast on the freeway. Too many cars out there. Too easy to spot. I tried to test my fingers—not that bad, I hoped. Too easy to report. Let's face it—I was just not that common a hood ornament.

Thoughts of the squashed, squished, smashed-up bodies of squirrels and birds, possums, cats and dogs ran through my mind. Blood and guts sometimes, or dried, flattened, smashed fur and goo, indefinable finally, but dead, past thought and memory. It didn't cheer me.

I looked over, caught the startled glance of a driver. Waving was out, so I hollered, hoped he wasn't the kind who wouldn't get involved. Out of the corner of my eye I saw a dark sedan with a ski rack or— My heart leapt. I squinted, trying to squeeze the wind-rush tears out. *Hot damn!* It wasn't a ski rack, it was a light bar. *Yes!* As I watched, it flipped on.

Red and blue flashing lights. My kind of party.

Buck floored the accelerator. Sirens. I held on. My future was looking a little more certain. More lights. More sirens. Shoot, I hadn't felt this cheery since Christmas.

POLICE. PULL YOUR VEHICLE OVER *NOW*.

It wasn't a voice or an attitude I would have argued with. I looked at Buck through the dirty windshield. His eyes were slipping wildly around. I could see three police cars. He could probably see more. They weren't slipping, they were hugging our fenders. It was the OK Corral for Buck and he pulled over. I hung on. Habit by now. My fingers might be permanently crooked but my spirits were rising. I didn't let go until Buck was out of the car and handcuffed. I didn't let go then, either. My fingers weren't responding real well to brain signals.

An officer helped me off. "You okay?" she asked. Her hands looked a lot better than mine.

"I want to press charges," I croaked. The pain in my hands and cheek was unbelievable.

"No shit. We do too," said a young hard-looking cop. "What the hell's going on?"

I sighed. I'd had about enough of tough guys today. Good or bad.

I looked around for the female officer, caught her eye. "Can I sit in your car?" Might as well. It was a long story. It would take a while.

Another cop walked over, his gun jiggling on a meaty hip, his face grim. "We found this on him. It mean anything to you?"

I read:

*Do her.*
*$5000.*
*DeV.*

The note was on Louden stationery. The initials were scribbled but legible. DeVito. It did, yes, it meant a lot. It meant I now had Buck dead to rights. And, by extension, Louden. Also dead to rights. It might not put Buck and DeVito away for ten years on murder for hire but it might. And it would look great in the newspaper, on *60 Minutes*, on *Inside Edition*, whatever I could push through.

It would look great on balance sheets: Amanda's, Roberta's, Jeanette's. Jude's and mine too. Sunshine.

"Miss? This mean anything to you?" he repeated.

"Yes," I said to the grim-faced officer. "It does."

# 40

Dear Charity,
Do you think a Band-Aid makes a person feel any better?

Anna-Belle

Dear Anna-Belle,
It depends. I think a Band-Aid's a big help for bruises and scrapes and no help at all for a broken arm or a broken heart.

Charity

~~~~~~~~~~~~~~~~~~~~~~~~~~~~~~~~~~~~~~~~~~~~~~~~~~~~

I got home late and exhausted but it beat being roadkill, so all in all things were looking good. Even the Bronco was limping along unexpectedly well. The cops had helped me pry a fender off my left front tire so I could drive it. The radiator was intact. The insurance was paid up. Looking okay.

I didn't figure anything would happen at the house tonight. Buck had been busy in midtown most of the evening and now he was in jail: assault with a deadly weapon; battery with great bodily injury; murder for hire; hit and run; speeding, running red lights; chewing stale gum; they'd thrown the book at him.

So I figured everything to be okay. Wrapping up time here. A few more loose ends but the investigation pretty much over.

Assumptions are dangerous things.

I checked the neighborhood, the house. Everything was okay. Except me. I was worn out, starving, beat up. My fingers looked like an advanced case of arthritis on a good day. They looked better than they felt. The message light was blinking on my phone. I noticed as I headed for the shower, noticed it again as I headed for the kitchen and a snack. It could be personal or work—I'd set the office machine to call forward. I picked it up on my second glass of wine.

"Kat, it's Roberta Heald. Call me, please, no matter how late. Please—I need to speak to you. *Please.*"

I looked at the clock, one-thirty, picked up the phone.

Roberta sounded a little sleepy but woke up quickly. "I have to talk to you," she said without preamble.

"All right." It wasn't just a ball game, it was a doubleheader. Fun, huh? Only I was too tired to pitch. Or catch. Or run. Way too tired to hit a home run. "In the morning, though."

"Thank you. Early?"

"Yes." I stretched and finished the last of my wine, thought about a third glass.

"I'm a member of the historical preservation committee for local landmarks. We save, repair, sometimes even rebuild—"

"Roberta?"

"Yes? Oh. I have to take pictures tomorrow of the old Meiss Road bridge. For the committee. We want to recommend that it be rebuilt and—"

"Roberta?"

"Yes." She exhaled. "Do you know where the bridge is?"

"Behind the Sloughhouse Inn off Highway 16."

"Okay. Six o'clock? I know that's early but I have early meetings at work and then my day and evening are full, too, and—"

"Six o'clock." I yawned. "I'll be there."

. . .

I was up well before five, lacking enthusiasm but maintaining forward momentum; it was enough to get me by. I shivered as I drove, the early morning cool still, the day's heat something remembered and expected but difficult to believe in yet. Traffic was sparse but picking up, little of it going my way, most headed instead into Sacramento, driving into another business day.

I cut off Highway 16 to the right onto Meiss Road, drove past the Sloughhouse Inn, a restaurant and bar built on the dust of California history and on the site of a former Pony Express stop. Legend has it that Joaquin Murietta, the nineteenth-century folk hero or bastard— legend differs—once roamed the area doing good or committing evil. There was no sign of either as I followed Meiss Road past the restaurant. Poorly maintained, bumpy, almost rutted out in places, the road was a reminder of how swiftly Mother Nature reclaims her own.

I dead-ended at the Old Sloughhouse Graveyard, no bridge, and thought about it, remembered then that the road was closed here now, that you couldn't get there from here. Back to Highway 16 and Dillard Road. As I turned off Dillard onto Meiss I passed a sign telling me there was ROUGH ROAD ahead. The road was edged with wood post and barbed-wire fencing, rolling grasslands beyond. Jouncing along made me acutely aware of my many bumps and bruises. I passed several old houses, one with sheets in the windows, all with beat-up trucks in the driveways and farm machinery wherever. The smell of cow was strong.

The bridge took my breath away, but of course I'm a sucker for bridges, water, early morning and primitive California structures. I parked the Bronco off-road. The steel bridge angled up gracefully into the sky, defaced now with mindless and obscene graffiti. The massive wooden planking that had been the roadway was partially burned out and the bridge, no longer safe for traffic, was guarded by heavy rusted-pipe fences that blocked access. I scrambled through them.

The stream bed twenty feet below was fifty or sixty feet across, but the stream was only a summer flow, trilling along, not dead and sluggish but alive, scintillating. The world around me sparkled with dew, radiance, and the promise of early morning.

Promise and life.

I wasn't here to talk about life.

I leaned on the bridge and breathed deeply, awake now. I thought of all the bodies, looked for answers in the flash of white water, the leaves that caught and whirled and eddied about before being spun relentlessly downstream.

Too many babies lost. Amanda's baby. The babies Jeanette would never have. Roberta's Emily. But it was the death of Amanda, not that of a child, that had started this.

I heard an engine, the spurt of gravel, the abrupt silence broken only by the rush of the stream. Far above, as the sun climbed in the clear light blue-white sky, a red-tailed hawk soared lazily on an unseen, unfelt upward draft. I felt a lump in my throat. Far away a bird called and another answered and then Roberta called and I answered.

"Kat, hello!"

"Good morning."

"I still think of you as Claire. Well, sort of . . ."

This was too polite. She had hated Amanda for doing what I was doing. It made me uneasy, put me on guard. "Yes. I'm sorry about the pretense."

"It must have something to do with Amanda Hudson." Accepting, not angry.

"Yes. You wouldn't speak to her, I know. Why are you here?"

In her silence I watched the flash of fish, silver-darting-white in the water below, and listened to the songbirds. The hawk had wheeled out of my sight. The dew was beginning to evaporate, the sparkles occasional now and not an iridescent blanket of jewels strewn across the landscape.

I heard her sigh but thought at first it was a breeze, a last teasing tantalizing breeze before the heat of the day drifted in and clamped down on us, stifling us, forcing us to turn from Mother Nature and worship at the altar of the air-conditioning gods. The second time it floated past—this small, sad exhalation—I knew it for what it was.

Not what. Who. Roberta.

I answered for her. "You came to see what I know."

"Yes."

"I know most of it now. Not all the details, not the unspoken feelings, but I know now what happened."

As I looked at her, she seemed merely an outline, a silhouette without internal detail trapped against the blinding light of the climbing sun. It was a halo effect that dazzled me and then blurred out everything else except for the dark, deep sadness I felt. I looked away from the sun.

This wasn't a beginning, this morning.

"Tell me." Roberta spoke softly.

So I did.

"I think you must have known Amanda better than I realized at first. I found your letter to her, Roberta, cool and formal in tone. I imagine that you thought that would end it, that your polite and very firm refusal would be enough."

I paused and considered Amanda Joan-of-Arc Hudson, eyes flashing with surety and courageous righteousness, sword dripping with the blood of the enemy as she held it upraised, triumphant, challenging. A polite refusal would not have been enough.

Roberta said nothing and I continued. "But it wasn't. I don't know exactly what Amanda said or did. Still, you must have come to realize that she wasn't going to go away, to disappear."

"She was a monster."

I thought I heard tears in Roberta's voice, but I kept my eyes on the stream below. I thought, too, how little difference there might be between a saint and a monster. There was little room in either for consideration or compassion, laughter or tears. I had seen Amanda bruised and beaten, feeling unwanted and unattractive. I had known the ugly duckling as well as the swan; I had seen both sides and I had loved her. Roberta had seen one side. And feared her. The seeds of Amanda's destruction were in Amanda's own heart. She had planted them.

"I hated her."

327

K A R E N   K I J E W S K I

"Yes."

"She threatened to take my privacy and self-respect away from me. From Nicky, too."

"No one can take your self-respect from you." I looked her full in the eyes then, those odd, beautiful gold-brown mirrors to her soul. I looked for a long time and saw nothing. One-way glass.

"I just wanted to be left alone. Every day for the first year after Emily's death I cried out *Where is my baby?* I woke on that thought and fell asleep on it. You can't imagine the pain, Kat. The grief burrowed into my heart like some kind of awful worm, gnawing, always gnawing. I had lost my husband a year before, my son had an illness that crippled his leg. Emily was my hope and beauty, the light in my future. And then she died because someone was negligent and greedy. It wasn't fair."

No.

"After a time, I started to heal. I was doing better and then—"

"Amanda."

"Yes. I said she was a monster. It's not true, really. I'd been driven by grief, I could understand how she could be driven by what she believed in. I understood—I just didn't want to be a part of it."

A diamond the size of a blueberry shimmered at me from a ring on her engagement finger.

"But she made you a part of it."

"I said she took away my self-respect, and in a way it's true. I was confused about what I'd done. She built on that, made me feel like a criminal, made me feel that there was only one way out and that was to tell my story, to warn others." She opened her hands helplessly. The ring sparked. "I couldn't do that. Some people are fighters and some are not. I'm a private person and I would die."

The sun no longer haloed her. Now it fell—stark and harsh—on features that were plain and drawn in emotion.

"This is a horrible thing for me to say"—her face got honest, sincere, uglier—"but I was glad when I heard that she had died. I tried to be sorry for her, and later, when I heard about her baby, I was truly sorry. But most of all I was relieved. I was freed. Do you under-stand? She was your friend, I know, but—"

I nodded. I understood. The Joan of Arcs of this world are not widely beloved in their lifetimes.

"The papers said it was an accident. I wondered, though. You know how you get an inside feeling about something?"

"Yes."

"From what she said one day—I can't even remember what it was —I suddenly knew that she had a boyfriend. Everything wasn't all perfect and wonderful in her life any more than it was in mine. A boyfriend *and* a husband. And that's trouble. People get killed for that. I watched the papers but I didn't see anything else. I really tried to feel bad about her death, but I couldn't. I guess I still can't. In a funny way, I admired her. But it is not difficult for me to imagine that someone would have wanted to kill her."

"As you did."

"Yes, I wanted to." She acknowledged it simply, easily, factually.

"You were right, Roberta. It was murder."

"Ah!" There was color in her cheeks now. "The husband? Surely not the boyfriend?"

"No, not the boyfriend."

"I thought not."

"Not the husband either."

"Who, then?" Her eyes were wide now, more gold than brown, the one-way mirror in place still.

Overhead the hawk circled again, waiting for a mouse, a lizard, a rabbit to move unwarily, for without that unwary movement there is nothing to pounce upon.

I tossed a pebble in a still water pool on the edge of the stream. The concentric circles widened, widened, then disappeared before I answered.

# 41

Dear Charity,
 In this busy world of ours, I think it's the thought that counts, don't you?

Full Of Thoughts

Dear Full Of It,
 No. I think thoughts are cheap, talk is cheap, and action counts.

Charity

~~~~~~~~~~~~~~~~~~~~~~~~~~~~~~~~~~~~~~~~~~~

"You left your sunglasses at the Hudson house. Ray-Bans. It was night but you wore them. Why?"

"Ray-Bans? A *million* people have Ray-Bans."

"Yes."

She relaxed.

I thought about Amanda, about good guys and bad guys and shades of gray, and about how Amanda's preoccupation with beauty had complicated everything. I said:

"The day I first met you—"

"The day you were Claire?"

"Yes. When you asked me to come upstairs to talk with you I saw an earring tossed in the jumble of your vanity table. Pretty enough but nothing remarkable. Except—"

"Except?"

"Except I had found its mate in the Hudson hot tub. It had been left there the night Amanda died."

Roberta didn't move, didn't speak.

The wary mouse was safe.

"What nonsense," she said. "An *earring*, for goodness sakes, as if there aren't dozens, *hundreds* of earrings that look exactly alike." She laughed, a false sound in the early morning air and beauty.

The mouse twitched. I remembered the earring I'd found in the hot tub. The pearl with the small gold beads that hung from a delicate gold wire. Amanda had just gotten her ears pierced. She couldn't wear earrings like that yet. You could only wear studs for the first couple of weeks or months, I'd forgotten exactly. Mine had been pierced for a long time. I did remember the pain when I tried to put a dangling earring in too soon.

"Ray-Bans, an earring—they helped but didn't make it certain. The fingerprint did that."

Roberta's eyes widened. Her hand flew to her mouth, covered it protectively.

"There was a print on the edge of the hot tub. A clear, perfect print." I spoke that clear, perfect lie in clear, perfect tones. "A million people may have simple pearl earrings and Ray-Bans, but only one person will match that print."

The mouse broke cover.

"I can explain," she said.

I felt immeasurably saddened, weighted down by those words. No infamy was too great, no incident too small, but there was an explanation excusing it. A fish broke the water, flashed silver gills and fins at me, disappeared with a flicker.

"I saw her, but earlier in the day, not in the evening, not at all—"

Transparent. Desperate.

"She worked all day, had a guest most of the evening," I said. "Her guest left at eleven. Amanda was alone then. She had been harassed a lot in those days before she died. She would not have allowed anyone whom she did not know to come over. But she knew you. You called and asked to come over and she agreed. She may not have trusted you but she wasn't afraid of you. And she very much wanted something from you—your cooperation in nailing Louden. So she locked the dogs up and waited for you, relaxed in her hot tub while she waited."

"Yes," Roberta said.

"And you killed her."

"No. It wasn't like that. I can explain." That again.

"Do." I dared her and then listened to the silence.

"She started hammering at me again, that even if I couldn't reveal the company's name I must tell my story, tell people about Emily. That I must use my personal tragedy to warn others. And I couldn't. I couldn't. I thought she was right—that was what made it so hard—but I couldn't. I am a private person. There is no way I would parade my loss and grief about like that. No way."

"No," I agreed. "Not your loss, not your grief. Not your one and a quarter million dollars."

She gasped. "No, it's a secret. I don't know what you're talking about, I *don't—!*"

"I looked into your background. The Kansas farm girl who was desperate for a better life, a life of sophistication, culture and ease. You went to school, worked hard so you could leave Kansas behind. Sacramento wasn't New York or L.A., but it was right for you. You came here, found a job you liked, married, had children."

"It was my dream come true," she said softly.

"Yes. And then your husband died. You had lived a life of some luxury, of ease, but on his death you discovered that it was all unpaid for. Borrowed money, borrowed time, borrowed luxury. When the debts were settled you had nothing."

"No, that's not true. I had my children, my health. I knew I could do it again."

"And then Emily became terribly sick. One operation followed another. Your dream—"

"It became a nightmare." The diamond sparkled at me in the sun, cold and dead and hard like Roberta's words. "And then I lost her. *Where is your baby?* this sad, lost voice cried in my dreams and I would wake in a sweat, heart pounding and breaking, listening for her in the night, as mothers do. But my baby was dead.

"I sued. It was a good case and I took them for everything I could. The money doesn't make up for Emily but it was something . . ."

"A nice house, a Mercedes, an expense account at Nordstrom's?"

"Oh yes. And a nest egg, a secure future for Nicky and me. I put a lot in stocks and bonds and carefully built it—just the opposite of what my husband had done. I had trusted him and hated him for mortgaging our security, our future. I wouldn't do that. I would make sure we were safe. We had to do it without Emily. Nothing made up for that pain or for losing her. It was just money. But money helps. I started to live again. The nightmares stopped. Nicky was happy. I met Ted. And then—"

"Amanda."

"Yes. She was like one of those awful alien things in a horror movie. Wherever you look or go, there it is. You think you're safe, and there it is . . ."

I liked the crusader image better, but I could see Roberta's point.

"She said I had to save other people's babies and lives."

"By telling your story?"

"Yes. Oh God, it was all I could do to save my life. And Nicky's. And the nightmares started again. *Where is your baby?* I would wake up night after night trembling and terrified, *Where is your baby?* ringing in my ears.

"She said she would tell about the money, that it wasn't right to profit over the death of your child."

I sucked in my breath. *Goddamn, Amanda. Goddamn!*

"Was she right? Was I such a horrible person and mother?" It was an anguished cry.

"No. She wasn't right. And you aren't."

"I was just trying to put my life back together, just trying to survive. And she? She was trying to take the peace I had fought so hard for away from me. And the nightmares got worse. Only they had changed. The voice was Emily's. *Mama, Mama, where am I?*" Roberta was crying. "*Mama,* her voice said, *where are you? Help me, Mama. Help me.*"

My heart filled up with sadness.

"Amanda made it sound so awful, my settling with Louden and taking the money, my refusing to go public about Emily's death. But she didn't know what it was like, she hadn't gone through it. And then she said *she* would tell our story, even if I wouldn't. Emily's voice cried at me all the time then, not just when I slept. *Mama! Mama!* I believed Amanda, believed that she would do as she said."

Yes. I believed it too.

"And I thought, that if she told, everyone would hate me. Ted, the people at work, the other charity volunteers, everyone. I had struggled so hard for myself and my children. I had made a new life after my husband died and again after Emily died. It was very difficult but I had done it. And I knew I couldn't do it again. Not so soon. I was too tired. It was too hard."

Roberta twisted the ring on her hand. I thought about the evil that is done in the name of good.

"She was threatening to take everything from me—oh God, what right had she?—and in my dreams my children cried out, the live and dead one—" Her broken sob was like a child's. "Oh God—I hated her!"

And now I knew I hated her too. I had loved Amanda, but I could also hate her.

"What happened?" I asked, less sure than I had been before, the hawk's eye more farsighted than mine, the mouse heading for cover.

"I went to her house just to talk. Just to talk . . . I thought she would understand if I told her everything. I didn't try to justify it, to say that my way was good. I just wanted to explain. To let her see how I'd lost my husband and then my baby, how my son had a health problem, how I was doing well now, building another life, but I was still so tired, so exhausted from it all. I wanted her to see that I couldn't do more. I wanted so much to be whole again. I couldn't talk to reporters and show them Emily's picture and be on the *Donahue* show and all the other things she spoke of."

The thing about people who are willing to risk their lives, their careers, families, and peace of mind for a principle is that they're willing to risk everyone else's too.

They? She. Amanda.

What she had done, she expected others to do. Perhaps she would have changed had she lived, borne her child, had to weigh the consequences differently.

"I couldn't throw away everything I had built. It would have destroyed me. I thought she would see that and understand, I really did."

*But she hadn't.*

"She was so stubborn. And we fought. I didn't feel like a person, I felt like a cornered animal fighting for its life."

"You fought physically?"

"No. I yelled and screamed at her. At first she stayed calm, but then she yelled back at me. She called me names, called me selfish—"

I put my head on my arms on the bridge rail. Oh, Amanda. So young and pure. So righteous. So impossible. *The seeds of destruction.*

"She got out of the tub, went into the house, came back with two sodas. I was still very upset. I almost stepped on the CD player plugged into an outdoor outlet and sitting on the ground. Without thinking, I picked it up and put it on the corner of the spa, out of the way. Amanda put the sodas there too and got back in.

"I was desperate. I threatened her, threatened to sue her for violating my privacy, peace of mind and anything else my lawyer could think of . . .

"When she started laughing at me something inside just broke. I screamed at her. I was crazy with rage and frustration and desperation. I don't even know what I said. I don't know exactly what happened next. I startled her, I think. She was watching me and reaching for her soda and somehow she knocked the CD player into the tub. Then—" Roberta's face contorted in a horror that was a pale reflection of what I had seen in the autopsy photos.

The mouse had broken cover.

But I was no hawk.

"Please believe me," Roberta whispered.

There was truth in there—most of it, perhaps—but lies as well.

"Kat—will you come to my car with me? I want to show you something."

I pushed off the bridge railing feeling older, tired. We walked in silence to the Mercedes, the dew gone now, the day's heat pleasant still but starting to kick in. Roberta popped the trunk.

Except for a cardboard box, the trunk was empty. The box was full. She lifted out a silver picture frame and handed it to me. "I wanted her to be real to you."

The child was snugly tucked into a baby swing. She was high off the ground, her hair a golden halo around the beautiful face, the laughing eyes and smile. Sturdy little legs stuck out straight, feet in tiny scuffed red sneakers. Little hands gripped the safety bar.

Not a principle. A child.

"This was the dress she wore at her christening." Roberta lifted a folded garment that had once been white, the linen and lace now faintly yellow with age. She was crying, silent tears that she made no attempt to stop or wipe away. "Nicky wore it before Emily. As I did before him and my mother before me. Emily was named after her. These are her first shoes." Little and white and leather, and scuffed with her first steps. "This was her blanket and her teddy bear and—"

"Robbie—" I used the familiar term for the first time.

336

"There is one last thing," she said urgently. *"Please.* Please, will you pick it up and look?"

Something heavy was wrapped in a lace-trimmed pillowcase. I knew what it was before I unwrapped it. A gun. A .25. I opened it. Loaded.

"I hoped you wouldn't be like Amanda, but I thought if you were I could threaten you, scare you—"

*Kill me?*

"But it doesn't seem to me that you would threaten or scare very easily, and besides I don't think I can do it. That was what Amanda did to me—I can't do that to someone else."

*Seeds of destruction.*

"Do you know how to use a gun?"

"Sort of. My husband showed me once."

I unloaded the .25 and dropped the bullets in my pocket. "Is there more ammunition in the car?"

She shook her head. "Kat, I thought about killing you. I'm ashamed of that."

Shame seemed to be a pretty lightweight word considering the context, but I didn't say anything.

"Kat, it wasn't murder. Don't you see? I couldn't, wouldn't do that."

"You should have called the police at once." And before them, medical help. Maybe it had been too late for Amanda—the autopsy photos slammed unbidden into my consciousness—but maybe it hadn't. And someone besides Roberta should have made that decision.

"I know. I was so afraid for myself, though. For Nicky, too." *I hated her. She was a monster.* "That's horrible, isn't it, but it's natural, don't you think?" *I was glad when she died. It was a relief. I was free.* "I'm still afraid."

Sounds from the present and the past bombarded me.

A bird called, a golden butterfly danced briefly in front of us. I watched as Roberta put the things back in the box, folding the blanket and garments carefully, tucking in the tiny shoes. The photograph went on top, Emily laughing at us, life and the future ahead of her then in an unbroken silver ribbon. Roberta closed the trunk.

"I'm so glad it's over." She looked at me through heavy lashes, brushed her hand across her eyes, though I couldn't see any tears.

"It's not over." I heard Amanda's righteousness in my voice. "Go to the police. If you don't, I will. Call Detective Zack Taylor, Sheriff's Department. Good luck, Robbie."

She straightened her shoulders but didn't say anything. I looked for the hawk one last time before I climbed into the Bronco. I didn't see it. Or a mouse.

Or hear a dead baby cry.

Just hatred.

Amanda hated Louden. And everyone who got in the way of that hatred. They obliged by returning the sentiment and including me in it. So Jude hated them too. Buck and the boys fed on hatred. Amanda loved Clem who disliked Jude who loved Amanda and disliked Clem. Amanda hated Roberta who hated Amanda. I forgot that hate doesn't solve anything and jumped right in, hating every which way myself. What was left?

The circle of hatred was complete.

It was time to break it.

# 42

That night I watched a western on TV. An old one, flickering and grainy and black and white. The black and white was figurative as well as literal.

The good guys wore white. The bad guys wore black. *Listen up, Zack.* The good girl (they were girls in those days, not women) was a fresh-faced wholesome virgin in a plain dress. The bad girls were in saloons and push-up bras and sassy attitudes and were no better than they should be, if that good. A man's word or handshake was his promise, and he would keep that promise or die trying. The government was not much good and a man was on his own with only his horse, his gun, and his courage and that was that, take it or leave it.

But the good guys won. Sure, there were ups and downs and it wasn't easy (it was a two-hour movie, after all), but they won. Their clothes were still white, their land still theirs, their virgin brides-to-be still virgin, their unblemished honor still unblemished.

Son of a gun, it never even rained. Yeah, those were the good old days when right was right and wrong was wrong and everyone over two could tell the difference. Even the horses. Even the weather.

Simple as that.

I made popcorn and cried at the sad parts, got mad at the get-mad parts, rejoiced at the triumph-of-good-over-evil parts. There weren't many funny parts. Laughter falls into the gray areas, I think. Maybe laughter can't survive in just black and white. That was too bad, but otherwise it was very satisfying.

There was one problem, an extra good guy left over. Well, he was only pretty good; it was kind of a mixed message. He had a white hat and shirt but a *black* vest. And there wasn't a fresh-faced wholesome virgin in a plain dress with a starched white apron left over for him. I hate it when the numbers don't come out right. But then he rode off into the sunset—a really spectacular one, though for sure it would have been better in color—so everything worked out after all.

I wiped my tears, blew my nose, and finished my popcorn. The kernels at the bottom of the bowl were loaded with butter and salt and that was a rush. Then I went to bed. Before I fell asleep I thought how much easier life would be if things were black and white.

But of course that's out. And we wouldn't laugh or have great sunsets, so it's really out.

I wore white in the morning, white shorts, white T-shirt, white Reeboks and socks. How can any thinking parent deny the influence of TV on their children? And then, because I'd unplugged my phone and slept late, I rode out into the white-hot glare of the noonday sun, staggered through waves of heat and climbed into the Bronco.

Jude was expecting me.

It wasn't going to be a black or white day.

I met Lynda coming out as I was going in. She was crying. And— this makes me look like a jerk but I'll admit it anyway—I had thought that it would be more fun.

"He asked me to leave. He doesn't want to see me anymore. Oh God, I am so bummed." She was sobbing by the time she got to the so bummed part. I was starting to feel a bit teary myself. "Oh *God*, he is absolutely the best, the greatest thing in bed. I am *so* bummed."

My tears dried up without even a sniffle. Someone should cancel that woman's subscription to *Cosmopolitan*. But *dang* it all (that's what the cowboys said in the movies when they were *really* annoyed), I should have known. She was wearing a black tank and matching sandals. So there you are. Maybe it was going to be a black and white day after all? My spirits soared at the thought of such endearing simplicity.

Of course I know better than to count my chickens before they're hatched. You betcha. I waved good-bye to Lynda, who ignored me, and walked in the house, looking for Jude.

"Hi, Jude. It's 112° out and you're building a fire. What a swell idea. Cozy."

"I spent the night going through a bunch of stuff. I spent a good part of the morning talking to a homicide cop." He reached into the cardboard carton in front of him, grabbed a handful of stuff, tossed it on the flames. The fire flared up. Sweat poured down Jude's face, muscled chest and arms. I stepped back, away from the heat.

"I'm starting to get a clue about how little I know. How about that? Starting to think I might notice more, hear more if I wasn't always blowing up, busting things up."

The framed photo that Charity had taken of Amanda was on the mantel. Amanda smiled at us.

"I decided to remember the good stuff, the fun, the love. I'm burning up everything else."

He looked at the photo of Clem and Amanda/Rosita and tossed it in. When he finished with the papers he burned the box too. So then it was 112° outside and 112° inside. He stood and smiled at me.

He was a sweathog but I hugged him anyway.

The smile changed to a grin. He touched my cheek gently. "That's one helluva bruise, Ms. Colorado. Look, I'm going to have a shower. Why don't you sit in the kitchen under the air conditioner?"

Good thinking. After his shower Jude came into the kitchen. I was on my third glass of iced tea. He walked right past me and out into the heat. When he returned there were piles of roses in his arms.

"I'm going to the cemetery," he told me. "It's time to say good-bye."

We walked out to the cars together.

"You think it was murder, Kat?"

"No. I did at first. Now I think it was complicated, but not murder."

"Will it go to trial?"

It? Roberta? "I don't think so," I told him.

Jude kicked a tire.

"How do you feel about that?" I asked.

"I don't know. I think it's time to move on. Mandy was a victim. It sounds like Roberta was too. The whole thing is just too fucking bad." He glanced at me sheepishly. "Sorry. What about Buck, the other guys, Louden?"

"Will they nail them?"

"Yeah."

"I think so, at least on the various break-ins, assaults, and the attack on me. With any luck, Buck will squeal and we can nail Louden. It will look bad in the press, I'll see to that."

Jude opened the door to the Bronco for me. I climbed in. "That Sunshine in the Courts bill? Might look into it. Sounds like something we oughtta have, oughtta work toward." He slammed the door, then leaned in the window to plant a kiss square on my mouth. "Thanks, Kat."

I watched him walk away all dressed up in a clean, starched shirt, ironed jeans, and cowboy boots. A *white* shirt. Maybe I was making too much of this, but I didn't think so.

I drove out to Charity's to say *hey* and see how the animals were, to see how she was and tell her the news. It was almost dark by the time Ranger, Kitty and I left. I came home to a HUGE bunch of roses on my porch. Clem's note said he was quitting Louden for another job, he'd decided to get into the loop, and he'd stay in touch if that was okay? I buried my face in the beauty and fragrance of the roses. Okay? It was great.

I pulled out a red rose.

The next day I bought a new bathing suit. A white one. Hank was waiting for me. Hawaii was waiting for us both. Icy fruit drinks made with too much rum, sand and sunshine and salt water, lazy happy days and hot sweaty loving nights, sunrises and sunsets, tropical flowers and lush fruit.

We would parasail and pretend we were flying. Sometimes it wasn't pretense, that's what's so wonderful.

And everything in color.

Life is not a black and white movie.